The four trained killers drew their swords and reined closer. Leitus's mouth was metal dry. He now understood these men were about to kill them.

"I want your lumpish skull, onion man," snarled Pug-face as he ripped a terrific slash at Subius. Subius's seemingly inert bulk moved with uncanny swiftness. He rocked back from the glittering blade arc and then sprang forward, slamming his thick dagger under Pug-face's gleaming breastplate. His blood spraying, the man sighed and crashed to the pavement.

Subius turned with that odd grace just as Leitus jumped from the cart holding a javelin. But the enemy on his horse was already towering over him too close, and the solid shoulder bounced him off the side of the cart. Leitus saw dark and light, then felt a cold crunching shock on his chest. Only as he fell did he comprehend it was a blow from the sword . . .

Other fantasy titles available from
Ace Science Fiction & Fantasy:

- Daughter of the Bright Moon, *Lynn Abbey*
- The Face in the Frost, *John Bellairs*
- Peregrine: Primus, *Avram Davidson*
- The Borribles Go for Broke, *Michael de Larrabeiti*
- The Broken Citadel, *Joyce Ballou Gregorian*
- Idylls of the Queen, *Phyllis Ann Karr*
- Journey to Aprilioth, *Eileen Kernaghan*
- 900 Grandmothers, *R. A. Lafferty*
- The "Fafhrd and Mouser" Series, *Fritz Leiber*
- The Door in the Hedge, *Robin McKinley*
- Silverlock, *John Myers Myers*
- The Magic Goes Away, *Larry Niven*
- The "Witch World" Series, *Andre Norton*
- The Tomoe Gozen Saga, *Jessica Amanda Salmonson*
- The Warlock Unlocked, *Christopher Stasheff*
- Bard, *Keith Taylor*
- Shadow Magic, *Patricia C. Wrede*
- The Devil in a Forest, *Gene Wolfe*
- Changeling, *Roger Zelazny*

and much more!

RUNES

· RICHARD MONACO ·

ACE FANTASY BOOKS
NEW YORK

RUNES

An Ace Fantasy Book / published by arrangement with
the author

PRINTING HISTORY
Ace Original / January 1984

ISBN: 0-441-73684-X

Ace Fantasy Books are published by The Berkley Publishing Group,
200 Madison Avenue, New York, New York 10016.
PRINTED IN THE UNITED STATES OF AMERICA

To the memory of
Vivian Strazzera

Special thanks to Jim Silbersack
and Gerald Earl Bailey

Deep appreciation for Terri Windling's efforts
Adele's hard labor
Robert Bongiorno's support

CHAPTER I

Dark trees sped past, looming in the evening mist, bouncing with the stubby strides of the powerful man who held her under one arm like (Bita thought) a loaf of holy bread. She'd already stopped struggling pointlessly in her captor's arms. He grunted as his splay feet smacked the sloping path that (she knew) ended at the water: a reach of what was already called the Thames that opened into the channel, which her people called the sea.

The man's stink enveloped her: sweat, musty rot, and stale garlic. His garments were leather and fur though it was mild spring. She knew he was from the north. Even at nine years old she knew there was no real hope of pity or help. The other raiders were bunched around them. To her they were massive, shadowy beings talking animal sounds as they panted along, weapons jink-jingling. There must have been a dozen. It never occurred to her how odd it was that they had captured no one else. But then, she'd never found it odd either that she, a mere girl child, was being trained in priestcraft by the village wizard, Namolin. Her parents didn't really discuss it with her. Her father, the chief, Tirb the Strong, was very fond of her. Always gave her an extra kiss or bit of sweet. He'd simply told her to go with the old man. Bita was frightened of him. Some said he never slept, wove spells continually, and had lived at the village outskirts for generations, barely speaking to anyone. He'd simply shown up one night outside their one-story, thatch-roofed dwelling. Just at sunset Bita had noticed him

1

standing motionless as a rock in the grassless yard. He was lean, knife-faced, with skin that looked lumpy and hard. Bita had started to retreat into the house but bumped into her father. She hadn't heard him come up behind her. He'd held her with one large hand. He hadn't kissed her this time. He'd told her to listen to the old Druid, that she had to go with him. She'd felt cold and afraid.

Old Namolin would take her to the forest cliffs behind the village and have her sit on a flat rock facing the last pastel stains in the west. He'd ask about her dreams. "What did you see before you woke, child?" in a voice like dry leaves scraping stone. "Omit nothing. Tell me everything." He would stroke his long beard and squat with the sunset behind him, dying in red flame so that his robed shape seemed a jagged boulder among the others there. "Infant of the moon's darkness." He'd sometimes call her that.

Later the young priestesses would walk with her down to the stream in the hush of twilight, instructing her to search for the plant that knew her name. The idea seemed quite real and serious to them.

She'd wander along the bank of the slow stream while mists drifted from the dark forest. The priestesses would watch her and sing in whispers while two or three young warriors leaned on their spears in the background. She'd poke around the spice-scented brush and wait for the tiny voice (as she imagined it) to call her.

But that night shadows suddenly leapt from among the trees and splashed across the shallow water—squat, demonic beings (she thought) with horned heads, charging the guards. Suddenly there were terrible noises of hysteria and pain. Sickening impacts. In her mind a voice cried, *This is something bad . . . bad. . . .* A shadowy swirl flung past: a priestess in a pale robe tangled with one of the demons, struggling. The speed of everything was scary; too much to take in. So she fled from the sounds and then hit what she took for a tree, except that it lifted her, had bright, gapped teeth, shook her, barking or laughing, as she screamed and kicked in its hard hands. A moment later the creature was loping back across the shallow water and into the solid-seeming forest darkness. He yelled or barked at the rest of his killing pack. She took away with her a last sound, a sighing sob, a pain that seemed to become the exhalation of the wind and earth itself: a woman dying in the twilight.

Coming down the coast road (two ruts slicing through tall weeds toward what would someday be called London) Bita's father ran in front of all but the youngest warriors. A few held torches that muttered and roared as the wind and dimming landscape rushed past. They kept their breath for the chase which Tirb already believed was lost.

When he'd heard the alarm raised somewhere out in the fields he'd snatched up his spear and iron-bound shield on the run, flinging himself out the door even before his wife had time to look up from where she knelt by the open hearth fire. He'd charged across the muddy yard and was running in the right direction by the time he'd met his frantic men coming across the wheatfield. He'd snapped, "I know . . . I know. Make speed!" Thinking, *We were betrayed. . . .*

Because of Bita. Because the priests were afraid of what the prophecy said about her—except none of it had been proven yet. Was his small daughter really meant to bear the children of gods? *They're afraid and mean to destroy her,* he thought. *And none of it has been proven at all.*

They had to have boats, Tirb reasoned; even a village idiot would know there was no hope of escaping Tirb's people on foot in their own territory. If the plot originated here, outsiders were needed or else the plotter's identity would soon be discovered. He grunted in self-agreement. They had to have boats and he knew where they'd have to beach them; there was only one cove in the estuary where a sizeable vessel might lie hidden. So he ran as if to a rendezvous, cutting down the sudden slope (the others following because he was their lord), plunging through prickly brush, tilting his spear clear, the branches lashing, catching, snapping around him until he could see the misty luminescence of the tidal water, just turning, and then the dim outline of the last long, low craft slipping away and melting into shadow.

He stopped, wide-legged, panting, as the others staggered to the shoreline in frustration's pointless momentum, as if it made a difference. The younger ones shook their weapons and shouted empty threats.

My child is lost to me, he was thinking. Because he loved

her, his youngest daughter. More than his son, who would be lord of the clan in his time and a fighting warchief, he loved slender Bita. He loved her face, the pale gray-blue, distant eyes that (they said) would someday be filled with the light of the queen of goddesses. He found joy in her when she'd ask him simple questions about the world or marveled at what wonders could be discovered in a summer's day.

He turned. Jumped. Someone had moved close behind him. He was shocked. He always felt man or beast that near. A woman stood there, a tall, pale-robed priestess. Young. There was just enough light left to hint at calm, remote beauty.

Magic? He didn't quite believe in magic, always had trouble with it at close range. Yet her shape might as well have solidified from the mists and shadow. Perhaps she was involved in the kidnapping plot. He felt himself harden within. His spear was up. He was a breath from striking.

"Who are you, woman?" he demanded, too loudly. "Your damned plan went well, did it?" He was thinking hard, chill thoughts. She'd confess. She'd speak her words.

"Follow them," the priestess said in a preoccupied tone. Tirb sensed how little of her attention was actually on him. "Beware the old wizard, Namolin."

"Tell me why not to feed you this spear for supper," he demanded.

"I have eaten, but many thanks." He felt her focus on him; she was amused now.

"You should have escaped with your cronies," he said, stonehard, "for now you face discomfort."

"Your daughter is far less childish than her father," she said, remotely. "Were it not necessary she be stolen from you, I would have prevented it."

"Before you die, holy one, you'll name the other traitors. Else your path to death's peace will hurt your feet."

She chuckled, mellow, faint as wind chimes.

"So you mean to urge me from this existence," she said. "But would you say to a man in his house: 'Go home'?"

"Eh?"

"I will aid your child despite your manners and youthful foolishness. I will pay her dowry, in days to come."

"I seem young, aye. But I've passed forty summers. And winters, too." He smiled. He was vain about his looks. "Holy witch, if witch you be. Enough of this nonsense." He let go a short, vicious thrust to wound her shoulder. Then he staggered forward because the spear met no resistance. He'd poked into a shadowy bush on the steep slope.

She was gone. If she had been at all. He saw and heard nothing but mist, shadow, and the waves along the rough coast. He looked back over the faintly luminous water, past where the baffled warriors stood motionless on the beach.

"*Follow her,*" he thought. *Advice from what? A spirit?* He rubbed his face, wanting to wail from grief and frustration. He sighed instead.

Bita was never certain how many days had passed before she saw the rocky coast that made her think of sharp teeth trying to chew the wild, gray billows of a violent, contorted squall. The rain sprayed sideways at them. Lightning flailed and tore the air to tatters.

She stared at the coast while the barbarian crew barked at one another. She didn't notice their hysteria as the reefs seemed to bite the smashing surf. She assumed this was another part of her homeland. These men (she'd realized they weren't actually demons) had fed her and kept her protected. It was just another mystery and she was thinking it might have to do with her training. Old Namolin told her she was going to have to do things that, up to now, only boys had done. Told her to expect anything, anytime, anyplace.

She was fascinated and unafraid as the jagged shore seemed to rush out to meet them. One of the blocky, ill-smelling warriors (she didn't know was the captain) squatted beside her, clinging to the boat's side with one hand, gripping her arm with the other as if to find security there. Each heave of the waves half sprang the boards.

He shouted over the storm din close to her ear:

"Lady Bita . . ." The rest was blown away. She was surprised to hear her own language. The craft was tilting up wildly now and the bearded man held her as if she, somehow, would save him from the shattering elements. Foam broke over their heads. The crew was panicked. They struggled uselessly with useless oars that snapped or were flung wildly. "Lady . . . true that you . . . cannot die?" he yelled.

She just looked at him as the ship wallowed and the square sails went to shreds as if invisible claws had ripped through them. Rocks snapped bites at both sides of the hull.

"Forgive me," he yelled. "Save me!"

"What?" It meant nothing to her. The world went dark as a swirl of scud streamed over them. The foaming shore thrashed insanely. The world spun and sank. Men screamed. Tons of sea slammed down.

They ground to pieces in a welter of shattered planks, cries, and struggles. The captain clutched her arm convulsively as rocks flashed by. Then, sucked deep, they drifted in sea-silence and she felt him bump, chewed off by a ridge, his desperate grip suddenly gone.

And then, somehow, she was standing in a wash of calm foam. She waded to shore. The others were gone. Nothing now but sheeting rain; low, smoky clouds that flickered like shadows; and the milling surf. No trace of the boat. The rain whipped and stung her bare flesh; her long, bright hair was plastered and strung flat over her thin neck and back.

She wandered up the shale beach to a coast road she assumed led to her home village. She waded through the running mud and sheltered herself under a dense cluster of pine trees, huddling there while the downpour smashed into the mucky earth. Only a few, cool drops filtered down through the netted mass of branches.

Soothed by the steady *whoosh* of wind and water, she might have actually been asleep when she heard the voice. She never recalled any actual words, but she knew the plants had finally spoken to her. Somewhere out in the gray rain they'd called her name, her true and secret name.

Then it was morning. Bita was sleeping curled on dense, damp, fallen pine needles. In her dream she was looking up at a tall, graceful woman whose face was lost in sunbright so that the features seemed to melt in light. She seemed to be telling Bita something as wondrous as music and the scent of flowers. She tried to rise to touch her . . . and then was awake, where stray threads of sunlight leaked into the pine dimness.

Short, stolid, dark men in brassy armor stood watching her.

One said something to her as obscure as the barking of the barbarians. She sat up. One of the men smiled. Gestured for her to follow. They waited as she did.

On the drying road there was a line of them. The sun was fresh and hot and the rainpools steamed. The sea down the hill was a stainless sparkle. She felt very good.

As she walked along with the Roman troops she wondered about the graceful lady in her dream. She felt she was connected to the voice of the plants. She was sure she had been trying to tell her something. If only she could have touched her. Her robe had seemed soft and her movements so beautiful. . . .

She kept thinking about her dream as she was marched through the lush countryside of Gaul into (though she had no way to know it) slavery.

CHAPTER II

Leitus felt his heart race as he climbed the low garden wall and dropped quietly into the sweet richness of spring flowers and cypress trees. He saw the reddish, slightly wavering glow in the window he was looking for. One or two lamps must have been lit, no more. Most of the rest of the long, low villa was dark.

She might be away, in fact, he thought, and wanted that to be true. But why the light in her room? Servants? It was late for that. He hoped her brother was still gone. There was a sallow, sullen, soft-faced gentleman he'd like to cork in a cask and float out to sea.

Thought he saw movement inside, a shadow. Froze. Waited, holding his breath.

No voices. Sounds in the distance, washed up the city hill by the spring wind: bangings, shouts, music, hoofbeats. Dark branches brushed against him as he moved closer to the window. Overhead the stars were like crushed sugar.

He was on stone now, crossing a kind of patio. Bit his lip. Heart banged hard. Felt sweat gather on his palm where he unconsciously clutched the dagger in his tunic belt. *Were she false,* he thought, *I could kill her* . . . . Though he knew better. Not if she looked at him. Never if she looked at him. He'd raged before and she'd melted him each time and drawn his jealousy into caresses where he'd lost himself completely. In a way, that was what he wanted now. It wouldn't matter if a lover had just left her arms if he could only press himself deep into her scented heat one more time. He realized he wanted to run away. Felt he might at any moment. He stepped forward

8

into the soft, blood-colored light. Ran a hand through his
curly hair. His coloring showed he was no purebred Roman.
Nervously gripped the knife's bone handle again. Sweaty.

This is stupid, he thought. *I'll go home now. . . .* Down the
hill and home, to pad barefoot past his sleeping parents'
chamber and roll himself up in his bed. And suffer worse torment for not knowing; lie there and imagine her making love
all night to some . . . to some . . .

Leitus bit his lip in sudden fury. *Enough, enough! She's no
doubt away, as she told me. . . .* He was a fool. A madman.
Madman and fool. He ought to trust her. Two days ago she'd
said she loved him.

He'd been in love before. Three times since turning eigh-
teen. Three times in four years. And he'd never really been
jealous before. The fact shocked him. Why once, with Lu-
pana, his second lover, her sister, and his friend Didus, they
had made love together on her family's pleasure boat at an-
chor in the Tiber. After a time, stunned by wine, drained by
exertion, he'd gone on deck to sleep untroubled by the last
sight of his girl sighing and struggling closer around Didus
—called the "dog" in his set because they claimed his sex
spear had a bone in it and never failed. He was topping her for
the third time that night. Leitus recalled thinking: *If she's
wise, she'll feign sleep and let him wear away to naught.* He'd
smiled peacefully across the dark water at the city lights. He
loved the city. Felt the boat rocking slightly in lover's rhythm.
Let the wind take him softly away.

But that was Leitus last year, and here he was now moving
on silent sandals, wincing to a stop when a hound at the other
end of the property whined and seemed to half bark in its
sleep.

The red glowing filled his sight now. The walls were stained
dull red and her sheets were purest red linen. She liked to roll
herself up and have him unwrap her naked; painted, pouty,
breath like wine.

What nonsense, he thought, rubbing his head nervously. He
forced himself to turn and took a half step away. Stopped.
*Even if she's with a man, that proves nothing since she loves
me. We all sport. . . .* Except he hadn't sported since meeting
her and had no real desire for anyone else. He'd changed.
Wasn't sure it really pleased her. *Why is this one so different?*
Or was it all in himself? His fellow student, Marcellus, had
said, "You ought to see a physician, and not our teacher,

either. He would probably advise powders to settle your bile
and cool the heart." Marcellus had laughed.

Leitus wasn't amused just now. He turned back to the red
gleaming. *Just a woman,* he told himself. With dark skin
that'd seem to sweetly sting his flesh when he'd press himself
along her firm but yielding length. He'd gasp as the hotness
melted open between her legs and he'd be almost desperate to
get inside and have her in private ecstasy.

He breathed deeply. Encouraged by the silence he went to
the window. She might just be asleep. Yes. But with whom?
His feelings went from calm to chill to fury, over and over.

The dull rose curtains were silk and thin. His hand parted
them, and at first he assumed it was the general hot, coal-
colored glow staining her sleek, golden-hued, naked body:
staining the parted legs, buttocks, slim back. His desire stirred
because she loved that position with Leitus behind pressing up
into her musk and pliance, nuzzling behind her neck, inhaling,
licking, biting, reaching back underneath until his rhythmed
finger caught the opened seam of her and she thrashed. Then
the wrongness hit him like a belly blow: too many slim arms
and legs. And then he actually understood and admitted into
his consciousness the blood, spray and spatter that the ochre
floor and crimson sheets absorbed into invisibility. Blood that
seemed a child's scribble over both bodies.

He never remembered climbing the sill or crossing the tiles.
He suddenly was touching her still warmish blood, smearing
his hands and wrists, tugging her in distant, desperate panic
until she flopped free from the boy (who couldn't have been
over fourteen) and sprawled off the low bed at his feet. She
twisted onto her back. He was sorry about that, because whoever had stabbed her had concentrated on the face.

He had no consciousness of making a sound except that
later he believed he must have; because, suddenly, there was a
skinny, long-nosed slave in the arched doorway. The man
hadn't even knocked, though he should have. He bugged his
eyes at the scene. Leitus must have still been making noise
because the bony man kept reacting, then shrieked himself,
over and over:

"Guard! Guard! Come quick! Help!"

Leitus took a few tottering steps, sweaty, panicked with
grief and shock.

"I cannot speak to you," he said, vaguely, at the servant. Took a step in his direction and the fellow fled. Lei-

tus dimly wondered why. Did he think the killer was coming back? Tears suddenly flooded over his smooth, fine-boned cheeks.

"O sweet lord Jupiter," he cried out, "unmake this horror. ...O..."

And then he was running from the terrible, unbearable redness and red pain and terror, scrambling through the window, tangling in one of the curtains so that as he fled across the patio into the shrubbery (hearing outcries, clash of steel) the fabric clung to him, flapping wildly as he tried to fling it away. Blinded for several steps, he crashed through a hedge and rebounded from a tree trunk. He finally left the stuff hanging from a branch as he levered himself over the low wall and glanced back. There were torches in the yard. Men shouting.

He shook his head. His shock was too much. It had to be nursed alone. So he wandered down the hill toward the main part of Rome. The pinpoint flickering of the city's lights blurred in his sight as he followed the smooth-paved street.

The houses were small and close together. The street was rutted, unpaved. There was a compound stink of sweat, animal musk, damp wood, waste, and cooked meat.

Leitus stopped by a horse trough. The stars gleamed in the unfractured water. When he bent over, his face was shadowy, blotting out part of the sky. He heard a woman talking on an upper floor; a chariot creaked and clanked on a nearby street; laughter around the bend.

His face was burning hot and he plunged it into the cool wetness. Shook his head. Blew spray from his lips. Bent again and washed his hands and arms, washing away the stickiness he didn't actually accept as blood. His toga was damp and he assumed that was water. Just water.

O lady Venus, he thought, *bring me peace and comfort.* He stopped his mind again. Blocked away the images. He stood up and went on, not really conscious of where he was. This was no neighborhood for a young aristocrat to wander in. Not at night. He went on, still following the now gentle downslope, carefully trying not to think.

The smells were thickening. Muck squeezed over his sandals. The wood and stone buildings here were pressed and jumbled together. He kept brushing his hand nervously through his hair. Oil lamps flickered in some windows, but the twisting street was almost solidly dark.

His foot hit something soft and he staggered: a woman lay face down in the soft street. He bent closer. Her robe was ripped aside. His heart raced. He imagined she was dead: saw the blood again, the hideously hacked face.

He looked up, blinking at two fat, dim figures emerging from a low doorway. He couldn't tell their sex; just dim bulks in pale robes. Then the woman at his feet stirred, made a choked, vomiting sound, and his overwrought nerves jerked him back.

Control yourself, he insisted. *Act as a man acts.*

He reeled away and found himself suddenly at the archway of a wineshop. The air was steamy, reeking of stale drink, fresh and old sweat, wet earth, vomit, and burning tallow from the oily candles set here and there. Shadows filled the low-ceilinged room like flooding water from some dark dream. Faces seemed to float there: grizzled, hard eyed, watchful, silent. Three bulky gladiators leaned against one wall. A bare-chested dwarf leered up at him, a wine jug over his shoulder as he tilted a drink into a grossly fat woman's unsteady cup.

A fire smoldered in the far corner. Someone lay there, a huddle of robes, making low, meaningless sounds.

"Thirsty, friend?" a voice said in the shadows. Someone had already moved to block the doorway.

Leitus turned and a spatter of candlelight filled the blossoms of blood on his tunic and forearms with color. Only his hands had washed clean.

"Is he wounded?" one gladiator asked.

The dwarf stepped close and touched the young man's body, lightly.

"No," he piped, "it's another's blood, Subius. And freshly spilled."

A pause.

"Ah," said the gladiator in a full, rich voice, "then let him drink. That's been earned."

The man beside him grunted assent.

"No. He's a stinking patrician," said someone else in the shadows.

"Never mind that," said Subius, "let no hand touch the lad . . . else touch me first."

That stipulation amused the dwarf, who cocked his head to the side and said:

"Better to first goose a lion."

Leitus only partly attended to the general discussion. His eyes were focused on Subius, who was a short chunk of muscle and bone and scars, compact as an orangutan, and virtually as strong. His massive brows overshadowed an incongruously delicate mouth.

"Give me a drink," Leitus murmured.

"Pour," said Subius.

A battered tin-cup was pressed into his hand. He gulped down the bitter wine. Felt no sting or taste. It was refilled.

There was a commotion outside: voices and torches. A hulking man shuffled outside a step, then stage-whispered over his shoulder.

"It's the watch," he said. "They are stirring like hornets."

"Piss on them, then," said the dwarf.

"The watch, is it?" the bald fighter beside Subius put in. "I took them for the temple dancers come to let us ass-fuck them end to end."

That sally brought down the house. The hulk suddenly drew back as a short, ax-faced centurion of the guard in brassy armor pushed through the archway, troops at his back, holding a sputtering torch in front of him like a shield.

Subius moved with astounding speed and grace, a ball of coordinated muscle. He whipped Leitus off his feet and effortlessly dropped him softly into the darkest corner and draped a greasy tablecloth over him—all in one movement.

"Make no sound," he hissed.

The centurion was just leaning in at that point, saying:

"Have any here seen a citizen fleeing, his body wet with the gore of a foul murder?"

"We see little else, Centurion, sir," remarked the dwarf, leering as he tilted a thin stream of wine from a flagon into his gap-toothed mouth. His eyes, however, were strangely gentle, ruminative.

"Well, so," said the soldier, "hard cases. We'll see about that." No one reacted. The young officer was slightly uneasy. "In the name of the Republic and for a reward of—"

"Ah," said the dwarf, "a sounder name."

"Be still!" commanded the officer. "I'll have you scourged for insolence."

"If any man have a stick, you can be certain he'll beat something with it," said Subius from where he sat firmly on

Leitus, who struggled now, thinking he was being robbed. The
bald gladiator was holding a hand the size of a human head
over the young patrician's face to stifle his cries for help.

"A reward, I say," the captain went on, "of one hundred
serterces for news of this villain."

"A fair-enough sum," someone said toward Subius.

"Well then?" the centurion demanded.

"He's right here," said Subius. "I'm sitting on him."

The officer frowned. Guffaws sounded around the room.

"I know your face, joker." He moved the flaring torch and
shadows weaved and played over the bare walls, distorting
shapes, as if unhuman beings showed their dark substance
there.

"You should," one of his men whispered, leaning in near
the captain's shoulder, squinting across the narrow, smoky,
cavelike chamber.

"Subius," he said.

"The same," responded the gladiator.

"Trouble them not," murmured the soldier to his captain.
"No point to rouse such men without real need."

The centurion kept frowning, but he was uneasy. These men
had no fear. Why should they? Ordinary fighters were chaff to
them. No one had forgotten the Spartacus rebellion of a few
years ago. Rome had tasted defeat, her armies in the field had
been thrown back again and again before Crassus had crushed
the rebels in the end.

"Well, well," he said, blustering slightly, "yet, if you see
this slayer of women, I trust, as good Romans, you'll come
forward and do your duty."

"You may rest on it," said the leering dwarf, still drinking.

Subius pursed his delicate mouth.

"Slayer of women?" he murmured. "What's this?"

The centurion backed out of there, flanked by two guardsmen. There were more in the street. Their shadows, amplified
by his torch, hovered around the entrance for a few moments,
seeming to claw the stone like blind and rapacious ghosts.

The bald gladiator unmuffled Leitus, who still struggled
hopelessly against Subius's compact bulk squatting over his
back.

"Free me," he said. "Free me, you dogs. . . ."

"Mind your tongue, O noble born," sneered the bald man.
He folded his huge hands and pondered Leitus's profile where

it was pressed against the wet floorboards. "We are no women."

"Peace, Crato," recommended Subius in his rich voice. "Well, young master?" he asked.

"Let me up," said the youth. His face was flushed.

"What woman did you kill?" Subius asked on. "Was it in passion?"

Others had gathered closer. The dwarf held a candle so that the soft, changing light emphasized Leitus's fine features, and slightly too-full lips.

"I don't have to talk to gutter waste," he announced. The image of the murder returned. He moaned faintly. "Let me go . . . let me . . . I don't . . . have to talk . . ."

"You loved her, eh?" suggested Subius. For some reason he obviously favored the young man.

"Turn him in," someone said. "We can all divide the price."

"Love oft has an adder's tooth," remarked the dwarf.

The barrel-bodied Subius stood up, and Leitus gathered his feet under himself. He looked at them without fear and, then, without anything at all. This was strangely impressive; he clearly didn't care if he lived or died.

"Love," he murmured to no one and nothing.

The dwarf handed him a brimming cup and he tossed it off exactly like the first, tasting nothing. He was blanked, just concentrating on holding away the terrible images, the red glow that kept burning his mind like coals.

The cup was refilled.

"Can you pay?" asked the dwarf.

"Fool," said someone, "he's not a mere dung lump like us. There's a man with land and horseflesh."

The bald gladiator felt for Leitus's purse, poking it while the young man stood staring, blinking, watching the shadows dance. Suddenly the wine struck him a dull blow and the room swayed. For an instant the shadows seemed to stand away from the wall and become palpable figures: strange, savage warriors, barbaric with wild hair and crude weapons.

And then he was fleeing straight for the arched door-way. He never heard Subius command, "Let him go," as he plunged out into the muggy, stinking night, running with a strange, blind certainty as if fate guided each particular step over the uneven streets past dim lights, smoldering watch fires, sleeping drunks, prowling thieves, as if fate led him along the slope until he reached the paved mainway that slanted up toward the house of his family.

He stood there, wobbling. The wine was a numb pressure on his eyes. The night, the streets, and the buildings were a single blurring. He kept thinking, *Home and sleep, home and sleep.* . . . So he really wasn't paying attention to the wavering lights coming down the wide road past the darkened state buildings. The lights winked, bobbed, dipped, and doubled in his sight. It didn't matter. He weaved along. He didn't notice the coppery glints of armor or pale flashes on sword blades.

"You . . . you there!" someone was shouting far away where the world melted into featureless dark and broken glints.

"You there," he echoed back at them, and then giggled.

"It's the one! Look at the blood!"

Blood, blood, blood, he thought. *Bl . . . bl . . .*

The torchlight hurt his eyes. He winced away from it.

"No more blood," he shouted.

The guards rushed forward as he staggered down the smooth paving. He fled warmth and light, thinking he could fly as he ran, the wind fluttering his tunic. He'd felt like this as a child playing on the hillside at his uncle's villa in the country-side, racing under the sun-sprayed orchard, leaping out over the soft, summery earth, trying to struggle into the sweet air. So he wasn't concerned with the clash of weapons and slap-slap of sandals behind him, much less the shouts. He was laughing now, fleeing faster and faster. A spear whizzed past and clattered over the stones, striking sparks. He was too quick for them. He'd never lost a foot race in his life. He'd taken the laurel a dozen times and won the nickname "the deer."

And then the road bent and he was over and down the embankment, treading air. It felt wonderful, until the world tilted, as if the hard surface had broken like water, and he sank under into soothing, blank darkness.

CHAPTER III

Grayish gleaming . . . floating up . . . out of softly clinging darkness. He was cold. Wanted to sink back down.

"No, let me go. . . ." And then a shock of chill grayness choking him.

"Easy, boy," a quiet voice said. The massive man set down a water bucket, leaving Leitus sputtering and spitting. He felt like he'd inhaled a cupful. "You can't sleep anymore."

Leitus sat up, staring at the wall and the statue of a woman with faint jets of water arcing from her breasts. He realized he was lying near the stables of his house, just off the flat stone path in clammy morning mist. The massive gladiator and the tall, bald, leaner man from the drinking shop were standing over him. They'd either followed him or carried him here. But how could they know where he lived, unless he had told them? He wasn't quite ready to think too much. His head felt like someone had run a short spike behind his eyes.

"What a fool," the bald one was saying.

"Which of us?" Subius asked, watching the young man.

"Me for coming with you. You for dragging this patrician gadfly home. Him for—"

"Peace, Crato."

"We'll be taken as accomplices."

Leitus stood halfway up. Pain jabbed him. He sighed. What did these low-lifes want? A reward? He stared at the house as he slowly straightened; the walls seemed half-melted in the foggy dawn. A rooster crowed down the hillside; dogs yapped in reply, faintly; a horse snorted and stirred in the stables.

"I can't remember. . . ." he said. "Oh, my poor skull. . . ."
Then he remembered the terrible, red images flashing. He
winced and pushed them away. "You brought me home."

"Yes," said Crato, "because we're fools." He rubbed long
hands along his greasy, leather tunic.

"The guard was here," said Subius, "and will come back. I
know this from your watchman."

Leitus wiped away water from his eyebrows and temples.
His head pain had stabilized. He felt shaky, cold but in control. Now he just wanted to go upstairs, to roll himself into the
warm softness of sleep. He felt he could wash away the red
pictures that way. And all his pain and soreness. He could
miss the morning lecture, he reasoned, as if nothing else had
actually happened, and turn up by midafternoon to watch his
teacher set broken bones.

"I need to rest," he murmured.

"Not here," said Subius. His gaze was dark, remote, and
calm. "Put on these garments." He held out a plebeian's tunic
in a bundle.

He frowned, rubbing his temples. Enough was enough.
Who were these coarse fellows to be giving him commands?
His head tilted with the unconscious arrogance of youth and
being a Roman.

They've obviously won their freedom in the arena, he realized. *This Subius is somewhat familiar. Some local champion,
I'm sure. He resembles a toad.* He was pleased to feel his confidence and irony returning. This was but a gradually fading
nightmare. Yes.

Against the tilt of the hillside, pale stone buildings and
flamelike cypress trees showed the first soft, warm rose of
dawn that slowly seeped into the misty air. He pushed the
madness of last night deeper down. He'd think about it later,
after hours of sweet rest.

Leitus ignored the bundle of clothes pushed toward him,
walking toward the side entrance of the house. The building
looked elegant in the diffused light; the cracks and weathering
didn't show. His family had just enough money to tread water
and feed the household slaves. Paying for his studies kept
them at the brink. He'd been training as a physician and had
years of apprenticeship ahead—if he got that far. He'd nearly
been sent down three weeks ago. Since he'd met Claudia
everything had started slipping. Claudia. Dead Claudia.

His friend Marcellus disapproved. Two weeks ago they'd been sharing bread and oil at noon in the scattered shade of a twisted olive tree. They'd rested in the flickers of spring sunlight. Marcellus had been watching a young girl pick flowers in the public garden next door to their teacher's massive villa. She was as graceful as a dancer. The sunlight on her face and limbs seemed a pure glow from within. She must have been eight or nine. Near her a wizened, leathery slave was chopping the fresh earth around a bed of herbs. The sweet smells floated across the lane.

"Hear me, Leitus," Marcellus had said, chewing, then washing the oil-wet bread down with a sip of plain wine, "this Claudia's a sweet-enough whore, but is she worth a career?"

Leitus had closed his eyes. The sun-heat had seemed to stir in his groin, as if the air were Claudia's caress and the grassy earth the rich female flesh itself.

"Ahh," he'd sighed, "who can estimate her worth?"

Marcellus had rubbed his slightly beaked nose, watching the barefoot girl kneel with her face in the yellow shimmer of flowers.

"If you are walked out by Clietus," he had said, meaning the doctor they were apprenticed to, "your father will pin your ears to the door frame."

"I won't be walked out. Not by the old fish. I've got the hands of a great cutter."

"Did he say so?"

"Would he admit skill in any but himself?"

Marcellus had chuckled and tilted up the wine. The young girl was moving in a quiet semidance, bare feet flashing the mellow sun.

"You'll end up cutting heads in the army," he'd responded, "like your father. If you follow your present—"

"Oh, peace," Leitus had insisted, stretching out on the warm earth, stroking his palms gently over the soft loam. He'd been imagining Claudia kneeling over him, her deeply painted lips pouting and parted, golden-hued body thrust at him, inching her groin's jet dark and silky hair closer and closer to his face. "Ahh," he'd sighed, a little to mock his friend, "cannot you leave me to my mental bliss? There was never such a lover."

"So I've heard. But they all have the same hole under their bellies." He'd watched the young girl suddenly toss up the laboriously gathered bouquet so that the yellow flowers scattered on the breeze and fell around her as she spun, like a rain from the world of the gods.

"You know nothing of her, Marcellus. Nothing."

"Yes. Which puts me in a select and shrinking group."

"I love a woman of experience."

"Yes, and what she's done to others she'll do to you, my friend, don't mistake it." Marcellus had bitten another hunk of bread off and thoughtfully chewed.

"No," Leitus had smiled, tasting her now in his mind, running his tongue along the slickness that subtly yielded to the aching caress. "Never. Impossible." The sun-heat on his face felt like honey spill that he could almost lick from his lips. . . .

Leitus reached the gray stone steps just as Subius took his arm in his overwhelming grip.

"There's no time for this," he told Leitus.

"What have you to do with me? Why are you here at all?"

"Putting that aside, for now," suggested the gladiator, "you'll be arrested soon enough. There's a soldier posted at your front gate as it is."

"This is all nonsense," Leitus said, blinking against his headache. "I would never have hurt her. Never." All he really cared about was sleep. Who were these annoying plebeians? He tugged his arm free and went to the door. "All nonsense and madness."

The bald fellow leaned on the wall near the statue and silently watched.

Inside was cool dimness. Leitus wobbled down the familiar corridor, almost banging into the bronze of Diana the huntress and her dog pack. Suddenly a black, icy grief gripped him:

O, poor Claudia, he thought. Cold despair.

"Leitus," someone said and he stopped, staring at the staircase where a large man stood halfway down.

"Father," he responded, feeling as if he'd just been caught at something. The dawn seemed to flow from the upstairs windows like blurry water around the solid man. "I—"

"Where are the men?"

"What?" Leitus blinked. He couldn't focus his eyes or mind very well.

"Outside. They had instructions to take you—"

"Who are they?"

"This is no time to make small conversation." Gracchus's voice was pure command, unshaken by events, the voice of a man who'd risen from the ranks, who'd fought in the vanguard with Crassus against Spartacus. No man to contradict lightly. He tried to be just. But, a true Roman, of all virtues and skills, in his heart he rated strength highest. "It doesn't matter right now what you have done," he told Leitus. "You are my son and will not be judged honestly in this matter."

There it was again. Leitus had heard things, growing up, but never anything substantial enough to form a clear question. Just hints that there was something in old Gracchus's past that was never mentioned but cast a shadow all the same. Something that wasn't quite a palpable disgrace but . . . something.

"Why not, father?" he asked.

"There's no time for that now. I have always loved you as a son and protected you."

"I am your son."

"There are suspicions that need not see the light of day. Whatever you've done, a trial—"

"I have done nothing."

"That won't matter. And there's no time."

"Where is mother?"

"I told her to keep to her apartment. Go with these men. They may be trusted. We'll do here all that can be done."

Leitus rubbed his face. "I need to rest," he said. "Don't you care if I'm guilty or—"

"There's not time for that, either." The voice had softened as they spoke and showed concern and great weariness. "Just go. For all our sakes." Gracchus was protecting the family; were Leitus to be accused and then flee, their property could be forfeited to the state.

"It was horrible, father . . . horrible. . . ." His hands suddenly shook where they held his cheeks.

The stern, full face was shadowed and vague. "You'll get money and help. Now, go. At once. The day cannot find you here." The pale, bluish toga slowly filled with the watery morning light.

Leitus turned to find Subius at his elbow, looking up at Gracchus.

"I don't—" he started to say, but his father cut over it.

"I want him safe. That's my charge and I pass it on to you, freeman."

"Yes, Commander," said the gladiator respectfully.

"In the name of the last man on the cross."

He heard Subius sigh, faintly, deeply.

What man? What cross? What . . . Leitus was baffled.

"Why cannot I have justice in Rome?" he blurted. Just to rest and sleep again. He yawned with the thought.

"Justice," snorted his father with contempt. "Do as I bid you. It may already be too late."

"Yes, Commander," repeated Subius.

And then the youth felt those irresistible hands grip again. That was that. He was part lifted and hustled down the smooth tile floor. He heard his father saying, not loudly, not softly:

"Farewell, Leitus, my son."

And then they were outside and it was substantially brighter. The air was damp but clearing. Details showed now: the broken arm on the statue; the scarred, bald head of the lean gladiator; the trampled grass near the stable. Leitus's head throbbed.

Subius helped him pull off the bloodstained tunic and dressed him in commoner's clothes. The rough cloth prickled his sensitive skin. It marked virtually at a touch. He was still stunned; he wasn't really asking the right questions yet, but Subius was answering:

"I recognized your name. I knew your father from the wars. And owed him a debt." *He didn't say "served with,"* Leitus remembered later. *Just "knew."*

The bald one was now squatting on a load of wood stacked in the back of an oxcart just outside the tradesmen's gate. He spat past the wheel and cocked an eye down the street. People were starting to stir here and there: a bent woman was tossing a slop bucket into the gutter; a gardener was pondering a hedge and drinking water from a gourd; two slaves were heading to market with wicker baskets hung on poles.

"You sit," ordered Subius, easing Leitus onto the wagon seat. "I drive." Subius chucked the reins and tipped the massive, dark oxhead with a flexible staff. "Move on, you fat, black bastard," he said, almost tenderly, at the immense, dusty behind, which drew flies, Leitus thought, as if its arse were a honeypot. Pouches of loose flesh trembled with each powerful step. The cart creaked and banged over the cobble edges.

Leitus glanced back at his home of twenty-two years. The

squarish building was now quite clear against the waking, purplish sky; the old street, the trees he knew, the shops . . . What was happening to him? This was a dreaming . . . a dreaming. . . . He felt flooded by memory and loss. His friends, everything. Claudia.

It was late morning. The stone houses sitting shoulder to shoulder gradually gave way to wider stretches of garden and field. They were rolling through a valley at the edge of the city. The sun was rising higher at their backs; they seemed to be catching up with the shadow of themselves.

They'd just come to the end of the paved way. A horseman passed, leaving a dust wake; slaves trudged along; citizens in wide-brimmed hats rode in two-man litters. The sun beat heat shimmers out of the drowsy spring landscape. The sky was spotless blue. Watching the scenery soothed him so he didn't have to think. Birds chittered; the ox broke wind and grunted every few steps; the bald man hummed and muttered to while away the day. A line of infantry in bright brass and gleaming leather crunched past under their eagle standards.

The suburbs gradually melted into rich and hilly farm country of olive trees and grape arbors, grainfields and distant villas perched on upper slopes. Somewhere along the way Leitus dozed off, slumping into the solid roundness of Subius; dreaming, in fits and starts, of a wild, barren, misty country with strange huts fenced in by rough palisades, peopled by wild-haired, wiry savages, half-naked bodies painted with garish blue streaks. He'd lose the images as the cart jarred and sunlight would burn away the dim landscapes. He went in and out . . . in and out. Suddenly there was a misty field where a long-haired, beautiful girl stood under a dark tree shape in muted moonlight looking over tangled, twisted, blurry heaps of dead men . . . a battlefield. The sun burned him awake again.

"What was that?" Subius wondered.

"That?" Leitus blinked, then remembered where he was. And why. Well, almost why.

They were just crossing a stone bridge high above a crashing river. An aquaduct arched beside them, part of the complex that fed water to the great city. The whitish stone gleamed in the afternoon sun.

"You were talking," Subius said to Leitus.

"My belly's talking," said Crato from behind. He stood up on the load, swaying, and urinated over the wheel to his own particular satisfaction. Leitus glanced at him with disgust.

"There's a market a mile or so on," said the gladiator. Leitus noticed he wore a long, thick-bladed dagger which seemed really a reduced version of an army-issue short sword.

"I know this country," Leitus remarked, mainly to himself, shielding his eyes from the hot glare and noting that his head felt better. Dozing had helped.

"Good for you," muttered Crato, sprawling back down on the bundled wood with hands behind his neck, humming.

"My uncle lives out here."

"So Gracchus told me."

Leitus studied the bent-nosed profile. Subius whipped the long stick and the ox snorted and swished flies with its tail. The water far below crashed steadily.

He was fascinated by a rope-thick, purplish scar that ran across the old fighter's halved right ear. *It might have cloven his head in two,* he thought. *What a blow to have taken and lived.* "Why does my father trust you? Who are—"

"Young Leitus," the man said, in his solid, quiet voice that calmed men down quickly, "I serve your father in this matter. Freely and with all my loyalty. Fear not." They were nearly across now. It was quiet here above the steady waterrush in the gorge.

"How did you find me?"

"Chance brought me to you. And now I must discharge an old debt."

"A debt to my father?"

This idea seemed to make the man thoughtful. And faintly, distantly, amused him. At least his lips seemed to smile.

"Yes," he said. "To your father. And to more still."

Again something mysterious. Leitus studied the expressionless face and learned exactly nothing. They crossed the shadow of the aquaduct and winked in and out of the sun at every arch.

"This pup," said Crato, sprawled over the wood, "not one hard Saturday in the arena, eh?" Snorted. "You'd of fallen like an ear of corn, boy. No time for questions on a hard Saturday."

Peripherally, Leitus noticed several mounted men moving up the sloping road. The hooves echoed as clearly as dropped stones.

"What sort of debt?" he pressed. He decided he'd never paid enough attention to his family's political ghosts and half-told secrets. He'd been too busy trying to make ten pieces of gold seem a hundred. And perfect the patrician lilt in his voice. He had never really wanted to think about the dim places in his father's past.

"The less you know," was the answer, "the less you can tell."

Leitus was getting annoyed now. "Listen, my fine fellow," he began, and was cut off in the middle of once again attempting to assert himself by bald Crato.

"Ar, Subi, I don't like this."

They all glanced back at the clump of oncoming riders with their light shields and brassy armor. They seemed to float, misty in shape, through the melting heat-shimmer beating from the stone road.

"Well," said Subius, "there's no outrunning the scum."

Crato sat up. One hand reached down between two bundles of wood and gripped something.

They weren't quite off the bridge by the time the soldiers reined up and blocked them to a creaking halt. Leitus noticed that Subius didn't really look at the men around them. Just sat on the driver's bench, big hands relaxed on his knees.

"We had word," said the captain in a detached, business-like tone, "that a young murderer has fled the city with two ex-arena men."

"And you just happened to follow us," said Subius, not looking at anything. "No doubt by smell."

"Base dog," said another man with a dark, pug face, "that would be easy. The odor of dead meat carries a long way."

Leitus sensed power building up inside the gladiator's body, a terrific concentration of force. But what could they hope to accomplish against five trained soldiers? Leitus had no weapon except for the short dagger at his belt.

The horses moved restlessly. The ox lowed. Hooves clack-clacked on the pavement.

"Look at this bastard," snarled another soldier, "he has a body like an onion."

Not an unjust comparison, thought Leitus.

"What did they use this lanky rat for?" asked the pug-faced man. "Caestus practice?"

These weren't ordinary soldiers, Leitus realized suddenly. Their armor and leather was marred and unpolished. And why

were such low types mounted? They should have been infantry
and looked too criminal even for that.

"Arena men," whispered Crato through his teeth.
"Dressed up to play troops."

"Don't underrate these fellows," suggested the captain in
his remote voice. "This is Subius Magnus."

"Who says so?" Crato wanted to know. "We're in trouble,
curse it," he whispered to the immobile man at the reins.

"And his fellow slicer, Crato," the captain finished.

"Are our faces on coins," asked that gentleman, "that we
are so surely known?"

The four trained killers drew their swords and reined closer.
The captain sat and watched, businesslike and aloof, as they
hemmed in the three on the cart. There was no other traffic.
The water roared softly below and a cool breeze stirred among
the trees on the slopes. Leitus could smell the water. His
mouth was metal dry. He now understood these men were
about to kill them out of hand.

*And they knew to send gladiators. Somebody knew that
much.*

"So you see," said the captain, "they are clearly resisting
the authority of the Republic and leave us no choice but to
raise arms against them."

"What are you saying?" Leitus broke in. The man had
almost yawned in pronouncing their doom. A patrician pose,
Leitus realized. He was surprised by some of the things he was
suddenly noticing. He'd read that danger sharpened a man.

"Ah," said Crato, "we'll resist, you need not fear."

"And you," declared the aristocrat, finally drawing his own
blade, looking at the young man with dispassionate eyes, "you
are Leitus Sixtus. How do you do?"

"Someone told them," he whispered to Subius, who sat
without stirring.

"They want you dead," Subius murmured. "Someone
does." Then he spoke to the captain. "Well, assassins, come
ahead."

"I want your lumpish skull, onion man," snarled Pug-face
as he ripped a terrific slash at the object in question.

He leaned in to do it. Leitus started to cry out, except the
blow sliced only air and tugged the man slightly off balance on
his stirrupless mount.

Subius's seemingly inert bulk moved with uncanny light-

ness. He rocked back from the glittering blade arc and then
sprang forward under the awkward following cut, clearing the
rump of the ox by a foot and slamming into the horse's flank
so hard that the animal gave ground and wheezed, so fast that
Leitus never actually saw the thick dagger smash home under
the gleaming breastplate. He just registered the spray of blood
which flickered back the terrible image of ripped Claudia for
an instant as the man sighed and crashed to the pavement.

One gone.

But it was already two. Crato (called the "snake" in the
arena because he hissed when aroused) came up with a trident
from the cart floor and impaled the nearest rider through the
bare thigh, jerked the weapon free and yelled with fury and
strange joy. The horse bolted and threw the man. The captain
frowned (the most expression he'd yet displayed) and backed
his mount a few steps aside so that Subius couldn't close
distance safely. The other two dismounted. One was almost as
broad as Subius. The second looked to Leitus like a human
dagger: a dark, oily-skinned fellow, possibly a Persian.

"Man on man, then," said the big fighter, taking a profes-
sional stance facing Subius. His partner crouched and said
nothing, moving sidelong as Crato stepped down to the road.
His breath hissed in and out. His stare didn't shift or break
into blinks as he followed the lithe man's movements.

Leitus seemed to see and hear everything with terrific clarity
in an unbroken perception: the flash of Pug-face's sword lying
near the ox's splayed hooves; the wounded man sitting up,
stunned, helmet knocked askew, clutching his punctured leg,
trying, quiet and desperate, to stem the blood pumping out in
loose jets between his fingers. His face, under dark, weathered
skin, went ghastly, greenish pale. The horse was still running:
one of the prongs must have pricked it. The captain moved his
mount closer, preparing to lean in and stab him.

Leitus backed off the driver's bench and half crawled over
the wood in the back of the cart, wondering if he should try
and run for the trees at the end of the bridge. He heard the
horse snort, the soothing water sounds, the grunt and clash as
the gladiators closed with one another . . . and then his foot
twisted on something. Looking down at two javelins, an ax
and a club, he realized that Crato had come prepared.

Crato, in fact, had just jabbed at the elusive Persian who'd
brushed away the trident with his small shield. He was trying

to work in close enough to use the short sword effectively. Crato kept the needle-sharp prongs in his face.

Subius (Leitus paused, as did the horseman, to see this) spun aside like a massive top each time his opponent thrust. The man had perfect balance and showed no openings for the famous fighter. They'd sent first-rate men, he realized. It was only sheer luck and surprise that had eliminated the first two. Otherwise they'd be dead. Leitus was certain of that.

The next time Subius spun from the neat, vicious thrusts, the dagger zipped from him so fast it seemed a flash of light caught the other man in the face. Leitus registered it for an instant as some magic blow, because the armored man dropped with a crash, hands feebly plucking at the blade buried in one eye to the hilt.

Subius turned with that odd grace just as Leitus jumped from the cart holding a javelin. But the horse was already towering over him too close and the solid shoulder bounced him off the side of the cart. He saw dark and light, the shadow of horse and rider flailing over him, the sword glint as he jabbed the javelin and scraped over bone, heard a scream (glimpsed Crato darting in on his Persian in a tangle, glitter, and flurry) then felt a cold shock on his chest. Only as he fell did he comprehend it was a blow from the sword. Then the horse shadow passed over him and his bright blood stained the stones. He felt himself draining away into dim gray nothing like water flowing into the thirsty earth. . . .

CHAPTER IV

Sweet, green hills were moving past a horse's nodding head. Leitus gradually realized that Subius was behind him, one arm holding him like a child on his father's lap. Blood was caked along his side. He always seemed to have gore on him, whether someone else's or his own. He felt cold in the baking hot sun. The pain was a steel claw locked under his ribs.

"Ah," said the famous gladiator, "you've come back to us."

Leitus sighed for answer. Subius was grim and quietly furious.

"We just lost a good man," he said. "It shocks me. That Persian was deadly. And in fighting trim, which neither of us were." He made a soft sound both of grief and acceptance. "It shocks me."

Leitus tried to concentrate. He leaned back into the firm ball of belly and chest. He recalled the flash of trident and zip of sword when Crato and the dark killer had clashed, just before the horse and weapon had hit him. So that lanky plebeian was done for.

"A miracle any of us live," he said. It hurt when he spoke. "Are we near my uncle's?"

Subius grunted. He was still lost in details of the fight.

"His foot slipped on a damned stone," he said to himself. Shook his head slightly. "It's always like that. Skill is nothing. When the gods blink you fall, try what you wish."

"You think there are gods?" Leitus wondered. Young

29

medical men were ever prone to doubt. He gingerly touched his slashed side. The nicked bones ached.

"Ah, no one leaves the arena an atheist."

"How about the dead?"

"Their views are kept close. The living could learn that much from them."

The road here was all fine white dust that smoked around the horse's hooves. They'd wound away from the stone thoroughfare. There was little shade in these open, coppery fields.

"I was meant to be a surgeon," Leitus remarked, "yet I am the one sliced." He suddenly realized he wanted to win this man's respect. "My left deltoid has been properly sectioned," he said, attempting a slightly gruff, manly tone.

Subius seemed unimpressed. He aimed the horse at a fast canter across a freshly planted field. Then up a grassy slope. Leitus recognized the gateless arch where the stone boundary wall opened to permit a short, brick bridge to cross a narrow stream. Memories welled up when he looked at the shallow blue water rush, the pure white stones, the stippled current. Childhood summers. He'd sailed stick boats here and followed them down the unwinding waterflow, sometimes tossing pebbles to spin or sink them. He felt again the cool mud under his feet and the excitement of play, the purity and freedom of it.

Then they were across and on a dusty sketch of trail.

"That other fellow," he said, rocking against the powerful man, "he was a gladiator, too?"

"Yes, young Leitus."

"You both fought together?"

"Never each other."

"You were famous, they say."

He felt vaguely proud of his own wound. *Jupiter, but much has happened in a little space.* He'd run and fought for his life. This fellow here was an amazing battler. He replayed how he'd spun and struck down his opponent as if with a thunderbolt.

Now he saw his uncle's place—pale, rose stone lushly set among groves of fruit trees and flowering gardens. A pair of female slaves stood up from their labors over a washtub, staring with the laconic watchfulness of country people.

"What happened to the man I struck?" he suddenly asked.

"The captain?"

"Yes."

"He struck you."

"Did he fall?"

Subius didn't exactly snort. "How many times have you fought to the death?" he asked.

"I?" Leitus murmured, touching his wounded side.

"It needs practice," said the gladiator.

When they halted in the walled yard, Leitus glanced at the people who'd just come outside: mixed servants, one Nubian male and a strikingly pretty young girl with reddish-tinted hair and a rose pastel tunic setting off her beautiful legs and bare feet. Leitus's eyes were blurred from sun and suffering so that the people suddenly went hazy, and when his uncle came through the big arched doorway he seemed a short, stout shadow and Leitus only knew him by his voice.

When his feet hit the hard-packed earth, there was a red burst of flame in his side that blazed into his head. . . .

When he came to this time, he assumed he was in the world of the gods: soft, perfumey, honey-gold light washed over coppery-fired hair and pooled in the pale eyes of the young goddess who floated above him. Her form seemed to be melting into soft, golden fire. He squinted and blinked to clear his vision. The face stayed lovely but went suddenly solid. It was the young slave girl in the rose tunic, holding a basin and napkin.

She pressed the cool cloth over his forehead. He sighed. The pain beat along his ribs.

"Are you better?" she asked. Her voice suited the smooth, calm expression.

"Mmm," he said and winced. At his side a pad was tied to the wound by soft cloths. "You did this?"

She shook her head, gravely watching him. "No," she responded. "Your servant." His expression prompted: "That man who brought you here."

"Ah," he said. He touched the damp pad. *I'll need this changed properly*, he thought. After all, he'd had two years medical training. He made a mental note to explain things to Subius.

"He said there was more pain than danger."

Easy to say, thought Leitus. *Dr. Subius.*

He looked around the room. The window behind the girl was open to the late, low sun. Treetops moved and shook the mellowing light.

"Where is my uncle?" he asked.

"He just went downstairs. I'm to watch you." She smiled faintly. "See that you keep still."

He nodded, opening and closing his eyes. She was very pretty, he decided. He took it as a good sign that he was conscious of it. Shy, perhaps, but she seemed strong underneath —or at least determined.

"What's your name?" he asked.

"Bita," she said. "And you're Leitus. I remember you."

"Do you?" He shifted in the bed and groaned under his breath.

"Yes. You were here three years ago. In the summer."

"True. Still, I don't recall you." He studied the calm eyes, richly gray-blue. "How old are you, Bita?"

"Sixteen."

"That's an odd name."

"I wouldn't know. It's mine."

"Where are you from?"

"Here. The farm."

"Before?"

"Britain."

"A barbarian." His stare drifted back to the shimmer of green and soft gold at the arched window. He vaguely registered voices outside over the drowsy *whoosh*ing of the warm breezes. After a few moments he realized they belonged to his uncle and aunt. He concentrated but only picked up drifts and fragments.

". . . be a fool, then," his aunt seemed to be saying.

"Hah . . . never so . . . his mother I . . ." his uncle said in turn.

"Nonsense . . . too many enemies . . . come here . . ."

"We must . . . send him . . . we must do right . . ."

Now her voice came louder and clear:

"So, my husband, you wish to discuss *must* with me?"

Just the breeze for reply. The voices had moved when he thought he heard them next and were finally swallowed by the day's murmur.

He realized Bita was staring at him with childlike frankness.

"You came from Rome?" she asked. *I wonder what sports he likes best?* she was wondering. *He looks very strong.*

"Yes," he said, shifting his head on the pillow. "I come from Rome." *These country slaves,* he thought, *have a lax manner.* He vaguely remembered hearing someone say that. It was almost a quote. Not his father. Not his schoolmate Marcellus. And then he remembered it was her brother, Iro. Claudia's brother. Poor Claudia. The hollow shock came back for a moment. She was really gone. Gone forever. He sighed without knowing it. He'd never liked Iro. He pictured his long, sooty face with a nose like a bent blade edge and lips like a thin flesh wound. He had an oversized mole under one eye that annoyed Leitus because whenever the man blinked it bobbed slightly. He had decided then that anything Iro said with certainty was worth doubting.

That cold bastard, he thought. *He used to spy on us whenever he could. . . .*

Once they were sitting in the garden by the fishpond at sunrise after a long, sweet night together. Claudia was kissing his neck absently. They were stretched out on linen cloth. He stared past her face at what he first took for one of the statues, except it was that pale, expressionless face with pit eyes staring through the low branches of an ash tree. He felt an unaccountable fury and malice.

"Who's that?" he'd asked her, because this was the first time he'd been to her estate. She'd rotated a languid glance there and away.

"That's mad Iro," she'd said.

"Who's Iro?"

"My brother."

"He's touched by the gods?"

She'd laughed, light and ever so faintly harsh.

"No god would put a finger to him," she'd remarked. "He's a perfect viper, my brother. Everyone fears him. Well, almost everyone." He hadn't been able to make out just how serious she'd been. When he'd looked up again the face had gone. A few days later they'd been introduced at a feast. Iro had looked blandly at him and said nothing in particular. He hadn't seemed dangerous or hateful. Bland, if anything. When he'd spent a week at their countryside estate, Leitus and Claudia had gone swimming in the river at sunset. She'd just gone back to shore when he'd noticed the face upstream, neck-deep, the vague, violet glow hinting the features, the mouth opened in a silent shout of shadow. Leitus had stood knee-deep and squinted, to be sure. Hadn't been sure. Almost called his name, but the head had gone under the surface. He'd waited but whoever it was, he'd decided, must have swum away underwater. After a while he'd wondered if it hadn't been a trick of vision.

"Iro," he muttered.

"Yes?" wondered Bita.

He didn't want to think about Claudia. He held away the red images and tried to focus on the petite, graceful slave girl, talking to him almost as if she were an equal.

"What do you do here?" he asked, unable to think of a better question.

"I?" She wasn't quite flustered. "I help in the garden. I'm learning the herbs from old Flavius."

"Ah. The herbs."

"Yes."

He nodded, trying to come up with a new subject. He was strangely dull. The wound and fever, of course, he reassured himself.

The problem was solved by his uncle coming into the chamber, perspiring, seeming flustered, angry, and nervous.

"How are you, my boy?" he asked distractedly, patting his plump hands together. They gleamed with sweat. "I see you've been fixed up quite well, eh?" He glanced nervously at Bita. "He's getting fit, eh?"

"I don't know," she responded.

The uncle paid no attention. His hands flicked in the fading daylight from the window when he gestured and seemed to stream long beams of darkness.

"Just a superficial cut, eh?" he suggested.

"Well," responded Leitus, "it may be so." His ribs still felt as if a red-hot saw blade had been drawn across them.

"Excellent. Excellent, because, you see, you must move on as quickly as possible."

Quickly? Leitus thought.

"Uncle," he began, "I—"

"Oh never mind, never mind," irrelevantly scoffed the older man, "I care nothing for your crimes. You're my blood relative. But, you see, Leitus, my wife . . . ah, my wife. Now, that's another matter, you see. She feels rather strongly. Yes. Rather."

"I did nothing wrong, uncle."

The hands moved smoothly, seeming to softly rip the deepening light into shadowy shreds.

"Yes, yes," he said, "naturally not. Naturally not." He coughed. "I am told the state authorities insist otherwise."

"Sir," Bita spoke up, "I think he should stay and rest."

The idea of his going so soon upset her. She thought of him suffering along the way. *They're going to call me to go to the kitchen,* she was thinking at the same time. *I'd better be quiet and just wait.* Because she wanted to stay here as long as possible. She didn't explain just why to herself yet. She wished her master would leave, because there was something she wanted to say to Leitus, except she didn't know what that was, either, or, at least, the words hadn't yet formed in her mind.

The uncle didn't quite take note of her.

"My wife, your aunt," he said, "has definite views on most subjects." He shook his head.

But we'd be safe here for a few days, surely, Leitus thought. Why was his uncle doing this? He sensed it had to do with his father, again. Wasn't sure, but sensed it.

Now Subius was in the doorway. Though his eyes were set too deep to read, Leitus felt their scorn.

"He should not be moved yet," the gladiator said. The corridor behind him was stained with the deepening rose color of fading daylight. His body was a silhouette.

"Nevertheless," said the uncle, "my wife has views."

Subius was stolid and blunt.

"Can you cast out blood kin like a dog?"

"It's for his own good, in the end. I'll provide what you need for safe travel. We dare not risk his staying here."

"His father swore me to keep him safe," said the gladiator.

"And so you shall," the uncle insisted, quiet and nervous. "So you shall." Hands touched the dimming, blood-colored light.

Leitus shifted his back. There was dull pain. He felt weak, but strangely confident. Decided to sleep some more. The discussion seemed remote and not really to involve him. Being sick or hurt made some things easier; he didn't have to care. He vaguely wondered if that had been his problem right along, as if he'd always been ill: not caring enough. Until Claudia, who'd crippled him with caring. Made him mad with it. He shut and reopened his heavy eyes. Felt like a child.

He looked at the little slave girl; smiled faintly; lost himself

in the glints of hair and the pale, gentle eyes. And next, as
he jerked down into sleep, he was afraid because the crimson
glow haloing her from the window was suddenly blood spilling
down her cheeks and across her slight bosom as if she'd been
slashed.

"He's resting," she murmured.

The uncle still stood with his back to Subius. "Take him in
the morning," he said. "There's no point arguing with me,
gladiator."

"Yes. I don't argue. Just stand amazed."

Why are you so silly? Bita asked herself. *He's just another
Roman.* Cinca always said the day would come when the
slaves would rise again, as they did under Spartacus. Whoever
he was. She frowned, thinking about Cinca. He was not tall,
with a bland face and pale, blinking eyes; he always seemed to
be watching her when he spoke. He was always saying something in the slave kitchen when everyone gathered for the evening meal, sitting on gray stone benches at the massive cutting
table. He would curse the Romans and promise revenge.
Flavia, the chief female slave of the household, would set her
jaw and ask him if life here was so terrible? They'd generally
argue for half of dinner. Despite herself, Bita was impressed
by his intensity. "The Romans," he liked to say, "are stealing
the world and putting the victims in prison!"

"Hear this then, gladiator, if you would be amazed." The
uncle turned around to face Subius. "Hear this: Our entire
family was once proscribed. What do you think of that,
gladiator?"

"When Sulla was consul?" Subius was thoughtful. Proscription meant the state had excommunicated you. You had
no rights and any man could rob and kill you. When Sulla
became dictator he'd made up lists of enemies of the state and
proscribed them. He and his supporters had become very rich
in the process.

"When else?" the uncle said, blinking and nodding as if
he'd won his point entirely.

"Why?" Subius wondered. Except he already knew why,
just as he knew this man wasn't going to tell him. He really
meant to ask, "I mean, why was it lifted?"

"A favor. Dearly bought. But the sword still hangs above us
all." He gestured toward his sleeping nephew. "Him, too. But
don't you know that?"

"Yes."

"Why are you in it?" The bulging eyes watched shrewdly through the strip of fading light. "Money?"

Subius snorted with disparagement.

"I intend to become rich," he said, "flying for my life with wanted men?"

"Well, I'll give you gold enough."

"Yes, to buy a night's sleep."

The dark eyes went lidded, as the uncle paced toward the window, hands locked behind his back. His toga hung askew and made him look stooped with age.

"I tell you, I have no choice," he said out into the gathering evening. The sun had dropped behind the garden wall and the pale twilight seemed to rise sourcelessly among the trees and shrubs.

"It isn't a matter of choosing," the gladiator said. "You follow your heart or you don't."

Bita had moved beside the bed. She reached out her hand before she realized what she was doing and with two fingers softly, fleetingly touched his cheek. He stirred slightly and she took her hand away.

"I do what I must," said Leitus's uncle. "Ask me no more."

CHAPTER V

He awoke this time to a tin-gray sky and a wet clinginess that a few moments later he realized was a drizzling rain. His sight blurred until he blinked the water away. This time he was in the back of the cart. He lay on damp straw. He vaguely recalled being carried downstairs and outdoors by torchlight. It seemed long ago.

Above him was Subius's back. He chucked the rein of a sturdy pair of horses. The slave girl was still there and that surprised him. Until that moment he wasn't certain he'd actually been at his uncle's estate.

She was unfolding a piece of canvas, obviously meaning to cover him. By the soft bumping he knew they were in open country on a dirt road. He stirred and his side ached but felt much better. He touched the soft packing on the wound. He'd told Subius to gather cobwebs and soak them in vinegar; the gladiator seemed to have followed instructions.

"You had fever," Bita told him.

He stretched and felt rested, though cramped on hard boards among sacks of provisions. She adjusted the canvas like a sheet around him.

"For how long?" he wondered.

"Two days now," she told him.

He sighed.

"So he's back," Subius said cheerfully.

"We left Uncle Flacchus . . ."

"Two days ago," said Subius. "Too much of a good thing there. Too much hospitality makes a man soft." He spat

38

carefully between the horse rumps.

Leitus was too dazed to react to his sarcasm. Bita never did. If she had one defect, he was to think a long time later, it was an almost total lack of irony in her nature.

What had seemed dreams came back to him. . . . His aunt leaning over him in the dark, holding what seemed a blinding candle over his face so that shadows stirred and hollowed out her long, lean face. She was talking, but it meant nothing. His uncle's soothing voice saying, quite clearly, "Bita will go with you and thus confuse pursuit." Then blank darkness . . . then bright sky and treetops passing overhead . . . then grayness and a feeling of floating out to sea. . . .

Bita leaned close to his face. For a moment he expected her to kiss him. She was quite lovely. There was fire in her slate-colored eyes. He could imagine her furious or sullen.

Very sensual mouth, he thought. He pictured erotic things.

He touched her cheek gently and held her eyes with his own stare. Felt his loin fill and stir slightly. Subius watched them, round head cocked to the side, delicate, almost girlish lips creased with humor.

"You're lovely," he murmured to Bita.

She blinked, watchful behind her smooth mask of expressionlessness.

"Thank you," she said.

Subius was grinning. "If you're well enough to notice," she said, "you're well enough."

She held a leathern flask to his lips filled with some sweet herbal broth. It seemed to instantly charge his body with energy. After a gulp or two he sat up. His side was stiff, but not really painful.

He held the canvas around his middle and stared across the misty, grayed-out countryside: steep cliffs, rocky fields.

"I feel better," he said to Subius, leaning on the wicker side of the cart. It gave and creaked under his weight. Bita had the hood of her cloak over her head. The warmish drizzle beaded on her cheeks. "Did you run away from my uncle?" he asked her. *The bastard,* he thought, *driving me from his door. What can one expect? Nothing much. The world is the world. Someday I will come back and show them all a few things.* The idea was small, but real, comfort. *I was too soft. A man has to be hard.*

"No," she was saying, "he gave me a travel pass."

"Why?"

"I suppose so I might tend your wounds."

"No," scorned Subius, "he merely meant to enrich me the more. Now I have two slaves when before I had only myself and my own ass to keep whole." He grinned at the damp horse rumps where the soggy tails kept mismatched time.

"Two slaves?" wondered Leitus. "I see but this girl here."

"Aye, so," chortled the gladiator. "You'd need a mirror to behold the other."

Bita smiled slightly.

"Mock me not," Leitus said, irritated. "Don't presume on my present state to—"

Subius cut him off:

"Peace, slave," he commanded. "For your relative, while a treacherous coward, which is to say, a noble Roman"—he grinned wider—"is, nonetheless, shrewd enough."

"Watch your tongue!" Leitus snapped, furious.

"Will you cut it from my mouth?" Subius mildly wondered. "Stem my insolence? Call the guard?"

"But I thought—"

"I am your friend and stand charged to preserve you," Subius said. "But my opinions are mine. You are safer as a slave. Old Flacchus was very afraid. There's more here than I knew, myself."

"More what?" Leitus was curious.

"Politics. Plotting. Murder. I'm not sure. Roman tradition."

Leitus reached himself another drink of broth from the flask. He was getting hungrier by the minute.

"You hate all Romans?" he asked.

Subius was amused. "Do I seem to?"

"I suppose not."

"I hate all and no one. But many have little cause to love you."

He sounds like Cinca, Bita thought. *But I like him more.*

"I never really thought about that," Leitus confessed.

"Where have you lived?" he snorted.

"At home." He took another swig of the rich, perfumey broth.

"Drinking and wenching and talking about nothing in the steambaths," said Subius. "Did you imagine everyone was as happy as you?"

Leitus frowned. "I'm not happy. Not really."

He doesn't look like a wencher, Bita thought. She had a

vague image of what that meant. She didn't like it.

"Not now," said the gladiator, "that's clear enough. But you were a happy little aristocrat a month ago, I'd wager."

Leitus thought about it. Pursed his lips. Stared across the misty, rugged fields. High on the hill slope a walled villa showed one wing of itself.

"I wouldn't say I was happy then," he remembered. *Claudia,* he thought. *Claudia.* . . .

"Well," said Subius, "whatever you were, I can tell you this: You won't be happy for some time, if ever. You'd better learn to be a slave if we're to find our way north in safety."

Leitus shook his head, frowning.

"And you're my master? How silly."

The massive man turned full around to look him in the face from under his overhanging brows.

"And teacher," he said intensely. "And you'll learn to listen because you're no medical sack of excrement now, boy, you're going to be trained for the stinking games. We're taking you to learn your trade. In the hill circuses."

"What?" He tried to see the eyes and couldn't. Of course. It made some sense. It would explain Subius being in charge. Promising slaves were often sent to outlying arenas to learn their bloody business. And die. He almost laughed at the idea. *Me, a gladiator?* He recalled hot afternoons with men and beasts ripping and slamming and chopping one another down while the crowd howled and hissed and shuddered.

"We will stay in Lirium," Subius said, "long enough to let memory of you fade." He yawed the reins as they passed a cart going the other way. They both gave ground. The driver was a squat black man, a sullen-looking slave, with gray hair. He didn't look up when Subius hailed him. "Hey, are you deaf?" he called after. The cart was loaded with flat stone. It sagged and squeaked. The black didn't shift an inch on his seat. "Stupid bastard," Subius concluded. "Unless he speaks no Latin." Spat past the wheel. "In any case, Leitus the younger, there's a sweet little arena in Lirium run by a friend of mine." He snorted and spat again. "A friend you keep one eye on while you hold your purse with both hands. Ah, you'll love Lirium. You can have educated conversations with drunken mule drivers. When I fought there no whore on the street weighed less than a bullock." Subius chortled. "Or had more teeth than a duck."

And it is fitting, the gladiator was thinking, quite seriously,

*most fitting. The hands of the gods are tugging the reins.
Lirium.*

"So this is exile," murmured Leitus. He thought of the
many famous men who'd suffered exile. The eminent com-
pany failed to improve his spirits. "Some provincial horror."

Subius craned his neck to stare back at him from under jutting brows that blanked the deep-set eyes.

"Men more worthy than you think, boy," he said almost
harshly, "learned their trade there. Learned to keep their
assholes tight in the jaws of hell." There was emotion in his
voice.

Leitus winced as he moved his left arm to grade the pain. He
felt much better.

"You have a nicely insolent manner," Leitus commented.
After all, he thought, *I'm from a famous family. This fellow
ought to respect what merits respect.*

"Have I?" Subius said, pleased. "That's troubling news. It
will rack my sleep to know it."

"Where is Lirium?" Bita put in suddenly, as if she really
hadn't been listening, which was true.

"Near the coast."

She thought about it. Tried to picture the sea, the place
where the ship carrying her had beached.

"You're just setting foot on the hardest road of your life,"
Subius went on to Leitus who was looking up at the trees that
overhung the road. "But you'll count yourself a man if you
come to the end of it."

"Is Britain far over the sea from where we're going?" Bita
asked.

"Britain?" Subius smiled, urged the horses over a hillcrest,
where they suddenly had a misty view of rolling, sloping country. "This is still Italy, little one. Britain is an adventure
away."

She kept remembering things: rows of people naked by
moonlight, kneeling before mysterious and massive stones; a
robed priest shaking a wand wrapped with leaves and flowers;
strange humming moans and chanting; the sharp face of old
Namolin leaning close to her.

"You're not serious," Leitus was saying.

"Do I seem a rich man's buffoon?" Subius wondered. "Or
a trip-foot from the marketplace?"

"About this arena business?"

The round face turned to him again.

"Am I breaking in two laughing?" he asked. He wasn't.

"But that's foolish!"

"No. We'll teach you to fight. That's the least I can do for your father. You won't live otherwise, not as you are, not where you'll be going."

Leitus blinked. The drizzle and mist closed in again, seemed to fold over the open country ahead. He had an impression that all the world had melted into (as the poet said) Hades mists of forgetfulness.

"I was almost a doctor," he said to no one in particular.

"Ah," said the gladiator, "I was almost a general. Once. Long ago."

Spoiled, he was thinking, *because these gents are all getting soft. Well, not all. But this one is barely his father's son. The women have done for him.* He felt it was wrong to compare but hard to resist. His father in battle: planning, fighting hand to hand like a fury; planning wisely for peace if it came and judging men fairly. That was a man—more than a man. Yes, and finally, lapsing into tragedy.

Leitus imagined himself fighting the way the Persian had fought Crato at the bridge: soft, quick movement and blinding strokes. Saw himself dazzling the mob, battering down opponent after opponent to hysterical plaudits in a rain of flung flowers. Yes. Saw himself, incognito, in the Circus Maximus, in the heart of Rome, winning a breathtaking triumph. Shut his eyes to play with the images. Perhaps Lirium might prove interesting at that.

"It seems a sound plan," he said at length. "Confuse pursuit. Give me time to make decisions."

"Ah, noble born, I'm delighted you approve."

CHAPTER VI

The sun shocked the sandy soil with brilliant heat. Hot sand grated under Leitus's toes as he planted his sandals, bent his knees, and aimed the short sword, the *gladius,* at his teacher, who was wearing a basinlike brass helmet and holding a target shield. Otherwise he just covered his loins with a cloth like a diaper. His body was smooth and powerful, thick as it was wide. A wooden sword was stuck in the ground between his squat legs.

Leitus was suited up in full Thracian armor. It felt hot as a griddle. Sweat kept blurring into his eyes. But, he realized, he was getting used to the weight of the sword. That pleased him. During the first few weeks of practice his arm had hung down like dead meat.

He pointed the stubby blade at his teacher. Behind him were the rusted iron cages that held men and beasts for the circuses in this small provincial arena. The curved walls sagged and were cracked in places.

A man in a misfolded, stained toga leaned forward over the first row's wall. He was shapeless-looking. His round head was swallowed in shadow; only his puffy, reddened, scaly-looking nose jutted into the violent sunlight.

"Well, Subius Magnus," he said in a scornful singsong, "we've enough scraps to feed the dogs; we don't need this lad."

"Insolent pig," said Leitus.

"Be still, slave," Subius said. His foot lashed out and caught the young man on the hip. Leitus staggered two steps, turned, furious, sword poised.

The arena master was amused.

"That's the way," he encouraged. "Go on, then, chop off the great Subius's other ear."

Subius held a wooden sword. He waited.

"Come on," he commanded, "cut my head off!"

Leitus scowled and set his teeth. He wanted to, for a moment. He knew he probably couldn't succeed, but he was in armor with a shield and ought to be able to make it interesting for his teacher.

He tried. The arena master jeered. Subius rolled aside from each stroke and whacked the youth alongside the ears with the wooden sword.

"Come on, boy," he suggested. "Slice me into steaks!"

No one was working out now. Everyone was watching Leitus pant and sweat and charge the massive master with empty cuts and stabs.

Then Leitus, without thinking, slashed, knowing he'd miss, and, instead of recovering and taking a whack on the head, he kicked viciously with his rear-planted leg and caught the pivoting gladiator behind the knee. Subius went down in the sands and rolled out of range before Leitus's following back chop, crouched to his feet, and nodded approval.

"You see," he called over to the arena master, "even a goat learns not to chew stones, in time."

Leitus stood there, running sweat, panting hard. The armor seemed forged of lead and the sword dragged his arm to his side. The sun-heat beat at his head.

"Save you were fighting Samite," said the arena master, "he would have slit your gullet, Subius."

Leitus understood: If Subius had been armored he could not have escaped the downcut. He'd impressed these experts, but he was too miserable to care. He walked a few steps into the shadow of the wall and rested in the coolness. He imagined himself in the Coliseum in Rome, the stands packed, the yells and stink of the crowd, the raw odor of blood on the sand. Saw himself standing over a fallen champion and unmasking himself to drink in the cheers. Heard himself calling up to the lord of the games in his flower-decked box: "I am Leitus, son

of Gracchus." And the shocked murmur of the people:
"Leitus . . . Leitus the murderer . . ." "Arrest him!" went up
the cry, soon dinned over by shrieks of: "No! No! Free him!
Free him! He's the greatest fighter in Rome!" Yes, a triumph!
The charges against him set aside. But what was he thinking?
He was innocent, by Jupiter and Pallas. Innocent! Yes.
Disguised as a gladiator he'd ferret through the city and find
the real killer. He wasn't sure of the exact method, thought
vaguely about asking questions in wineshops, at the arena. He
nodded to himself. He'd find a way.

"Stop talking to the air," Subius commanded. "Get over
here. Is the sun set already? Is it time to rest?"

Leitus turned. The shadows hollowed his face; inside the
brassy armored hat he seemed the image of death. *They're go-*
ing to want him to fight, sooner or later, Subius was thinking,
watching him flex his sore arm as he walked back. You never
believed it would be you, he remembered. Not until you stood
in the glare of Saturday's harsh sun on grating sand, while the
brute animals cheered in the stands, and faced another savage,
frightened man like yourself who had to kill you to live. *How*
do I teach him? And how do I save him?

Bita swept fine dust from the rough plank flooring out into
the dried ruts where a street should have been. There were
about two dozen wooden apartments set along the outer brick
rim of the circus, what Subius called the Circus Minimus.

The blinding afternoon sun highlit her bare arms, face, and
honey-colored hair. The hot glare winked with shadows as the
broom scraped and tossed yellowish fluffs of dust-smoke to
hang in the windless air.

He'll like some cold meat, she was thinking, *and greens.*

She stood the broom beside the door frame and blinked out
at the rough-hewn little town that sloped down toward the
western sea, visible between the squat stone and wooden buildings.

She closed her eyes and let the tingling sun-pressure bathe
her face. Bright spots leaped and whirled in the darkness of
her shut eyes. She remembered childhood suddenly: the mists;
the rough huts; the deep, dark, murmurous woods; the smells.
Her pale, black-haired mother working leather with her hard,
polished-looking hands. Her father holding her in his arms,

carrying her into the sea, laughing as the wild spray broke over them.

And then, suddenly, it was as if the light were a voice touching inside her head. A voice like the beautiful lady's seemed to wordlessly speak. She understood not to be afraid. She understood that something mysterious was opening inside her. A doorway she could pass through into safety. She was changing. Terrible things would find her, but she would learn to defeat them.

And then she blinked as Leitus came through the door out of the sun-dazzle. He was tanned, sweaty, and looked tired. The voice that wasn't a voice seemed to tell her: *"This, too, is necessary."* And she nearly asked "What is?" aloud.

The training, she could see, agreed with Leitus. He was lean and strong from all the running, leaping, and endless practice thrusts and parries. "You're dead meat," Subius liked to tell him, squatting in the slant of shade from the empty animal shed near the arena gate. "Dead meat, unless you never tire. There's a power in some men to never tire. Worth more than a sword."

"You're back soon," Bita said. She wished she'd already started the meal.

He grunted and set his sword down in the corner. He was thinking how far away his life of a month ago seemed. He hadn't actually forgotten anything, but the blood and horror of Claudia's death had faded somewhat in the bronze, violent sunlight of the arena. Always a poor sleeper and tormented by dreams, the sheer physical effort of his present life had purged his nights. He awoke refreshed at dawn. He had less taste for wine, and the plain foods he would have scorned seemed rich and satisfying. *The gods know,* he'd thought, *this life would almost be worth paying for . . . a finer cure than the waters of Mantua.* Except, he preferred not to think, for having to die, sooner or later.

"I fight this Saturday," he told her, smiling slightly. He felt like fighting. His body was ready, poised, tensed.

"Fight?" she said, upset. "But—"

"My contest is not to the death." He realized he wouldn't have minded if it were.

"How can they promise that?" she pressed, watching him, seeing him fall, sticky with sand and blood, and for a moment she wondered if it was imagination or the other seeing, the strange seeing.

He shrugged. "How can anyone be promised another day's life? Yet we go on in the face of that."

"That's different."

"We use blunted weapons." He smiled again. "Anyway, I'll knock the bastard on his ass." He was studying her legs and feet, looking up from the dusty, pretty toes to where the slim thighs were covered by the tunic. He pictured her legs folded up around him. "I'm an arena man, now," he said, catching his breath slightly, picturing. "We have privileges."

She didn't follow where his words pointed. She was trying to find a way to say "Don't fight" that might actually stop him.

He was remembering something Subius had talked about the first day he'd wobbled out into the practice area in drizzling rain, the sword weighing his arm down, the armor pieces grating, clumsy. The other men, novices and seasoned veterans of (as his teacher said) a dozen provincial "dance contests," all seemed to Leitus lithe, smooth, ready, and solidly powerful.

"Maybe," he'd suggested, "we should forget this and head straight north, Subius."

"Sooner or later," his teacher had said, "we'd have to stop."

The fat arena master had been standing in an unhitched cart, soft hands gripping the side. He'd shaken his head at the crop.

"And this," he'd said to Subius, "is what you want to add to this stew of cripples and old men?" He'd snorted and spat with disgust. "By the gods, I'll have the goats fighting the three-legged dogs this season, instead." Subius had guffawed.

"Or," he'd suggested, "have infants wrestle like the Greeks."

"Ar," one mature, hairy, long-armed gladiator had snarled behind a rude gesture, "you're worse than a Greek yourself, you fairy!"

This comeback had been met with wide approval. Subius enjoyed this sort of thing. He'd swigged some wine from a flask, winked, and had answered:

"Do they pay the crowd when this one fights?"

Leitus had just wanted to go home. Even to Rome where they waited to arrest him, or worse. What was he doing there in a miserable provincial dungpit, treated like a slave, bullied, scorned? . . . He'd sighed and only half heard the arena master declaring him to be "dead meat, Subius, I tell you. I can smell him already. Look, the flies know it." Referring to the fact that Leitus had kept brushing the little buzzers away from his face. He'd used some scented water Bita kept to soothe his face after shaving. Walking over, Subius had informed him he smelled like an old whore.

"Hey, slave," a young hopeful had said, wanting to join the general banter, "the buzzards know your name."

"Enough wind-pumping," the arena master had snarled, "Let's see some work here!"

And, muttering about the rain, the men had begun to pair off for sparring. Men fighting Samite, with net and trident; others Thracian with heavy armor and thick swords. Curses and clanging sounded in the wet, dull day.

"One thing you'll like," Subius had assured his charge. "You get your pick of slave women the night before you fight." He'd sneered. "We, who are about to die"—he'd spat into the wet sand—"piss in your face." That was a saying where the deadly men waited on benches for the arena call.

"Women?" Leitus had been vaguely interested. "But the ones I've seen here would sour a dog's milk."

"In Rome," Subius had said, grinning, "even noblewomen would often disguise themselves as slaves to be roughed under by one of us." *As was the fact with you, boy,* he'd thought, *though I shall never tell you so. . . . As was the fact with your mother, which led to you, boy. . . .*

Leitus had raised a cool eyebrow, watching the novice and expert gladiators work into their warm-up drills.

"In my experience," he'd remarked, thinking of Claudia suddenly, distantly, and bitterly, "women in heat can snap any chain."

"Some seem to like sweat and garlic."

Now he was studying Bita and thinking, *Why not?*

"There's a custom," he told her, "before we die on the sand."

"Custom?"

She was lovely, young, tender: smooth oval face, glinting

hair that fluffed in the slightest breeze. Fresh and young.
Possibly a virgin. His loins suddenly tingled and warmed.

He kept his eyes focused on hers. Moved closer. *Before we
die,* he said to himself. Touched her cheek gently with his
palm.

"What did you say?" she asked.

"About the custom?"

"No. Just now. I thought you said something."

He hadn't. Not aloud. He frowned, then stroked his fingers
along her neck, marveling. "Ah, but you're beautiful," he
whispered.

She was slightly flustered. Her hands felt awkward. She
clasped, then unclasped them.

Oh, she thought. *Oh.* She wanted to hold him. She'd kissed
one boy: a kitchen slave. She'd been scrubbing the table when
he'd leaned over her, turned her around, and asked if she'd
ever done it, and she'd asked, "Done what?" He'd showed
her and she'd pushed him away with both hands after a brief
taste that was salt, sour, and sweet, too. A tingling had
touched her in mysterious depths, for an instant, and then
something like fear had flung up her hands and tried to push it
all away. She'd shoved the slender boy into the cold hearth in
a dark puff of ashdust that stained the scrubbed stone floor as
if a vaguely human shadow had been frozen, clutching at
nothing.

She was remembering the kiss as Leitus leaned forward and
took her lips with his in an experienced, softly sure nibble and
firm, gentle suck. Her arms went to his chest. He pressed her
closer. She did nothing, feeling flooded up.

"Oh," she tried to say.

He was considering parting her legs, picturing the sleek line
of flesh he'd seen more than once. He pulled his face an inch
back. His hands did things. He was good at this. Very good.

"We who are about to die," he whispered. She just watched
his eyes. Troubled because there was a shadow in them. A
shadow of something she didn't like. She felt they didn't quite
see her. "You're so lovely," he told her. His hands were firm
and gentle. At home, he realized, he could have commanded
her to submit. He wasn't thinking of her as a slave. Slaves
often married, and, though the forms were not strictly legal,
some endured together for a lifetime. Others were cut short by

sale, caprice, fury, or a master's whim.

His hands gently cupped her buttocks. They were strong and small. He softly eased her loins into his own. Her pale eyes seemed startled. He kept wetly nibbling her mouth. Her eyes finally shut and the sweet scent of her roused breath seemed to hit him a tender blow behind the knees.

"Ah," he murmured into her mouth, "you are fragrant . . . ah . . . wondrous . . ."

He moved her rhythmically into him, standing there in the blurred and diffused hot glow from the open doorway where the sun shattered down outside on sand and stone.

Still holding her mouth with his, he eased her a step back. Her tongue, as if fearful, touched his. Withdrew then returned. He sucked it gently. He eased his hands and felt her still keep, ever so slightly, the rhythm he'd started. He squeezed, then moved his hands up under her light tunic, amazed by the feel, the always new feel of living smoothness, of living heat. He met her rhythm now.

"I love you," he said and meant it. For that moment.

"Oh," she said back, kissing him. "Yes, Leitus . . . yes . . ."

She felt him there, shockingly there, his fingers soft and sure. He was skilled in touching, though she didn't know yet it was a skill or could be. She took it all for tenderness.

He gently eased her back into the sleeping chamber and knelt her down on a soft bed of sacking and rushes. She was lost in his mouthwork and the stun of his tongue opening her lips. She only distantly felt her tunic being loosened and lifted aside.

She knew he was naked down below when he placed her long, soft fingers around what she'd only seen soft in children or glimpsed on men at the baths or when drunken plebeians went on the wall. She was country bred and thought of a bullock first because she'd seen that. While she was thinking her feelings deepened and her fingers closed a little too hard, but he didn't quite mind that just now.

She knew she was bare below when his fingers did something that she'd done herself without anything like these results. She heard her own voice as if from far away asking without actual words for something she didn't know, something dark and sweet and slow as tides, and terrible, too. Something she didn't know but somehow remembered. Lifted

herself to press up to touch it. Knowing it was in him, too, and
that they had to bring it to one another. Without words she
demanded it. Reached her strong, slight arms around his wide
back, gripped as if the strong, smooth flesh were in the way of
it, opening herself as if to be a door to it and a door to him,
too.

The pain was just a sting, a flash, a blur, because she melted
them together. It didn't matter. She heard him cry out.

"I love you, Leitus," she almost sobbed, pushing, wrapping, struggling with the bodies, the interfering flesh and
bone. "Oh . . . I love you! . . ."

And something opened that wasn't only within her. She saw
a shaft of incredible light, intense yet soothing, fire-flaming,
yet sparkling wet, somehow pouring down from a golden
blaze of sky. The beam streamed through her body and then
into the earth itself. There was a voice in the light. She knew
the voice. She understood and trusted. Her mind seemed to
float free, riding the penetrating shaft through the surface of
the world. Floating in the lightbeam she looked out (in all
directions at once) at a thick, billowing landscape of shadows
where glittering, black, flapping shapes with terrible fire-eyes
swam through the pasty atmosphere on taloned wings above
lifeless spears and sawteeth of basaltic-looking rock. The
musty darkness seemed to fill the heart of the earth.

The voice told her to see and then forget, because eventually, when she was strong, she would have to go there
again. . . .

And then she was back in the clay-walled sleeping room.
Her legs were strained, opened and already sore. Leitus was
relaxing, smiling and spent, leaning up from her strong though
fragile-seeming body. His lips felt blood-swollen, loins still
pulsing as the last glimmers of his pleasure died into tiny
spasms.

"Mmmmm," he sounded deep in his chest like a purr.

He looked at her pale, oval, tender face where the blurred
and slanted light from the doorway touched it. His own was
above the light so that his features were blotted together. For a
moment her staring eyes gave him the impression she was in a
trance. Then he blinked the odd feeling away and glanced
back under at where he joined her body, fitting together at the
pale, honey-gold fluff of hair at her leg's juncture and his own
coppery-gold tuft.

A sweet virgin, he thought. *Now she's been done. . . . How sweet. . . .* Her cries and gentle struggles had been strange and sweet, too. He'd drunk them in. *She needs some tricks,* he thought. He pictured her small, full-lipped mouth sucking where it would do the most good. He shut his eyes, and in the darkness of his mind he saw Claudia again, alive, kneeling between his bared legs, wearing a golden neck collar with a golden chain that he held in his hand. She was naked otherwise. He tugged the chain and drew her face into his aching groin. He remembered the feel of her silky tongue, the frictionless wetness of her blossoming mouth. He sighed.

What a woman she was. . . . The terrible image of her ripped body didn't surface this time. He just remembered in remote, dreamy lasciviousness.

The only sour note was that strange look in Bita's eyes. The remoteness that didn't suit the moment. He almost would have preferred it if she'd wept . . . almost.

CHAPTER VII

Actually he never had to fight in the arena because the next day it was raining. All the sandy ruts were running mud by gray midafternoon.

Bita watched him silently. She wasn't sure what she expected him to do about the day before, when they'd made love. But he hadn't seemed to react at all. She still felt him in the hurt down there. And the blood. He acted, she felt, as if nothing had really happened.

The old gladiator slept away the morning. He had a weakness for wine. A serious weakness. It would build up for weeks, and then culminate. Last night he'd danced, naked and massive, from the town wineshop almost to the door of their little apartment space. He'd sung a few strange songs, Leitus had noted, trying to sleep, wrapping his covers around his head while the gladiator had serenaded the moon.

The rain had stirred Subius at dawn and he'd crawled from the street through the doorway until his head had hit the far wall, where he'd dropped instantly into a snore. Once in a while he spoke at considerable and unintelligible length.

Leitus was sitting on the doorstep just clear of the steady, warmish downpour that was gradually running all the puddles together so that the street had the look of a sluggish tropical river; he saw the soldiers first. Because of the rain they'd paused under the archway across the open plaza. The arena master was with them, pointing.

The young man's heart sank. He eased himself back on his haunches into the room.

"Subius," he said. "Wake up! Subius, wake up!" *They're here*. He shook the massive sleeper, who sputtered to consciousness. Bita stood near the doorway, watching him, big-eyed, silent, sinking inside with a fear she didn't understand, because suddenly she knew he was lost to her. Like something in a dream when you wake. Lost like that. No way to get back. She'd been imagining a life ahead for them both: cooking for him; having his children; somewhere in the hills in a cottage with olive trees and a little waterfall. Like remembering a dream and losing even that as waking burned away the subtle light of its own ghosts.

And then something happened to the young seer: the scene, rain, Subius, Leitus, the room, all gone instantly, as if sucked away into a bottomless hole in her mind and she was looking down (as if she were a flying bird) on a misty field, where Leitus, wearing soldier's armor and a brass helmet, was holding and kissing a girl whose face was blocked by his head yet seemed familiar. He was on top. She was bared, her robes pulled aside. Bita felt a flash of fear and hurt. While she watched (unable to move or feel her own body) a cloudy clot of darkness that seemed to have a heart of blood-colored fire flapped into the wavering landscape and overspread the couple like demon's wings. Bita felt chill fear as she struggled to move or wake. She had a sense that the darkness was looking for her. Had been called to her, sensed her intrusion into the vision world. The wordless voice she'd known from childhood, suddenly soundlessly sounded, the voice in the flowers the Druid Namolin had trained her to listen for (mistaken because he'd obviously meant for a darker speaking to touch her mind). The voice seemed to say: *"Do not poison your vision. Look and learn."*

She did, and saw images more vivid than life: battles in those misty British hills she recognized from childhood; Romans and her people crashing together in blood and fury; Leitus with a bloodstained sword. Darker views: three hooded Druids standing over a misty altar stone. Night. A young woman lay naked and seemed asleep or dead. She was about to give birth. Bita couldn't focus the face but felt it was the girl Leitus had lain with. Namolin, the chief priest (a glimpse of his knifelike face under the hood), raised a silver dagger which burst into greenish flame as he ripped the blade into the full womb. The mother spasmed when he tore out the bloody child. Then the mist billowed and she pulled her mind away, because she felt another mind watching her, cool, distant, edged like a razor. Her last glimpse was of long, impossible arms reaching up from the churning flame and shadow under the earth, reaching into the dying, tormented woman. . . . No, not the woman—the newborn infant, filling the babe with dark thick fire; swelling, formless hands trying to take the shape of the child, who began to twist and struggle in Namolin's grip, its eyes glowing, smoldering red for an instant. Bita felt she screamed aloud, staggering backward to escape, actually rebounding from Subius as he stood up. She'd thought she'd bumped one of the horrible priests. She shuddered.

"Wants to be born," she whispered.

"What's this?" asked the old gladiator, setting her aside and squinting out the door through the sheeting rain. "Bloody shit. We've been sold again."

Leitus was suddenly calm and in command of himself. Even groggy Subius noted it. The boy was finally showing steel in his guts.

"The wall in back," he said. "The mortar is rotted." He'd noticed a few days before. "Bita," he commanded, "sweep in the doorway." He flung the broom at her. "Go! Now, you stupid slave!"

Without pause he charged into the rear room followed by Subius, who was still shaking himself awake, his round, massive body swaying.

"No need to be so—" he began, but Leitus cut him off.

"Here. Look." He was already prying the clay bricks loose with his short sword point, levering hard. "They'll wait for a letup in the rain if she seems unconcerned."

More and more his father's son, the gladiator thought.

They broke through and the sagging wall partly collapsed.

Sweating now, and shaking his head to try and clear it, Subius said:

"I'll get the girl now."

Leitus stood staring through the hole where the rain fell dimly between their apartment and the back building wall. Something turned him cold inside. Bita. How awkward. Now the little slave would expect attention. In another place at another time it wouldn't have mattered. The coldness seemed to come from outside himself, but he was breathless and tense and didn't notice that. He'd never love again, he found himself thinking, not after Claudia. He started out into the rain.

"Wait," said Subius.

They'll just send her back to my uncle, he told himself. Kept going. Subius stood, torn. He leaned out into the alley space and called after him:

"Wait, I say! We can't leave her here."

Leitus glanced back.

"We can't bring her," he said and went around the bend into the misty spray and spattering roof runoff.

Subius hesitated. "The cowardly bastard," he muttered. But he was bound to Leitus. There was no choice. Furious and hung over, he cursed his vow while every step jarred the sharp nails he imagined were holding his skull together. *Bastard. . . . All these snobs make the same broth.*

"Bita!" the old gladiator bellowed, stepping through the hole in the wall. "Bita! Come quick!"

He paused a breath longer, long enough to see her in the doorway, to know it was already too late. Too many loud voices and clashing weapons behind her. Hopeless. He gestured and then ran. *Bastards. All cursed bastards. Gods, you have no feelings to see what you see and do what you do. . . .*

Leitus trotted through the alleys with Subius behind him. Mud spattered under their feet and they splashed through puddles that ran like little rivers. A dog barked from a doorway and kept mournfully yapping after they were past. They jostled past a few stray citizens who happened to be out, holding pieces of shaped leather to cover their heads and shoulders.

Leitus suddenly felt upset. *What was I thinking, leaving Bita behind?* he suddenly wondered. It was as if he'd been drugged. He hadn't been himself. He paused under an overhang near the edge of the town, panting, and waited for Subius to come up to him. But the gladiator just stood there, watching him, standing out in the rain that beat over his round head and plastered-down dark hair.

"I . . ." Leitus began.

"Keep going," Subius said. "We have no time. I told you the man who tires dies."

"But . . ."

"But what?" He was cold, furious, wincing from the beating pain in his skull.

"Bita, I . . ."

"Too late for that now, boy. Too late."

"I should have . . ."

"Move," commanded the other, shoving him along. "Keep moving. It's too late."

"I don't know why I . . ."

"Be quiet. I don't want to talk to you. Move!"

On a barren hillside, dense mist flowed around massive standing stones. Three Druid priests stood spaced around the rim of what seemed a small stone pit or well. They peered down into the gape of darkness, swaying in perfect unison, left hands hidden under their robes, where they gripped ancient black stone spheres. Magical lenses for unseen power. Ancient, deadly, focused down the well-hold where a shadow rose, hinting a face that milled like smoke, changing as if the incomplete features had infinite expressions. They conferred with the face without actual words. The power of the spheres had called the face. The face of Aataatana. In the pit hollows of its lightless stare were images of Leitus and Bita.

"We have parted them," the three expressed as one, swaying, nodding, while a long arm of insubstantial darkness reached through time and space, subtly tugging at Leitus's naked mind, tugging him away from the girl.

Namolin, the eldest Druid, glared from his razor-face at the shifting outlines. He hadn't seen Bita since he taught her as a child. Namolin had planned her abduction for his own purposes but not the shipwreck on the Gaul coast which only she had survived. The hand of his enemies, he believed.

The three of them clutched the redly pulsing power stones. Possession of them marked the inner circle of the dark lord's surface minions. The globes were no gifts. He'd have taken them back himself, if he could. No possessor of one ever gave it up willingly. They were had through cunning, stealth and violence. The stones were said to have been made by Aataatana and his wizard-scientists in remote times. These Druids knew almost nothing about the talismans. The dark lord told them only what he carefully chose. These were the black grails of legend. Namolin sensed what a deadly peril they were for the user. But their power was addictive. The globes could take over your soul, he believed. If your concentration wavered. You had to be fierce and fearless.

"Now we strike, now we destroy!" And they tried: sped a shaft like a spear from their combined selves and thrust it at Leitus's heart. The stroke glanced off as if hitting a shield. *"Ah, he is well-defended, but soon his guardians may sleep. May nod. May blink. Then we strike again!"*

"Fools!" a thought like a shout blasted into their minds. The ever-changing face was speaking. *"You are weak. You are small. Grow lest your enemies destroy you! Yes, even as you prate of greatness."*

"O Lord," the three supplicated, *"help us. Grant us power. Teach us your secrets."*

"Fools again." Scorn spilled from the features of darkness. *"You must win power. The weak perish. Slacken and your enemies take you. Your union is feeble. You blend crudely together. My least fighters could shatter you."*

"O Lord," they intoned, hungry and fearful, tasting his raw strength, *"we will never slacken. When, Lord, will you be free and rise to our world?"*

Because he wasn't. That was still the bottom of the problem. He could no longer physically come to the surface. He and his people and their servants had been trapped ages ago when the color and radiance-thinned earth could no longer support them and they'd sank gradually, level by level, to dense depths in the heart of the world. Aataatana became the thinking, brooding, dreaming darkness down in the pit that his very being had created and shaped. Driven down by the shafts of slashing light that had once been sweet to his strange senses. Held down by unrelenting pressure from above in the higher worlds he hated, watched by minds that never slept, that kept the edges of the dark kingdom melting into dawning so that the thickening shadows never fully spread.

"The time is near," the face explained. *"I shall fill the earth with myself."* Smoky darkness billowed and fumed in the well shaft. Something like a half-formed hand, long and narrow, groped at the twilight as if to claw down the first stars that were, to it, the eyes of its enemies. The face cried out in fury and strange, frustrated grief:

"Fill all earth and boil the heavens into one solid, rich substance! Destroy those flimsy butterflies!"

Next the hand reached for slender Bita, who was facing the
Roman soldiers in the narrow room. She was just remembering the first time she'd seen men like this. They'd marched her
out of the sweet pine forest into captivity. She felt a tingling
(as when she combed her hair and held the charged implement
near her soft cheek), and knew the golden, wordless voice was
back. In the same fraction of time she perceived a shock of
darkness all around and a terrible numbing. Shadow talons
clutched at her thoughts. Golden light flashed and the blackness recoiled. She felt it shudder and flail away with a thunder-
ing pseudosound that shook the earth into voice. An actual
word. A word that cursed and shattered. If that brightness had
not shielded her, she sensed, that word alone would have burst
her bones.

Then another blow: the room vanished in a roaring rumble
of darkness, claws ripping at her. She saw her own body glowing with golden fire and she struck back at the huge, smoky
paw, straining her will against it, pushing, twisting, the pressure of it smothering her. For an instant she felt the thing give
slightly, then heave back again with sudden weight behind it.
She glimpsed massed and terrible shapes, fang-filled, shifting,
pressing behind the hand. Her defense sagged, the shapes
roared at her. Her soul was suffocating. Her thoughts slowed.
Then a shaft of blinding gold stabbed down like a sword from
heaven into the shadowy, roiling fury that seethed around her.
The shapes wavered at the impact. Burst to nothingness.

Only an instant had passed in real time; the Roman soldiers
had just reached her as she reeled away from the door, half-
fainting, sitting down hard on the packed-earth floor. To her
still changed vision the men seemed mere colored outlines
without real solidity. Their voices meant nothing.

"Where is he?" demanded one. The rainwater dripped
from their gear and faces.

"Search this hole," commanded another.

One of the soldiers smacked her face. "Speak, slave!" he
demanded.

The blow was dull and blank and she was gone again. She
never felt herself hit the floor face down because she'd already
fallen deeper, dropping past dim, ancient scenes of titanic
warfare in vast spaces, in a twilight between the black void and
red, glowing earth. Her consciousness was high above, watching strange armies clash in the air in something between a vi-

sion and a memory. She saw the earth as it was then: a dark
fortress shot with volcanic flame, its atmosphere all smoke
and hot mist. Boiling seas were peopled by strange, scaled
creatures somewhere between fish, snake, and dragon, ruled
over (she somehow knew) by the quick, winged beings partly
human in shape, that seemed carved from dark, polished volcanic stone. The beings were swarming into the primordial
skies, bearing up the racked earth's flame in their hands and
hearts, ripping and blasting at the fainter, pale, almost gauzy
warriors sailing down from above. The pastel warriors (she
thought of butterflies) were forcing the dark ones back while
they themselves were being destroyed in masses, seeming to
focus the beams of the glaring sun through their clear, glowing
heads, melting away the thick, dark, sooty, cyclonic clouds
that sustained the denser, stonehard opponents.

Then the focus shifted and she witnessed the great dark lord
Aataatana, at the height of his glory, spouting into the sky,
riding the blast from a tremendous volcano that had just
blown hundreds of miles of brackish sea into blackened steam
. . . riding up . . . up . . . on mile-wide wings, claws strained
wide, vomiting lavic flame at the frail beings floating above,
raining down their concentrated sunbeams. He was driven up
into their midst (to the stone-crashing cheers of his following
warriors), burning and smashing them to tatters and mist,
riding the boiling gout of smoke and fury that rose like a
waterspout from the seething world below.

Behind him his lesser but no less vicious children flapped
and spun up the fuming, superheated shaft, riding the new
density to close with their ephemeral enemies.

Bita's mind went dark here, so she never saw the ending of
this battle—or what had gone just before: because he was losing, the great lord Aataatana hurried across the blasted, acrid
soil of his favorite park where zigzag fissures steamed and
rumbled endlessly and twisted, half-charred trees decorated
heaps of slag. He favored this place for his meditations: the
smoky wildness, bleak, brooding ruins, fitful play of deep
fires and molten slopes. The flamelight in the perpetual fog. It
pleased him.

His huge, glistening, ebon, stonehard body dwarfed his captains. His gleaming, batlike wings flapped in slow strokes,
fanning the burning air.

He was addressing his warriors in soundless speech where

words were flame. Incredibly solid creatures. The surface of latter-day earth could not have supported their mass anywhere. So dense, their darkness seemed to suck away all light without reflection. Their only glow was a dull, dark red; while their enemies were invisible to normal human senses, too faint to show even a shadow.

The cloudy images that manifested in Bita's time to the three wizards and others, the deadly hand and hollow face, were mere projections of the dark ruler's mind, amplified by his strange science.

"Bear in mind," he'd lectured his troops, *"even if held in check by these countless weaklings, we can always"*—He pointed a talon at the dim, swirling sky where the battle raged. Faint flashes of light flickered here and there as the sunbeams broke deeper into the cloudmasses—*"push out again until our people dominate above as well as below. Time favors us. We will shape other races to fight for us. We will breed champions. Whisper to our vassals in their sleep. We will never surrender."*

They understood. Turn the world into a boiling sphere until the fuming thickened into space and they could reach the hated sun itself, invade, smash the delicate cities of their enemies, sink them in endless clouds. They dreamt of a porridgelike universe where their hooked wings could carry them to all the circling worlds.

One of the chiefs responded:

"We will win now. We can win this fight, great leader."

The great one was unimpressed.

"Overconfidence, Hade, is the mark of an inferior will. A childish weakness. Never underrate the enemy." He'd stopped rushing forward at the rim of a vast, smoking, volcanic hole, measuring miles and miles across, blurred by gouts of twisting fumes. Another creature like themselves, only shorter and twisted to one side, stood there. His wings gave slight, nervous tremors. His eyes rolled around the desolate scene restlessly. He held a spherical stone in both clawed hands dull red, glowing bright, then dim, over and over. It seemed immensely heavy to him. His arms trembled with strain.

"Well, Luvnac," demanded the king, who stood at least double his size, wings wide-spread as he frowned down into the fuming pit where dim flames pulsed and seemed to gather in rhythmic unison with the pulsing of the polished stone. *"Is all prepared?"*

Luvnac shrugged his wings.

"What can be done has been done, Aataatana," he replied. He paced a step, body stooping to the side in a severe limp. *"All the available pools of fire have been diverted and are streaming to this point through opened channels."* He hooked his long, pointed chin at the crater below. Deep under, molten rock was in fact pouring through tunnels, directed by beings made of rock, eyeless, earless, massive, flat, swimming sluggishly in the fire like sea-skates of a later age; when the flow was checked by a narrowing or blockage they chewed through the solid rock with their own incredible heat while their proximity kept the lava molten at all times. *"The Zugs are at work."*

"They'll have their reward."

"They'll expect it."

"How long?" demanded the king.

"Prepare yourself, my lord," Luvnac the Wise said.

"Excellent." The great wing stirred the greenish fumes. *"Excellent."*

"When I release the touchstone," said the cripple, indicating the dense globe he held, *"all the inner substance in the earth will press to this point, and you and billows of the world will be exhaled into the midst of the enemy."* The wings shrugged. *"The rest is up to you and your warriors, Lord."*

"I have read the pictures in the melting rock," the great lord said, *"and I see this war will be long. But I shall never relent."* He rose and floated over the miles-deep chasm. He was comfortably filled with dark fury and joy. This was the great race. They would fill the universe and create dark wonders and immense triumphs still undreamed. The vision never left him. *"Now is the time of battle and purity!"* he thundered down at his captains. *"Now we ride the boiling earth to rip down heaven!"*

They cheered and flapped up into the wild, hot updrafts to hang beside him. Smoke billowed and thinned, then clogged dense again. The world trembled steadily, rumbling.

The brooding cripple lifted the pulsing stone above his head, frowning, grim, straining. Its pulsing light maintained the rhythm of the fury in the pit.

Now the lords of power, led by their king, swooped down to the raging bottom. Overhead their forces were being pressed lower and lower as the concentrated sunbeams dissolved the thickened atmosphere. Some dropped in spinning ruin where the shimmering light broke completely through, blazing down almost to the surface, before the deeper smokes absorbed them.

At bottom the warriors hung just over the bubbling slag, wings barely tipped into the blasts of smoke and fire, just holding their positions against the updraft. Miles above, Luvnac slammed the full power of his mind and will into the pulsing rock, which mysteriously restrained the now fully concentrated underground fury that drained the blazing heart of the earth. The stone went dark, and instantly the supervolcano burst with an unthinkable blast. A miles-deep plug of dark and hot earth flew upward, followed by a tremendous expanding cloud. Swirling, dense substance spread and thickened the atmosphere, blanked out the streaming sunbeams that passed through the bodies of their ephemeral opponents.

Luvnac could see his violent brothers and their king riding the boiling darkness up among them, lashing out at close quarters (where they were virtually irresistible) and rending the bright ones into shimmering, pastel tatters.

Because he had the same gift of vision, Luvnac saw what his lord had seen: unending ages rising up in tides of war until the semisolid surface cooled and thickened enough to support strange, fishy, lizardlike beasts and strangely intelligent amphibians who lived in the warm mists, perceiving life with eyeless sight and earless listening, as the great war between the races shifted to the surface creatures and the inner earth became a vast fortress hive. The dense, dark race became increasingly ghostly, seen only in shadowy projections. Became demons to the surface beings who were taking human shape. The new war was for the human consciousness. The cosmic races fought virtually unseen for eons to shape and breed them. There were climaxes when the smoldering war would break out in the hidden dimensions, and humans (like Leitus, Caesar, Pompey . . .) would mirror these battles among themselves, unaware of what dark dreams influenced them. Only poets and seers, like Bita, sensed these things.

Bita opened her eyes, still filled with the dying vision. What she'd just seen was overwhelming. She blinked and sighed as one of the blocky soldiers shook her.

"Has she the falling sickness?" another wondered.

"Am I a leech, to know?" the shaker asked. His cheeks

looked like reddened stone. "I see what I see, Marius."

Marius had a thin, grim, amused countenance. Bita stared at him merely because she was facing that way.

"Are you mad, girl?" he wanted to know. "Where is Leitus? Speak up!"

But her mind was flooded with incredible images. The powerful armored men seemed vague, their speech distant murmuring. Even the first slap that slammed her head sideways came through a blurry numbness. After the second blow her voice seemed to say of itself:

"I don't know these things . . . don't know . . ."

After a third blow she felt nothing at all.

CHAPTER VIII

The sea and sky were a single, seamless gray. Dank gray. The Roman soldiers huddled under their cloaks as the trireme pitched in the choppy channel. The chill mist condensed on everything. The ship's sides were lined with swaying, clutching vomiters.

Leitus had a greenish face himself. He held the mast, leaning forward on the hard bench. His knotted stomach pinched only pain and bile now. Subius sat facing him, watching the waves shake the men along the rail. He kept swallowing and sucking breath.

The ship rolled sickeningly. A soldier seated behind Subius snorted a curse.

"Give me the paved roads," he shouted over the roaring, conversationally.

"Give me German Gaul," cried another, "over this."

Leitus didn't look up. *Give me death,* he thought, feeling the bile churn in his seething guts. He sat clenched around his misery. Subius glanced back at the men on the adjacent bench. Down below he heard the boom of the timing drum and the banging of the oars. A thin, blond barbarian squinted at him. A dour turnip-face didn't.

"Press on for the glory of Rome," Subius told them, not smiling.

"Glory of my asshole," said the barbarian.

"That as well," returned Subius. He was in a blunt mood. A goodly number of things bothered him. He was disap-

pointed. He was thinking about the girl Bita. Grim as his life
had been, she had touched a soft place in him. He'd been
thinking about his childhood in the rugged hills of Thrace: his
sister had looked like the girl. He'd gone to sea and been taken
by the Romans and made a slave; then fought his way to
freedom in the arena. Gained everything by blood and pain.
But he kept remembering the sweetness: playing in sunlight by
the well, his sister showing him how to make a wooden boat to
sail in the long puddle from the overspill. He remembered her
intent, serious look as she fitted the chunk of wood with a
little rag sail, the sun scattered by the broken water rippling
her face with gold.

He'd lost respect for Leitus when he'd left Bita behind.
They'd argued two days later in Naples. He'd half convinced
Leitus to turn back and try to find and free the girl. A hopeless
idea, of course, but that hadn't been the point. For all he knew
they would have tried it, except while bargaining for bread and
apples in a marketplace, three soldiers had ridden up to water
their horses at the central fountain. Their armor had gleamed
with the silver and gold of high-ranking officers, their robes
shot with rich purple. Leitus had paused to stare with the rest
of the crowd. The stirrupless mounts had been big and restless. The man in the center, shorter and slighter than average,
had clearly been in command. The dust of the coming legions
had been visible beyond the city walls.

While his animal drank the leader had seemed to stare
thoughtfully at Leitus and Subius. Leitus had suddenly feared
recognition, turned to go, nervously. The noonday sun had
gleamed on the man's high forehead. The burly general at his
side had suddenly boomed at the desultory crowd:

"The Roman army needs men of courage!" He'd looked
around to gauge the effect of his words, tilting his chin at the
people. Part of the effect had been that several of the taller
citizens tried to crouch down behind their fellows. "The pay is
ample!" he'd added.

"Aye," Subius had murmured, "if you coin wounds, sore
feet, and watery shitting."

"Hear me, brave men," the general had continued. "Follow great Caesar to victory against the Gauls. Join the Third
Legion, the best and the bravest!" Some of his audience had
seemed to be setting their feet to flee.

"Aye," Subius had put in quietly, "note well the bravest.

You ought to join them, deserter of women.''

"Task me no more, Subius,'' Leitus had rejoined. "I—''

But he'd never said further, because the crowd had scattered, ducking and dodging in panic, and even as they'd turned they had realized the street behind them opening into the marketplace had been blocked by soldiers who'd gone the long way around. A pair of them, big and solid in their brassy armor and thick leather, were a few steps away.

"So I'm caught,'' Leitus had said.

"Us, you mean,'' his companion had added. It was too late to break away. "We've been recruited, by the brackish piss of Saturn.''

"Recruited?''

"I'll just reason them out of it.'' The gladiator had spat into the dust. Outside the wall it had turned into a mounting, yellow smoke, as if the earth caught fire.

"Here we are,'' Subius said, as the mists lifted enough to show a rocky coast walled by cliffs, where the waves were chewed into wild foam by the jagged stones.

"Anything's better than this,'' muttered Leitus.

"So you think now, deserter of women.''

"Peace, for Jove's sake. She was a slave, in any case.''

"Hah. So was I, once. So might any man be, were he captured by his enemies.''

"And don't tell me again how my father would have done differently. I weary of hearing.''

"Your father.'' Subius spat across the wind and watched the gob of spittle fly into mist and nothingness. "You know nothing of that man. Who deserved the name 'man.' ''

"I know him well.''

Subius frowned at the wind.

"You know nothing,'' he muttered darkly.

"Peace.'' Leitus's stomach chewed itself. He felt the bile gathering. "What matters any woman?''

"Hah. Unless it be Claudia,'' said the gladiator, "over whom you moon and mutter in your sleep.''

"But she's dead.'' *Dead* . . . And he realized she'd faded into the mists and shadows of his recollection. To keep her image vivid he had to concentrate.

"When will you be a man?'' Subius asked, without looking at anything. "Even an asshole has a beard.''

• • •

Three cowled priests stood facing one another. Just above them the gray and stormy sky ended as if the heavens had been torn in half. The loose wool of the stormclouds was frayed and strung out by the winds. On the clear side the sun was setting behind bare rock hills, outlining, in melting red fire, the two tremendous stone pillars that stood on the near crest like a gateless doorway into the twilight.

Long shadows carved up the bleak, damp landscape. The three men paid no attention. They faced one another, and suspended in the center of the triangle they loosely formed was a globe of mistiness in which shadows moved, swirled . . . then suddenly focused into a view of the channel coastline where the Roman army was disembarking, unopposed, onto stony beaches.

The scene tilted and swayed as the point of view changed, as if the priests were looking down from a few hundred feet in the air . . . drifting higher . . . then lower . . . swooping in a long curve down to where a line of soldiers was toiling up a wooded cliff face. Suddenly pine branches whipped past, and then the scene was almost still, just swaying slightly with the branches a few feet above the men, focused down through the shifting, misty pine needles.

"There he is," expressed Namolin.

"Yes," responded another.

"Shall we have the beasts attack?" The third. He pictured stirring masses of hawks, bears, and wild dogs into a frenzy, sending them tearing into the thin line of Romans to slay Leitus.

"No," insisted Namolin. *"We will do better than that. The Master has whispered to me. We will make him ours. We will love him. His power will serve us."*

Close at hand, was the weary, pale, distracted face of Leitus as he dragged himself along behind Subius.

He glanced up at the dark bird that seemed a hesitation, a cusp of shadow. Except the eyes were too still, seemed unnaturally strained with watching.

"Un," he grunted. "Shoo!" He slowed and grimaced at the creature, just out of reach, following him with that unsettling stare. He waved his arm, but the crowlike bird stayed almost motionless on the slightly swaying limb.

"What's this?" commented the man behind, a short, thin,

restless-eyed private about Leitus's age. His tone and accent
(noted the other) was cosmopolitan. "Practicing for when we
meet the barbarians?"

An older, burly veteran guffawed. "That's it," he put in,
puffing a little from the climb, "the Gauls are like damned
birds. Just say 'scat,' boys, and you'll be fine."

Leitus stopped, frowning, as if to outstare the shadowy
crow's jet eye. "Won't move, mn?" he said, flat and irritated,
more than he could explain to himself. He drew his short
sword.

"Get along up there," someone said farther down:

"That's it," counseled the veteran, as Subius turned and
slowed to take notice. "Display the might of Rome!"
Chuckled.

The line jostled. A sergeant downslope rattled off a list of
memorable, staccato curses.

"You shithole," Subius remarked to his charge, "what are
you about this time?"

He and the slender youth actually saw Leitus stab the bird,
which was within a blade's length. The vicious jab touched
nothing but a branch, which *clack*ed and *swoosh*ed.

"You missed," the young, slender one said. But Subius had
seen better. He raised both eyebrows in his bald face.

"Damned if I did," complained Leitus, leaping, slashing,
and ripping, scattering needles and twigs in a rush of sweet
sap. His heart was pounding. The near eye still watched him,
just out of reach, somehow higher, its movements blurred.
Then he was jostled and staggered as the sergeant came
furiously abreast of him on the narrow path.

"Move on, you senseless bastards born of ass-fucking!
Move, by the gods!!"

They moved. Subius frowned in thought. Leitus went on
nervously. The strange, black, penetrating eyes haunted him
as they wound to the top of the abutment.

He jostled close to Subius as they formed up on a rutted
roadway. The barbarian scouts moved noiselessly ahead. They
were supposed to know the territory. Mists gusted up from the
water and billowed softly into the dark, wet pines that walled
off and overhung the road.

What a wild and dismal place, he thought, shuddering. The
wind wailed and hissed in the trees. The other men were silent,
seemed to feel the same strange dread of that unknown land.

They gave an impression of huddling together. Then, naturally (thought Subius), it began to rain again.

"Well," Leitus said to him, quietly, "this is a perfect hiding place for us." Subius grunted for reply. "If you dislike me so much, great gladiator, why don't you transfer to another hundred?" Subius spat this time. "All right," said Leitus, "all right. I was wrong. Yet we would have lost the damned girl in the village when they took us."

"Recruited, you mean," said the slim, upper-class soldier behind him.

Leitus ignored the comment.

"We would have lost her and you know it," he insisted.

"As you like," was the indifferent reply.

"Do we march soon?" someone asked.

"Shut your hole," the bearded, blocky noncom advised. "Save your wind for work and farts."

"Better to march," commented the slim one, "than to dig."

"You'll dig, too," assured the noncom, "dread nothing different." Paused. "All right, you witless cunts, jiggle along, and quick!"

He paced them as the line formed up and moved into the dense mist that now gleamed under the rising moon. The road curved in from the coastline and soon the massive, dripping tree shapes walled off both sides of the road.

The smell was damp, rich, and pine-sweet.

The country felt forbidding, mysterious. The men saw little, trudged steadily, churning the slick mud, hoping the baggage train would keep pace so there would be hot food by morning, trying not to think about the unknown dimensions of this land.

Leitus kept remembering Rome. The images were vivid: hot baths, perfumey steam; warm, dry villas; restaurants; music in the city; warm flamelights everywhere; cypress trees on the stony city hills.

"Some of them out here," a soldier said up ahead, "eat human flesh."

"Said who?" Another shadowy form in the moon-hinted mist wanted clarification.

"I heard it."

"Ah," breathed the ubiquitous, blocky noncom, seeming to swim with stiff steps and arm swings through the almost buoyant fog, "dread not, jackass, I'll have first feed from your soft behind!"

Guffaws all around. Leitus felt a firm, solid hand briefly grip his shoulder. Subius.

"What?" he murmured.

"It's a lonely country," the gladiator said. "Lonely as death."

"Yes. I feel that."

He sensed the older man was dissolving the tension between them.

"Stick close to me, Leitus. When the time comes."

"Yes."

"I have an oath to keep. I'm to die before you."

"Is this oath or prophecy?"

"Leek and turnip in the same soup," said Subius.

They were silent after that, squishing along through the semimud weapons and armor jingling, creaking, and pinging faintly as the fog filled and melted around them.

CHAPTER IX

There was a bodyguard in front and behind, both stolid ex-soldiers in leather armor with brass disks at key points. The two men they protected went along arm in arm. One was hugely fat and labored to breathe and speak at the same time. They'd left the sedan chair at the gate of the villa that over-looked the city. The air was clammy and warmish. The torches the servant leading the way carried in each hand shook out long, strange shadows over the garden. The flowers smelled faintly sour, rotted. Man-sized statues of gods lined the brick and mosaic walk; the torchlight fluttered and flashed on the face of what obviously was meant to be Neptune with stiffly uplifted trident.

"Mark that, Flacchus," the slim, very dark younger man said to Leitus's uncle, who'd put on nearly thirty pounds since he'd chased his nephew from his country estate.

"Mark what?" responded the garlic-scented, balding man whose stately toga was swelled out by the handles of his hips and the bag of his belly.

"The face on the sculpture. Hold there a moment, fellow," he called to the torchbearer, a bent, limping slave, who turned his pointy profile to them so that the fireshadows seemed to beat the flesh to tatters.

"It's an ill face," offered Flacchus, patting the sweat from his cheeks with his draped sleeve. His mind was far from aesthetics at the moment.

"That's all you see?"

"That's all I care to see." He frowned. "What's the point, Pompey?"

"It's Iro Jacsa's face carved on Neptune's statue."

"Eh?" Flacchus squinted and frowned deeper, squeezing his bulbed nose with two fingers. It was true; the same soft, leering look.

Of course, Flacchus was mainly thinking about which senators were absolutely won over to Pompey's cause. The vote couldn't be postponed past a day. Thanks to Iro he'd come to the forum and was anxious to make the most of it. Now was the time, he reasoned, with Caesar lost in Gaul somewhere chopping up barbarians. Now was the time to consolidate their forces here in Rome. All these great soldiers seemed to care about were battles, triumphs, and preserving the social order so they could keep fighting. Flacchus thought mostly about gold and control of shipping. Let the great ones amuse themselves by telling everyone what to do until some rebel or other cut them down so that now *he* could take over the telling. Meanwhile, Flacchus would own everything. When you felt the urge to command he'd even sell you the citizens. There was, he'd often reflected, a certain basic kind of loyalty that could only be bought.

"On all of them," Pompey said as they continued walking, studying the rest of the faces.

"What of it?" wondered the fat man.

"Look." Pompey pointed at Jove, as the mist-softened, wobbling light brought out the next carving. "Here again."

"Yes, yes, well, we all know Iro is self-loving. He's hardly unique in that respect."

The young governor wasn't really listening.

"His face on all the gods?" He wasn't amused. Not in the least.

The subject of that exchange was occupied at present: Iro sat naked on the cool tile floor, eyes like pits in the shadow of his thin, wide brow. His thoughts boiled and surged in red fuming. Things in his mind were torn and shattered. He kept humming, dull, repetitive, with each shallow breath.

The taper glow showed a young slave boy tied face down on a low couch across the room. Now and then he sighed a cry, muffled by the cloth crammed into his mouth. He didn't struggle anymore. No one could have been sure that Iro was actually looking at him. Sweat beaded around his shadow-hollowed sockets. He stared and made his strange, rhythmic sounds, watching the red things in his mind. A trickle of saliva creased down from the corner of his mouth. He didn't wipe it. He squatted like a monkey, palms resting on the cool floor. Hummed . . . watched the red things . . . rubbed his palms on the tile and watched. Then there was a whisper that might have been the wind muttering around the slatted shutters. He cocked an ear and eyebrow. It could have been words, words that didn't distract from the burning images like embers on hissing blood . . . yes, words . . . soothing, vibrant, subtle words that absorbed his attention. He nodded slightly. Stared at the bound boy and hummed, tuneless.

The words were promises. He understood the promises. Kept nodding agreement and so didn't actually hear the new voice for several moments. "My lord," it was saying. "My lord . . ."

Then Iro looked sideways at the doorway where a slave woman stood, poised as if to flee. His eyes terrified her: dark depths that seemed unconnected to any expression on the face or meaning in the mind. *Dead windows,* someone had called them.

"Yes?" he responded, toneless.

She didn't quite look at him. She didn't want to see the boy clearly, either, where he was straddled over the couch—or Iro's puffy, naked shape. "The girl, lord Iro."

"Hmm?" His eyes wanted to stray back to the redness within and his mind to the whispers in the wind. "Which girl?" A tic creased his cheek and shook the loose mole under his left eye.

"The new slave, sir. The one they—"

"Get out of here," he said.

She did.

Iro stood up. Cocked his head. The wind was telling him that the girl was important. Blinked and remembered. He paused by the bound boy, thoughtfully, before rushing out of the chamber.

"I'll see you in a little time," he whispered without expression, humming as he hurried down marble corridors, through darkened rooms, and down narrow, bent staircases to the windowless basement chamber.

In the light of feeble tapers set along the walls he studied the

pale, slight girl sitting on the stone bench. She came into focus
from the wavering flameshadows. There was a guard just outside the door arch.

Iro kept sucking his lips, first bottom, then upper. She
watched him with a blurry, stunned look in her slate-blue eyes.

The soldiers had brought her straight here. Much later she
realized why that had been strange; they could have sold her
ten times along the way at a good price.

Her voice was small and muffled, saying:

"What will happen to me here?" Because the voice in the
light was silent and she'd had no pictures of this scene or of
this strange, soft-bodied man with a stare (she thought) like
dark stones. She seemed to have no control over the pictures.
She'd been told to watch and wait and that someone would
contact her. She longed, suddenly, to flood out of herself into
the image worlds. She was changing, wanting the pictures
more and more. She tried, but the world stayed shadowed and
gray. Wait . . . Could this chilly Roman be the one she was to
contact?

Iro seemed thoughtful, inward. He concentrated on the
redness in his mind. He, too, was listening, waiting.

"You," he finally said, slowly. "You were the one with the
great lover."

"Who?" She didn't follow.

"I'll have him soon. Very soon." She waited, blinking,
tired. The week's ride had worn her down. Iro smiled with
part of his mouth. His eyes did nothing. "He'll die." Wet his
lips. "Foul Leitus, who sprayed his watery come into my poor
Claudia." She came alert as he said his name. He didn't miss
it. "Where is he hiding?" he suddenly cried, reeling slightly,
and for an instant the redness filled everything, all time and
space, and he perceived her through a burning light that
showed something gathered around her not visible to normal
sight: a golden glowing that stung the crimson consciousness
into fury. Somehow Iro felt It reach through himself (as if he
were an opening in an unseen wall) with red talons clawing at
the soft, pastel, hated shimmer of the girl—except there was a
shock, as if he'd slammed his own locked fingers into stone.
The grinding pain jarred him back and he found he'd staggered forward so that he was actually standing over the little
slave. The redness had dimmed again and just flickered in part
of his mind. He felt weakened and lessened and suddenly cold.
The red had filled him with power, carried him forward like an

irresistible wave. He tried to call it back. . . . Nothing.

Bita shrank on the old seat, terrified by the dead, empty stare and snarl of uneven teeth.

"You're strong," he whispered, with hate. "Oh, yes, yes," and he hardly recognized his own voice, because something was swelling to force sound through his throat. "Yes, you are strong. But I have your body. You can't do anything about that. So you'll feel things . . . things . . ."

She didn't understand. Didn't try. He was rapt, seeing in his red mind what he would do to her, sighing with strange pleasure.

And then he whirled at the voice in the doorway: the slave girl again. She was holding a torch.

"Lord Iro," she began.

"Yesss?" he hissed.

"General Pompey is here with—"

"Shut up, you whore," he raged, for no apparent reason. "Put this . . . this *thing* here in chains. Call Vertas and have him wait with her. Tell him not to amuse himself without my leave."

"Yes, lord Iro."

He stormed past her, snatching his garment and awkwardly wrapping himself as he went up the long, twisting, narrow staircase.

What a ridiculous fellow, thought Pompey, as Iro came across the marble-floored chamber passing through the overlapping shadows of several candelabrum. His eyes, thought the general, were like pieces of dark metal. He didn't like to actually look at Iro, his fellow plotter. He didn't like him, period.

"Ah, Iro," said Leitus's uncle. "Good to see you." He was sweating. Iro made him sweat.

"Good evening, Pompey, Flacchus," Iro said, faintly derisive. He feared no one. His vast wealth, Pompey realized, was not enough to secure him. His enemies had a way of dying or vanishing. It wasn't the sword that mattered but who swung it.

"Good evening, Iro." *I need him. For now. To help hold back that vicious little woman.* He meant Caesar, picturing him as he'd looked in the baths a year ago, glimpsed through the billowing steam in a hot rock chamber, belly down on a stone bench. At first Pompey had barely glanced at a familiar

sight: a muscular young bath boy thrashing himself into the
patrician patron pinned beneath him. And then the ecstatic
face turned his way and Pompey recognized the general, lips
and eyes painted like a whore's, red and gold, a cheap wig
askew on his head. Then the steam billowed up as another boy
threw a bucket of cold water on the stones and the scene was
covered over in hot fog. . . . He'd just lost the thread of what
the fat senator was saying. Picked it up again:

". . . so, I'm sorry to report they lost him. Near Naples."
Pompey knew they meant Leitus. *We're supposed to believe in
this revenge? His sister . . . could this bastard feel so deeply or
have normal pride? And this desperate fat fool anxious to sell
out his own flesh and blood. What am I doing with these
dregs?* Except he knew what.

Iro shrugged with his too-large, too-soft hands. The
embers in his mind soothed him. He knew Leitus could never
escape. The real meaning only Iro knew. The real reason for
taking and destroying him. "In good time," he said, watching
Pompey, "I'll find him."

"That's really splendid," Pompey said. "Now, to business." He arched an eyebrow. "I suppose you're dressed and
ready for business?" He half imagined there was a feral flash
of dull red somewhere behind Iro's flat, unreflecting eyes.

"Caesar is out of the picture," Iro said brightly. "He may
never leave that Gaulish island alive."

Pompey locked his hands behind his back, squinting at the
shifting, crisscrossed shadows on the marble walls as the
candelabrum swayed in the draught. A slave girl with a limp
brought a tray of wine and goblets. She looked nervously at
her master. He paid no attention to her.

"Let him win his battles first," the general said. "Less work
for us later. Still, I doubt Caesar will fall in combat to please
us."

Iro giggled and took a goblet. He sloshed it around, staring
at the contents. "No one will be more surprised than Caesar,"
he said.

Flacchus was sweating. He rubbed his stubby hands together as if warming himself at a fire.

"Well, gentlemen," he placated, uncomfortable with their
tension, "we're all working to the same ends, I think, eh?"

Iro offered them wine and then drank deeply himself, staring cross-eyed to watch the ruby liquid spill into his mouth.
Pompey mentally shook his head with amazed disgust. The

crippled servant tipped back out. Iro reclined on a low couch and tucked his bare feet under his misfolded toga. Pompey was disgusted. His toenails were dirty. With all the baths in Rome how could anyone have soiled feet? Above the couch was a dark mural. Pompey pondered it so as not to look at Iro: it seemed to be a crude landscape where hills smoldered and strange, shadowy shapes flew or possibly crawled; he couldn't be sure. The candlelight was too unsteady.

What a senseless picture, he thought.

"Ends," Iro murmured. "Ends and beginnings of ends." He seemed amused. His eyes looked at nothing. "Ends are beginnings." He licked his lower lip with just the teased tip of his tongue. "You hope to rule, yet in the end others will rule. If you only knew their names, eh?"

"Look now," said the general, "I like plain speech and action."

Flacchus rolled his eyes and moved his hands as if to say, Yes, yes, of course. We know you have said that.

Iro tugged at one big toe with his small fingers. "You have the money," he said, "the men. And the support of the Senate."

"Well, well," put in Flacchus, "we can't entirely promise—"

"We can indeed," Iro cut him short.

"You forget Senators Casca and Guardius. They oppose any—"

"They are already reconciled," Iro told him. Sipped wine, close focusing on the wash of red as the goblet drained. A droplet spotted his lumpy white and black garment.

What does he see when he stares like that? Pompey wondered.

In fact, at that moment, he saw Bita. She was outlined in the dull redness smoldering in his brain as if he watched through a lens of fire.

"That's impossible, I'm afraid, lord Iro," said Flacchus, uneasily squeezing his knees with both thick, soft hands.

"Notwithstanding," the lord replied.

Pompey sipped some wine and found it faintly bitter and thick for his taste. "So you've slain them, or mean to?" he asked sharply, prepared to object. You didn't arbitrarily slaughter members of the Senate. How stupid. What bad taste.

Iro giggled, rubbing his stubby toes with one hand, and

shook his head. "No," he said. "Not necessary."

Pompey was coldly furious. "See here," he said suddenly, "why are you so . . ." He paused. It was hard to put, because the reasons were always so plausible. But he was sure there was something unclear, twisted, about even Iro's seemingly honest revenge for his sister's death.

"See what?" Iro smirked as if he read his mind. In fact, the red glow now lit the slight general's intense features. The dull, heatless light whispered things to Iro. Things . . .

"You spend so much time seeking that boy . . . that . . ." He glanced at Flacchus, who responded by lifting his hands from his knees and shrugging.

"My unhappy nephew," he said. "What can I say."

What kind of man sells out his own kin for any cause? the general wondered. These men were all strangely tainted and each time they met he wished he'd never joined them to begin with.

"Do you object, Pompey," said Iro, tucking his little feet under his body, "to my just revenge?"

"A terrible thing," said Flacchus, wrinkling his bald head.

"Yes. As is betraying one's blood, I should imagine," said the general. The man looked outraged, in the way a politician looks outraged.

"But think what a crime it was, sir. Think." He was sweating. The armpits of the pale toga were stained. "Atrocious."

"Where are you aiming?" wondered Iro.

And then the flame filled, flared in his mind and the room so that, to Iro, all of them shook as the fire shook. His voice went up in pitch and he spasmed to his feet with a boneless uncoiling. His jaw went slack, a trickle of wine-stained drool oozing from his lip corners.

By Venus, thought Pompey, *as I feared . . .*

Except he didn't topple. The jaw snapped shut and the slight, soft man straightened as if an unseen string had erected his spine. The thin epileptic's cry became a voice whose penetrating, shrill force seemed to shock every nerve in Pompey and Flacchus, as if their nerves had been gripped by unseen, cold, soft hands.

"I speak the truth," the voice shrilled. "Listen when I speak!"

CHAPTER X

Leitus had been so exhausted he'd simply dropped face down near the campfire in the damp field. The rest of the army had more or less done the same. Groans, curses, and snores competed with the raving night bugs while the moon culminated and softened, enhaloed by mist.

They'd had to build a wooden palisade before sleeping. Leitus's arms were numb from the work. As he'd dropped into blankness he'd felt the muscles cramping.

He began dreaming. Subius was chasing him around an arena in the rain—nude, huge, and growing, swelling out and up until he darkened the sky, towering over a shrinking Leitus, bellowing immense words that explained everything; all human distress and fear, except that the meanings were lost in a deafening bull-roar.

And next he was coughing and fully conscious, squinting at a lantern flame illuminating a bleary, bleak-eyed, wedge-shaped face, inches from his own, growling:

"Arise, Legionary. You're late. Your beautiful lady is tapping her foot."

Leitus sat up, rubbing his face.

"What? . . ." he wanted to know.

"Come on." A bony hand slapped his shoulder. "Headquarters wants you."

"Why?" He blinked at the misty night. The bugs were silent but the snores went on. The bony hand pinched his cheek.

"Get up, young goat dung."

Leitus managed, and flexing and rubbing his sore, stiffened arms he wobbled along behind the noncom. They picked their way around the torpid bodies as clammy fog swirled close to the ground. Leitus shivered and thought about a cup of hot wine or herbed water.

Then they were at the big lighted tent, passing two guards. The sharp little noncom parted the flap and stood aside for Leitus to enter. He didn't follow.

Inside, it was bright. There were several officers plus a tribune with a quizzical, soft-featured face half-seated on a map table, gazing into a goblet, kicking one leg slightly. His eyes were jet-dark and hard.

A smaller man was just rubbing oil on his hands from a bronze bowl. Leitus knew him, of course: Julius Caesar. The general looked up from under thick eyebrows holding the young man in an intense, brooding stare.

He's going bald and gray, Leitus observed nervously. He felt transparent under that stare. If it was a trick, he considered, it was a good trick. He belatedly saluted. Was he in some serious trouble? What could the commander want with him?

"Yes, General," he said.

Caesar gestured. He shook his hands and wiped them on a cloth.

"I know your father," he said.

"Gracchus," said Leitus, "sir."

"Have you more than one?" Caesar smiled. Leitus shook his head. "I respect Gracchus." The man frowned. "But what do I do with you?"

The soft-faced tribune spoke up:

"Send him back to Rome, Julius." His stare was strange, Leitus thought. Dark, blank, as if the eyes were opaque as stones faintly hinting the candlelight reflections. "As is right and proper."

Caesar never looked away from Leitus. After a pause he said:

"We slay savage men out here. And women and children may perish in a siege or when a soldier's blood runs hot." He shrugged. "Not fine things, you understand, but they happen and are even necessary at times to make a point." He waited again, the eyes unrelenting. "But what I'm told you did marks a beast and not a man." Pause. "Yet you seem fair enough to look upon."

Leitus blinked and controlled a yawn that was half weariness and half nervousness.

"General," he began, "I—"

The tribune stood up, scornful, hands on hips. "Back to Rome and justice, murderer and carrion," he said.

Leitus sighed. The world was small. What could he do?

"You don't deny it?" wondered Caesar.

"I wish I were guilty," Leitus said. "Then there would be justice."

The tribune shook his head. The blank eyes watched. "If you could be flayed and burned and still live on to suffer," he said, "there might be justice, too."

"You deny," Caesar pressed, "that you slew a woman and her lover and drank blood and devoured part of their flesh?"

Leitus sensed the others in the tent shudder when the details were named. His eyes went wide.

"What?" he demanded, shocked and disgusted. "What nonsense is this?"

"So are you charged," said the tribune.

"It was well witnessed," Caesar said, "so I was told. And you say no."

Leitus looked at the roof of the tent where the pole poked it upright. "No," he whispered. "What else but no? God, what horror." He shut his eyes. Distant as it was now, the red image came back to him. He'd never looked closely enough to know what had been done in detail beyond the running wounds he had noticed in a blur of shock and fear.

An older man in civilian toga looked up from the map he was seated before. "He says true," the man added quietly. "As best I can tell."

Caesar grunted, stepped near, and peered up into the young man's face. He smelled of oil and scent.

"Persuade me in three heartbeats," he said.

"But Governor," the tribune began. He was silenced by Caesar's raised hand.

"I killed no one," Leitus said. "I loved her. I still love her."

The tribune made a low sound in his chest without words.

The older man went back to poring over the outspread map. His beard was curly and tipped silver.

"Perhaps so," said the general. "Your fate, in any event, is a hard one. You are now an officer, since you are patrician. You can fight in the first line of the first cohort." He smiled

. . . and frowned, too. "Let the gods judge you until we come home again."

The tribune wanted to speak, but the commander didn't have to tell him to be quiet. His eyes did that. The older man seemed vaguely pleased. The tribune glanced at him with a slow, smoldering hate. Leitus realized the man was a soothsayer, by his dress.

"So," Caesar commented to him, "you approve, Trebonius. I didn't think you thought anything without consulting the entrails of something or other first."

"Ah, Caesar, but I have already looked and seen. He glanced at the tribune. "In the entrails of my mind."

"More like the anus," Caesar remarked.

The tribune shrugged. Even if his sense of justice was sore, Caesar was Caesar. The last man, seated on a camp chair in the shadows, armor glinting faintly, had just reached for his wine cup when Trebonius began leaping to his feet, the chair already flying backward, face pale, eyes startled—which was the only reason Caesar turned in time to react, because Leitus had moved to exit when the tribune in one violent, jerky, somehow unnatural movement, spun off the table, whipped out his dagger and chopped a downstroke at Leitus's neck. Caesar barely managed to kick the tall, lean man and deflect the blow to the shoulder bone. The tip scraped aside in a spray of blood and bone chips. The pain hit Leitus like a fireburst, and he went to his knees, half-fainting, black shapelessness ripping his nauseated consciousness. He clutched his wound and winced in shock.

The tribune had spun into the tent pole from the force of the general's kick. The man in back clutched out his short sword. The tribune snarled and howled with insane and feral hate and fury. The guards were already pushing through the flap, swords flicking the flamelight. They hesitated as the tribune flung himself at Leitus again as if jerked by unseen wires, foam and drool flecking backdrawn lips. He dove with the blade again, except this time the old soothsayer yelled and zipped his own dagger in a deadly toss that caught the killer under the exposed armpit, twisting him to the side with terrible screaming that was mainly frustration. Trebonius averted his eyes like a man blinded by an unbearable heat or brightness. The tribune, blood spurting wildly, was crawling toward Leitus, who'd managed to stand up, reeling from waves of sheer pain. He staggered back, clawing out his own sword.

The tribune lunged forward again.

"Stop him!" yelled Caesar, but the nearest guard, in an extreme of zeal, took a stocky step and smashed his blade into the back of the skull, splitting the bone to shards. The impact knocked the tribune flat on the rug floor. His legs twitched absurdly.

The soothsayer still covered his eyes. Leitus sank into a crouch, holding his pulsing wound. Caesar frowned, thinking hard and fast. The guards paused, waiting. And then the seeming corpse spasmed to hands and knees, babbling hoarse and horrible words that were not words, a language of terror and doom that froze everyone more from the sound itself than from the incredible fact that the brain-cut man actually stood upright.

Trebonius cried out in what could have been the same insane, violent tongue, rushing at the destroyed tribune, screaming, then shouting in Roman fragments:

"You . . . go back . . . go . . . into silence!"

The soothsayer clutched the dead man and fell with him, the two shrieking so hideously that one of the guards panicked and fled the tent. Caesar drew back with his hands before his face. Leitus blacked out.

The two were suddenly still, clinging to one another. After a few moments Caesar disentangled the soothsayer. The tribune's blood had sprayed everyone and spattered the fabric walls.

"Trebonius," the general demanded, stunned, "what has happened?"

The pale lips gaped, gasped a few almost breath-lost words:

"Hell . . . hell . . ."

"Speak plainly, if you can."

". . . from hell . . ." was all the failing old man could get out, because the corpse with the split skull, Trebonius's dagger buried in his ribs, actually lunged to hands and knees, head dangling senselessly, and clenched one big hand around the old man's frail neck. The body went limp then except for the terrible hand. Caesar and the other guard and the officer who'd been seated in back strained to free the strangling man until the guard hacked away the wrist, then pried each finger off with the blade. The guard grunted with fear and satisfaction. Caesar turned away. There would be no satisfaction for Trebonius. Not in this world.

•   •   •

"Where is it?" a terrible voice whispered to Leitus in a dark
dream of pain where glaring eyes burned his mind.

"You were shown. Where is it?"

"What? What?" he tried to ask as clawed fingers seemed to
grip his naked, agonized mind. *"Where is what?"*

"Vermin, open to me!" Empty eyes burned coldly into him
above the gripping talons. The long, blurry face loomed close
and he half saw or remembered something, some place or object that was pure and bright, so that the dark mind around
him could not actually grasp its shape. A memory of pain,
long, long ago. Confused images of a golden, glowing white
figure, male and female blurred together, holding the blinding, unbearable thing in its hands.

"Where is it hidden, vermin?"

Leitus wasn't sure if these were his own or the creature's
memories. But he understood somehow that *it* had fallen to
earth, long ago.

Then the beautiful being raised the thing. A sword of light.
Its radiance was sucked away to nothing by the grim, skyless,
black landscape.

Leitus realized he was trapped there. All around him dim
creatures beat heavy wings, floating on gusts of semisolid
shadow, creatures hard and glossy as beetles, flinging themselves in frenzy at the lone figure who struck back with the
blinding, golden brightness. Then gigantic wings and fury
loomed above, striking down with a mass of concentrated
blackness that shattered the subtle body to glowing mist.
But when the huge hands clawed for the shining weapon it
dropped straight down, burning a hole through the darkness
that covered the world like a swollen skin, dropping down,
down, out of all perception into the nighted folds of that
ancient earth. Only then did Leitus realize that the battle had
taken place far above the actual solid surface on the surrounding, thickened clouds.

"The sword!" his mind cried in pain, because he somehow
knew, too, that he'd been there, as if the memories of that
glorious warrior were mixed with his own. And he understood
that the dark terror ripping at his mind this moment had never
perceived the actual shape of what he'd seen: he felt it gloating
now, knowing more, reaching deeper.

"I have destroyed you, vermin, before, and will again!"

Except, as if he'd actually been that warrior from unthinkably long ago, he felt a rush of willpower pour into him from some incomprehensible depth, and he flung back the shadowy invasion, the spidery, groping talons and penetrating, empty eyeholes. . . . And then he awoke in the tent, staring at Caesar, the high forehead and calm, small, inquisitive eyes.

"Can you explain any of this?" Caesar asked him, obviously not really expecting an answer. The others in the tent stood silent, uneasy. The second guard had returned.

Leitus sat up, pressing his hand to the slow, welling blood. The vision or dreamscape was fading in the candlelit tent.

"I . . ." he began. "No. I cannot."

Caesar pressed his lips together. "When the dead strangle the living," he reflected, "it gives one pause." To Leitus he said:

"There's something here that bears investigation, young man. I think I have much to learn from you, if I survive the process." He reached a hand and helped the young man to his feet. "Fate brought you to me, I suspect, for some deeper purpose than seems plain." Caesar stared at the bodies and shook his head. "Amazing . . . poor Trebonius. He didn't foretell his own end."

Leitus shut his eyes briefly and saw the warring shadows again. *God Jupiter*, he thought, *what next?*

CHAPTER XI

Marc Antony winced and let his jaw go slack. He closed his eyes over the numbing pain and spat the offending olive pit onto the pale blue tablecloth, where the remains of the feast were scattered. The pit had caught in the bad tooth, the third time that evening he'd hurt it. There was little point in trying to enjoy food anymore, he'd about decided. Starve, or face the surgeon with his damned pliers.

Several guests were watching him where he pressed back tensely against the pillows of his eating couch, shadows moving over his face as a draft fluttered the hundreds of tapers that lit the big domed room. The kneeling lyre player glanced over without missing a strum.

The molten iron that had seemed to fill his jaw was gradually draining away.

"Are you unwell, my lord?" asked the plumpish, dramatic-nosed woman beside him. He suddenly decided he'd spent too many days with her. The pain focused the thought.

"What a question." He exhaled; he was half-afraid to speak for fear the pain would burst in his jaw again.

"The tooth?"

He cursed softly. "No," he muttered, "a gnat bite on my big toe."

He reopened his eyes and blinked at a bony man in a soothsayer's robe with knees you could take for nutcrackers standing just beyond the low table. The fellow seemed to be in his thirties—lean, with a greasy, bristly beard that looked, to Antony, like fleas would pay top prices to nest in it. Who let him in and what did he want? Something boring, no doubt. Look at his eyes, small and vague, unfocused-looking. Watery. A Gaul, perhaps?

Antony glanced at the guest of honor, Senator Livian Argenteus Saccus. He seemed content to loll his bald head drunkenly while a young, nervous woman stirred one slim hand under his toga in the vicinity of his secret delight. Antony smirked and thought it would take more than natural skills to bring that organ from its wine-soaked, flaccid sleep.

This barbarian was patient. He studied the man: the lean cheek line. There was something chilly and distant in the expression. Probably needed a bath, too. Would a woman relax the stiff line of his spine, he wondered? He smiled. Perhaps he should offer him a taste of Liela's mouth.

"Who is that?" he asked the guard just behind the thin priest.

"My lord," said the guard, "he has a pass from Brutus."

"Indeed," he addressed the man. "Why?" *That sweet sister Brutus*, he thought, noting the rich gold trim of the otherwise plain robe.

"Antony," the man said in a scratchy voice, "I need your ear."

"You have it, though I'd prefer you took my tooth."

The deadly serious fellow went right past that.

"I have come . . ." he began slowly.

"I can see that," Antony overrode.

"To speak with you."

"And not to dance?" Antony grinned.

The priest moved closer, dropping to one knee and leaning across the low table. His voice was a whisper.

"Your enemies are our enemies."

"Really? You and dear Brutus? Are you some loyal Roman? Your accent gives me pause. So many barbarians harbor resentments for the small cause of having been broken and put to the sword." His lips were quite grim as he spoke. The priest still didn't react.

"You and your cause are in grave danger. Deeper than you could imagine."

"You came to warn me. How kind." Still nothing in those unfocused-looking, pale eyes.

"Yes," responded the priest.

Antony glanced away from the brooding, lean face to where the senator had fumbled the girl's breast into view. The nipple was rouged cherry-red. He kept trying to playfully lick it, and she kept avoiding his thin-lipped, greedy mouth.

"All right, priest," he said, "enough bantering. Whom do you serve?"

"Truth," said the man.

"Then you'll have little work on your hands in this world."

One of his personal bodyguards had come from behind his couch and stood over the man. This was an unarmed, massive Persian wrestler in a bulged-out tunic. His thighs were oily and thicker than the priest's torso.

"Take outside?" he asked, deadly serious. His puffed cheeks gleamed yellowish in the wavering light.

Antony waved the suggestion aside.

"Tell me some truth," he commanded the priest. "Or else I'll let this noble-born lad here escort you to the rear gate to meet the drainage ditch." He was still probing for reactions, almost bored now. The woman beside him made a wry face and tapped her silvered fingernails on the tabletop. The senator (to much amusement around him) was now trying to get his toga open and mount the half-bared girl.

"In the house of Iro there is a lovely young girl."

"What a novel idea," Antony sniffed. *As we are all forced to live for a time*, he thought, *we might as well laugh when we can.*

"This girl," whispered the priest in his scratchy voice, which was starting to grate on the Roman, "can penetrate the mists of the future better than any soothsayer."

Antony chuckled.

"My impression of soothsayers leaves that," he said, "a weak recommendation at best, fellow."

"She has powers that can help your cause."

"What is my cause?"

"To best Iro and Pompey."

He says Iro first, then Pompey, thought Antony. *That's interesting.*

"You hit somewhat nearer the mark now," he told the priest. "But I have enough girls." *And women, too.* "And one soothsayer, to me, is a surplus."

"There is more." The gaunt face leaned closer.

"Excellent. Because I warn you, your gist seems hardly worth serving at my dinner." The Persian wrestler looked hopeful and impatient. Behind him Livian Argenteus Saccus was getting nowhere.

"She has the power," he told the Roman leader, "to change what will be." The remote eyes weren't really looking at anything.

"So," he replied thoughtfully, "I hope, have some of the rest of us, priest."

The eyes didn't react. The long, thin angle of his face twisted as if to listen to more than the laughter surrounding Argenteus Saccus.

"No," he said. "Even what the gods have wrought, even that she may bend aside."

"He's starved his mind," said the woman at Antony's side, "along with the rest of him." She squeezed the cream center from a honey cake into her wide, rich-lipped mouth and sucked at the sweetness. Antony paid her little attention. He leaned back on the couch and made and unmade a thick fist.

"Why tell me about this, then?" He was serious now, for some reason not entirely clear to him. The Persian bodyguard looked pleadingly at him, trying to catch his glance and get permission to act on that dry, bony-looking body. "And what are you called?"

"In my land or yours?" the priest asked.

"Yours."

"Ion."

"Ah. A Greek. But why tell me? If this girl has such powers, surely Iro is either doomed or favored. You said she was with him, did you not?" The gauntness nodded. "Well, then?"

"She is still a child. Her powers are not yet ripe." Pause. "And she could serve you. Iro is . . ."

"Yes? Or is this school and we must all answer?"

"A puffy pig," said the woman, licking the thick, creamy yellow stuff from her fingers.

"A worm," someone else offered, half watching Antony and the senator's struggles to mate. "Look at that," he added, pointing to the sad, bloodless state of the dignitary's organ.

"That looks more like Iro," said the woman, "to tell the truth."

"Did he spurn or fail you, Calpurnia?" Antony asked, grinning. "Or both in turn?"

"I leave that to you, Antony, my hero."

"To spurn or fail or figure out which?" he wondered. He turned and the priest's face was there, too close. It annoyed him. "Are you finished, barbarian?" The Persian wrestler brightened and opened his oiled hands.

"Iro," said the man, "is a monster."

Antony raised eyebrows. "We all agree on that. And a fool, too. And much more. But Pompey is the fellow I fear."

"No. He is a true monster. And far more dangerous than Pompey. The girl is born of a goddess."

The man was so serious Antony was drawn in against his will; almost.

"I find that . . . interesting," he allowed. Then shook his head. "Enough of this conversation."

The massive Persian looked relieved as he finally fell upon the lean man and heaved to yank him into the air. He grunted and wasn't the only one shocked when the bony limbs and body failed to budge. The wrestler cursed, puffed, and heaved. Nothing. The priest's eyes shone as if the flame reflections had ignited the lenses themselves. A strained smile seemed to cut his narrow head in two. Then he rolled his body slightly and the strangler simply slid aside and crashed on the table. It cracked in half.

Antony looked interested again. The wrestler scrabbled to get his blocky limbs under him.

"Can you be slain?" Antony wondered, because the guard had drawn his sword and even the senator was blearily peering over at the action. Not being contradicted by his master, the guard thrust at the priest's back. It appeared he couldn't be slain. The priest shrugged again and the guard's blow missed, stabbing the wrestler's bulging buttocks.

"Not by these fools," the priest remarked calmly. "Have I impressed you a little yet, Antony?"

The Roman nodded, staying the next wave of attack with upraised hand. The strangler was clutching his behind and bleeding over the table linen. He gnashed his teeth with pain. The senator had given up and was just watching now.

"What do you want me to do?"

The priest stood straight and folded his arms under his robe, head bowed slightly as if listening hard. "Go to Iro's home and bring the girl away," he said.

"And then?" Except the thin man had turned and was moving rapidly across the banquet room. Antony let him go in peace. Brooded.

"That won't be easy," Antony murmured.

One of the guests was pressing a thick napkin into the wrestler's wound. The woman beside him said:

"A man like that could spoil our party."

If he won't sell her, Antony was thinking, *then it won't be easy*. It would have to be by stealth and trickery. He lidded his warm brown eyes, immersing himself in plotting. He liked this sort of thing. The girl was clearly worth something if a fellow like that priest spoke for her. He wanted to see more of him. For one thing, he had talents that might be taught. A trick, yes, behind the obvious. There was nothing so unsettling as the obvious, most of the time. Any blow against Iro and Pompey was worth the doing. Anyway, he'd had enough of parties for a while. The lanky senator had gotten his feet under him and weaved closer. Antony barely noticed, so deep was he sunk in his tactics.

"Hey there," said Saccus, waving long, lank arms at Antony, "I'm sick of women." The senator blinked hard and shook his head. "I like wine, though. . . ."

"Women," said the one beside the brooding host, "may have a touch of the nausea from you, too."

Saccus noticed the bleeding strangler. Blinked at that now.

"Ah," he remarked, "that's an ass with two holes. . . ."

Oblivious to the buzzing party, Antony tried out various schemes. There was always the likelihood that Iro knew nothing of the girl's true value, assuming there was one and the priest (or whatever he was) spoke true. No reason to assume that, but . . . the only way to weigh her value was to hold the goods in hand. He frowned. Could there be a trap here? He shrugged. There were always traps everywhere. This one was worth falling into just a little to see if it really masked some machination of his enemies. Jupiter, that priest could have slain him where he'd stood and walked back out through his guards!

He smiled wryly, looking up at Senator Saccus. He liked the man: excessive but intelligent. A little scattered and vague at times. He made him laugh often, which was inestimably in his favor: humor showed the flutter of divinity in men.

"Saccus," he said, "we have a call to make."

Saccus lolled his balding head, the pale hair catching the flamelight. His eyes were blurry.

"Call?"

"On Claudius Iro Jacsa."

"Mn?" The Senator swayed and wrinkled his nose. "That bug?"

"The very same," said Antony.

CHAPTER XII

Leitus was still getting the shock of battle out of his system. The madness in the tent, the death of Trebonius and the tribune, had been blurred away by the violent, sleepless days and nights of marching, digging, charging, defending, marching, marching, marching on, until the Britons had finally broken and scattered inland.

He was walking alone. It was gray twilight compounded of dank mist and chilly drizzle. The summer was sinking and draining away. He was wandering along a dense stand of dark pines and hemlock which the fog blended into a single, wet wall. *War*, he was thinking, *is worse than I'd imagined. What dark gods drive men to it?*

He focused his bleary, burning eyes across the shadowy field where the last battling tribesmen had made a final charge into the shoulder-to-shoulder bronze wall of Romans. He'd been beside Subius, just behind the first rank (because he was an officer now and he'd made the gladiator his orderly), when the last charge of desperate, painted warriors actually cracked the massed line in a pure frenzy of steel clash. Clubs, flying stones, spattering blood, curses, howls, shrieks, women, priests, even children in the fray. Subius had just been telling him:

"Caesar promoted you to the first, eh?" He'd spat dryly. "A good spot for a man of questionable future."

"Why?" he'd wondered, nervously watching the Britons prepare their charge, led by horses drawing crude but effective chariots.

"Because what was a questionable future is now likely to just be a short one."

Leitus touched gingerly behind his left ear. He'd taken a stone there during the fight and it still throbbed. Dried blood spotted his short armor and bare limbs. He'd ducked under a spear thrust and stabbed a yelling, bony Briton in the groin, then vomited as he'd crouched by the struggling body. Another missed cutting his head off by inches as Subius's blow shattered the barbarian's chest. "Vomit later!" he'd recommended. Leitus had managed to get to his feet and chop a few parries before the ranks had closed again and the legion's mechanical advance had crunched on and over the ragged barbarian line.

Now he looked at the heaped bodies blurring together in the clinging mist. Spears poked up here and there as if to pin the carnage down to the blood-soaked earth.

We are all just meat, he thought, *brought to the butcher's block.*

Behind him most of the soldiers were eating and drinking around cooking fires. Victory songs vied with scatology. The fires were uncertain spots of reddish glow.

He paused, stared down at a young Briton lying on his back, arms outflung as if clutching the vapors steaming from the cold ground. A sword pinned him there. Blood had pooled a dark shadow around torso and legs.

Always death, he thought. Life seemed, suddenly, incredibly precious.

He turned suddenly as a shadow swirled toward him from under the trees, billowing the mist so fast he barely had time to twist aside as the lean arm of terror and doom clutched at him. The arm sprouted a dagger and a slim body followed, hair wild and long, and then he was wrestling a panting, wiry-strong body to the earth before actually realizing it was a young woman about the size and shape of Bita.

Her breath hissed in wordless fury. Teeth ripped his ear in a blinding red flash of hurt as he slammed his elbow across her skull in reflex. Her fur and leather garments bunched and pulled part-loose as they struggled. He mounted her, kneeling at her thighs, pinned her arms there beside the corpse.

"Damn you," he said, "be still."

"You," she said in her tongue, "slime!"

"Well put," he reacted, "whatever you say." He winced, felt blood dribble from his ripped ear. "Bitch," he said further, squeezing her wrists until the bones grated. She made no sound. Her dark eyes glared at him. Her breath hissed in and out.

"All you," she insisted, "all will die. You bog slime! You slew my brother and came to steal from his body. Slime, unspeakable!"

"I might agree," he returned, "if I understood your barking."

She wrestled again, spat, tried to bite and claw, and then rolled him over several times across the wet, soft, mossy earth. Holly bushes were thick and dark around them.

Her body was lean and strong. Their legs locked as they struggled. He'd never been rough with a woman: always slow and silky, soft, languorous, tender hands and hot, nibbling, sucking mouths with sometimes touches of refined pain. This was new and strange. The thrashing, lean-muscled thighs kept rubbing and beating along his groin, and he realized, as he wrestled her almost motionless again, that there was a sudden probing heat gathering between his legs. He was almost annoyed, at first. What nonsense.

"Calm yourself," he pointlessly insisted. The last glimmer of twilight was swallowed in mist. The dead were only shadows now.

She cursed. He assumed she was cursing him. He didn't care. He tried kissing her, distantly surprised at himself, at the body's blind reflex. She bit his lip and he butted her chin. Her breath was hot, scented sweet. Spicy. He heard himself moan: all the long weeks of chill days, loneliness, and terror of battle built to that sudden need.

Pinning her with one hand gripping both wrists, he levered around so that his free hand found the bare length of her thigh, a sudden shock of smoothness. His fingers plucked delicately between her legs where the coarse fabric could be edged aside with his thumb. He felt the secret, bristly fluff. Despite the strain of holding her he was able to keep a smooth light touch working until he felt the crease of the actual gash of wetness. He heard the familiar catch of a woman's breath as he made contact. Her eyes were bewildered through all their anger and frustration. His lip was swelling and his ear hurt numbly. He felt the blood drip. It didn't matter now. She writhed and jerked, but he kept one finger lightly moving, inching in, fraction by fraction.

"Stop fighting it," he whispered. He didn't wonder why she wasn't shouting. (She was afraid that she would only attract more rapists.) He realized she was weeping. His finger probed smoothly. He knew he had her.

"I need to have you," he said. "It's not so important, why struggle so?"

He knelt aside, taking a chance releasing her arms so he could expose her body. She swung, punched him hard in the face. He saw bright flecks, tasted fresh blood from his lip. He ignored it, ripped the fabric so her legs were parted and the elusive, hinting light showed the dark shadow of her groin.

The second blow rocked his head but she made no effort to roll away or sit up. He understood that. He fastened his lips to her. Felt her body shudder, tense, then loosen. Heard her gasp again, far, far away because he was lost in it now, lost.

In a landscape formed by their united wills, the way a dream is made of dream-substance, the mist of consciousness, three beings floated. Blue-bright and crystal-green trees spread over silvery grass stippled with violet flowers that gleamed like afterglow when the eye has been shocked by brightness. They drifted above a golden pool that softly roiled in muted pastel tones.

Two female; one male form. Naked, golden-bodied. Tranquil yet troubled. Their eyes were spots of faded gold, ancient, ancient gold. Softened sun colors seemed to fill their translucent heads. They existed far from the dense pattern of the earth dimension, but they could tune themselves from world to world. These were adepts, even by the standards of their ancient race of sun-dwellers called the Avalonians. This place was their private world where they met to screen away any (they believed then) questing mind.

The shimmering pool was a lens and they had it focused on the earth. A tighter aim would have penetrated deeper into the dim domains of Aataatana's race; but not far before, that subworld's sheer density would blot out the view.

The golden voice that Bita knew, the shielding brightness, happened when those three forms united into one overlapped consciousness and the resulting supernal fusion reached across spheres of time and space to touch her. This joining was what the three Druid wizards had tried to mirror but only mocked.

They were observing Leitus raping the young Britoness on

the misty battlefield. They were exchanging ideas that were actually images, patterns of color with more force than words. Had those intensities been tuned down to the level of speech, the results would have resembled:

"Neither chance nor fate bore them to this meeting," expressed the pale, lovely female whose hair was warm waves of russet and peach-glow floating around her as if she drifted in some sweet tide. A current of honeyed atmosphere flowed around and into their subtle bodies.

"Agreed, Lillila," expressed the pale violet male form. His eyes were like compacted starlight, hard and bright. *"I feel the enemy and sense his hand in this event."*

"The question," put in the third, a pink-and-blue lady with a gaze where golden-tinted water seemed to pool, *"is always, How deep is this current?"*

"You mean, is there a purpose deeper than any purpose we can know?" he responded. *"It may be. We cannot trouble too much with that, because, clearly, there's a dark touch of the enemy here on the surface where we must deal."*

"Aataatana," expressed Lillila.

"The foul name in the foul tongue," put in Adellee, the other female perfection of shadowless shape.

"Obviously," said the male, Olloa. *"Foul, yet he was once my brother."*

"And," expressed Lillila, *"you still admire him, I feel, in your heart, lord Olloa."*

"Ata was great once. He let the light of truth fill him. Who can say otherwise? You have to respect his energy."

"No," she replied, *"I do not."*

In the pool the dim shape of Leitus was now pressed between the ghostly legs of the barbarian girl. His back was arched as he moved into her. They glimpsed others watching: shadows in the mists of that distant field of death. Servants of the enemy. An ambush? They were not humans. Did they expect, perhaps, Avalonians to try and intercede?

"This mating should never have been," Adellee said. *"But it is too late now."*

"Unless," Olloa put in, *"we touch the womb itself."*

"That is forbidden," Lillila insisted, *"as well you know."*

"And how will we bring him to the sister," he asked her, *"and what will it mean?"*

Because it was Lillila who had been working with Bita,

watching, leading, protecting her, unseen.

He meant "mean now," because they all perceived that Leitus's seed was being planted in the Britoness. The wrong Britoness. Which meant the dark race knew all about him, about Bita and the Avalonian plans.

"We must do something," Adellee expressed. *"This is a key moment. They chose it well. They tempt us to strike too early. They want us to appear there."*

"That's obvious," declared Olloa impatiently. *"And they wait in force for us. We'd never get out of there once on the surface."* His colors brightened because now he was focusing, seeing into the future and past, down currents and winds of time and space. *"My brother is thorough and deadly."* Then he saw Lillila move and he cried in image: *"No!"*

She'd plunged into the pool (that was also a way between worlds), instantly appearing on earth. They watched her change her form to seem dark and dense with deep boilings of flame—a cross between man and bat. They watched her appear on the hillside, manifesting to old Namolin, taking a terrible chance, pouring a burst of furious energy (that they knew could be easily traced, revealing her presence in the fortress of their enemies) into the old master, which she hoped he would believe came from his dark lord. Then she was back, floating with them, herself again, glowing rich gold.

"I risked only myself," she told them. *"I succeeded. I told the old man to capture Leitus."*

"But," interjected Adellee, *"that's playing into their hands."*

"It's quite subtle," contradicted Olloa, with admiration. *"But it could fail."*

She shrugged in light.

"Humans have said 'Feed a tiger and he will let you close enough to take him.' "

"Explain," requested Adellee.

"Our sister," he told her, *"kept me from the simple fight I confess I still long for. We give them honey and turn it to poison in their mouths."* He brightened, flaming with focused intensity. *"But the fight will come in time."*

"We cannot force the flower to bloom," Lillila reiterated. *"The boy and the girl must come to it naturally or all our hopes will mean nothing. We would be no more than Aataatana himself."*

"Yes," agreed Adellee, *"but neither will a rose prosper among weeds."*

Olloa made the last point, as he usually did:

"Some do, as we have seen." The bluish fire of deep seeing ignited the gold in him, his shimmering substance. *"The light cannot be destroyed or extinguished, only obscured for a time. All we can do is show it, clear away the walls of darkness and let it shine. Whisper it to the humans, touch the light in their sleeping minds, hint until they awaken. They, too, are born of light and made of light, yet know it not!"* His colors flared.

In the mirror pool Leitus was still riding the girl. Olloa was almost amused by the subtlety of Lillila's plan. He felt the future with his enhanced senses and was aware of a chance of success. The Druid Namolin was rushing to the spot, "bending his staff," as the saying went. He believed his master Aataatana had called him. Lillila had indeed totally deceived him.

The key to regaining Leitus had to do with the gangly, spiderlike apprentice who'd awakened when Namolin left and was following, just out of sight. His every wobbling step expressed greed, fear, depression, and strange tenacity. The plan was subtle, perhaps too subtle. But that was ever her way, Olloa reflected. The hound might bite the master if she were able to work through this sad creature.

"In the end," he told his two companions in radiance, *"we have to get the lost weapon to him or this is all for nothing."*

"Not for nothing," Lillila responded. *"Even trying in vain spreads light."*

"When the child to be born holds the blade again," he insisted, *"then can I draw mine."*

The holly bushes parted and a white-bearded face set in a hood seemed to solidify from the mist.

Leitus looked up, eyes rolling back, feeling his loins pop and pour melting ecstasy. At first the face had no reality. Then he flung himself back on his haunches, groping for his sword, which had gotten twisted around behind his back. Even as he fumbled to free it, the Druid's eyes caught his own, gleaming like a cat's. The stare was like a soft blow. Leitus was stunned to stillness in the act of drawing the blade. He strained to move, broke into a sweat, then, as if underwater, slowly drew the sword out and took a crouch-step forward, thrusting, feeling caught in the slow motion of a dream. The priest stepped aside effortlessly, saying in his language:

"Astonishing that he can move at all."

Then he brought up his staff and poked Leitus under the heart so that his breath seemed to freeze in his lungs and blackness rushed up into his brain. He cut, hopelessly, at the snow-bearded face. As he fell forward into darkness he vaguely noticed another face peering through the wet bushes.

CHAPTER XIII

Antony leaned on the chariot railing as they rattled, bumped, and clattered along twisting, uphill streets. The burly driver kept the thick reins humming and crackling as he wrenched the two horses along.

Antony thought carefully and long as they crossed the hilltop, passing trees and walls now, lost in the moon-stained night under sharp stars. Iro's villa was just ahead where the road made a long, smooth curve across the crest. Senator Saccus was dozing on the cramped floor, head lolling and banging on the boards.

They left the team with a slave at the gate and walked under squat olive trees, past the line of statues of the gods with Iro's likeness. As they approached the marble front Antony decided that the sack of gold he'd slung to his belt would buy him exactly nothing.

He glanced back to see if the senator was still following. He was, in a sense, going as far left, right, and to the rear as forward. One of the slaves hovered near him with a sputtering torch. Another led them.

Well, he'd made two plans, though Caesar would have made four. He missed his friend. He was one of the few people who really liked the general. He should be in Rome, not wandering off to invade worthless barbarian fastnesses for tainted glory. Now was the time, Antony believed, to elbow Pompey and his crowd aside in the Senate. Anyone could sense Pompey (and Iro, too, crouching in the shadows of greatness) was about to make a major move to take over the

republic, which had become (as Caesar liked to say) a damned
debating society riddled by corruption. It was time for someone with the will and energy to create a crisis—an uprising,
anything—then push through special powers to deal with it in
the time-honored (or dishonored) style. Bring an army into the
city and that would be that. They had Caesar cut off in the
north, he brooded, and once he surrendered his sword,
anybody they disliked or worried about would be arrested. It
had been done before. The trick was to do it first.

And here he was wasting his time over some obscure slave
girl while he should be gathering a secret legion and joining
Clodius and the mob for a surprise strike . . . or was that
senseless? He sighed.

They were shown into the reception hall where Iro was
waiting, half-naked, barefoot, fresh from the steam, bleary
and puffy-looking. He was sipping wine from a long basin
that he tilted to his pursed, pouted lips. Some spilled and
beaded like blood along his chin and oiled, hairless chest.

The domed room was painted glossy-black. The low
couches were deep red. The candlelight was bunched on a low
table before Iro, so that his outsized shadow was humped on
the wall behind him, shifting as the flames moved.

"What a pleasure it is to see you here, Marc Antony. And
the delightful Senator Saccus." Iro smiled with faint scorn.
The senator weaved and blinked.

"He's in formal attire," he muttered.

"What's that?" wondered Iro.

"I smell vomit," said the senator.

"You scent yourself, then," Iro said.

Antony wondered why the little fellow kept no guards in
view. What made him so confident? *He could be smitten here
like a toad.*

"Never mind the pleasantries," he said. "We all know how
much we love each other. There is little need to paint hearts on
the door."

"Yes," drawled Iro. "Well then, what?" He cradled the
wine with both hands in the elongated dish.

Antony unslung the gold from his belt. "I want a new slave
girl," he said.

"Is this the trading block?" Iro looked around as if to make
sure.

"For the moment." Antony smiled. He felt he had one ad-

vantage: There was a trade to be made and his extreme
caprices of taste were known. "I want to buy that new little
girl, with the blue eyes. A tender young barbarian." Antony
grinned widely and, he hoped, ingenuously.

Iro leaned forward, arching his eyebrows. "Do you?" he
asked. "Why tell me so?"

Saccus swayed a little closer and shut one eye to better focus
on Iro.

"*I* have breeding," he declared, with some satisfaction.
"What do you have?"

"Antony," said Iro, "why do you bring this winesop with
you?"

"To get the price lowered," was the reply. "You'll sooner
be rid of us if you come to terms." He chucked the money
sack on the table. Iro grinned. The man was already rich; what
would money matter? Except to some, the more they had the
more it did. Antony knew Iro was just waiting, so he said,
"Just a gesture."

"Ah," said Iro, the grin starting to tic ever so slightly at one
corner. "Why go to such strange lengths for some bit of
fluff?"

"Are they?"

"What?"

"Such lengths? I merely follow a . . . a tip."

"I just got her myself," Iro admitted thoughtfully. "And
what reason have I to sell her to you?"

"Why not?"

"It's far too pleasant to deny you." The smile jerked.

"I'll owe you a favor," Antony tried.

"Favor," muttered Saccus. "Do him one . . . cut his—"

"Peace, friend," said Antony.

Iro just shook his head. "No." He sighed. "It's still far too
pleasant to say no. You understand." The grin twitched wildly
in one corner, then the smile went away.

Antony bowed slightly. "Very well," he said and started to
leave, taking Saccus by the arm. The senator was glaring blurrily at the little, catlike man on the couch, who was now looking uncomfortable.

"Wait," he said, "is that all you've got to offer?"

Antony glanced back.

"I don't bargain like a merchant."

"That's right," added Saccus, waving one arm in a wide
and meaningless gesture.

"You forget your money," Iro told him.

"I always pay," Antony said, going out the archway into the hall to the door. "For everything." And went out.

Iro stood up, fluid, concentrated, almost angry. He sucked in some wine and then spat it out on the white tabletop, where it spattered. He stared at the splash for a moment. It reminded him of a face. "But this is senseless!" he called after Antony.

He stared down at the winespill again: a long face, yes . . . there were the eyes and there a long nose. An omen, perhaps? He wondered what the message might be. Smiled secretly. Went inwards to look at the spot, the drop of redness that was his power and joy. Made the soft, unsteady hmmming sound as he stood and swayed.

Antony headed quickly for the gate, holding the lanky senator by one arm. They brushed past the slaves holding torches and kept ahead of them down the long line of dim statues.

"He's disgusting," Saccus said, lurching slightly against Antony's grip.

"Peace, my friend." He looked up at the sky. Clouds had massed, leaving it utterly blank and black. "It was worth the gold to find out she's important to him, too."

"Important," murmured Saccus, closing one eye so that the two Antonys melted together.

"I say the goods may be worth their price."

"But you don't have any goods. . . ." Saccus smiled and made a show of patting Antony's cloak and toga. "Unless you've got her underneath here. . . ."

They were back on the street again. As his eyes adjusted, Antony could make out the outline of the chariot.

"I hate to pay for nothing, Saccus, old friend." He raised his right hand over his head as if to stretch, held it for several steps, then dropped it back to his side. They had reached the chariot. The driver said nothing as they mounted up.

"Is your arm sore or something?" Saccus wondered, using both hands to get aboard.

"I was simply saluting fate," Antony said. "Hail fate."

Saccus stood uncertainly, gripping the wood. He kept trying both eyes open and giving up quickly.

"Are we moving?" he asked, amused.

"We're making great progress," said Antony.

Two black men, nearly seven feet tall, dressed in dark

cloaks and barbaric skins, short, thick spears slung across
their backs and four daggers in their belts, watched Antony
from the dense hedges that enclosed the side of the villa. When
his arm went up they padded noiselessly along the building
wall, giant shadows moving into a vacant, lightless window.
Soundless as time passing they crouched down an arched
hallway. A house slave in Antony's pay had explained the way
and where the girl would be kept.

Underground, the slave girl they sought was naked, spread-
eagled over a raised, platform six feet across. Golden chains
held her ankles and wrists. The chamber was low-roofed,
square, and set with thick, square pillars that clashed with
the Roman architecture upstairs. It was clearly an ancient
structure that had become the foundation of the villa, an
underlevel from a lost city that had fallen before Rome was
even a dream.

Iro had been active down below. He'd once pried up loose
stones in the basement (thirty feet overhead) because he'd had
vivid, recurring dreams about an incredible treasure held
there, a stone so rare that the richest king of the east would
give all he had to possess it. Not one of his few confidants
knew anything about what he might have actually found. Not
even his sister Claudia. The chambers and passageways he'd
discovered had become his favorite resort. There were sealed
doors that none of the few slaves who actually returned from a
visit down there even considered trying to open.

There were rumors that he made human sacrifices to a god
he never spoke of—except for unconscious mutterings and
brief bursts of fury . . . and what he'd said to his sister (which
she barely hadn't laughed at, much less believed) about a great
deity of infinite power who lay trapped and who, once freed,
would destroy all lesser gods. Only Iro, himself, he'd told her,
would be able to free the great lord, because he would learn
the rites to raise him from ages of darkness and semisleep.

A small, smooth, unsexed deaf-mute in a loincloth sat on
the edge of the strange altar along with Bita waiting for Iro,
his master, to return. He'd become the chief assistant. He was
meditating on the festivities to come: how Iro would enter,
oiled, perfumed, and nude; begin by a whipping that would
gradually lace the smooth, soft limbs with lines of blood and
welts. Then Iro would amuse himself with his mouth and
tongue for a while (if the fancy took him) and then proceed to

other things. To that extent he understood his master and approved, even looked forward to these intimate sessions and the pointless but pleasant silent struggles of the victim. Life was a void to this slave and he'd come to need extreme events to pluck the deadened strings of desire in him. He knew that at a certain point his master would demand the whip to streak the skin of his own pale buttocks while he thrust himself to a climax that meant nothing at all to the eunuch. He'd shake his head while Iro mounted the victim (male or female or even, at times, animal) and shouted (unheard by the mute) chants he'd learned in dreams or found in his mouth at moments of inspiration. Cries that were (he believed) sacred to his faceless, formless god. He prayed to see the face. He'd prayed since late childhood when he'd first seen the redness that no others could detect. He'd smile over his secret knowing.

The best time, the slave reflected, was when Iro would spontaneously decide how to finish the flayed and violated sacrifice. That was the best part: the impassioned inventiveness of his master.

The Nubian warriors slunk to the last doorway that the informer had described through the interpreter. These men spoke no Latin for good and obvious reason. The lower levels of Iro's palace was virtually a maze set with few torches. These men, however, saw well in nearly total darkness, as if it were a quality of their own substance.

The door was iron-banded and shut. Left and right the dim corridor curved away, dank air sucked past them up the stairs they'd just descended. No sounds. The thicker-bodied of the two hooked his thumb at the door and made a low, tongueless sound. The other warrior nodded. He tugged the ring and the door opened. Cold air fluttered and tugged their fur and feather ornaments.

They hesitated, then went quickly and silently down the rounded, greenish-stone stairs that were eaten by time and smoothed by unnumbered steps over lost ages. They were both sweating from tension, controlling their breaths carefully. The stairs curved sharply, the wet walls dimly showing reflected firelight from below.

They stopped in unison, soft as shadows, when they could see around the last bend into the low-roofed chamber where Bita lay bound to the altar stone.

The slimmer one (though both were lean by any standard

but their peoples') made a low, unhappy sound in his throat.
His big eyes showed white as he glanced at his partner, who
nodded to show he felt it, too. Then a grunt and they went
down fast, spears unslung as they split up and ducked from
pillar to massive square pillar, watching the round-bodied
eunuch, who had his back to them because his master had
come down and was already into his play and ceremony, nude,
praying to his god of redness, the redness that was beating in
his head, burning, filling everything with a deep, beating, demanding glow. The redness was showing him things, nearer
than ever before. He felt his faceless god slowly stirring, finally stirring and radiating his needs. O needs! Needs! Needs
that burned slow and deep and forever. Iro called and it
came, craved and demanded. *"Show your feet, Lord,"* Iro
begged in his brain, *"and I will lick them clean and submit
myself to Thee."*

The thicker warrior was a gleam of sleek, supple blackness
charging from behind the closest pillar to the puffy, absorbed
slave holding the whip.

Iro was kneeling over Bita now, her head between his knees,
feeling the red demands pouring into him, filling his mind,
draining down to the bottom of his body.

Bita, bleeding from dozens of lashes, rolled her head. Her
eyes were glassy and vague. She'd pleaded for the golden voice
and she'd sensed it groping for her, trying and failing, lost
somewhere out of reach. She felt something like a vast wing
moving above them, blotting everything out. She shut her
eyes, even her mind, when a black denseness squeezed her
down, pressed her soul into a hopeless corner.

Now, numbed, she saw only the shadow squatting over her
and never noticed the glossy, water-smooth attack of the
seven-foot warrior, who in one graceful lunge ripped the fat
eunuch's neck and dropped him squealing and spurting blood
at the foot of the altar. He became a loose sack of sudden
nothingness.

The second man closed on Iro a heartbeat later. The Roman
didn't quite look up, intent on degrading Bita and mumbling
prayers. The spear jabbed hard and sure for his putrid heart.
But the great shadow seemed to thicken around the nude man
so that the spear appeared to melt into darkness. The savage
reacted instantly: he turned to run. But Iro twisted his head
and all the darkness in his gaze now had a glint of flame that

seared the African's mind as he tried to move and found his body melting. Iro crawled toward him on hands and knees, licking his lips. The warrior's shrieks faded into nothingness.

The other giant stooped and snapped the thin chains that held Bita to the cube; when Iro was done enjoying his companion's dissolution, the second African was already at the stone stairs with the slight girl slung over his shoulder. He heard Iro's screech of fury. Too late. He felt the chill darkness pluck at his retreating back, shivering him to his bones, and for an instant he felt his substance thin so that he seemed to race the last few feet suspended in space by his desperately beating heart alone. . . . And then he was at the top of the stairs and panting, charging down the hall, rebounding off walls, until he staggered into the night air and began to recover his wind and sanity. . . .

Ju'ja, he kept thinking, *Ju'ja*. He'd been raised to fear Ju'ja, who cast webs of darkness in the jungle shadows to snare souls of the unwary. He'd just felt the actual breath and heatless touch of Ju'ja.

The thought spurred him over the wall in virtually a single leap, the girl flopping like a sack over his shoulder. He was sure he felt the chill claws at his back as he fled into the road, not realizing he'd lost his spear somewhere until he whirled to stab with it when something moved in the moonshadows along the street. Then he heard a voice he knew and saw several armed and hooded men.

"Good work," Antony said, stepping into the moonlight. His even teeth gleamed. "My trusty little fellow." He grinned, touching Bita's down-flung hair where she hung across the giant's back. "So here's my magical wench. How do you do, young witch?" She was still unconscious. He noted the wounds and frowned. *Degenerate*, he thought.

Antony looked at the glossy, sweating, mute black whose expression was lost in its own darkness. "So, was your brother lost?" he asked him. Another, smaller Negro man in an ankle-length robe translated and the panting, shaken warrior answered with a nod.

"We best move off," said one of the soldiers, looking across at the wall of the estate. "Why wait for trouble?"

"Get her in the chariot," commanded Antony. The translator spoke and the giant effortlessly slung her up alongside Saccus, who stirred from a doze and cleared his throat.

"Ahha," he muttered, touching the bare flesh. "Never too late for love. . . ." He touched her back and pulled his hand away. "She's all wet."

"She's bleeding, old Sacc," said Antony. "She's been weekending with Iro." He glanced over at the wall and the black warrior followed his look. As Antony turned away and mounted into the chariot the warrior stared at the tall tree shapes that blotted the stars where shreds of night mist seemed gathered into a loose and empty face with depthless hollows for eyes and mouth. The man made a terrified tongueless sound and bolted straight across the road into the open field across the way that sloped down overlooking the winking city lights. In seconds he was a vague stir in the night, and then he was gone, as if melted away.

Antony and the others looked around but saw nothing. Saccus pulled himself to his knees.

"She's too thin," he said, "for my taste."

"Move along," ordered Antony, backwatching as the soldiers pulled in close around the chariot.

CHAPTER XIV

Subius jolted awake. The last thing he recalled was dropping the wineskin. He remembered his thick, dead fingers groping hopelessly at the too-tiny bag (it was, in fact, bigger than his head) that had dropped somewhere far away; it had been so, so tragic. He'd wanted to weep because he was falling a long, sickening distance that seemed to have no bottom. He recalled passing Leitus on the way down and trying to tell him about the problem. He wanted to tell him about his father, his real father, his father who'd been a slave and killer and a great man. A great failure, too. Maybe that all mixed together.

So the first thing he did when he awoke was to reach for Leitus with lost words on his tongue. Nothing. He sat up, head pulsing with the effort. Nothing but embers, mist, and moon-shadow.

"By Saturn's chill cunt-stirrer," he muttered, climbing up to his uncertain feet. He belched hard enough to cross his eyes then peered around, shutting one squinty eye so there would be only one of everything else, too. One smoldering fire, one moon above the stained mist. "Where is the bastard?" He weaved vaguely toward the outskirts of the camp where the sentries were at half-mast on their spears, slumberous over a won battle.

Led by something he couldn't have explained, he weaved out across the field, stepping and sometimes tripping over the dead and pieces of the dead. He was still drunk, which was no surprise to him, because every chance he got he set sail on the grape sea (as he liked to call it). After half a wineskin had softened the miles and stiff joints, he was able to forget all the long, harsh years.

Suddenly he remembered *her*. Her. Gave a growl that was a sigh, too.

Why you? Why are you still in my head?

Because she came one night (she was bored, she told him) before the deadly Saturday when the fighters had their pick of slaves—or whoever wanted to offer themselves to the terrible and tragic killer/entertainers. Slim, dark, beautiful, obviously patrician, she was wearing golden chains tying one ankle to the other, thin enough to bend with a hard step, in strange, sensual mockery of actual slavery. It was an emblem of her real thralldom. When he led her to his hard pallet in a corner of the low room with barred windows he was stunned by the rare, sleek beauty of her naked body, stunned to see her kneel as if to do votive service, bare feet delicately touching one another, the golden chain knotted tight around each calf, glinting. She tossed her hair and took his hot, hard thickness and swallowed it into her painted mouth, the color staining the shaft. His massive body went limp everywhere but there and he sagged to the bedding, gasping as she wet, nuzzled, licked, bit, worried, squeezed, lip-nipped him into a sweet agony that he never was to forget. . . .

Because it wasn't that at all that haunted his memory; it was later when they were just lying there, bodies melted together and she laughed softly and talked and was gentle and understood until he was like a knotted cramp gradually soothed in a hot bath by probing, skillful fingers until he finally slept peacefully with a trusting arm across her body. . . .

He sighed, weaving into the woods, watching the memories so intently the present was a formless blur, not really feeling the tears spilling over his round cheeks as bush and branch whipped past his lurching body. He was trying to remember her name now as he crossed a knoll where the trees opened into lines of saplings that bent and snapped back behind him.

He didn't really come to himself until he glanced off a massive standing stone block which he first took for the side of a building.

The impact brought the misty night scene into better focus. He peered at the stone, then noticed others, standing on end, jutting up from the slow coiling fog on the glistening hillside, starting, he realized, to outline a vast circle.

For some reason he followed the line, thinking about the woman, trying to recapture her face, the way she actually looked. . . .

"Ah," he muttered, "what's wrong with you?" *Why do I suddenly dream again? Here, in this dreary place?* Where was he going? To find that boy. His charge. That foolish, inconsistent, sex-ridden lout. *Yet he's brave enough and means well at heart. But it's not enough to mean well; you have to do well.* There was a fact to pick your teeth with. He passed another massive stone, lost in ruminations and fog. *They'll use him if I let them; they'll destroy him too, like his father . . .*

He was weeping again, tears burning and brimming with a sadness that had never dimmed. Because he had only his honor and vows to keep. There was no glory and nothing could be held forever; but something could be left unstained in the heart—because that terrible, scarred man loved. He had never learned how not to love.

At the next stone he saw figures that seemed to melt into form from the blurred, moonstained air. An old man with a white beard, a slim girl, two tall warriors, and someone—a Roman soldier—sprawled on the ground, a spear point near his neck aimed by one of the Britons. The girl was talking. Both soldiers were talking at once. The old man was watching, motionless.

Subius drew his sword and wobbled closer. There were just two fighters. Where were two opponents who could trouble him?

"Well, people, what's this?" he asked.

The priest had just brushed aside the spear from the soldier's neck. He gave a command. The taller warrior cursed; the girl knelt and stared at Subius, who was just lurching from the mist. She pointed and said a few words the gladiator didn't understand. The tall Briton shoved the Druid back and prepared to finish spitting Leitus. Subius had just recognized him, which brought the fighting squint to his smallish eyes.

He had no more to say. With his surprising agility he slid his great bulk into striking range as the first spearman stabbed at his round, taut belly. He chopped the shaft in two, slicing part of the fellow's ear away and a piece of his beard.

The shorter, stronger, bowed one snarled and leaped to the attack. He was good, Subius noted, making a casual backhand

parry, gliding closer and closer as they circled around Leitus.
The Druid leaned on his staff and watched. The girl slowly
stood up beside him.

Subius was starting to enjoy himself, in a drunken way. The
circling spun his head. He laughed a little, which did nothing
for his opponent's nerves. The other one was moving carefully, trying to fix Subius's shifting flank.

This is serious work, thought the gladiator. Except it was so
easy. Nothing like his battle with the one-armed Nubian on a
decades-lost but unforgotten violent Saturday: sand spray,
blood shouts, steel on steel, lungs torn by sucked wind. . . .
Fighting had become a thing done without normal fear or full
attention; the moves worked of themselves and seemed natural
—no, normal. He never doubted he'd be killed sometime, but
that had no effect or meaning while he worked.

He relaxed, set his teeth, squatted under the next full thrust,
grabbed the shaft with his free hand, and simply pulled the
Briton onto his sword point. In the same motion he stood up
with the spear in his hand and tossed it at the other, who was
already running uphill into the mist in pure panic. The point
glanced off his shoulder and the spear spun unto the nearest
stone pillar.

"You're prisoners," he declared to the priest and the girl.
"Yield to me." He gestured at them; he didn't know if they
understood any Latin. The Druid shook his head, smiling
faintly. The girl pointed to Leitus and said something clearly
unflattering.

"Bind his hands," Namolin told the girl, indicating Leitus.
They acted as if Subius were an insubstantial image.

"I want to kill him now," she said, paying little attention to
anything but the young man's throat.

"No," said the priest, "he comes with me."

"There are enough dogs in the camp already, Namolin,"
she said, grim, furious.

Subius made large gestures, hoping to communicate.
"Come along, now," he boomed. He stooped to study Leitus
and noted he was alive, sighing in seeming sleep. Subius
frowned. "What's been done here, Britons?" he demanded.
The old man's staff jabbed at him faster than a lizard's
tongue, the tip just touching his forearm as he jerked
backward. His arm went numb, and, as he struggled to rise,
his body was already gone . . . and then his sight and thinking,

too, in a single, dull wave of darkness. The last thing he actually heard was the girl saying, in that tongue which meant nothing to him:

"Will we make him suffer before he dies?"

And Namolin:

"Most mortals do."

CHAPTER XV

Leitus opened his eyes and blinked at the fangs that gaped near his face. Bright sunlight slanted over the hut roofs and trees around him and throbbed into his head. The jaws worked, slavered and showed a drooling tongue as the dog yawned and flopped down beside him in the dust.

He sat up, holding his head, trying to get a grip on what had happened. He'd lost everything when the cowled old man had pushed through the underbrush with staff extended.

There were some children naked, smeared black with mud, kneeling in a puddle, slapping the thick, sopping clay into a crudely man-shaped mound. They smeared, patted, and lumped the thing as if it were a matter of life or death.

He frowned and remembered the girl under him, the misty night . . . and then his mind went to mist and blurred shadow. He shook his head. There were images that formed and faded: scenes of a strange, warm city with masses of bright-painted stone buildings mounted on hills beside a big river; men in long robes; soldiers in bronze armor. . . . Somehow he felt it all connected to him but couldn't remember how.

He stood up, squinting into the mildly warm sun while the serious children shaped the mud.

The blood tingled in his legs. He blinked. A couple of Briton warriors in furred loincloths and furry boots were sharing a ladle of beer, leaning on a hut wall a few doors down. In the next yard two fat young women were pounding the dust from a huge hide rug. They'd strung it over a line and were hitting it with sticks. He'd first taken the sound for his heartbeat.

Inside the hut the chief of the tribe, gray-haired Tirb the Strong, kept his eyes on the old Druid rather than on his youngest daughter, who was now doing most of the talking.

Namolin, in turn, was watching Leitus through the unshuttered window.

". . . so," the girl was saying, furious, "I'm to be sacrificed to that Roman animal?" She clenched her fists in her father's face. "Are you mad? Or did only your other daughter matter to you? You have never been the same since she was slain—"

"There's no proof of that," he cut in.

"And long years ago it was. Yet it poisons your life. Don't say no. Mother says the same thing. And now you let me be—"

He cut over her again:

"Bita was a sweet child."

"This pig should be sunk in the bog for his crime against me!" she concluded.

The chief pursed his lips thoughtfully.

"There's some substance in what she says, Namolin. The young soldier should perish." The priest didn't react. "Yet you hope to persuade me otherwise."

Namolin was remembering that dawn when he'd gazed into the black crystal stone that sat in the fireplace where the flames were never allowed to die. His young disciple had slept in the room and tended to the fire and his master's food. The boy, Ulad, had been built like a man of twigs set in a farmer's field, so frail and thin his family had pushed him into the priesthood. The boy had squatted on his hams, barefoot in a sooty robe, and watched Namolin kneel with his face close to the stone, the pulsing red coals stirring his long, greasy, gray-white beard.

"What do you see, master?" the boy had asked in his shrill voice. Whenever he laughed (which was rarely enough unless some other's misfortune happened in his sight) it was on the intake of breath.

He half suspected the master saw nothing at all. Had a nagging idea most of the magic was a sham. He was desperate to learn the tricks himself and take revenge on everybody, starting with his unfeeling peers who liked to mock and scorn him at feasts and play . . . and then on his master, whom he hated for more reasons than he could have numbered—not that

Ulad was capable of counting very high. He daydreamed of
Namolin falling into mire and sinking to a boggy doom; or
being blinded by his own magical fires; having his heart fail
suddenly.

He had been forbidden to move or stay near when the old
wizard gazed into the stone, but he'd tilted his head and
strained his sight for glimpses. He had seen the dark, smooth
sphere like a hole in the embers, heatless, unreflecting. At
times he'd imagined he'd seen a red-eyed face hinted by the
flickers and hollowed by the blackness. Something seemed to
move there. He told himself later it had been his mind. But
several times while his master had rocked before the hot
hearth, he'd felt a chill, as if a cold breath had been impossibly
exhaled from the fireplace.

His master never answered him or looked up for slow
minutes. Ulad had tried to pick up what he'd seemed to murmur to the stone and had caught fragments:

"Yes . . . I see . . . yes . . . give her to him . . . I see . . . burn
his thoughts . . ."

The hole in the throbbing coal-heat had drawn his focus
deeper and deeper until the room had become shadowy and
faint and he'd left his flesh and heavy bones and seemed to be
drawn down to the heart of the earth, and taught there by the
ones he never named. . . .

"This is an important Roman," Namolin now explained to
Tirb. "We will teach him things that will help us."

"But why must I be—" she began again. Namolin overrode
her:

"He has been cleansed of his memories, for the most part.
He is a pure child, in a sense, with no memory of his offense.
What sense to punish a body when the mind knows nothing?"

Namolin didn't want to force things and reveal his true
powers. Not yet. He went on playing the role of a feared, but
not awesome, wizard of the backcountry.

Tirb turned to the window, thinking about his lost Bita
again. Remember chasing the stealers right to the shoreline,
watching the boats fade into the offshore mists. He watched
the children idly building a mudman. One of them propped a
wooden-tipped spear under its lumpy arm.

What was this priest really after here? He obviously had
reasons. He'd been adviser to his father and had performed
the necessary rituals, trained young men in the minor mys-

teries, and so on. Never made a pressure of himself until now.
He was bending the code, taking a little risk, no matter how
you looked at it, forcing the chief into an uncomfortable position. If he wasn't careful, the Druids would have all the chiefs
dancing like trained bears, he reflected.

"Do you mean to use the custom," he said carefully, watching the children shaping the mudman's head out in the sunny
street, "that a man who knows not his deeds may be claimed
by the priests?"

"But, then," she tried again, "he cannot—"

"I know, daughter," her father interrupted. "There's no
law to join you with—"

"Excuse me," said Namolin. "She will bear his child."

"How—" she began.

"Do I err in such matters?"

"One error would be enough," said the chief. He studied
the young Roman in question, who was now pacing across the
muddy street, looking curiously at everything. "Still, I might
slay him as an enemy."

"And break the treaty?" Namolin arched an eyebrow, expecting something cleverer from the man.

"Treaty." Tirb spat out into the palely sunny street.
"Hardly an agreement to trust your life to after sundown."
That was true. The Romans stayed encamped or moved
around in small fighting units.

"We will use him," said the priest. "He will make a perfect
husband." He smiled. "A blank slate for your daughter to
write what she pleases on." He held the chief's gaze with his
own dark, secret stare. "And for us a perfect tool. The invaders have us at their mercy, for the moment. I will forge this
boy into a weapon to smite them with." He bent the pressure
of his stare on the girl now. "We will all profit. You need not
admit the fellow to your bed, unless you choose. I mean to
teach him what will profit us all."

"I don't trust priests," she said, making a face.

"A horse may throw you," her father put in, "if you lack
care. Yet one must ride at need."

Namolin nodded, pleased. He'd won the easy way. No sense
in bending men's wills and risking backlash.

"What better revenge for his outrage?" he asked her,
rhetorically. He'd won. She was looking out the window now,
appraisingly. *The ordinary mortals*, his own master had ad-

vised him, long ago, *ought to believe they rule themselves.*
Thus they serve us best. Because when the final victory came,
the great race and their servants would rule openly. Forever.
Until then, be patient.

When Namolin reported to the master of the hidden land,
he sat high in the upper tier of the inner council. He and his
two fellow adepts were responsible only to the great lords
themselves. So while he might have compelled these two as
easily as wiping away Leitus's memory, Namolin chose to convince. And mirrored the secret ways of his lords.

The sunset broke through the clouds and wanly sprayed the
village with softened brightness.

"I will marry them myself," said the wizard.

The chief grunted and chewed his lower lip. His daughter
watched Leitus watching the boys working the clay mud
shape. The head kept falling off, melting in the muck. The
whole image was visibly sinking back into shapelessness
despite all efforts.

The child of this bloodline, he thought, *is essential to our
purposes.* Decided he could safely leave now.

Hours before his goosefaced disciple, Ulad, had squatted on
spidery legs against the wall of the firelit hut. He had watched
his master finally turn away from the dark stone with an effort. His long face was pale with strain, stare lost in unfocused
depths. His master seemed drained and strangely content. He
hoped, sometimes, he would die from the effort.

Sensing the weakness as a good moment, the disciple
pointed his long, uptilted nose at the suddenly frail, hard
breathing old man and demanded:

"What is this stone, master?"

Namolin didn't react. He sat staring, his cowl fallen back to
reveal an overlarge bald head knotted with twisted veins.

Ulad blinked his squinty eyes and levered himself to hands
and knees as if to crawl. No reaction from Namolin. Was the
master ill? He'd never left the stone out in the flames before
like this. Normally he put it instantly under his robes. What a
chance! He had no idea that the wizard was, in fact, still far,
far away among the shadows and flames of a lost world.

He crept past the old man and peered at the jet surface of
the sphere. It was twin to the one held by the winged black
scientist in Bita's vision of the time when the world-emptying

volcano erupted and spilled the dark army into the warring stratosphere.

Wisps of reddish reflection shifted and squirmed over the surface of the sphere. His eyes tried to follow the rhythm and hinted shapes and were suddenly caught. He tried to look away, but his eyes kept tracking the intricate, fascinating patterns so that he barely reacted when the pictures came. The dark globe grew and suddenly swallowed him into its darkness. He fell into rock and rubble landscapes, fitfully lit like hot embers where winged beings flapped and labored over vast constructions, strange machines with wheels and angles dripping dull fire. He saw pale, naked, humanlike figures, male and female, chained and suffering, seeming (in his blurred impression) to be roasted and eaten over banks of fire or whipped and torn, kneeling and groveling to worship the winged ones who ruled them.

He sailed to a vast, dark peak under a sky like blood, circled by thousands of the creatures whose red eyes burned into him, draining his strength. Poised on the squared-off summit which had been carved into a cyclopean fortress was their giant king, Aataatana, perched with outspread wings. Suspended above him was a hollow globe of metal rings that glowed red and dim green and slowly rotated. He glimpsed the hundreds of miles of cavern, rock, flame, massed activity, and pale suffering . . . and then the great eyes fixed, took him, seared his consciousness. His soul screamed and flailed in frail terror.

Namolin was smiling with half his thin mouth, watching his disciple rocking on his knees, caught by the gleaming stone. He was pleased. He'd come back to himself a little sooner than Ulad had thought. The repulsive boy had taken the initiative. That was something. Now, if he survived, he might be useful.

He stood up and went outside, slamming the heavy bronze-bound door behind him. The boy would be unconscious for at least a day and useless—no, *more* useless—to talk to for longer still. If he survived.

In any case, Namolin knew what to do now. He headed straight for his strange rendezvous with Leitus and the girl. He needed the child. The child who wasn't born yet.

CHAPTER XVI

Antony sat at ease, drinking wine from a jewel-studded goblet and eating spongy cakes soaked in honey and wine, licking the sweetness from his lips. The soft sunlight filtered through the trellised grape arbor and mellowed his smooth face, kindling soft fires in Bita's coppery hair where she sat on the grass facing him. She was barefoot in a blue tunic with gold trim. She held a flower in one tapered hand and idly turned it by the stem, angling it into the nearest drizzle of sunlight to study the golden petalwork that reflected soft speckles across her pale cheeks.

Across the fields slaves were tending the gardens of his country estate. The white marble buildings, half a mile away, gleamed in the sweet sun. Insects hummed and strummed in the rich air.

He was satisfied that the girl was healthy and recovered. She seemed to have surprisingly little memory of her experiences at Iro's villa. He didn't think she was keeping anything back. Not intentionally. He was waiting to see how she might prove useful. Except at that moment it wasn't an issue, because the blood was now running thick and sweet in his loins as he studied the graceful curve of her instep on the bluish grass and the sleekness up the calf to where the smooth thighs curved under the delicate fabric.

"What of my future?" he'd just asked her, sucking down another mouthful of wine. "Do you see what will happen to me?"

She shook her head, not looking up from the flower. She was content here, waiting for the pictures to return. She awoke dreamless now night after night. This frustrated her. Her need for the pictures was an ache, a craving. Sometimes she thought about Leitus, but that stung a little. She hoped he'd come back and find her, though she knew that was foolish. It had simply been one moment that was lost in the harshness of life. How could it come again?

Where are you? she asked, thinking about the golden voice, the formless light that counseled her and opened the world of images, and then: *Leitus . . . Where are you?*

"I don't know anything," she told her new master.

"Ah."

"I don't *see* anything." She sighed. He liked the way she sighed. Liked her mouth. He'd waited but now felt it had been too long.

"Come here, girl," Antony said huskily. She looked up. He gestured with one smooth, soft hand. "Come," he repeated. "You are adorable."

She was thoughtful as she shifted and stood up beside him. He gestured at his lap.

"No," he said softly, "kneel."

She blinked and tried to hear the secret voice or see the light. Nothing but the shadowy grayness. She hadn't really expected results.

She knelt and he smiled and opened his toga. She stared at the slowly filling prong of smooth flesh set off by the shadow of his bared legs.

"Put it in your mouth," he told her, "sweet little slave."

She might as well start serving me, he thought. He gripped the hardening shaft with his left hand. *And this is generally the best way. . . .*

She blinked again. The soft sunlight misting through the leaves lit her bluish eyes with golden traces. "But . . ." she began to say.

He reached over and loosened her tunic so that it fell away and the slim young body was sweat gleaming.

Her arms partly covered her. She was baffled. Leitus had made her do things . . . and the captain of the soldiers had made her touch him one night while camped on the way from Naples to Rome. An alarm had cut the incident short.

"Come," he insisted, "take it in your mouth." It pained

him a little now, tense with desire.

He took her by her long, sun-fired hair and bent her face to his groin. Her lips strained to admit the somewhat bulbous tip. The taste was salty and his perfume seemed vaguely sour, like overripe flowers in a damp place. She wrinkled her nose as he pushed more of himself into her small mouth. She gagged briefly and tried to pull free but his smooth hands were very strong and firm in purpose. He adjusted her head as he wished.

She wondered (among other things) what was so desirable about this. She was uncomfortable and wished the dream pictures would come back.

"Ah," he sighed, gazing at her bare feet, rounded buttocks, small swaying breasts. "Just a little pleasure," he whispered. "And then to serious business." He pulled himself clear, and then, turning her on her back, spreading her legs open, he knelt between them to mount her. "I must have you, little whore slave."

She lay there, pliant and abstracted. The corners of her lips were sore. She felt no sexual excitement at all. Even with Leitus it had been tender but muted. Had someone described an orgasm to her it would have been meaningless.

She was wondering what was going to happen, what she was going to do. Would she spend her life here? It was peaceful but there had to be more than this. Couldn't there be something in life like the dream worlds? With Leitus it had somehow seemed possible. . . .

The first poke of Antony's outsized organ startled her with fear.

It will rip me apart, she thought. But there was more: Suddenly she felt a sparkling power filling her, welling up (she felt) somewhere near her heart, matching its rapid beats.

"No," she said quietly. Her voice had power in it; she felt the words were almost vibrated away. The voice stopped him. Just the power of the sound. "No," she repeated, though she didn't have to because Antony was already back on his haunches, trembling.

She felt so good she sat up and smiled. It was like a song in her. Like the color of flowers and sunlight. Suddenly everything she looked at was like the dream pictures: she was enraptured by the wonders of the afternoon. The sun sang in the shifting brightness of the wind. She felt something, a tiny touch, a pulse of life inside her and her hand strayed to her belly. She could feel life there, a golden rush of warmth. She sighed.

"No," she told him again. "You cannot have me."

His erection was a failing memory. He gaped and was already thinking how the priest hadn't lied. Here was a potent little something.

"Naturally not," he said wryly, fascinated. "You mistook my actions. My manners fail me, at times."

She listened without focus. She lay on her back, naked, innocent, and content. Her hand kept touching above where the precious spot of life lay.

Antony went on studying her with amazement and calculation. He didn't see the man and woman stepping out of the glowing arbor. They were both quite young-looking and beautiful, with long, oval faces, small chins, and large, slightly tilted eyes that weren't quite Oriental-looking. Both wore robes more in eastern than Roman style and almost might have both been of the same sex—except her hair fell in soft, sun-pale waves to her waist.

Bita noticed them first and to her they seemed to have gathered the vibrant sweetness of her fading vision into their startlingly graceful movements, so that, to her sight, they both seemed to shape themselves from the tinted shadows and trills of shattered sunlight, melting into exquisite form and stepping, fluid as a breeze, into the heaviness of earth.

"Well, well," Antony was saying to her, closing his toga over his shrunken desire. "Now I know what I have here. Not a toy but a weapon." He nodded, pleased. He could have sex anytime.

Their hair, Bita was thinking, and eyes . . . all the colors were there. As if the subtle sun-glimmer had been strained and refined into edgeless pastels.

"Hello," she said, pleased and at ease.

Antony turned, startled. *A pretty pair of doves,* he thought.

"Where did you come from?" he wanted to know, standing up with his arms folded, ready for any surprise. The question happened to be one the couple was bound to answer by a cosmic and eternal etiquette—no, not "answer," *respond to:*

"Close by," the woman said, in a fluid voice that matched her melting eyes.

Antony tilted his thoughtful head, taking in her beauty and grace. He didn't notice that he'd failed to view her sensually—which was unlike him.

"From where precisely?" He smiled. "You are, after all, on my lands. Are you slaves? Messengers? Guests?" He chuckled. "Creditors?" She shook her head. "Well," he went on, "I have guests here who've been getting fat and drunk on me for so long I've forgotten who invited them or why." He thought of Saccus. "My parties and feasts can go on for generations."

"Which question do you want answered?" wondered the male. His eyes were calm, remote, luminous.

"All right, then. 'What do you want' will do to start with."

"Need we prove first to you, Antony," said the girl, "that we have authority to speak as we shall speak?"

"Let me first hear," he suggested.

She inclined her head. "A sound reply."

Antony liked them and sensed they were quite extraordinary, though he wasn't sure just why yet. His experiences with the priest and then Bita had opened his mind somewhat, and he learned very quickly—something his enemies always had cause to regret.

"We cannot stay long," said the male.

He glanced up at the sun and the Roman noticed he didn't blink. In fact, after that, he never caught him blinking at all, during the conversation. Antony felt vaguely like a child for the moment, free of all responsibility (which is the pressure of time), absorbed in his curiosity and these fluid voices whose sounds were strangely, sweetly satisfying.

"What are your names?" Bita asked. And to the Roman soldier the question seemed fascinating. It was something like being in love where anything about the beloved had almost equal weight with anything else.

"We have been called many things," the male told them. "Imi is one . . . and she is Jem."

Jem's long hair rippled in the soft breeze except the movement seemed greater than the vagrant fluffs of air should have accounted for, as if she actually stood underwater in some strange, dreamlike stream.

"We cannot stay," Jem said tenderly as if she spoke to her dearest love.

Bita was still rapt. The more she looked at their eyes the more the landscape around them dimmed and seemed to tilt strangely as if they were, somehow, more real than anything around them. She understood that they were not present in the same way as she and Antony were.

"I know," she said.

"If we are caught here by our enemies," Imi explained, "we will be destroyed."

"You are under my protection," said Antony.

Imi smiled; a ripple, old, tender, and sad.

"And will you hold the dark claws from your heart, fair-speaking mortal? Have a care what you promise."

"So," murmured the Roman, "you say you're gods?"

Jem spoke:

"No time to debate these matters. There are ancient powers in this world. This is their fortress and will become their garden of smoke and shadow, if they are not held in check."

"Speak," he said, "beautiful ones." He was uncertain but impressed.

Imi:

"We have come to help. The black ones sense us here on the surface and seek us. What you believe changes nothing. So simply listen."

That was easy. Their voices were music and soft flowers. He smiled and bowed slightly.

A shadowy blurring seemed to cross their forms, shifted their outlines. Even he caught it.

Imi:

"We cannot stay. They are close. This girl must be protected. She will become their bane."

"I don't know these dark . . ." He tilted his head, bland, curious.

Imi:

"Her seed will battle the lords of darkness. And you *do* know them. Protect her, let her develop her strength. You, Caesar, and others must fight for us in a war you cannot imagine." Pause. "The dread armies are preparing to march."

The shadowy ripple shook their substance again, though only Bita actually perceived it. Antony thought his sight fuzzed for an instant.

"Dread armies?" he wondered.

Bita saw them. The memory was vivid from her visions. She saw the winged, black warriors with long, fierce faces, flinging themselves up at the fragile defenders of the open sky. She felt the dream power gathering in her again.

And then she felt fear, because she'd sensed or guessed into what dark places she was going to have to bear the light. A shapeless, imageless flash of understanding.

"Under your world," said Jem, "or within it, if you prefer—"

"To truly explain it," put in Imi, "would confuse you, because, of course, if you dug straight down forever, you might never find the dark ones."

"Yet," said Jem, "they fill all the heart of the world."

Antony shook his head, amused still, and raised his hands in a what-can-I-do gesture. "Give me something solid," he requested, "and I'll push and pull awhile."

"Your enemies will be thick enough," said Imi, "to test your temper."

"You, and your friend Caesar," amended Jem, "and others, will hold the surface of your world while this child—" Jem's eyes were now glowing with a light that blurred away the actual shape of her body. She was slowly fading, dissolving into soft light. Imi, too, was mysteriously leaving. Bita sensed a dark, shapeless, groping movement coming from deep underneath, reaching like a hand and arm, coming closer as if more certain of its target. "—this child will battle for its soul."

"Protect this girl, O Antony," ordered Imi, "from any who would destroy her. In time you will be rewarded for your services beyond any dream you might have of payment." His voice (if voice it was) came from a pale mist of golden rose-violet.

But to Antony's eyes, the two of them walked gracefully away through the cool, hushed arbor. He felt strangely passive, vaguely wanted to follow. He'd never altogether denied magic and the gods, but he'd never expected to see much in that line. A week from now he'd probably lay his present feelings to a mood and the wine.

"Wait," he called after them. "Will Caesar and I rule Rome? Will I ever gain a woman who will bind me in love forever?" The questions spilled out, surprising him.

He had an impression that Jem called faintly back to him from the far side of the arbor where the sun was a blinding dazzle and hurt his shaded eyes. "More than you can imagine. But all mortal blossoms grow in nests of spikes."

He tried to follow now, managed a step or two as if wading in deep mud.

"Wait," he called into the sun-streaked blur of vines and leaves where there was only wind now. *Magic tricks,* his mind tried to reassure itself. "Wait!" And then he stopped, shook his head, and was himself again. Almost. He stumbled and went to his knees, breathing hard, thinking hard. *More than I can imagine?* he asked himself. He looked at Bita. She was still just standing there, not really looking at anything. "So you're a witch, in fact." Antony rose to one knee. "Yet why should I put trust in your spirits? Why believe a thing just or wise merely because it is not flesh and blood?" Except he did and knew he did.

A war, he thought. *Well, that's something I know how to dress for. . . . So poor Pompey is a tool of darkness. How pleasant to think so. One's enemies should always be tools of darkness.*

Still, he looked around uneasily at the familiar fields and the long, low, secure villa, half expecting to see terrible, cloudy creatures swarming across the sweet day in stains of terror.

Bita felt the vague horror that had groped for them fail and withdraw. The nearness of it angered her. She wished she could have struck at it, somehow. And then she went weak and reeled. Antony stood up and caught her.

"Very well," he said, as she recovered and he patted her shoulder, strangely fatherly. "I can't say I understand even a part of what went on here. For all I know I've been fed a potion of vision mushrooms. But I'll help you, if I can." *One assumes there's a choice, naturally.* They hadn't, he noted, told him which side to join because it wasn't necessary. The other was obviously so bad there would be no temptation. Or maybe it was just too late to matter. He suspected something had been done to him, something obscure and deep. So he held the suddenly drained young girl and stared at the empty spaces between the lush vines that draped and entwined the trelliswork.

He wondered if he'd ever quite be Antony again. He felt something ancient, a sense of long-lost wonder and mystery, the magic of living, of breath. A voice he'd heard as a child, he was sure—a wordless, soundless, speaking stillness in all the perfect movements of the day. A feeling that shrank ambition and lust.

He suddenly had a sense of what had been missing from his life. He'd been dulling himself for years with wine, meaningless women, even a boy now and then. . . . Meaningless. *The years flee past. How many to waste?*

Bita stood firm now, but he still held her arm.

"Well, little witch," he said, "what do we do first? Or is it my move?"

She was very serious, looking up into his ironic face. Her focus, he noted, came and went like the subtle shifts of light in the arbor leaves.

"I don't know," she replied. Except she had a sense now, wordless, as if what they'd said was superficial, while the real meanings touched her beneath the surface, like tidal shifts compared to ripples. There was something in her mind now like a gateway opening into a pure and hushed place, washed clean like the first landscapes of childhood when every stir of water, leaf, or air was a breathless wonder and surprise and delight. "But there's something . . ."

"Yes?"

"More."

"More? Jove be kind. How much more? Any more and, I think, my wits will break in half."

"They didn't say everything."

"Who could? Wasn't it enough to tell me an army from Hades is on the march?"

She stepped away from him.

"I'll have to. . . ." she said, remote again behind her slate-blue eyes.

"To what?"

"I . . . go back there. . . ."

Antony cocked his smooth head to one side.

"To Iro? What—"

"I don't know. . . ." She saw things, as through a doorway into time, swirling, confused: a pit of darkness, herself naked, bound, lightning flaring in some huge chamber underground. . . . "That's not his real name."

"Iro? But I've known him since—"

"Not his *true* name. Not true . . . I cannot say his true name." She reeled again and he feared she'd faint. She folded against him and he laid her down gently. She seemed to simply fall asleep. He knelt over her with an almost tender look on his world-weary, cynical face.

CHAPTER XVII

"The child ran out of her belly in blood," Ulad told his master. They stood in the muddy yard. The puddles and the crisscross ruts boiled whitish in reflected gray as the rain seethed and pounded down, chill, autumnal. Two roads crossed here close to Namolin's stone and log hut, set like a cave into a mound of mossy earth. The village proper was perhaps a half mile further at the base of a jagged semicircle of forested cliffs.

Namolin stood bareheaded in the downpour. The rain broke into mist over his bald skull and soaked his floppy beard. His robes were sopping. Spidery Ulad crouched under a dense, bushlike tree.

"I know this, Ulad, you fool," he said abstractedly, not looking at him.

Ulad cocked his head and made a face at his master's back. One arm shivered in a strange, prolonged tic, a mark left by his hours with the black globe. He'd survived (which had surprised the wizard somewhat) but acted more fearful, like a wild creature, so that Namolin suspected he was likely to turn out to be a shape-changer. Inwardly, Ulad had a peculiar new confidence: he longed to gaze again into the strange and terrible worlds of the stone. He thought about it constantly, schemed the way another man might have obsessed over a woman. He hated his master for keeping It from him and liked to think about ways the old man might perish, slow ways involving hot coals and deep, mucky water, snakes and wolves,

saw-edged knives and other delights. And how he loathed that
greedy fool who sucked the sweets of darkness, a babe
mouthing the breast. That filth, that Roman filth, favored by
his master . . . What deaths he would enjoy meting out to him!

His craving had given Ulad a new purpose. He had what
amounted to a passion now, something to hate for: the stone,
the black wonder worlds, the endless unfolding images of its
inner flames, the subtle promises of untold pleasures.

He'd become devious and careful, a willing student alert for
advantages, for even a glimpse of his love, his dreams. Only
part of this was lost on Namolin. Only part (so the old wizard
was amused), but enough to change history.

"Maybe his juice was sour," said Ulad.

His master stared into the crossroad where a snake had just
come from under a waterfalling hedge, sloshing and struggling
down the road as if meaning to crawl to the village on some
urgent business.

Everything means something, Namolin mused. Snake in the
rain. Snake on a road. An omen was like the small movement
in a man that betrayed larger purpose. His head felt thick and
the suggestion eluded him. *Treachery, coming this way,* he
decided. *But whose?*

Normally the rain cleared his head. He sighed and blew the
wet from his lips.

*Let me go in and do what I must do. This news sets me
back. Could some enemy coward be draining her womb?*

Namolin shut his eyes, trying to feel any subtle influence
operating in the area. He felt nothing. He wondered whether
to call on the council for help. That was another power the
stone had: to send thoughts to other stones. He decided there
was no reason to draw criticism. Still, it was strange.

The priest opened his eyes to the rain-blur. The snake had
writhed out of sight in the foaming muck. He glanced down
at Ulad under the gleaming, dark bush. Might this hopeless
creature be controlled by one of them? He was weak enough.
He should never have been shown the sacred window. *Look at
him there,* he reflected, *sick with lust for what would drink the
last dribble of brain spittle in his dark skull.*

Pity about the young Roman. He would have made an ideal
student. He had the power. Still, the crisis was coming, the
great night drew close. Then Namolin would have his pick of
helpers and learners. The great race would ascend again, the

dark sun would smooth the world, and the best of the humans would be made great themselves, changed, tempered into cutting steel, tempered in the sacred heat.

He saw the coming man: tall, gleaming, incredibly strong with immense powers and wings and iron limbs, eyes burning like volcanic flame, mastering a clean world, purged of sex and cowardice and meaningless vaporings and confusing colors. A stark world, black and red, polished . . .

His lips went grim, his teeth ground together, setting his face in a glowering frown of fanatical fury.

"Now there's no child," said Ulad. "Just blood. Maybe *I* should be the one."

Namolin stared at him, the water rippling and beading over his long face.

"What's this idea?" he asked, amused.

Ulad writhed under the bush. His long, twisted toes curled and uncurled, dead pale in the rainstreaming.

"Maybe I should, ah, produce," Ulad muttered, "the child you want."

"What would you use?" his master asked, smiling, as he turned and marched across the muddy road to his low hut.

Inside, Leitus was sitting cross-legged facing the embers of the hearth. He wasn't thinking about anything. Time was no longer an issue for him. When there was nothing for him to do he simply waited, empty and patient. Waited for the teaching and the thing that showed him the dream places. He had resources, words, knew what things were called, but there was no clue to himself, no name or picture of people talking to him, no mother or father, just objective scenes and strange, deep feelings attached to nothing. He wasn't bored. There was no pressure on him to go or come, nothing behind to urge him to action, nothing before he desired—except to drink, eat, wander around the fields, watch the days flow past, some warm and bright, others gray and damp, chilly. At the end of each day there was the hot fire and the black, sleek, glossy globe that opened a window into the dreams.

Namolin entered dripping and steaming in the hot, windowless room.

"Stand up, little Dagger," he commanded.

As Leitus did, the old man slashed his staff viciously at his face with a *whoosh* and spray of water.

Leitus caught the stick effortlessly in one hand, would have tugged it away, except the old man, with remarkably fluid strength, kept his grip. They locked wills along the shaft, both motionless, straining with more than mere muscle and weight (of which the master had but few strings left tying his bones together), with an energy that Bita (with her special vision) would have seen boiling around them.

No advantage. The stick began to bend from the terrific strain when Namolin said:

"Enough." The priest took back the staff. "You have learned well, Dagger."

"Is that my true name?"

"Do you like it?" Leitus shrugged. What did it matter? He waited. "You have the power. Now you must learn the claw."

"Yes?" It felt good to do these things. Tingling force rippled through him. He liked the learning. Wanted more. It was almost as satisfying as the dark images in the stone.

"You feel the power enter you?"

"Yes." Leitus arched his back and breathed deeply. It tingled, filled him, like strange wind gusting.

"Let it enter. Make no resistance." Namolin reached under his robes with his left hand, drew out the sphere, and held it on his sinewy palm. "Make no resistance."

Leitus was pleased. *The dream places,* he thought eagerly, staring at the dead jet surface, waiting for the first red stirring to appear and begin to trace the pictures. Nothing moved or changed. He frowned.

"Where is . . ." he began.

"Silence!" commanded Namolin. "Stand still!"

Leitus's body was filled with beating blood and gathering power that boiled to burst out. It was suddenly incredibly hard to stay motionless. Neither of them noticed the door part slightly so that a little wind and stray rain fuzzed and burbled around the crack. Neither of them saw Ulad's pale eyes peer around the edge.

"Now!" yelled the wizard, voice like thunder. "Reach and take the globe from me! I command you!"

Leitus's left arm shot up to shoulder level as if to salute, fingers outstretched, straining. His legs seemed rooted, numb, so his reach was a foot or so short, like a prisoner behind bars clawing for a fallen key.

"Take it or perish, fool!" screamed his master.

Trembling, sweating, the young man tried, heaved against

the unseen bonds that locked him helpless. He strained, knowing some terrible death was behind him, tingling his back with
a dread touch, moving closer to destroy him.

His eyesight was shot with black flutters as he came near
fainting, feeling the shadow behind him. Now a clawed limb
reaching from the darkness, reaching from the stone through a
hole, gripping his hand and somehow he went forward, pulled
or freed, and had the cold sphere in his grip, pouring a bolt of
power like black lightning into him. When he let go, he whirled violently and glimpsed a winged something looming over
him. In a sudden fury he ripped his left hand at it, tore its
shadowy fabric and heard a faint, thin cry of distant pain. The
shape flapped and fled. Leitus turned, cold within himself,
feeling as if his head were scraping the ceiling; then, somehow
higher still, out among the weighted clouds. He felt he could
rise and rise. . . . That nothing in heaven or earth could resist
him.

Leitus turned. Looked at his master. He could rip his
stringy flesh from his rattling bones. He sneered as the wizard
quailed and fell back behind his upraised stick. Outside the
door, Ulad whimpered and scuttled around the corner,
sloshing on hands and knees in terrible fear, wanting only to
hide.

"Kneel, mortal!" demanded Leitus in a voice that shook
the stones and earth, concentrating on the crouching old man.
"Kneel and adore me!" The force of his command drove Ulad
flat on his belly in the muck so that he wriggled now as if to
burrow under the muddy ground to escape.

Namolin sagged but caught himself on his staff. Then he
hummed a low tone into the black sphere and a moment later
Leitus's eyes changed again and he seemed smaller, though
still vibrant. His fury at these lesser beings had subsided to an
ember. What did they matter? They would serve him well or
suffer for it. He withdrew into the empty center of himself,
deeply content, because the sphere was inside his mind now.
That was his new secret. It floated there, small, round, perfect, shot with flame that dripped and showed him scene after
scene and a long dark face with blunt eyes of terrific fire. The
face whispered to him, confided, promised him greatness over
men, showed him his kingdom to come, a world of slaves to
gratify hungers he was just learning about, that were being
stirred into need by the voice in his head. Because, otherwise,

there was only the distance he watched from, the strange emptiness where the days flowed past, gray or bright, wet or dry,
with nothing urgent, nothing to really fear or feel a need over.
The spell on him was like a drug or wasting sickness that
thinned the world to a kind of mistiness without filling him
with some compensatory inner richness. So only the black
roundness, the roundness like a hole in time, became a passion.

"You are strong now," said Namolin. "You are a ready
dagger. Soon you strike a blow."

What did he mean? Leitus vaguely wondered, concentrating
on the rich ball of darkness in his mind.

"Meanwhile," said Namolin, more or less to himself,
"your bride needs some little time to heal. Then you will
play the groom again. Ah, and then back to your people." He
smiled. "A serpent under the pillow. A hornet in the flower
petals. . . ." Nodded, still catching his breath from his terrific
effort to resist Leitus. "The hour is coming." He saw it: the
shadow armies gathering in the dense depths of lightless earth,
waiting for the child to come, son of the great father, born
through the physical agency of this young Roman whose
blood (he'd been told by the vision being that had sent him to
the scene of the rape on the battlefield) carried the strain of
power from the old, great race. For ages these bloodlines had
been prepared, nursed, the weak ones destroyed, the best
preserved and mated with or without consent, as with Leitus.
The child to come, after seasoning in the underworld, would
burst to the surface and open the way for the dark race to walk
above again. The glossy, gleaming armies would be free at
last. The higher realms would fall quickly, the sun dimmed to
an ember. The weakling, glowing races would lose their power
to subtly sap and poison the vital strength of the humans.
Those pastel corrupters of primal force! The world of dark
gods and godlike men would reach out to the stars, limitless in
power and beauty!

The sphere was showing Leitus something new now: a
woman, nude, glossy-limbed. He vaguely recalled her from
somewhere, somehow. . . . She floated in something dark like
star and moon-stained water; deep, lustrous, gleaming silver
eyes. She smiled, cupped her breasts, lifted one long, perfect
leg, bare foot pointed to him, silver chains circling the ankle
and upper thigh. She released a flood of memories without
focus, a flood of needs that triggered bursts of heat. He was

suddenly desperate to lick and suck that perfect, gleaming foot, to immolate himself in adoration.

He clutched his groin with both hands, stunned by the heat of what suddenly grew there. All this had been lost in the gray, amnesiac mists of Namolin's *geas*.

The woman turned smoothly in her silvered night-colors. He could have wept, dizzy with wanting to press his face between those full, smooth buttocks and adore.

He didn't notice Namolin go back outside to stand in the downpour, the chilly impacts soothing his feverish head. The witchman tucked the fist-sized stone back under his soaked and frayed robes.

Namolin noticed movement in the swampy stretch between his windowless hut and the swollen, spreading stream. He peered, blinking water, imagining (for an instant) that it might be some strange creature roused by the burst of psychic energy loosed during his initiation of Leitus—one of the risks of liberating such potent forces. Another was the drain on himself. His nerves still hummed and sputtered in protest. His heart ran too hard. He sensed this body was nearing its end, at least of real usefulness. He considered that while watching (what he'd just realized was Ulad) the muddy lump, rising to his knees in the bog like some primal creature taking tentative spidery, human outline, resisting the general shapelessness that sucked him back down . . .

He'd been promised the secret of endless youth. The sphere was a storehouse of power and knowledge collected through unremembered ages. It amplified the will that controlled it (unless it were too weak, in which case the forces within would destroy the wielder) but could never be trusted: it had drunk the minds of humans and nonhumans until it had a kind of malicious pseudointelligence. If the user slipped, the stone would betray him. He held it in trust for the great ones. Trust . . . A loose term, since he'd stolen it to begin with from an ancient loremaster and left the old man dead. He'd only scratched the surface of the thing's powers, but he knew (from the loremaster's lore) that at a certain time and place following certain grim ceremonies, with the help of the masters of the great race, an old man could be restored to childhood, keeping his full knowledge and capabilities intact instead of dying and smoking out into fuzzy afterlife in a tattered mist of dissolving memories.

Soon, he thought, watching Ulad slog back toward the hut,

a featureless mud stick in the gathering twilight. *Soon, great ones, I must have my reward. . . .*

The rain washed over him. It seemed to melt Ulad so that at each labored, sucking step he seemed to sink deeper into shadowy blurring.

The old man rolled his eyes as if trying to see under his own forehead. A red spot suddenly burned there, tiny, intense, like a star.

Hear me, he thought into the jewel-hard spark, *I must have my gift soon. . . .*

CHAPTER XVIII

Subius was enjoying the thin sunlight pressing warmly into his face as he walked along the hillcrest looking over the autumn landscape: yellow and red leaves filling the valleys, pale grass on the rounded slopes. Here and there massive stones marked special hilltops, he assumed. The other two soldiers with him walked twenty or thirty paces on either side. They were under his orders since Caesar had unexpectedly elevated him to acting captain of ten. He'd been surprised to be called out of line. The legion had been marching back from the farthest inland outpost. Caesar was preparing to return to Gaul. The campaign was winding down. He'd made his treaties and set up a system of tribute.

Caesar had talked to him, alone at sunset in a pine grove where the last light had gradually gone gray and melted the dark trunks and interlaced branches into a depthless roof and wall.

The army had been settling down not far away, digging trenches and pounding in posts for a palisade.

"Soldier," the commander had said, sitting astride his white horse. It stood very still except for the tail and an occasional side twist of the long head. "You joined with the young Leitus." Subius had nodded, waiting. "The deserter." Subius still waited, trying to make out Caesar's expression in the failing light. "And, we hear, murderer of women. Eater of human flesh. You were his companion on the road, yes?"

"Yes, lord General."

139

"Do you object to what I say about your friend?"

"Did I say he was my friend?"

"So you agree he's a monster, unnatural?"

"No. Not at all. I believe he's quite innocent of the charges, lord General."

"Ah, so did I." Caesar had leaned closer, stooping from where he'd sat the sleek horse. "You were a great fighter, Subius. I remember you from the arena. I never really liked the games. I prefer the field, where events lead to something more substantial than entertainment." Subius had nodded again, his still massive but trimmer body resting solidly on his planted feet. "I want you to find this young fellow whom I made a lieutenant before he ran off. Take some men and follow after." He'd sat up straight again, one hand on his hip.

"Why do you care so much, if I may ask, sir?"

"I hate a mystery, Sergeant. I want to talk to him. I want to know more of his story." Because he'd been thinking about a letter that had come that day from Mark Antony in Rome. A letter in code:

> Caesar: Unnatural events mix with the
> ordinary schemings of our enemies. Pompey
> has joined Iro and Flacchus, the fat. And
> young Leitus Sixtus seems of undue interest
> to them. Something strange in all this.
> In haste, A.

The commander had been haunted by the terrible deaths in his tent when the half-headless tribune had strangled his soothsayer after failing to kill Leitus. He'd had forebodings and dreams he'd tried to shut off. There'd been a shadow in his mind and over his actions.

"He didn't desert," Subius had said. He hadn't reported his encounter with the priest, had seen no advantage at the time. "He was taken by Britons."

"It seems everyone wants him." Caesar's face had been just an outline in the last glimmers. "Find him and bring him to me before I quit this land. I'll give you my best native trackers."

Subius squinted now down the sunny hillslope at where the Briton scouts moved on ahead. *If I find him I think we'd both do well to retire from this army.* Rebellion was fermenting in

Rome again, and Subius swore the boy would have no part in it. He remembered the old rebellion all too well, the terrible, wild days when they'd almost won the world, when the gladiators had broken free in the circus and, backed by a city full of armed slaves (who'd chopped down their masters in great style), marched from Rome, raising the countryside in a tide of blood and fury. They'd gathered into an army to stand against the greatest military force in the history of the world. They'd been led by a brilliant warrior, slave, gladiator, general: Spartacus. Subius had stood at his side the day he'd broken the best army Rome could muster, moving on to the sea where their ships had been lost to treachery; then had stayed with him, fighting all the way north the length of Italy. Then, despite Subius's arguments, Spartacus had turned back because he had believed he was invincible and had been granted divine power to create a new, free land. He'd been possessed, in the end, by a grand and unreasonable vision, which finished on lines of crosses measuring the Appian Way with markers of suffering, a dying rebel on each. The line of agony had finally ended where the bleeding leader hung. . . . Subius had escaped, with Gracchus's help. Gracchus owed his life to Spartacus; before that general had even been a soldier he'd been sentenced to the arena on conspiracy charges (unproven), and during a mixed melee Spartacus had spared him the fatal cut, saying later he refused to slay so incompetent a fighter in full daylight. And so each had been bound to each. . . . And now, the old survivor reflected, Leitus's fate hunted him like a deadly black hawk dropping in a blur of wing and talon, keen, remorseless. . . .

He spotted the Briton scouts moving up the gradual slope ahead. He realized they'd moved back toward the coast. He could smell the sea. The bearded scout had told them, in awkward Latin, that he'd heard of a young captive being taken to some coastal town. The place was nearby, well within the pacified area, but the gladiator had no illusions about that or the temper of the population. It didn't feel like a conquered country.

The Romans were preparing to withdraw their main forces back across the channel. From now on the scattered garrison towns would have to do the job alone and incline the stiff-necked natives toward Roman ways.

•   •   •

Hours later the reddening sun was nicked by the smooth old hills. The scouts and the three soldiers stood on a hilltop earth mound looking down at Tirb's village set inside a semicircle of palisade that backed against dense pine cliffs. Long shadows stretched over the rough country. Subius was tired of walking.

The taller Briton gestured with his head. Subius nodded.

"They don't waste words, do they?" said the lean, skew-faced, slightly pop-eyed soldier who reminded Subius of dead Crato. The second, very wide across the back and narrow of head, was sparing of speech himself. He just stood there, somber, chewing a strip of dried goat meat. Both these soldiers were considered outstanding fighters—which was faint comfort to the gladiator.

"What now?" he demanded of the ruddy-faced scout. The other was right-eyed (a scar had obliterated the left) and red-haired with pale, bony features.

"Mn?" responded ruddy face.

Subius gestured, unconsciously raising his voice. "Do?" He tried a fragment of native tongue, then back to Latin. "Do! Get boy!"

The Briton nodded, then shrugged. "Pay," he said, holding out a big flat hand. He pointed to the village. "Pay," he repeated.

Well, Caesar had given him a small sack of silver against need. But that would be too easy and went against Subius's forty-five years of experience.

"What dull assholes," put in the lean soldier, hand on the hilt of his sword.

Subius sighed and unstopped his wine flask, sloshed the contents, then sucked a long, coolish slug down into himself. That was better.

I drink too much and care too little. . . .

"Pay, mn?" reflected Subius.

The native nodded and grunted, squinting. The reddish sunset gleamed on his pale cheeks. The gladiator took another swallow and squatted down on his haunches.

"Well?" wondered the third soldier, chewing the dried flesh. "What?"

Subius eased himself down onto his outsized, powerful buttocks. "We wait until dark," he said. He gestured to the scouts, who took a few moments, then sat, too, leaning against the trees that strung along the hillcrest.

Subius passed the wine. Everyone got comfortable. The town down there reminded him of childhood: youthful shouts on the breeze in the gathering twilight; barkings; banging sounds; parents calling children. The smell of cooking washed up to them.

At moonrise, he thought. He felt a nip in the air. A taste of winter cutting through the thin autumn wind.

Leitus followed Namolin along a wildly twisting path that cut through the cliffs behind the village. They were wrapped in their robes against the chill, suddenly much colder than the week had promised. There was a feeling almost of snow now.

As they went under the dense pines and hemlock, ending at the stream that separated the village from the rocky hills, Leitus was intent on the sphere of dark wonder in his mind. He saw a dimly glowing land where tall trees carven from some glittering stone, with interlocking leaves of a reddish metal, arched over the gleaming road that slid under him as if he now walked in two places at once.

They were crossing the little stone bridge into the village proper. Namolin held his staff loosely, not leaning on it. His step was silent and spry. From behind he could have been decades younger than his actual age—which no one living knew.

Leitus followed vaguely, lost between worlds. He glanced at the low huts as they crunched over crusted, iron-hard mud. Moonlight gleamed on thin ice in wheel ruts, hoof- and foot-prints. He watched the dark circle in his mind. Stared into that faintly gleaming emptiness.

"Wait here," Namolin told him, as they stopped outside the chief's long, low hut. Across the twisting street, firelight fluttered around rough shutters. Inside someone was snoring loudly. In the hills a wolf bayed.

Leitus faced the door that the old man went through into a hearth's coal-lit dimness, leaving the door wide so that the embers in Leitus's line of sight mixed into the images in the circle in his mind. He wasn't aware that a few houses back Ulad crouched like a spider in the shadow of a bush and peered at him.

The embers seemed to glow inside a vast square block above the luminescent roadstrip. The block was hollow. Everywhere the blackness was pressure that the glimmering barely held away so that the haunted illumination made that utter night even more oppressive.

Something gargantuan squatted on top of the block, something with immense wings and miles-long, thin, angular limbs. It seemed to be brooding over the block as if it were a square egg. Inside, where the dim redness flashed and flickered, he felt anguish, terror, frustration past imagining. Pale, human-like forms were visible there, crushed flat at the bottom under the immense weight of that bitter night. He understood it was a prison. He perceived the victims laboring to pile heaps of glossy stone . . . others crawled aimlessly . . . others embraced, ignoring all circumstances, trying to lose themselves in one another. . . .

He was being drawn in. He was so close now the sides of the vast cage loomed over him.

No! his mind cried. He felt the vast presence become aware of him, waiting for him now. He strained to pull himself out of the vision. A voice was calling him. *No!*

"Dagger," it whispered, "come to me."

It was Namolin calling from just inside the hut door. The picture in the dark circle changed: the floating woman was there, the silver-tinted perfection who swam in liquid delight, beckoning him, licking her parted lips, stunning him with desire so that he almost tripped over the nude girl on the floor (lying on a furry hide rug), legs smooth and opened (he didn't realize it was his wife, Tirb's daughter Abti), and the image in his mind blurred over the real flesh at his feet. He felt both were vaguely familiar from somewhere long, long ago, but no names leaked back to him.

On his knees now, he reached for the glowing image. His hand touched warm flesh instead. He was barely aware of the old priest squatting nearby, muttering and humming under his breath in the semidarkness. He ran his hands over the bared, unmoving body. He thought she was sleeping. Then the vision beauty turned, showed him her secret, a crease of dark and silk and moon-stained light, and he gasped and tried to reach it with his mouth, and then a deep male voice (Tirb) came in, raging:

"Priest, what foul thing is this?"

The clank of a sword, a curse, and Namolin was moving, slashing his staff. Tirb screamed. The two figures reeled together while Leitus paid no heed, matching himself to the girl as the arms in the image reached up to embrace him and his body thrashed into ecstasy. He never heard or cared that his father-in-law went crashing past in a flash of greenish fire. He was lost on the unresponding body of his wife while the silvery, gleaming woman held him in a thrill-shock of smoothness and rapture. In the grip of it his loins burst white fire and spilled out his soul. He tried, gasping, to hold the already fading image in the coal-lit dimness, tried to float and follow her into the subtle world above the unmoving girl he was hunching into. He touched nothing but smoky air.

Ulad had crept up the frozen street and was now kneeling at the corner of the open door. The eye he risked around the door frame saw vague shadows stirring on the floor, then pounding feet, a crash and a cry, a blinding green flash, the hum of a sword stroke, and next, too many arms and legs spun out the door. It took Ulad an instant to realize two men were locked together: a sword flailing, a stick clacking; robes flapping. When they fell and rolled he recognized his master's bald head glinting in the cold moonlight while the chief tried to get his blade cleared for a stab. The wizard's staff impotently beat air and frozen earth, flashing deadly green fire when it hit.

Ulad heard a muffled groan, took it for the last breath of some fearful death. He crouched to flee, took one step, wrenched his ankle as something hard and smooth zipped his foot out from under him, and he fell on his face hard enough to flash red sparks in his head and spring blood from his long, bony nose.

What he'd slipped on now lay under his throat choking him. He scrambled to his knees, gripped the thing to throw it away in frustration. It was slick, jet-dark, perfectly round in his hand. His heart pounded because he had it at last.

In the street they still rolled and fought and raged.

Ulad stuffed the sphere into his bosom without a glance. *The dreamstone,* he kept thinking, *he dropped the dreamstone. . . .*

He limped and shuffled to a run, ducking around the nearest house (like any thief), not looking back. He never saw Namolin win by snarling a word of power that checked his opponent long enough for him to bring his staff into play, rolling aside and poking the chief in the ribs. The green flash spun Tirb over and left him twitching in the chill moonlight.

Crouching there, snarling without rage, Namolin didn't actually register that Tirb's sword was missing. He felt cramp and cold pain in his side, but it took a long moment before he realized the blade was sheathed in his body.

Furious at himself for laxity (though he didn't yet grasp the extent of his losses), he jerked the chill metal free and concentrated on holding back the blood flow. The instant he lost the sphere his power had begun to diminish, so that even the deadly staff blow (though he didn't know it) had failed to kill his opponent.

The wound was too deep to ignore. He could barely stand. Internal things had been severed and punctured. He cursed, muttering. (Later he would believe he'd been attacked by unseen enemies because all this could not have been coincidental.) By the time he leaned in the doorway Leitus was gone.

He had no time to look for him. He had to heal himself or leak his body's life away.

"Master, help me," he whispered, clutching his side. He had to get home and recover. There was no time for anything else.

Doubled over, raging every painful step of the way, forcing himself to go on, he never thought about the sphere that should have been rocking against his body in the pocket inside the robe—until he realized he was going to have to contact the other two wizards. Then, on the rocky slope above his lair, he knew and howled like a stricken wolf.

The two Briton scouts had melted away somewhere back in the forest leaving Subius and his two men to enter the village alone. *Not,* reflected Subius, *that the two of them would make much difference if it came to chopping.*

The silvery moongleams on the frosty ground guided them to the narrow bridge where Leitus and the others had recently crossed. They crouched in a screen of stiff holly bushes as a gangling man (Subius thought of a stick figure in a farmer's field) limped across, murmuring and chuckling steadily to himself in high, nervous glee. He headed back into the wooded slopes.

Subius looked down at the thin stream, saw the white glitter of frost along the dark, unrippled surface. Reeds were stiff, crisscrossed shadows. He wanted a drink. He wrapped his heavy cloak closer around himself against the chill, thinking about mulled wine steaming in a copper bowl. He sighed.

"What?" asked the lean soldier with the bulging eyes.

Subius shook his head.

"Peace," he said.

"That isn't my trade," said the other with the too-narrow head and wide shoulders. "What do we do?"

"Wait for the next one to pass."

"Which next one?"

"Coming now," whispered the gladiator, pointing across the stream. "Busy little spot we picked."

A dark-robed, long, bearded outline staggered quickly over the bridge, clutching himself (Subius noted) and drawing hard breaths.

Hurt or sick, Subius thought. *Something's up.*

"Come," he said, "we'll do it house to house." *Or rather,* he went on internally, *hovel to hovel. . . . What am I doing working for Rome? I hate Rome.*

Except for his vow to Leitus. What would he be without it? The purpose kept him drinking until he could sink past and present into final obliteration—because it was hopeless. The blind machinery of the world ground on like a vast iron millstone, grinding all good and hope and real purpose to dust.

And then, he thought, *they keep the chaff and toss the wheat away.*

Leitus rolled off the motionless girl. He felt the cold draught on his loins. He was still lost in the fading intensity, trying to call back the vaporous, silver-lucent female into the dark circle of focus in his head. The struggle outside was vague and meant nothing to him.

After a time he felt only the cold and lumped hardness of his body on the planked floor. Desire had faded. He had no particular idea why he was there. He got up and wandered outside, wondering what had happened to Namolin only because he was used to seeing him.

He glanced back into the room before he shut the door; the girl lay perfectly still in the dull emberlight.

He paused in the icy street looking down at Tirb. Tirb also lay perfectly still.

A pair of warriors on guard duty, short and blocky men in horned helmets, spears over their shoulders, entered the street. They came up to Leitus, who was on one knee now peering into his father-in-law's face. He hardly noticed them at first.

"What's this?" one guard wanted to know.

"Who's this?" asked the other.

"Looks like that old shit-ear wizard's little Roman pet."

"Arr?" said the first, "you mean the chief's son-in-law."

"Is that fact?" The other poked his bearded, bulb-nosed face close to Leitus, and peered past him at Tirb sprawled on the frozen ground.

"By the shit pits of the gods," he whispered, "here's a thing."

Their spears came ready and Leitus faced the tips.

Bulb-nose spoke through slit lips:

"You Roman bog-slime," he remarked, cocking the spear for a full thrust. "Doing murder, are you?"

"Kill him, Olod," said the other guard. "Who's to know?"

"A rare good point," said Olod, thrusting low and hard for the young man's groin.

A strange thing: Leitus actually felt the spear head over a foot from his body and he wasn't facing the man. In fact, the dark sphere had opened in his mind again and he saw the guards there as reddish glows. The man on the ground was dimmer than the others. Further glows showed down the street and inside huts. He even perceived wounded Namolin stumbling home along the cliff woods and Olod, Subius, all living beings in the area, as if he watched from high above in a dream where near and far and time all blurred together.

The spear thrust seemed absurdly slow, and he reacted, feeling a dark, furious, wind of force gust through him. He felt immense anger at these pitiful worms as he turned and struck at them.

Olod's thrust met nothing. What had appeared human, he instantly knew, was a demon. It whirled too fast for mortal sight or flesh, blazed like a flame, eye pits like holes in a forge-furnace, suddenly ten feet tall or more. A long claw tore him literally in half as the other guard bubbled a shriek of total terror, starting to turn and run as the thing sprang, engulfed in searing rage, and crunched him with a single blow that broke his back and burst his lungs.

Subius peered around the hut wall, having followed voices. He saw three men. One jabbed with a spear, but his target whirled with astonishing speed, a blurred shadow in the moonlight, and struck both men down with incredible fist blows that reminded him of a Nubian gladiator he'd once fought beside.

Here's an athlete, he thought, loosening his sword in its sheath.

The narrow-headed recruit at his elbow gave a low growl. He was impressed.

"There's a raw son-of-a-bitch dog," he muttered. "Why don't we let him go his way?"

The other one agreed:

"A few like him and who knows how that last battle might have gone."

"Maybe they was saving him in reserve."

"Save him for fifty years, so please me," said the pop-eyed youth.

"Quiet," hissed Subius, "the fellow comes."

Which was true. Having already forgotten the two fallen warriors as if they'd dropped into a pit and vanished from the earth, Leitus wandered back the way he'd come, trying to stir more images out of the black hole that seemed to float in the center of his forehead. It was just cloudy obscurity again. He felt lost, hollow. *Show me more things,* he thought.

"Leitus," Subius whispered. He stood up and moved out from behind the edge of the house. Inside a baby squalled and someone hushed it.

The young obsessive stopped. Sensed no real threat. Wondered what "Leitus" meant—was it a word or a name? The other two soldiers came cautiously from behind a wall. Inside the baby choked out a cry again. A female voice began crooning.

Leitus felt the cold killing power pumping up inside him again. This time he was sure it was pouring up from the ground into his body. As he raised his arms to slay these men, the cloudy voice spoke through the empty circle in his mind and stopped him with: *"No. Go with these men. I will tell you when to kill."* And it preluded the feeling that would come: killing would be ecstasy, a burning deep pleasure that would fill him thick and full like touching the silvery woman. *"I will tell you when."*

"Good," he faintly voiced, blinking at Subius and the others, dropping his arms to his sides.

"What's that?" the gladiator wondered.

"I will go with you," Leitus said.

"Well, that's generous of you, you young slop pail," muttered the wide-shouldered soldier under his breath.

"Come on," said Subius.

They headed back the way they'd come, crossing the bridge over the frosted stream, leaving the sleeping, dark village, the scent of wood smoke, sweat, and stale broiled meat.

Moving into the rocky, cliff-step woods, Subius spoke:

"When last I saw you, Leitus, you were on your ass beset by an old man and a girl, among others. Now I find you wandering among the natives and smiting them left and right."

"Must be the damned climate," muttered the pop-eyed soldier. "Though it don't prosper me."

They followed and twisted and dipped with the ragged path.

"Eh, Leitus?" Subius nudged him.

"What is it?" Leitus responded.

"I spoke to you, Leitus."

"Did you?"

"Did I?"

"What is that word?"

"What word?"

"Leitus. I don't know what that is."

"Ah," put in the bug-eyed soldier with understanding and a certain satisfaction, "he's daft."

"What," said Subius, "do you only answer now to 'fool'?" He shook his head.

"He's been bewitched," suggested the bearded, stocky man.

"Or hit on the head, more like," the other reasoned.

Blurs of moonlight leaked through the pine branches. The air was rich with their scent. The cold nipped at them as they plodded along.

It was too easy, Subius was thinking. *And now this. Too, too easy. . . .*

CHAPTER XIX

"Caesar is preparing to come back," Antony was telling the two senators, standing in the pale autumn sun-splinters that sprayed through the trees lining the front steps of the forum.

Cassius, thin, nervous, with slit, downturned lips and restless eyes; Casca, stocky and hairless, not looking at anything while he listened and rubbed his front teeth together gently back and forth.

"If he comes with troops," said Cassius, "then we'll have civil war."

"And if we do nothing?" Antony asked, hands on hips, looking up the slope at the white, bright blue, and yellow painted capitol buildings and triumphal statues. The sky was cool, faded blue with streaks of high clouds. He watched a flock of birds circle slowly above the wooded hill dotted with estates. Iro lived near the top there. He idly wondered if the birds were vultures or buzzards keeping hopeful vigil above his house. Iro continued to obsess him. He'd dreamt of him a few nights ago, trapped in some cave, naked, feeble, at the mercy of the little monster.

He squinted. It had to be a trick of the atmosphere, he decided, because the birds seemed too large and dark and ominous for a moment and put him in mind of some deadly omen.

"Then we work out our differences," suggested Cassius, "and keep the peace."

"No," said Antony. "I don't think so. If Pompey and

151

his—" He paused. What *was* Iro, properly speaking? "—his *creatures,* come to power, there'll be blood shed one way or another. They'll pick us off one at a time."

"Hah," said Casca, "did your little whore witch prophesy this, too?"

Antony wasn't amused. He brushed a curly oiled lock of hair back behind his ear and set his lips.

"She is nothing to jest about."

"Are you in love again?" pressed Casca, smirking.

Antony blinked. Who could fall in love with a woman who could stop you with a glance, read your future, and draw down spirits? He shook his head.

"She's a tool," he responded. "A valuable tool." Except he knew there was a problem. He kept asking what she could see, pushing her because she'd been getting fragments, flashes, blurs: a scene where a Roman general in some obscure and misty forest, his army around him, was in deadly danger. Antony believed she was seeing Julius Caesar on that Gaulish island. But the threat crept behind a shadow in time she could not penetrate. Perhaps she was just too young in her art. He didn't pretend to understand nor she to explain. There were blurs wherever she looked with her strange senses and she felt things, beings, lurking even in Rome, whose actual form and purpose were lost in the same shapeless shrouding.

He sensed she needed help. But then they all needed help. Some tremendous climax was building and strange things leaked into even his solid Roman, normally pornographic dreams, so that lately he'd been waking up in a sweat, clutching the covers, startling Dia, his bed companion of the moment, the woman from the banquet with hooked nose, tight ringlets, dark skin, and honed tongue.

"What's the matter now?" she'd demanded, twisting around on the bed in the semidarkness of the predawn. "What are you doing? Why is your head down there? Are you sick? Why don't you speak, Antony?"

He'd been shaking his head, trying to jar away the images that'd been like a black, foul muck seeping through the bricks of the clean, solid house. He'd wiped chilled sweat from his forehead, controlling his nervous breaths.

"Are you sick?" she'd repeated. "Why is your head down there?" She'd sat up, naked, short but deliciously curved. "Did you vomit? Oh? Oh?"

"Be still!" he'd snarled. And then he'd forgotten her and

the dreaming, staring into the grayed shadows as dawn ghosted softly around the shutters into the sleeping chamber. He'd remembered a point she'd made. She'd seen Clodius battered and stabbed in the streets of the capitol. It had to be he. Which meant defeat for their side. With Crassus gone, the triumvirate was broken, in any case.

Clodius had organized the mob (originally at Caesar's instigation, to help keep a balance of power while he was in Gaul) and had decided simply to strike as soon as possible. Take over the city and let Caesar return in triumph to settle the unrest. Antony had said no a dozen times but Clodius had not been obligated to listen.

"Pompey will destroy him," he'd muttered.

"What are you saying, my love?" she'd wondered, somewhat subdued by his temper.

The sweat had dripped down his nose, cool and unpleasant.

"He'll have the excuse he wants," he'd said, not really to her, "to push us under."

"Go back to sleep, why don't you?" she'd said, frustrated.

"Shut up!" he'd snarled, leaping from the bed and pacing, staring intently at nothing.

She has to see more. The little witch has to see more. . . .

And then the whole dream had come back to him. It was Iro's face shaping itself from the darkness as the mud and shadows overspilled his home. Iro, except the eyes hadn't been eyes at all, just holes. Iro's face billowing up like smoke in the wind rising over the city, towering, filling all the air, and then he'd screamed and struggled to awaken. . . .

"The city is leaderless," Casca was saying, "in any case. The mob is stirring and boiling. We need order." He patted his hairless dome with a wide, soft hand. "We cannot risk tipping the steaming pot."

Antony wasn't really listening. He was too nervous. Suppose Iro took the witch back? He'd assumed she could see enough to save herself but she kept insisting that Iro had always been unclear in her vision, a finger of that impenetrable darkness.

"I'm a fool," he whispered, brushing by the senators, aware he was offending them. He half ran past the long row of cypresses and statues that flanked the pristine white processional wall where heroes and their chariots finally halted to greet the Senate and receive honors.

He had two problems, he realized. He had to help her perfect her gift as well as protect her, if he could. But the dangers were not always palpable.

He realized how much he'd changed. The world had always been a machine to him, a thing of massive gears, grinding wheels, and often subtle adjustments, but all solid and subject to cunning and strength. Now he hardly knew what to fear, much less what to fight.

At the arched gate where he'd left his mount he almost walked past the robed and hooded man leaning on a free column. He paused. Frowned. A slant of sunlight showed the lean, remote-looking face in the hood. Ion.

"You," said Antony, stepping closer. The old priest just waited. *By Juno,* Antony thought, *you began this, now you'll explain.* "Listen to me, you—"

"I understand your problem," the man said, calm, untouched, but not quite disinterested.

"What?" He grinned lopsidedly. "Which one?"

"Take me to her."

"To whom?"

"The princess."

"Any particular one?" Antony cocked his head to one side, hands on hips, and glanced over at the row of the huge statues rising in file behind the soothsayer: dead leaders and gods rising to the top of capitol hill.

"The girl, Bita."

"So she's a princess. But all barbarians are princesses."

The remote, pale stare came close, focused like blue fire. Antony was shocked.

"Be serious, youth," said the priest, who suddenly seemed old in a way that made Antony very uncomfortable. He wished he'd never been drawn into this whole business.

Go be a plain soldier again, he thought. *Forget these intrigues and empty politics. . . .*

The old man answered his thought:

"You are involved. It is too late to complain. You could remain a pawn moved by what you know not." He stepped away from the column, eyes locked on the Roman's. Antony was reminded of the power in Bita's look that day in the fields when he had attempted to make love to her. The man was sharp as a clean sword edge. "But you are no longer quite a pawn. So you must be serious. You must help the princess. She's not ready yet."

Antony shook his head. *Ah,* he thought, *when this is over*

I'll live in the provinces, drink, make love, listen to music, sleep in the sun. . . . "Not ready," he murmured.

"Honey is sweet, yet if I fed you a vat of it you would be sickened and maybe die. A blow is painful, yet skillful massage heals the soul and body."

"I don't exactly follow you." Antony was scornful. "I'm no philosopher."

"To say as much makes you one. Be serious. You've a role to play, play it well and with a good heart."

Antony blinked against the man's stare. "You," he said, "you are of the old blood."

Ion nodded. "That is true. Now you know something."

Which meant he wasn't really a barbarian at all but rather a descendant of the Etruscans who originally ruled this country. Almost all soothsayers were once of the old blood. Men from the lost land across the western sea. The priest's eyes were distant again.

"Very well. What must I do?" This girl had changed him, like it or not. Even Caesar was no more than a piece on the vast board. But, he realized, Caesar probably had always understood that. *I'm the simple fellow.*

"Protect her body," said the soothsayer. "She'll know when she's ready to act."

"Please answer me if you can." Antony suddenly stepped closer to the man so their faces were inches apart. "I was already rushing back to see to her safety."

"Yes?"

"You are a seer?" The priest shrugged. "Do you know all that will befall us?" The man shook his head, eyes remote, serious. "Will she see all?"

"No. None ever sees all."

"What about the dark forces?"

"You know about them, do you?"

"Do they see, too?"

"Of course. But only pieces. We all muddy the water. Nothing is certain. One lies to another, makes errors, blurs his sight. Dark or not dark, it's all the same."

Antony nodded, thoughtful. "Very well, priest. What *can* you tell me?"

"The dark master wants this world. He wants this girl for the child she will bear." Antony's eyebrows went up. The priest nodded. "He knows she is pregnant."

"More than I know. Or she herself. As far as I can tell, she discourages the process."

"Notwithstanding. This child will be a great lord and ruler. He will live, then sleep for hundreds of years, then awaken to rule. His brother will love the dark lord."

"You have seen this?" Antony was half-believing, half prepared to laugh. As at a good drama.

"In part and piece." The old man shut his eyes and rocked his head. "The girl will see more. But this lore is written in stone, for those who can find it and read."

"So she will have two sons?"

"No." The blue-fire eyes reopened. "I charge you, Antony, for your part in this, to help her and the father of her child, Leitus." He touched the Roman's shoulder. Antony was amazed by the strength of that hand.

"Leitus who?"

"Leitus Sixtus. You knew his father."

"Old Gracchus." Antony smiled. "So you tell me that young fellow had his way with Bita? Son of Gracchus the slave lover. They say he killed that whore, Claudia, Iro's brat sister." He shrugged. Murder and sex were nothing of note. He'd met Claudia a few times. She was the type of woman he didn't like, as a rule. Yet nothing was ever proven. And now new rumors: that Spartacus wasn't truly dead, was coming back to smash Rome. Except Antony had seen him die. He'd been a boy then. He'd gone with the other boys to the Appian Way, where they knew the slaves had been crucified as a warning. They'd been forbidden to go. He'd been frightened and amazed by the sight, the bleeding, wracked lines of dying men. If he'd been alone he would have run away; one of his fellows did, in fact. He'd hardly noticed because he'd been staring up at the last one. Spartacus himself. He remembered having been surprised by the slim, corded, weathered-looking man bleeding and sweating out his life. He'd expected to view a giant with a terrible, savage face. The leader, even in agony, had seemed thoughtful, with mild, hurt eyes. The man had looked up at the steel-gray sky and Antony recalled thinking he was hoping for rain to soothe his thirst. A new crowd had gathered when he'd moved and jostled the boys aside. The citizens and soldiers hadn't mocked him, just watched as that long, scarred, intent face had seemed to listen to the sky, with one ear cocked. Then young Antony had seen no more behind the wall of adults.

"I see imperfectly, Roman," the soothsayer told him, "but you have a part in history. . . . You pitied the man on the cross."

Antony's eyebrows went up and his heart rate sped. "Now wait," he began, "how did you know—"

The old man cut him off:

"Spartacus. I've seen some things, bear in mind." He smiled. "I'm not the old hoax you'd like to imagine, am I?"

"I don't say so, but—"

"That pity marked you. There are wheels within wheels and plots within plots. Your outer life concerns you and will make great tale-telling. But you were chosen by your own goodness." He started to walk away. "I'll see you soon." The eyes shut. He whispered, almost too softly for Antony to hear, "I may perish with you, Roman." Then, louder:

"Follow your heart, when in doubt. I charge you to follow your heart and you'll not fail."

Bita couldn't rest. She'd had too much warmed wine and milk. She got out of bed and paced by the floor-length window where the setting sun was a blood-red spatter behind a mounting mass of deep violet clouds. The shapes suggested a face to her, for a moment: long chin, long nose, a dark gape of soundless mouth.

She sighed and turned her back. She wore a light linen robe the color of milk. Her slim, strong legs were bare and tanned. Her eyes were strangely older and her expression more serious, concentrated, and yet remote.

The young guard, Selenius, had just found another excuse to tap on the partly opened door. He leaned his strong, pleasant face around the jamb, smiling. His brass breastplates were mirror bright. He thought about Bita constantly. He assumed she was his chief's mistress because the other one, Dia, had been retired a month ago in a barrage of crockery, taunts, curses, clawing slaps, wild-shaken hair, burning tears, battered furniture, and endless fury. Antony walked her out into the dusty street. She raged. Several times she walked away, then flung herself back to shout a few more words about his manhood. Selenius had watched all this from his post. He'd seen her squat and urinate into her hands and sprinkle the bronze gate bars. Cursed Antony's member. A skinny boiled carrot. Selenius remembered this and took heart.

"Bita," he said.

She just stood there, facing the blank white wall above her bed. She'd been thinking about Leitus. It seemed so long ago . . . so long . . . Yet she remembered, she felt him, saw him, heard his voice.

She had stopped living for her visions, the shifting worlds where she could drift and forget. Oh, sometimes, just before sleep, lying very still, she'd slip away and wander in fabulous landscapes where strange suns and moons woke liquid light. Sometimes. But more often she tried to touch the image-fabric of the future. She understood she had a mission. She really didn't want to have a mission. She'd had no real childhood because of that. Dreams, voices, and people had spoiled her life with hints of some great purpose. She wished she could find Leitus and love him, stay near him, let her body awaken to him again.

At this moment, staring at the blank wall, she was trying to find him, letting the images form, reaching out into the unseen world, looking for a trace, some subtle wash or blur of his passage or pulse of his distant life. . . .

She turned vaguely when the young soldier spoke.

"Good evening, Bita," the guard said, stepping into her room.

"Hello, Selenius," she responded absently. She stared at the blank wall again. *Where are you?* she asked. *My love. . . .*

Then something moved in the blankness: a world of trees and rocks, mists, a strange yet familiar countryside . . . Then a young Roman that might have been Leitus.

"Oh," she whispered. She strained to focus, to concentrate, except shadows filled the vision again, spilling over the scene like dark water.

"Are you hungry?" Selenius was inquiring. "I brought some pigeon stuffed and well roasted in honey."

"What?" she murmured.

"Pigeon."

She refused to give up. Shut her eyes and strained to break through again. *Leitus,* she thought. *Leitus . . . I feel you.* But had he even cared at all? she almost let herself think. And then the shadows changed, shifted, gathered like an overflowing pool and seemed to shape their darkness into a form, a face. A soft, smooth, hollow-eyed face. *Iro,* she thought. *Iro. . . .*

She opened her eyes. Then blinked at the guard. His face was close. He touched her shoulder.

"Bita . . ." he began.

She understood. Innocently, she pressed his hand. "I'm sorry, Selenius," she told him.

He winced, nodded. "All right," he said. "Still . . ."

"Yes?" She studied his face. She felt his energy. It was pleasant. She liked him.

He bent close and kissed her quickly on the lips. She didn't react one way or the other.

"All right," he repeated. "I'll leave you alone." He paused, hopeful. She could feel him hoping.

His family was vaguely noble but poor. Because Antony was democratic in everyday matters (as was Caesar, for that matter, a characteristic of dictatorial temperaments), he'd been able to get into the guards as a junior officer. He hoped to rise in the army.

He kept thinking about Bita. He liked to imagine her as a wife and mother. The idea that she was technically a slave didn't bother him. Well, he wouldn't have been the first one to "marry someone up."

She didn't look directly at him, but not for the reason he might have believed. She didn't like to look straight at anyone anymore, because she never knew what she was going to see.

Sometimes there would be flashes, scenes from some past or future, sometimes horrors, deaths, suffering, heartbreaks. Human beings and their destinies would become strangely transparent to her in images more real than flesh and blood. So she tried not to see these things.

"I need your help," she told him.

He paused, then said:

"Must I ask with what? Or must I agree in advance?"

She nodded, glancing partly at him. There was no flash of anything strange.

"Yes," she said, "you have to promise."

He hesitated. "Aye . . ." he began. "Well, that's much to ask a man."

She just looked at him. She trusted his eyes. She knew there was no way to lie to her anymore. Lies were a greenish darkness in her mind, unmistakable, as love was pale pinks and blues, and terror gray, horror black and void.

"Perhaps," she said.

He worked his lips around as if tasting something. "What are *you* promising?" he finally asked, looking around the room nervously. The bare walls glowed deepening rose around both their shadows as the sun seemed to burn into the molten horizon.

"Nothing," she said.

He'd known that, of course. He realized he ought to go back on duty. Why risk Antony's displeasure? Clearly, if she needed his help it was probably for something the master had refused or wouldn't even consider. He decided to leave, convinced he'd head over to the kitchen and wangle a loaf and a chunk of cheese or maybe even eat the roast pigeon he'd carefully wrapped in cloth. But instead of "good evening," he found himself saying:

"All right."

He felt her eyes come back to him again and then she asked: "Vow?"

He nodded. "Yes."

Just indulge her and then go about your business, he told himself. Except he knew better. He felt himself being drawn along. *What wonderful eyes she has,* he thought, wishing she would look at him more often.

"Antony," she said, quiet and serious, "protects me."

He nodded, waiting, studying the deepening red glow in her light hair like melting gold. "I have to leave here for a time."

He nodded, unsurprised. "Of course," he said. "So I'm to betray my lord."

"No. Just come with me and bring me back, if you can."

He absorbed that. Frowned.

"Come where, Bita?" He liked saying her name. He knew he was doomed, fated, lost. . . . He sighed. The night seemed to flow up from the still gardens under the window and spill in around the frame.

"And bring me back," she repeated.

"Yes. From where?" he asked again.

"That horrible place." She went to the window. In the distance she could make out the capitol hill. She pointed one slender, long finger. "There. That horrible place."

He squinted to follow her direction, leaning over her, inhaling her slight fragrance. The last smear of sun was melting behind the capitol buildings and monuments.

"The Senate?" he wondered.

"No. Iro's house." She shut her eyes, seeing it: herself and the naked, softly shaped little man in some dim, windowless place, something huge and dark rising over them, shutting the scene out. She was sweating, heart pumping hard. She'd managed to see him. She was getting stronger. She had to go there. She knew she had to actually touch him, physically. That would burn away the shrouding blurs. Touch him and find a way to survive. "Just bring me there and take me back," she repeated. "Please."

He sighed again. Doomed. "Yes," he answered. "I promised."

It is this, she thought, *or nothing.* When you were given power where could you hide? Isn't that what the priests and voices or whatever they were had hinted and suggested and put into pictures all her life? Something was different, changing inside her; her body was changing. She never mentioned it to anyone. There was no way to escape from the power. Because she had to sleep and she was open then. Even the brightest noonday could be changed to a view of worlds past understanding in colors no human eye ever saw.

So, she'd realized, her quiet pride was her best ally. She knew sooner or later she'd have to face terror and darkness. She was afraid but she had pride.

Antony was thinking about something the Etruscan soothsayer had said. He wished the man had not disappeared. He'd said none of them could be sure of what they saw in the future. They just had flashes, fragments. Like Bita. There were times when it was clear and times when it was obscure.

He was crossing the huge lawn heading toward his residence. The last stains of sunset were lost under mounting, boiling, dark clouds that were laced and stitched by distant, violent lightning flashes. There was a strange, tense calm in the atmosphere.

He noted the oil lamps were showing in the kitchen windows. He wanted soup. Soup and bread. It had been a long day, arguing with senators and getting nowhere at all. Not enough to act. He had to write Caesar, he decided, get him to come home. Things were reaching a crisis. No doubt about it. He didn't need mystics and soothsayers to tell him that.

He'd reached the large, circular patio. He stopped to think. Why had the fellow set him on Bita? Why not protect her himself? Why him? *Whom does that priest serve?*

Because he paused, Bita and the guard slipped away successfully. They'd just come out of a side entrance and crossed to the long hedge timed to miss a pacing sentry. The first flashes of the speeding storm flickered on the marble as they crouched low exactly where Antony would have crossed into the house.

Bita followed Selenius quietly through twisting lanes that cut down into the densest part of the city. They moved through a solid stink of offal, sweat, spice, burned meat, dung, and decay. The wind before the massing storm front cut viciously through these alleys, shaking thatch and drumming hide roofs and flimsy walls.

Selenius held a lantern as did others who passed them or sat in doorways. It was unusually quiet tonight, he noted. There was, he thought, an expectant feeling or readiness, very tense. It puzzled him.

"Stay close," he told Bita more than once. She kept a dark coat over her head and picked her steps carefully over the broken, filth-spattered stones. "There's no better route," he explained, as they crossed an open place where women were moving slowly in a circle around a bonfire, humming a low, wordless dirge. At the next narrow intersection a man was selling roasted chestnuts from a low brazier. The coals flared fitfully as the wind gusted. The man was squat, plumped on a bench, his back to a brick wall covered with painted scrawls, names, dates, crude faces, and sexual parts. His nose, mouth, and eyes were tiny in a ballooned, hairless head. Selenius bought a handful of chestnuts for a penny coin, gave Bita a few, and walked on peeling and munching as they crossed the lowest point between the adjoining hills. She tucked the warm nuts into a pocket. He glanced back at her.

"What," he wondered, "are you going to do when you get there?"

She wasn't sure. She believed she'd know when the time came. She'd have to get close to Iro, that much was obvious.

"Is it far?" she fended.

He shrugged. "I told you it's the best way without horses. I wasn't going to steal horses for you."

"I didn't ask you to."

Before he could respond he stopped suddenly and lifted the lantern high. Something had glinted in the muck beside the narrow path and soggy planks. The houses here sat partly in a bog. In summer the insects, the locals liked to say, would strip a soft-skinner (a patrician) to the bone in half an hour.

There it was again: a flash of gold in the narrow space between two sagging buildings. Inside one a woman was coughing. He heard her gag and spit and mutter. A baby wailed across the street. The mounting wind made most other sounds uncertain. A thunderclap came rolling, hollowing down the hills. Sputters of lightning showed people scurrying indoors. Shutters (where there were any) could be heard slamming closed or just banging in the erratic gusts.

"Wait," he told her.

He squeezed between the two houses. It stank there, he thought, like a fly-blown corpse. He stooped over the brightness. It was a coin. Gold? Here? Incredible. Perhaps a lost bit of loot.

He picked it up and backed out, amazed, thinking it an omen. The next shudder of electric brightness over the low roofs showed too many figures around them and he groped for her hand to hurry her on—except three hooded men, their cloaks flapping out in the gale like great dark wings, moved toward them. He glimpsed what had to be cudgels and a long barbarian sword.

"Run," he told her, shoving her ahead. Why had he stopped? That glint of gold (it was probably copper at that) was going to cost him all breath, all hope, all future.

He drew his sword, casting back his cloak. The lightning flashed on his body plate. He moved back step by step, blocking the twisting lane. He could touch either wall with either hand.

"One at a time," he muttered, unconsciously.

The tallest pranced forward behind a long spear.

"We mean no harm, O soldier." He laughed. "Just let us weigh your purse and kiss the little whore for luck."

Selenius backed around the first twist. His heart hurt with pounding. His mouth tasted like metal.

"Leave us in peace," he heard himself say. His voice seemed high-pitched in his ears.

"O soldier," came the reply, "you are a fierce warrior, we're sure."

A massive near-dwarf kept pace crowded under the first man's shoulder where they were wedged into the little lane. The last languished in the rear, chewing a piece of something, putting hand to mouth and taking bites, visible in the wild light.

They were too relaxed and patient. It wasn't until he realized the girl was still close ahead that he understood there had to be others waiting. He cursed. A neat trap. They must have been stalking them, he concluded.

"There's a cross street ahead," she said. "More of them there, I think."

"Listen," he said, as the tall one leveled his spear and mockingly moved inches closer. A sudden gust rattled the roofs. "Listen, we'll give you our purses. What sense in risking blood?"

"But it's only your blood at risk, O soldier."

Selenius was sweating. Chill sweat. The building walls on either side were blank brick. A few flicks of rain spatted here and there. One stung his face. He wondered remotely how the drop had found its way into this slit between houses.

The little dwarf scampered forward, slamming his cudgel into the muck, howling, spattering everyone.

At the next bend the young soldier, glancing behind, saw the other hooded men waiting where the lanes crossed and opened out somewhat. The flashes were brighter and the figures seemed to leap in the sudden light. The wind flailed and spun. Voices were sucked away and blotted out.

"I'm sorry," he told Bita. "I led you badly. We should have found a horse." Thunder rolled over the last words.

"Don't be upset," she told him.

"Why not just take what we have?" he tried.

"We will," the tall one called over thunder echo and wind rush. They were in the open now, ringed in. The wind hit so hard that Bita skidded to one knee and they all leaned and tilted to hold position. Pieces of things whirled by with gouts of dirt.

She felt the strange energy pressure building inside her again. She saw the figures surrounding them, tall, short, skinny, wide, brandishing weapons, closing in. She noted Selenius (seeing color glows again), a pale bluish aura streaked with gray fear, a glimmer of yellow around the head. Then she was shocked because the six plebeian street killers had no light at all! They were like holes to her special sight in the flashing, shaking, torn night. Hollow shapes.

"They're not real," she whispered to him.

"What's that?" he asked, arching back from the spear thrust that cut inches away from his face. The dwarf hopped two-legged and thwacked the mud again. The spatters hit them.

"Not real?" he said, wiping his face.

"They're not," she insisted, holding his arm to keep balance. "Not people." But they could kill, she sensed. And were meant for her, drawn by her energy. None spoke but the tallest one. The robes flapped around their seeming bodies. Their emptiness drew at her, at her warmth, youth, and strength. Such creatures were byproducts, leaks from the general darkness. Wizards often controlled them, put them to work. She'd been taught these things as a child.

Lady of light, help me, she cried to herself. Nothing. And then she spotted it: They were wincing, hoods pulled closed, wincing at each lightning flash. Just a little, but she noticed.

They howled, high, cold, keen, and rushed, robes billowing madly. Selenius staggered in a semicircle trying to protect her. He slashed wind, flicked rain, yelling in fury and fear. She raised one arm and cried out something surprisingly loud, somehow sad, sweet, and strong. Selenius caught the flicker of her gold bracelet as she saw the light downpouring, slow and soft, into her opened hand, a white-yellow sparkle, each slow, gentle beam melting the darkness, baring the shapeless things in the dark hoods, exposing their terrible emptiness. She felt them wail and shudder. *Let the light fill you, ignorant children.* Then they were wisked away like rags on the wind.

Selenius caught only a glimpse, falling to his knees as the tremendous bolt of lightning hissed, ripped, shattered into the bracelet, and then rebounded from her, crashing into their opponents. His own shouts were lost in the wind and crashing blows and then a wall of almost solid rain. His forearms locked over his eyes. He glimpsed flaming robes and shattered weapons.

Gasping, half-blinded, he reached for her. He felt sad and sick, expecting a scorched and blasted body.

But she was standing, leaning on the wind, still raptly watching the incredible light fade. She was thrilled, yet calm. She felt pure. The flash had burned away fear and dreaming.

"Come," she told him. "We have to go on."

He blinked around at the now vacant intersection. The rain billowed and whirled and stung. He thought he saw smoldering cloaks in the now almost constant flashes. And still, from the sound alone, he knew the heart of the storm hadn't yet reached the city.

"Incredible," he shouted.

"Yes," she agreed.

They were climbing now, braced against the shifting gusts. They were soaked, ploughing up lanes that had already become rivers of mud.

"What a night," he kept saying. "Incredible." He was still blinking violet afterglow from his sight when they reached the hilltop and found themselves on wide streets under storm-shaken trees.

"Is it much farther?" Bita wondered.

"No," he replied. "I used to have duty in this section." He wiped the rain from his eyes. The trees leaped, the street jumped as the huge lightning bolts slammed closer and closer, hissing and ripping.

At the wrought-iron and brass gate they crouched under the square arch. The ground within looked like a pond. The surface boiled with downpour and spattering waves as the terrific, unrelenting wind slammed across the open places. Smaller trees were down here and there. She was shivering slightly.

"Well," he wanted to know, "do we hit the gong?"

"You can go back now."

"Um?" He half grinned. "And not pay my respects?"

She shrugged. She tugged the gate and it swung open. A bolt crashed to earth nearby.

Selenius knew he should go back to duty. This was madness. Why add trouble to trouble? But Bita slogged toward the massive main building, wading between statues that shifted insanely in the shuddering light. He followed. He was still trapped in it. The more he was with her, the more he cared.

He sloshed behind her right to the wall of the villa. There were no lights showing. A shutter banged wildly around the side. They moved together in the relative lee of the overhang.

He put his mouth near her ear, feeling a slight thrill at the wet scent. He caught a flash of her pale eyes looking at him, then, too quickly, away. He misinterpreted her look again, had no idea she'd started to see something she didn't want to see.

"Aren't you going to knock?" he asked, wiping his face with his saturated cloak edge. "It looks deserted, in any case."

"I want to surprise him, if I can," she said, close to his ear. "I think you should wait for me out here." Because of what she partly saw. A flash.

He shook his head. "Better *you* wait out here," he suggested.

"I have to see him."

"Iro?"

"That's why I had to come here."

The spray from the flooded grounds was beaten to foam in the next terrific, shuddering gust. Lightning bolts bounced and walked all around. He'd never seen such a storm. He had a seaman uncle who'd told tales of the like, but tales didn't blow in your face and half drown you. He kept imagining strange, unnatural shapes forming and unforming, dancing in the jarring overlaps of wild light.

He had an idea Iro's household were all huddled around a fire in the basement. *He* would be.

"Here," he said, prying at the soaked shutter, easing it open. The wind slammed it and him behind it against the side of the house. "Dung!" he cried. The drapes inside were sucked out; tiny things rattled and banged as the gusts poured into the room. "Go on!" he cried, forcing the panel back in a semilull. She did and he climbed in after her, finally slamming the thing shut again and relatching it.

He stood there, panting a little, dripping in the dark. Well, he consoled himself, no candle could have stayed lit, in any case.

"Now we're in," he said needlessly, with some vague idea of holding her close for a moment. Outside, the storm shook the very bricks of the massive place. He groped around for her. "Bita?" He went a few steps aimlessly into the big room. "Bita!" he hissed louder. Nothing. "Saturn and Venus," he murmured, "what next?"

CHAPTER XX

By dawn they'd reached the coast, just behind Caesar's main forces. Subius was first to the cliff edge. The fleet was moored close offshore, vague gray shapes in the first light. The bushes were wet with dew. The day, he noted, promised to be clear.

Leitus (though he still hadn't done more than provisionally accept the name) and the other two soldiers worked their way down the incline together.

"There're the lads," said the stocky veteran, meaning the massed troops camped along the beach under their brass standards. "And ain't we all glad to see them ships."

"Aye," said the younger one.

"Most," grunted Subius, swing-sliding down a few steps by gripping the end of a flexible branch, "will be cursing through their puke in a few hours."

"Right enough," said the first, "but coming home vomit is sweeter than going."

"Home?" asked Subius. "Back to Gaul, you mean. Or did Julius himself give you special orders?"

"Well, what do you think, simple killer?" The younger one with the small head spoke to Leitus as they reached bottom and crunched across the dark, gritty beach. The morning mist was melting fast under the first golden-red touches of sunrise.

"Go easy with him," advised the blocky elder.

Leitus paid scant attention. He was trying to remember things. He knew this place, these ships, but still there were no images with himself visible in his mind. His memory had been selectively sectioned.

The hazy, black outline of the sphere that seemed to float in the center of his forehead was gone again. That bothered him. He wanted to see the pictures there, the strange, uncanny places, the languorous, silver-veiled woman. He frowned. The woman. That had been very good. He wanted to feel it again. Somewhere there had been a promise about that, about her.

"That's what I want," he said under his breath as they went past the sentries into the camp.

"What's that?" Subius wondered. He hoped Leitus was coming out of whatever spell or concussion had dulled him. "What you need is some sweet wine from Pisa." *No, that's what I need. . . .*

"Subius," said the blocky man, "there's my hundred. If you need me further look under a blanket. Or, better," he amended, veering off toward a campfire sheltered by a massive edge of gray rock, "don't look at all."

The younger soldier had already stopped to gossip with a sentry he knew. Men were gathering around the breakfast fires. Some were bathing and yelping in the chilly water.

Subius smelled pigflesh roasting. He made a note to seek it out as he marched Leitus straight to Caesar's tent, yawning ten times on the way. He'd spotted the rich purple banner from the slope.

There had been no choice but to come back, because Leitus wasn't fully Leitus and couldn't be consulted. *A man is mainly what he remembers.* He'd decided there must have been a blow to the head, except he hadn't noticed a wound or scar. Very odd.

Caesar was half-naked, wet with steamy water from a heated copper basin. An orderly was toweling him dry when the guard admitted Subius and Leitus.

"Ah," said Caesar, "it appears I picked the right man for the work."

As Caesar spoke the black circle returned to Leitus, the hole in the world, Namolin had called it, and he instantly knew what he was supposed to do. The suggestion was more a reflex than a command, though he had a brief impression that an actual voice spoke through the hollow into his mind.

He moved toward Caesar, the deadly thrilling force filling him again, his killing hand already lifting to strike with that terrible, impossible speed. . . .

Ulad fled, panting, sliding and rolling down the slope,

clutching the black sphere as he jarred and scraped over stones and banged into tree trunks.

He was heading down to the edge of the swampy lowlands. He knew his enraged master was following. He sensed that the stone might give him the power to withstand the deadly old man, but he had only vague ideas about how to use it. Now he had it and was stuck with it. There was no going back.

At the bottom he dusted off his spindly body and winced, touching his ribs. Tucked in his leather vest, the sphere had ground into his side. Each step now stung as he tried to walk softly over the mossy, boggy ground. He developed a kind of halting limp. He kept craning his skinny neck to peer back at the slope. He paused and crouched in a stand of marsh reeds, waiting for the familiar cloaked figure to come stamping over the crest. He waited. No results. Ulad felt better and decided to go on.

He followed a ridge of high ground, the wall of a natural dike that humped across the bog like the back of a gigantic serpent. As the sun cleared the treetops, the bog began steaming, which may have pleased the frogs and snakes but did nothing for Ulad but slow him to a cautious, lurching amble. He was already sorry he'd ever taken the thing. His nerves sputtered under his skin. He was tired, thirsty, and the ridge kept dipping into the marsh so that he was caked to the knee with slimy muck. The sun-fog was blindingly bright now.

His idea had been to cut across and reach open country far from any road Namolin or his people were likely to use. His deeper idea (as deep as Ulad went) was to join the invaders and be well rewarded for using the stone's power for their benefit.

Ulad hated his people as much as he hated his master. He'd dreamed of controlling the stone and subjugating Namolin. Now he just wanted to get away. Dreams were one thing, reality was another.

As he slogged along like some nervous mantis, feeling a little secured by the mist that still boiled up whitely from the bog, he took out his stolen treasure and held it on both palms, blinking and staring, trying to recall some of the spell fragments he'd overheard. In sunlight the thing seemed more than ever like a hole, a color-sucking void, reflecting nothing. He thought of Namolin. Namolin had made him grovel, made him plead in the mud for pity. The list was long of his master's wrongs. He pictured Namolin, focused a sudden seethe of hate into the stone, hissing what he hoped were power words, pic-

turing the old man's eyes bulging, swelling out onto his
cheeks, then bursting in blood. Something like the beat of a
wing seemed to bend deep in the sphere's suddenly red heart.
Other things moved in there, caught his attention. A moun-
tainous landscape rose up under gigantic dark clouds, a blood-
colored sky. A vast fortress on a peak overlooked countless
beings who labored among green-flaming wheels and blocks
and the grinding beams of strange machines where stone and
metal seemed to melt under huge hammers and massive blades
of black steel. Ulad felt drawn out of himself into the landscape. He seemed to float in the thick, pressing atmosphere,
drawn toward the immense castle. He felt something (he
couldn't see) like a hand reaching for him, tugging him irre-
sistibly forward until he actually stood on the highest square,
flat-topped tower. He found himself walking forward, gazing
up at a device of spokeless wheels that revolved around an
utterly lightless center, floating in the smoky air high
overhead. Near him was a throne; vacant. The voice that made
no sound seemed to be telling him that seat was meant for
him. He would rule this kingdom and have domination over
all the subjects! (Namolin had observed more than once how
truth and fiction were mixed in the pseudomind of the sphere.)
Ulad gazed down and saw pale women, fragile, nude, chained
near carven mouths of black rock where (he was being told
somehow) at his command flame would flare out and consume
them; or he could command the dark, winged beings (he suddenly noticed them the way something in a dream is suddenly
there without coming) to whip them with hot wires. All he had
to do was sit on the great throne. He reached the massive steps
. . . and then, as he mounted toward the seat of power, the
true owner arrived on vast wings that shook the blood and
black sky, a terrible face looming over him, pouring a chill
breath of stifling, solid darkness, blotting him out. He tried to
scream but was clogged, and as the scene vanished, insane
with fear and fury, he clutched the ball as if it would sustain
him, because he'd walked out into the bog and had already
sunk to his long nose. His eyes glared back through the thinning mist at where Namolin now stood, panting from the
chase, edging out on the last hump of solid ground, yelling,
begging him to toss the sphere (which he held above the slimy,
sucking, rot-flecked surface) to him, vowing that he'd save
him. Ulad tried again to scream his hate and horror, but only
bubbles of muck and greenish water blurped to the surface,

and then his mouth and throat were filled solid. His eyes
bulged. His head went under, the bony arms upraised, the
hands locked on the dark ball while Namolin limped wildly
back and forth, wading knee-deep until he had to struggle
desperately back to save himself. Finally the arms went under,
hands still holding tight as if expecting to be buoyed free by
the stone. Then it was gone, too, with a last, soft splash. . . .
Smooth mire again.

. . . and Leitus—poised above Caesar, tensed to casually kill
him with the irresistible edge of his power-charged hand—
He choked on terror, a dark flutter, a chill sense of death.
Something dying echoed in his consciousness. He reeled, then
dropped to one knee on the thick fur reminding Caesar of
when he'd fallen wounded in the shoulder by the demented,
almost unkillable Tribune. No one had known that Tribune.
On his chest were tattoos associated with the Druid cult. But
he seemed a perfect Roman.

Leitus blinked at the sunlight streaming through the parted
tent flaps.

"Are you all right?" asked the commander. Subius supported the young man under one arm.

"My god Jove," he whispered, with wonder and pleasure.
"I think so. . . ."

"You remembered yourself?" Subius asked, turned to
Caesar when the young man nodded. "His memory was wiped
away when we found him." Subius was very tired. His eyes
hurt. He thought mainly about sleep. He wanted to go away
from here, find a warm hayloft, a peaceful farm, and drag a
woman (any woman, if need be) with breasts bigger than a
poet's ego from her clothes and rub everything out of himself.
But sleep first of all . . . sleep. He yawned.

"Where did you find him?" wondered Caesar.

"In a village, General."

"Captive?"

"Not that I could tell. I think he'd just escaped, in fact."

"Well, Leitus?" Caesar asked him.

He shook his head. "I'm not sure. . . . It was like dreaming. . . ." He touched his face, forehead, eyes. Shook his
head.

"You're quite a mysterious character," said Caesar, stepping to the entrance of the tent and looking out at the blue

channel. He stretched in the sun. "You'll accompany me back to Rome. We happen to share some enemies in common." He smiled, but his brooding stare was fixed on the horizon where the distant, rounded peaks of dark gray thunderheads were gradually mounting under the bright, warm sun. "One mark of a man's importance is his enemies." He clasped his hands behind his back and rocked on his toes, the high-strapped leather sandals creaking faintly. "The time is coming when I'll have to deal with mine. I'll need every weapon I can sharpen, however unlikely looking."

"Back to Rome," whispered Leitus. He thought about past loves and deaths . . . family . . . what might happen to him. He thought about his lost life: in the classroom with Marcellus; feasts by the Tiber; boating, fishing. . . . Could he ever go back to it again? He had a feeling that his fate would carry him further and further from any hope of that. He wondered if Marcellus was still studying with the old leech. Too many memories came spilling back. And then, surprising him so that he frowned, he had a clear image of the slave girl, Bita. Yes, Bita. He remembered her smiling, for some reason, holding up a plant she'd potted, gently touching the new green leaves. Then she'd set it on the window ledge. How tender she'd looked, he thought now.

"Yes," agreed Caesar, "back to Rome in easy stages." He was feeling very sure of himself again. He felt he could not fail if he willed a thing. He squinted at the horizon. "Easy stages."

Subius suddenly decided to unburden himself soon. He would tell Leitus about his real parents. Then they'd figure out where to go and what to do. Rome was all danger.

"Home," said Leitus, thinking now about his mother and father. Then he frowned, trying to recapture what had happened to him during the last weeks, the missing, blurry time. Very quickly his head hurt with trying. Too many shapeless, dark things there, but he didn't want to live with pieces missing. And then, something else: "General?" he said.

"Yes?" responded Caesar, not turning.

"I want to clear myself."

"Yes?"

"Of the murder."

Caesar glanced over, remembered.

"I see."

"I want to be free. Will you help me, General?"

Caesar nodded, once. The young male servant handed him the undershirt of heavy cloth that kept the leather and brass armor from chafing.

"If I can," he told Leitus.

"I want my life back," Leitus said, frowning. "I think . . ."

"Yes?" asked the commander.

"I remember . . ."

"Yes?"

"I think I was supposed to kill you." His frown grew deeper. It hurt, thinking about it.

"Whose idea was that?" Caesar raised thin eyebrows.

"I don't know. . . ." The shadows in his mind hurt. But he knew it was true.

"Interesting," said Caesar. "The more I splash the pool, the more fish jump into sight." He smiled and raised one thin, arched eyebrow. "Will you be trying again, young Leitus?" he wondered.

"Trying what?"

"To have his life," put in Subius.

An orderly approached, limping slightly on the gritty sand. His side was bandaged. Across the strand a number of wounded men were being helped aboard one of the boats.

Leitus shook his head.

"I was not myself. . . . Like a spell," he said. "But it's broken, I think."

Caesar took thought. "But you're not even armed," he pointed out. "Am I become so soft a target?"

Subius was thinking, too. "He could slay us both, General," he said. "Or, at least, he could have a few moments ago."

Caesar remembered the scene in the tent. He couldn't altogether dismiss mystery and magic from his practical considerations anymore. These were strange times. And getting stranger. "Wizardry?" he asked the gladiator, who shrugged massively, and replied:

"I saw speed and power only. But there was something more than human in it. I have no explanation. This lad was a good fighter"—Subius shook his head—"but nothing like what I witnessed."

Caesar nodded. Well, well, a weapon was a weapon. You could slice your meat with the dagger once held to your throat.

Leitus wandered out past Caesar and stood in the thin autumn sun. *What a life,* he thought. Accused of foul murders, driven from home, captured by Briton barbarians and put under some strange compulsion. . . . He shook his head and tried to remember again past the hurt and darkness. He glimpsed a girl, remembered pouring himself out between her legs in the misty night on the battlefield, clutching her in a kind of horrible desperation. Then the old priest striking him with the staff. . . . Then the real shadows began, the red flashes, the hurting, the strange worlds drawing him. . . .

He shut his eyes, oblivious to all but the warmth on his eyelids and face; wanted just to sleep now; didn't hear Caesar command the guard outside the tent flap just behind him. Or see him hold a restraining finger up to Subius.

"Slay him now," Caesar ordered, indicating Leitus.

And Leitus didn't see the man quickly draw and take a short, driving step, jabbing (before Subius could finish reacting) a pistonlike thrust (the kind of blow that had won the world for Roman arms) at his unprotected back.

CHAPTER XXI

Because in his dimension his will controlled his size and shape, the great lord Aataatana was presently looking just a few feet taller than most of his subjects. He stood with folded wings on one of the squat towers of his fortress. He leaned over the parapet, chin in hands, gazing thoughtfully down, eyes dimmed to ashy coals by meditation.

He overlooked one of his favorite views where rivers of red fire crisscrossed down ten-mile-high cliffs in smoldering waterfalls to feed a long, glowing lake. Along the shoreline he could see huge statues hacked from the glossy, dark, green-tinted rocks: images of himself and other heroes, past glories of their race. Out in the lake several flat, powerful Zugs, the rock creatures, splashed and dove into the molten stone. The Zugs were Aataatana's pets and helpers, vaguely resembling sea-skates.

A whisper of flame curled from his mouth as he considered his main regret again, a regret that went back before the days of the first men on earth, before the ethereal intelligences found ways to mix themselves with earth and vapor and so take incarnate form and become prisoners of the world's time. A regret for the lost female. The mysterious, alluring, palely shadowed loveliness. They were lovers before his body changed, became hard and winged and dark, setting the form for his race, which then wavered between matter and pure energy. Ah, they'd loved! Mixed their insubstantial selves together in silvery, dim, half lights on long-lost worlds. His fire sighed again.

He didn't glance up as two of his officers moved quietly to each elbow.

"Why do you trouble me? What new stupidities must I hear about?"

"My lord," responded the lord Laabba, *"cannot you perceive all things in your domain?"*

"Do you mock me?" The long, brooding head didn't move. *"Had I such powers I would see even what was in your mind, Laabba. Then, would I not have destroyed you already?"*

The other general, Zeleb, was amused and showed it in the manner of his kind: his eyes dimmed and flared rhythmically.

"The news, O dread lord," he expressed, *"is that we lost contact with the breeder human."* He meant Leitus. He would never have used a human's name.

"That must have taken some skill," the master responded with scorn, *"since he was held by a power globe wielded by our"*—a slight hold—*"former chief priest. And overseen by one of the inner circle."*

"The miserable human erred," put in Laabba, the member of the inner circle in question, *"and lost the stone.* Shrugged one wing. *Nothing could have been done from this side."*

"I assume nothing was tried," declared the king, turning, still leaning on the battlement. Above them a guard of perfectly schooled killers circled the tower. Smoke boiled around them, shot with dull flame. *"Now I know who was operating from this side,"* he mocked, eyes flaring slightly brighter, like wind over embers. He stared at Laabba, who shifted his feet nervously.

"He lost it," Laabba declared, *"to a weak-willed creature."*

"Who was, I presume, too strong for you to overcome?"

Zeleb was amused again by the heavy irony. His fellow general was frustrated and barely controlling his fury. He had less sense of humor than most of his fellows. And jokes were as rare in that world as common sense on the surface.

"I, Lord, was concentrating on the human breeder. He was about to slay the warrior whom our forecasts indicate may overcome certain of our allies."

The king's eyes seethed with heat now.

"Was about to?" he expressed.

"Yes, Lord. And by the time I reached my will into the puny thing's brain to hold it, he was already dead and the stone was lost."

"Lost." In words the king's expression would have been a baleful murmur. *"And 'about to.' "*

Because the warrior (Caesar) lived. Not a major problem. He began to visualize the full situation.

"The stone is in a bog," Zeleb added, almost with glee. Then he realized his master really wasn't paying attention.

"Attend me later," he told them both. Then he leaped up into the black-and-red atmosphere, beating powerfully, kicking up to where the machine of overlapping rings that made a hollow globe hung, spinning slowly in the contorted billows of smoke clouds.

This was the real center of his realm. In the heart of the spinning, suspended rims, unimaginable stresses and forces were concentrated. This was the inmost point, the focus of all the universe, dimensions layered, sphere within sphere. The immense pressures had made it a hole, a channel to mysterious dimensions that his vision powers could not penetrate. He sensed intelligences in that inconceivable void that even by his standards were cold . . . cold, remote, and fearful. . . .

Now he hung in the air, alone, staring through the rotating power rims that glowed blurry green and red. He stared at a spherical something that seemed solid. No color. Not even blackness. That was the plug in the hole. By pressing his will on this plug, he troubled the unknown beyond, stirred strange things to touch at his eager mind. He believed they existed beyond all possible space and time frames. He suspected they had powers that could rewrite the laws of any universe. At times, these powers seem to help him, even leak him whispers of energy. This was his secret weapon: secret knowing, inner, inexplicable darknesses within darknesses, here at the bottom of his impenetrable kingdom. His accident, his freedom, the hole in his prison.

Focusing on the hole, he sometimes picked up future patterns. He did so now. But he wanted much more. These beings (if they were actually sentient in any sense comprehensible in the known universe) were to help him break out and control the surface world again. To do this, he'd have to alter the laws of nature, thicken the earth to support his mass and furious heats. And he'd need the child, the special child, who would be both human and yet like himself. His true son, with whom he, Lord Aataatana, could corule all worlds. His enemies were unwittingly helping him to produce this child. Now all that remained was for him to bring the girl, Bita, to his kingdom.

Aataatana stared into the place where all his knowledge and strength failed utterly. Called for help. Moved as close to the plug as he dared. He knew enough not to actually touch it. The rims slowly spun inches from his brooding face. If he displaced it seriously he would free the unmakers. The final destroyers. The world enders. He knew only ancient hints of them, imprinted in the structure of the universe itself: in living cells, molecules, atoms, written on ripples of energy in ancient scars and stresses. Aataatana was very wise. He had deduced that the unmakers, in the unconceivable emptiness of their lair, had once sucked the very stars dry of light and heat, unmade the eternal soul of all existence. . . .

He sometimes wondered why this power was in his keeping. Why was he the one who could pull the plug and let all life run out? Because he would be the least tempted. The idea of his own death chilled him and made him very angry.

But without this risk, he told himself, *there is only defeat and stagnation.*

He glared, eyes pouring red beams onto the plug, rocking, shifting it infinitesimally with the pressure of his stare, demanding: *Manifest!* His will cried: *Manifest! Manifest!*

Namolin was seated, collapsed, on the narrow spine of the damp, bristly ground that twisted out into the swamp where Ulad had gone down clutching the power globe.

The old wizard was soaked and spattered with slime, exhausted from wading and poking his long stick into the bottomless mire, trying to contact his lost disciple's body. He hoped to somehow drag it to where he could free the precious sphere from the death-locked grip.

His body hurt, his brain ached. He'd gone past his limit. He'd tried raising spells, howled himself hoarse, thrashed the pole—to no result. The setting sun spread a blood glow over the standing water.

Crouched down there he resembled the crumbling mud figure the children had slapped and shaped in the streets of his village. He gradually faced the facts: without the stone his power was severely limited. His problem was that the other two master priests still had their globes. They weren't likely to share them.

He frowned. The chances were they'd destroy him or drive him off. He tried to wipe the muck from his beard and succeeded only in smearing his cheeks.

There was no room for weakness in the inner circle. He sighed and let his chilled weariness make a lump of him. Insects buzzed and cut near his head in the crimson light.

He didn't want to think about it, but he had to. Had to do something. Before the great eclipse. The day when Lord Aataatana would rise. In Rome. He sighed again and sunk his muddy head in his mucky hands as the light bled away and shadows floated in from the motionless trees.

He had to go there. He'd have to get his hands on one of the other two stones. But the chances were poor. No direct attempt would penetrate the guard of either of the wizards. He would be weak and transparent to them. He'd have to spend the night here and try again by morning light, maybe get boys from the village to help. He'd have to resort to crude means. His raising spells had drained away to empty gestures and dull words.

He'd become too dependent on the stone. He was addicted to its amplification of himself. Without it, his self shrank. Even if he now managed to directly contact members of the great race without the stone, by using the old rituals of blood and herbs (and he was long out of practice), they would probably only help destroy him. Or drive him off in disgrace. Weakness was a sin, as he well understood.

Namolin knew that his only real hope was the fact that the stone had preserved him, had been part of him for a long, long time. It would, in a way, know him. It had a life, an energy, a mock consciousness of its own and might seek to return to him. A very thin hope.

He sat up, excited. That was it! The spell of calling!

Namolin stood up in the pale, washed-out ruby hints of twilight and drove his body back toward the village along the humped, winding ridge, pushing on through the thickening shadows and arms of fog. No time to lose. He needed to get back by midnight, and with a human being. He couldn't risk using a mere animal, not for this last hope, this calling. Someone young, a child even. Yes, a child.

CHAPTER XXII

So Selenius, in a quiet sort of panic, groped down the darkened halls of Iro's rambling villa. The wild lightning flashes flared around the shutters in the empty chambers.

He'd lost Bita. In a blink. How could he face Antony? How had he let himself get into this?

"Bita!" he called into the hollow, rattling din of thunder crisscrossing and reechoing. "Where are you? Bita!"

Down a flight of stairs, touching the wall. Wild draughts tugged and twisted. All lamps and tapers had been sucked out. Another level down and no lightning glimmers penetrated.

He cursed. This was hopeless. The thunder crashes were distant, dulled. And where were the inhabitants?

Then a faint light ahead . . . down a hall. He followed. Deep red, wavering, then it dipped down and he hurried to another flight of stairs. Winding this time. The flamelight stained the walls ahead. He followed, faster now, but carefully . . . and then found himself in a tremendous, vaulted chamber. He'd gone down hundreds of feet, he was sure of that. What a place! This villa was a labyrinth beneath the surface. Things smelled damp and ancient. This was no Roman construction, he realized.

He hesitated on the last few steps and watched shadowy figures walking with a torch whose dulled splashes of color touched no wall or ceiling. The place was immense, he thought.

And then the lightning jumplight showed again. How could

that be? He squinted up and discovered some kind of hole or
shaft in the roof. Yes. There was even rain. The shaft was
about fifty yards out in what was probably the center of the
hall. And then he made out another hole or well right under
the one in the roof that obviously went straight down . . . to
where? Why? He blinked in amazement.

There were figures standing around the lip of the pit or
whatever it was. The bright bolts that hissed and slammed
above flung their shadows around the chamber.

He would love to have fled right then. There was chill fear
sweat on his face and hands. He sensed formless terrors from
childhood nightmares. He was trying to convince himself Bita
couldn't be down here. *Because,* he thought . . . except there
was no because.

And he'd stood dreaming too long and so it was already too
late, he realized, cursing, clawing his short sword free,
twisting around because there was reddish torchlight behind
him now, too. It stung his sight an instant and then he registered the massive, oily, bald block of a man filling the twisting
stairwell, looming over a smallish, pale Roman he recognized
from senatorial feasts: Iro. Iro, naked, eyes lidded, dark pits
of emptiness.

Selenius's mouth went dry. His heart pounded. The weapon
in his hand seemed heavy and feeble. An inexplicable oppres-
sion pressed down on him suddenly. He sensed it was a strange
presence, a spell. . . .

"Who's this?" Iro whispered.

"I . . ." Selenius began, realizing the vacant eyes weren't actually looking at him and that nothing he could say would
make much difference. He wondered whether to fight or run.
Wondered if that would matter, either. All this in a flash.

And then Iro walked quietly past him, ignoring his sword,
heading for the open shaft in the center.

"Bring him along," Iro ordered over his shoulder, not looking back. "With the female."

"Which female, Lord?" wondered the oily bodyguard. He
looked around, holding up the torch.

"The one following," his lord replied.

"You act as if I'm unarmed or a child," protested Selenius,
shaking his blade at the massive man. He felt that way: weak
and vague.

There were other, smaller men behind the chief brute on the
stairs.

Iro was still saying things, his high-pitched voice carrying over the thunder booms:

". . . she's a tool of the weaklings. They mean to spy on me here." His soft feet padded almost noiselessly. "We will let her see a few things this night."

She must be a tool of mine, then, thought Selenius. He backed up a half step. He admitted again, in a kind of hopeless wonder, that he loved her.

He heard her cry out up around a turn or two of the stairwell. He charged the killer, who stood on bowed, massive legs, a torch in one hand and a cudgel in the other.

"Out of my way, dog!" he shouted, feeling as if he struggled underwater, voice high and tense. The fellow grinned, showing no teeth, a hollow gape of empty mouth. Selenius knew it was hopeless down here in this stifling darkness, chilled by fears he couldn't explain, feeling trapped in a terrible dream. He knew it as he stabbed at the sleek, massive belly that pushed out above the loincloth, because something seemed to come out of the mouth, a freezing, whirling breath that filled his body and head with instant numbness. The open, grinning hole seemed to expand until its blot of blankness covered everything and Selenius never knew if he actually fell or simply froze, lost in some limitless, lightless space.

Above the glowing pool that was a window into myriad worlds (reflecting the violet-and-golden skies of Avalon in a landscape blown like delicate soap bubble shapes from perfect imagination), the three beings floated, equidistant, and slowly rotated around the perimeter of watery light.

"Will she do what must be done?" asked Adellee.

"We cannot force her," added the male, Olloa.

"We will not," responded Lillila. *"She understands."*

And then their minds united, became a single fusion, melting together, their radiant shapes overlapping, forming a globe of soft, slow, lucent pulsation.

Their single consciousness now expanded and touched countless others like themselves as the armies of light gathered in the sun. To them, the solar fires were soft gleamings. They literally drank brightness to forge an incredible spear of light. All their wills concentrated on shaping a bolt of almost solid brilliance. Together, mind to mind, they would fling it through the lens pool into Aataatana's underworld. Inside the sun the long shaft took form. Their wills reached out like hands to hold it, tensed and tempered, ready to strike. It was aimed, not outward toward the spinning earth, but inward to the core of the sun, where, in the magical inner sphere, the land of Avalon, the gateway bridged the literal distance between worlds instantly.

The fusion spoke to the thousands on thousands of radiant forms, like themselves, drinking light like cups of glory.

"Expect no victory, O kindred. We hope only to blind them while we look deeper into their defenses and schemes. Victory enough if we keep them in their lair and distract them from the human children."

They understood that Iro meant to free the lord Aataatana, who had poked a dark, insubstantial red-tipped claw into the paffy Roman's shadow-haunted brain.

They knew he thirsted for Bita. She was bait, in a sense. She had a hook in her, put there by the Avalonians, who believed that when the dark lord reached from his dimension to clutch Bita there would be an instant of vulnerability.

The Etruscan priest was explaining a version of this to Antony, who was arming the full century he housed on his estate, forming them to march in the madly storm-wracked courtyard where the gusts beat the flooding grounds into foam and no torch lasted thirty seconds. Lightning flailed the sky where clouds billowed, ripped, and whirled. The storm, many believed, was beating the city flat and drowning all the lowlands.

Antony was furious.

"I want that girl back," he raged at the priest, holding his mouth inches from the long, narrow face under the hood. The wind flapped their cloaks like banners. "Did you have a hand in this business?"

"No. But I think . . ." The rest was lost in gust and thunder. The soldiers had their shields tilted against the downpour.

"What?" demanded Antony.

". . . hints. I have seen . . ."

"What?"

"It's an inexact business," he shouted, wiping his face with a long-fingered hand. "I did what I had to do."

"Who commands you in these things?" the Roman soldier wanted to know, waving the men out the gate, his centurion at the head of the ragged column.

"The truth," yelled the adept, slogging beside Antony in the wake of the troops whose tracks in the mud were instantly blurred away. "So much as I can see and hear."

Antony leaned closer. Cupped his ear. Waterspatter echoed in the flap of flesh.

"What's that?" Antony said, leaning closer to the priest.

"I have seen hell rising."

"Ah? Where?"

"There's a hole in the world."

Antony heard enough this time to make him frown. They moved down the muddy slope toward the city. The men's curses and complaints were fragments blown past like rags spinning on the wind.

"There may be," he muttered inaudibly, "a hole in my skull because I have wind on the brain." He didn't dare ask too many questions. He would simply see this through without asking too many questions.

"She's being drawn there," the soothsayer said. "To the hole." He had a dim, confused impression of gigantic wings cramped, claw-beating in a too-narrow shaft, struggling upward in spurts of fire, of a slim, pale girl falling into the unfolding darkness. . . . Then the scene burst, blindingly bright. "To the hole."

Aataatana gazed into the round emptiness that was somehow more than solid, the dimensional plug suspended in the rotating rims that hung in the center of the underworld. He was watching the earth's surface. Watching Bita and Iro—amused, because the Avalonians expected to fool him. To hurt him with their pathetic colors and hideous brightness.

He grinned. Flame rimmed his lips. He had a surprise or two left for them, he reflected, watching the images in the ball of emptiness.

Time was passing. The stars were wheeling above the trees and the low roofs. Namolin crouched nearer the open window. He could hear snores. He knew this family. Their crumbling shack was on the outskirts of the village, close to the common dungheap where collected slops were dumped—the perfumed glade, as it was known.

They were poor, numerous, with a blind father, sluttish mother, and various cousins and uncles crammed under one sagging roof. He knew the one he wanted: the plump teenager impregnated by Thor-knew-who. Seven months along, last he'd noticed her at the well, barefoot in tattered leather that exposed patches of grimy skin on the belly bulb.

He drew breath carefully, moving closer. Dawn would be too late. He couldn't take more than an hour more.

Body and face caked with drying muck; a stink in his nostrils; beard standing out front and to the side as if suspended underwater; eyes a wild glitter. The recent wound hurt his side. He crouched over the sill and let his sight adjust until he made out the sleeping bodies crowded on the hay-strewn dirt floor. A reek of sweat and sexspice, stale meat and ripe pockets of human gas.

There she was, a bulky man beside her, face down, out like the dead.

It was a desperate thing, but he was desperate. His powers should still be equal to these swine, he assured himself, climbing inside and moving, stepping over the nearest, concentrating his power of voice and hand, sweating with effort, stooping, clamping his palm over her soft, moist face and hissing with full power:

"Obey in silence!"

She choked, gasped, squawked, and bit his finger. The bone grated between her teeth. His heart sank. She sat up.

"You've had all you're going to have this night," she cried, "you Viking bastard!" Except the Viking was flat on his face. Namolin made a desperate grab, clutching her around the neck and dragging her with wiry strength toward the window. Hopeless, but he was utterly frustrated.

Have all my spells slipped? Is all my power gone?

She took one look at his face, his stare, she inhaled the noxious swamp stink, and she protested.

The room stirred into hubbub: crashing, curses, and her continuous shrieks of fear and outrage. Even the illegitimate Norseman rolled over and grunted, burping beer. He groped one ham hand for her body and found straw.

Namolin fled. A fight had broken out between two men in there. The wife of somebody was howling. Chickens fluttered and dogs yapped, echoed (as he fled across the yard in the first subtle hints of false dawn) in the rest of the village.

He paused for breath at the bridge, cursing the morning stars. As he leaned on the railing, he heard a click-scrape of claws and then a silent lump of shaggy fur and ripping teeth hit his thin chest. He staggered, felt the pinching, sickening pain of a bite, rolled with the skinny dog, clutching its small throat and, in near panic, commanded:

"Obey! Obey! Obey!"

And it worked this time. The animal went passive.

He got up, holding it under one arm and shuffled into the wooded cliff area that walled off the wild swamp. The dog would have to do. No choice anymore.

He thought vaguely about the other girl, Tirb's youngest, who'd lain tranced under Leitus the night before. His plan to use her baby as an offering to Aataatana seemed very remote just then. All he could think about was the spell of raising and the pain of his stab wound. He could only hope the little beast he carried would have enough vital force to carry the spell. . . .

The guard's sword thrust was right on target and Caesar almost shouted "Stop!" at the last moment; except Leitus moved. Spun. None of them there (including Subius, who was frozen in the act of trying to reach the guard's arm) had ever witnessed such blurring speed in a human being. Leitus effortlessly caught the extended wrist and snapped the bulky man's arm the way one might crack a whip or snake a rope. Subius winced as the bones popped and the soldier rolled his eyes and screamed.

Leitus was blinking, surprised himself.

"Well," said Caesar, "I think you are worth my attention." He gestured across the beach where the sun was just managing to stay above the advancing line of dark cloud mass on the horizon. "We sail and will return to the city together." He smiled. "Centurion, Leitus Sixtus, commander of my guards."

Subius watched and thought: *It has to be the blood of the father finally manifesting in the son.* But even Spartacus couldn't have matched that speed. Strength was one thing, but that speed . . .

The man on the ground managed to rise to one knee, cradling his shattered arm, sighing in pain.

"Attend me, Centurion," Caesar said, walking ahead, crunching down the beach toward the waiting ships.

Off the coast of Gaul the storm hit. It had mounted over them, walking in pale, greenish lightnings and massed, boiling clouds. The strange thing was the virtual absence of wind. The rain just fell, almost dead straight, in bucket drops, a sloshing wall of gray. The thunder seemed oddly high and remote.

The men bailed constantly. There was a real danger of the hull filling up. The slaves manning the oars below decks were near panic as the water foamed down the steps and waterfalled through the hatches.

Shoulder to shoulder at the oar holes, soldiers toiled with buckets, flinging water into the solid gray sea and air.

Subius was beside Leitus, scooping from around the slaves' chained feet while the timing drummer beat his steady, driving rhythm.

Leitus glanced at the straining, scarred backs, some bleeding from fresh stripes inflicted by the whipper, who waded along the center passageway.

Subius and Leitus were snatching a rest, leaning on the side. Officers worked side by side with the men.

"What a terrible fate," Leitus commented.

The gladiator took his meaning. "Here," he said, "you see it naked."

"See what?"

"The soul of the empire."

Leitus thought about that. "It's the way of the world, I think," he finally came up with. The incredible rain *whoosh*ed and pounded the sea outside and the deck above, cascading down the hatchways.

"No. It's the way of some men." Subius spat salt water from his lips into the overflowing scupper. "Your father . . ." he began to say.

"What about my father?"

Subius jerked his head at the benches, the cracking backs, scraping oar shafts poking at the sea, keeping the time of the massive, jet-black barbarian beater in dark red loincloth and copper hoops.

"Your father was one of these," Subius told him. Finally.

"Gracchus? He was never a—"

"Not Gracchus."

"Back to work over there!" yelled a noncom. "You, Subius! And the fine centurion. Stir yourselves! Is this a picnic in the grass?"

Subius gave him the upraised thumb to mouth. The man pointed to his own backside. Subius grinned, and picked up his bail bucket. The water was sloshing around their calves again.

"What are you saying?" demanded Leitus.

"I'm talking about your real father."

"Real father?" But it fit. Leitus had felt it, or something like it. There had always been something strange between them. "Real father?"

Subius nodded. "Bail," he said.

"Then who?"

"You're part of a legend." Subius pursed his delicate mouth. "Gracchus protected you from it."

Legend? That sounded as meaningless as anything else. People were always implying things.

"I only tell you now," hissed Subius under the water's white noise, "because others soon will. Don't let yourself be drawn into . . ."

"Into?"

"Madness. Refuse all offers of greatness. Live small. You cannot win. Your father couldn't win himself." He gripped the young man's arm, his big hand circling it. "Rome is the world and the world will crush you in the end."

Subius turned and bailed powerfully now. Leitus half-heartedly scooped water, then let it trickle back to the flooded floor. The slaves groaned and leaned into the rowing. Leitus glanced at the black drummer at the far end of the low-roofed hold, lost in his slow, steady, double beat.

"Greatness isn't one of my worst problems," he said. "Who did you say was—"

"I don't lie, boy. I may keep close counsel, but I don't lie."

"Who was my father?" He wasn't sure he even wanted to hear and Subius sensed that, too.

"Spartacus." Subius paused, stared at nothing, kneeling in the warmish water. "Ah," he sighed. "He nearly did it . . . nearly . . . and he was a fool, too." Spat and scooped again. "He was. A stubborn fool." *And I loved him. A glorious fool, a dreamer with a sword.* "Worse than you."

Leitus was quite amazed.

"Spartacus the rebel?" He shook his head in wonder. "What an idea. . . ." He stared again at the black man, his long, bony arms lopping the sticks down on the taut hide. "That's amazing," he said. He had no doubt it was true. All the loose ends of his life were being pulled together and knotted. "Amazing. . . ."

CHAPTER XXIII

All that lived now was hate. There was just that under the massed tons of darkness pressing him down. But to say "him" was meaningless, because there was no consciousness of sex or past or actual self. Pressed down to nothingness. Hate in blind, silent, flat blankness. Hate without words or even actual thought. Rage stirred like a crippled worm at the bottom of the world.

The hate formed an image, a face and form, the object of the hate. The hating knew the object, the sharp face, the bald skull, the hunched-forward body; knew the feel of the object's soul. Stirred, struggled in painful fractions, like the worm, crawled, strived through the infinite muck mass. Wriggled to find the object.

How long, how long? "How long" could never be measured in a place where time had died, crushed to blankness that could eat any movement, blink of light, everything . . . except hate.

The Avalonians knew there were intelligences who existed in dimensions their powers could not reach. They had hints, subtle touches, unclear contacts with these worlds. As they were gods to humans, so these beings were archangels to them. The least contact was a sacred event. They had no real evidence, but they believed the "Great Ones" almost never took substantial form. Tradition held that these universal spirits saw and touched all time and space at once but rarely interfered in the struggles of the lower worlds.

Lillila was walking alone, meditating among crystalline trees by soft falls of rainbow liquid, each drop a pure, clear, bell-like spatter, spilling down sheer walls of golden-blue, jewel stone.

When she heard a voice in the singing liquid, instantly she understood and stopped. And listened. This was a rare moment, a blessing, a gift. Her colors showed awe. Because nothing ordinary (good or ill) could penetrate this sanctum, the heart of Avalon.

She looked, silently, at the rainbow liquid spill and saw the outline, a figure incomprehensibly perfect and intense. She felt fear and love which was awe.

The being's light flashed and all her world trembled and seemed dim. Thin, brilliant beams sprayed into her head in a single flash and wrote there, intimate and terrible. Traced an indelible message. Was gone. The being vanished. But she wandered for some immeasurable period, absorbed in the message. All her colors were heightened; her awareness keener, wider than she'd ever imagined it could be. The inconceivable touch had changed her. She had been kissed by eternity and its message was written in her substance. Forever. She glimpsed what waited for her beyond her universe, what she'd called her life. Everything would always seem narrow and somewhat dull after this.

The part of the message she passed along to the others contained a caution:

"Consider," she later told Olloa and Adellee, *"precisely when that creature Ulad died, clutching the foul globe; Aataatana was loosening the gateway to the destroyer world . . . beams of chaos leaked out and touched the foul power stone."*

"Ah," Olloa responded. He was struck by the new intensity, star-bright in her eyes.

"Namolin, that ignorant magician, never actually had to raise his disciple. Ulad would have followed him in any case. The final doom is loosened."

"Ah," sighed Olloa again. *"And we're doomed."*

"No!" she insisted, her fierce, shining eyes flashing, full of the incredible message. *"No, we go beyond . . . beyond."* Expression failed. Glory blazed in her soul.

• • •

At a certain point the pressure of the darkness lifted. The voracious hate that had once been called Ulad broke the surface and what had once been eyes or ears or brain itself felt the shadowy outline of fear and hope, ambition, need, anger, and disgust that was still called Namolin. Felt as if seeing and moved (it knew not how) toward it, the object, the thing that stung it by merely existing. Drew it forward to stop the pain in the hate Namolin's very being created.

Namolin stood there, weary legs wide apart, holding the drained body of the dog by its hind legs. Its slit throat gaped in an insane, mock smile. The taller trees across the open, water-topped muck were touched by the first light. The glow showed arcs of widening red stains where the wizard had anointed the surface with blood. His throat was raw with shrieking his demands at the dull mire.

Now, reeling, he raged numbly. He should have tried to get another child at any cost instead of depending on this miserable dog. He flung it out into the swamp so that at first he thought it was an impact ripple. He stared and watched dully as the sun widened its brightness and sky started to show pale, pure, wet-looking blue.

Defeated . . . defeated . . . defeated . . .

He noticed the slight movement, still thinking it was a ripple, until there was an actual lumping, as if a mole moved through the pasty stuff. It was coming straight toward him. And then a roundish lump broke the brightening surface. A moment later he recognized (stunned, heart leaping in uncertain joy) the globe, caked with black and greenish slime . . . and then, horror, the skinny arms upholding it, still extended, locked above Ulad's head as if in mirror replay of his sinking.

Namolin cackled, his sore throat rasping laughter as he forced his wobbly legs to caper on the hump of solid, mossy ground.

"My powers," he whispered, "they were but bent, not broken."

It was not until his former disciple, festooned with lily pads, decayed vines, and packed thick with black and greenish muck, had almost reached the shore that Namolin felt the first fear and hoarsely gave the command to halt to him, who now seemed an animated length of angled sticks and mud shaped in senseless mockery of humanity. Ulad's spidery arms still locked overhead as if he were about to cast the stone, wading knee-, then calf-, then ankle-deep, sloshing slowly but inexorably forward.

"Stop! Obey! Obey! Stop!"

He said this in the secret language. It should have held back a charging bear, even a falling stone, if uttered well, with the will totally fixed.

It did nothing. The horror with plugged eyes, mouth, nostrils, ears, slogged closer. Namolin felt his doom like a chill from the heart of hell.

He stepped back, now yelling the commands. He expected his throat to bleed. No effect. The heap of muck came stiffly on, holding the globe high.

Namolin flailed, arced his staff. Hit the long head. Slime spattered. The wood shattered. Ulad kept coming. Namolin felt the choking wave of hate and annihilation. He took the hint of reason and fled, forcing his sore, hurting body to stumble back along the uneven ridge, brambles plucking at him, reeds flicking past. He glanced back to see the horror, gathering a mantle of flies, never pausing, uplocked arms still holding the power sphere. He tried to plan through his panic, thinking about knocking it loose from that deathly grip . . . thinking desperately. . . .

CHAPTER XXIV

Iro's two sleek, nearly naked guards padded quickly around the curve of the staircase, responding to his command to take the girl. He minced past Selenius and across the vaulted space. The lightning reflected down the shaft that pierced both roof and floor.

Bita saw them coming before they actually moved. She'd discovered she was seeing things in her mind (where only dreams used to show) in flashes, more and more vividly. Sometimes just moments ahead; other times some distance she had no sense or measure of. . . .

So she was thinking, as they came (to her suddenly hyperactive sense in slow motion) how she should have stayed at Marc Antony's and let all this pass; how she still might escape and forget. Why was she here? Because some beautiful, perhaps imaginary, beings promised peace and hope?

She imagined a small, cheerful house in the spring countryside when the flowers were bursting from the warm earth under powdery, gentle skies. Pictured herself with Leitus; small children playing in the sun while she gathered herbs and garlands.

Her body wanted to turn and run away, but she told herself: *They asked me to bear light into darkness, and as much as I have I will carry. . . .*

So she didn't try to smite them motionless with her stare (as she had Antony), just let them take her. They stripped her and tied wrists and ankles together. One oily brute who smelled,

she thought, like a sour pond, lifted her. She glimpsed what
Iro was and would do and knew that if she physically touched
him she would pierce the last shadow that veiled his purposes.
She kept the spring image in her mind, the lush colors, the
children playing, Leitus. . . .

She would lift the shadow tonight. She was confident of her
power to stun these men. She was angry, nervous, and impatient. She'd always prided herself on doing the job and keeping calm, but now she was having difficulty not blasting Iro's
minions into waking nightmares. That wasn't like her. She
hated suddenly. Kept losing the bright image, the colors. . . .

They unslung her nude, bound body and laid her facing upward at the lip of Iro's pit. The opening of the shaft above the
pit showed swirls of cloud and lightning flare. Bita noted how
she could see the sky. She lay almost at Iro's feet. Her altered
sight saw the shadowiness swimming around and within him,
possessing him.

He stood above her head. Rolling her eyes back she could
just distinguish his outline tilting up in the constant jarring
light. The hissing crashes shook her body. She expected he
would bend down (as he had the last time she'd been in his
power) and touch her body. She'd counted on that, to some
extent.

But she was wrong. He gave some command, and the fat,
oily strangler knelt and rubbed his big, stubby hands over her
torso. She had been gaining weight. And her breasts hurt. For
over a month now. The meaning of these and related facts
(because no one had ever told her) she missed completely. The
slave rubbed some tingling salve into her flesh. He had an expert, soothing masseur's touch. The salve tingled and she felt
it speeding up the glowing outline of herself that she now
thought of as her true body. She sensed this was some kind of
potion.

Next they unbound her and raised her to her knees. They
seemed to think she would be too weak to manage herself. She
decided the potion must be a drug. She concentrated her
strength into the glowing body, felt it brighten and vibrate,
washing away the tingling numbness. She overcame the drug
and waited.

Iro had gone to the lip of the pit. Bluish bolts flailed down
from the insane storm outside and poured into the hole. She
looked down and saw the sight-stinging flashes lighting the

shaft until it was just too deep to see anything. *Bottomless,* she thought, heart quailing a little. When she looked up she was shocked and horrified to see two of the guards carrying Selenius unconscious and undressed.

Selenius's feet had been bound to a T of wood, which they raised like a flagpole over another shrouded figure which the violent, leaping illumination showed was laid flat and stiff and straight. He hung upside down, his dangling arms just brushing the cold stone flooring.

She was riveted by the sight of what they unwrapped, pulling away the muffling cloths to reveal a shrunken body, dried out, with long dark hair. *A woman,* she thought, stunned. Saw the withered limbs and a face that seemed all hollows.

She hadn't had time to react before one of the squat, powerful servants slit Selenius's throat so that the dark blood pumped and dribbled and sprayed over the dead body underneath. Iro giggled, capered, and shrieked into the hole at his feet:

"I bring you, Lord Aataatana, whose name is terror and mystery, a tender gift! Restore my sister to me. May all her body quicken, her heart beat, her brain think, limbs be full and round for my pleasure! This girl for my sister, O mighty lord!"

His voice rose. Bita stood up, in grief, pity, disgust, and anger, seeing with terrible clarity the clawed hand of shadow that reached from far, far below in the bottom of the pit to grip Iro's brain and soul; saw the red-jeweled ring of flame (the red Iro always felt in his brain) on the dark finger that poked up the mushy little man's spine into his head where its fire filled his skull and reflected in his eyes. Iro, she suddenly understood, had been emptied. He was a puppet. With only his amplified and twisted desires sustaining his worse-than-dead flesh.

She wanted to hit the thing with the light that suddenly filled her heart. Golden, soothing. She felt the oily men fall back from her as she ran at the now chanting, rapidly bowing little man that Aataatana's dark hand had squeezed empty. It would be grace and kindness to destroy him.

She raced around the rim to where he bounced and shouted over the thunderbolts. She passed the corpse that had been laid under poor Selenius. She refused to look. Felt terrific blasts of updrafts, billowing and *whoosh*ing from the pit's depths. Selenius's body rocked wildly on its cross beam, sprinkling Iro's sister, Claudia, with the last drops of his blood.

And then Iro leaped (or was caught by the wind) and was out over the opening of the pit, held like a feather on the puffing uprush that made her think of heaving breath.

She began to weep with pity and thought distantly of Leitus and a lost life long ago and far away. She saw (in her second sight) the shadows reaching for her, beating like wings emerging from the pit shaft. Red ember eyes. The great king whose one hand held Iro reached his other out to grab for her. Vast wings beat the air into cyclonic madness (or was that illusion?), struggling to break free. While she knew these were projections from his dark mind, yet they could wrench a brain to death with their vivid force. She was trying to watch carefully, calmly, in the eye of this violence and hallucination for what was really happening.

"Claim your bride!" shrieked Iro from where he seemed to hang, tumbling in space. "Give me mine!"

"You false monster!" she cried. "Stop your lies!"

The wind caught her, plucked her toward the center of the pit. She screamed silently for her golden allies to save her. She rose, spun, and then, desperately, clung to Iro as she passed him, like a drowning swimmer. She felt jerked out of herself into a strange, ominous silence. She didn't dare look over (or couldn't) but had a sense that her physical body lay somehow sprawled at the lip of the well of darkness. Iro's form felt spongy, oddly damp to her touch. They were falling now down the pit, together, wind a whirlpool . . . down into smoky shapes . . . spinning into nightmare like a lost leaf. She heard Iro's terrible thoughts as she was caught in his memories of secret horrors, rites, murders, the fantasies he'd had while his victims suffered. Games he'd played from childhood, sacrificing sheep and household pets. His frenzy when he'd seen his sister, Claudia, with a man. His hate for Leitus, glimpsing them from behind bushes, over window ledges, silently witnessing Claudia and Leitus having sex with gymnastic abandon. And then the red spot in his head, that Bita now saw, too, whispering promises and revenge; because he, Iro, alone, loved Claudia—sleek, dark, Claudia. He'd knelt at her bare feet that night while she'd lain groggy in her bed, makeup smeared from lovemaking (it hadn't been Leitus,

though Iro hadn't known that, either) and he'd kissed and
worshipfully licked her arch and insteps and soft toetips, telling her how she would be a goddess with him in the red light,
in the red, glowing world to come. And she'd kicked him in
the face. He'd wept, shrieked, and shuddered. The red flame
had flared up in his already burnt-out mind and he'd flung
himself on her in frenzy, flurry, and terror, hurt and blood . . .
the salt-stinging taste of blood. . . .

And Bita felt that sense of fierce pity and fury again. Suddenly Iro was gone and she seemed to fall alone, twisting sideways now, passing through the boundary where the underworld's dense edges melded with the solid earth and sucked its
light and color.

"Help me!" she cried, falling in silence. She'd been tricked.
They'd all been tricked. Aataatana's hand cupped beneath
her. . . .

In Avalon, hanging above the shining pool, the three who
had fused into one single, flashing form neither male nor
female, gathered the golden energy of their entire race for a
thrust. Gathered and struck just when the dark had parted to
swallow Bita. They slammed the spear of sun and soul light
straight down the pit. Aimed for Aataatana himself. A milli-
second later they realized that the dark race had been prepared. Had expected the attack. From the deepest obscurity of
the pit came a counterbeam darker than darkness. A void. A
shaft of nothing that yet drank everything.

The dark beam winked out almost instantly. Aataatana had
not dared more. He'd teased a little energy out of the deadly
plug in the center of the world. Now he was satisfied. He knew
he'd dealt them a deadly blow. And they, the Avalonians,
knew as much themselves. Because they'd opened their defenses in order to strike at him. Aataatana smiled to himself.
All history on all worlds is altered now, he thought. *The laws
of the dark dimension have gained great power. The sun is
dimmed. A million sleepers on the earth's night side awoke
screaming in sweat and fear, shocked with a glimpse of what
had shown itself this night.*

The fusion of Lillila, Olloa, and Adellee understood: all the
worlds were hurt. The pool dimmed and they were flung
apart. The sun stuttered and their whole race was wounded.

And Bita was lost. Swallowed as the opening resealed

behind the blunted sword of light. She realized that Iro, or rather the hand that wielded him, had taken her, too. She could feel a vast intelligence, gloating.

It held her loosely for now, recoiling slightly from the sun-fire that pulsed in her heart ignited by the brief flash of the Avalonians' sun-blade, which the three, Lillila, Olloa, and Adellee, had focused. But as Bita sank toward the black bottomless bottom of the pit the dark projection squeezed tighter. The thickening atmosphere crushed her fire to a spark. Her mad fall was slowed by the gathering density. Her fear was like fear in a dream: screamless, detached. She watched the harsh landscape under her: molten rivers, flame-tinted billows of smoke . . . closer . . . smudged movements on the ground, green sparks, things with wheels and gears and metal limbs crunching . . . closer . . . lakes of violet-red embers, huge fortresses, countless beings swarming on roads or fluttering and flapping over the razor-jagged hills, closer, slowing faster now. She was a golden wisp engulfed by the vast image of Aataatana who seemed fifty miles high and a hundred wide from wing tip to wing tip. Tumbling sluggishly through hot, ashy gusts of cloud, she saw pale humans, slaves, trapped and toiling, suffering, their very presence and movements a soundless wail.

She struggled, tried to rise again or fling the light in herself at the winged creature, but the golden glimmering that sustained her consciousness was being stifled. The blackness was too thick now, like choking muck, pressing her until her mind and perceptions could barely move or shine the least light on anything. She'd never conceived such heaviness. She hardly knew when she actually touched the harsh surface at the base of the vast wall that had been seamlessly melted to form the lord's palace.

She tried to stand up. It was so hard to move or think here. She tried to remember where she'd come from, her purpose, but it was all vague and far away. She sensed another world but couldn't see it. Couldn't shake a dreamlike impression that she really wasn't where she was.

The ground was hard. This had to be real, she thought. She felt as if she were being closed into herself by an unrelenting dark pressure. Yes. There could be nothing else . . . nothing but this. She heard things now (though she still sensed there were no sounds here) the hiss of flame, rumbles, wind moans, beating wings, and sighs and racking sobs.

But it was so hard to move, to concentrate. She'd already forgotten the last few moments or how she'd come here. She stared dully at the other pale, nude, human forms sprawled on the harsh rocks; farther down the slope in the light of a geyser of molten stone, thousands seemed to be striking iron bars on iron wedges. She wasn't sure she saw anything correctly because her eyes hurt terribly and, as if they were unused to the light, missed all nuance, just capturing the stark outlines. The clanking was terrible and a vast tilted wheel seemed to spin at an angle, moved by the lavic stream. Hot sparks fell. A few drifted up to where she lay with the others. She turned her head. It took great effort. Saw two men. *They must be Romans,* she tried to think. Then couldn't decide what "Romans" meant. Her mind hurt with the effort. The two men were pressed together, one on his face, the other pressed to his back, hunching into him. One of the glossy, black, winged masters flew up and gracefully, powerfully, fluttered to a stop as if the soupy atmosphere were ethereal. He hovered, poking the man on top with a long, thin staff. She sensed his amusement. He poked the stick into the crease of the buttocks. The man writhed. The one beneath echoed his movements. Then she realized the two men were translucent, vague, and that there was no real contact between them. The act was phantasmal. Yet there was suffering, desire, desperation, hopelessness. She tried to look away, absorbed by the awful, wonderful strength of the glossy master; how he ripped through the thick darkness. She felt something that was dimly like a desire to worship them, their power . . . but felt the idea wasn't hers . . . sensed another mind, strong, vital, cruel, sharp, hard, like a voice at her ear:

"Adore me," it commanded. *"Adore!"*

Bent into the blasting rainstorm, Antony and his troops staggered along the flooded road toward Iro's villa. He still wanted answers from the soothsayer who struggled for footing beside him.

"You hold too much back!" he complained, shouting in the wake of the insane gale. "I don't care my testicle's weight in dung for what you cannot see. Tell me what is clear! I am earning the privilege." He grimaced.

The Etruscan leaned closer beside him.

"We're probably too late as it is," he said.

"I'm always too late, I think," Antony muttered.

"What's that?" The sharp-faced man cupped an ear. The lightning burned their shadows on the boiling ground and wracked trees in amplified angles.

"Why am I about to risk my unsteady head for a runaway slave girl?" *Which head never was much comfort to me in any case,* he thought.

"I know little for certain—"

"Yes, yes! Damn you! Sing new notes or be still!"

"There are gods who hurt and gods who help."

Antony's sigh of disgust was lost in a drumroll of thunderclaps. A fork of greenish-blue lightning walked along the road one hundred yards ahead and kicked over a tree in a spurt of flame before fading out. The troops huddled along, drenched, chilled, miserable, wading in running mud.

"Say something, will you!?"

"The gods who help have been breeding humans. For ages on ages."

"Breeding humans? Why not rats or snakes or something useful?" He shook his head. *There's the wall,* he thought. The back end of Iro's tremendous estate that sat with a smooth slope in front and steep cliff side in back that opened (Antony remembered) into a rural valley.

"Breeding warriors who can overcome the dark ones," the priest was saying.

"The dark ones? The Africans? I think the legions can do that job satisfactorily."

Cupped ear. "What do you say?"

"Tell me!" Antony commanded.

"This girl, this Bita. She is the female half. She will produce a great hero."

"The world needs more heros the way it needs more sins." *With enough heros there's never a shortage of wars. . . .*

"What did you—"

The next flash showed the wall clearly and the huge trees that flanked the villa within.

"Who's the father then, master?" Antony wanted to know, wiping the rain from his eyes. "Anyone I know?"

The knife-faced priest shook his head. Looked uncomfortable. Kept wincing as the bolts cracked, stuttered, rattled, smashed overhead. "But," he yelled, "the dark ones want

her, too. I think they led her here with spells and false hints
and befuddlements.''

"As I am led in most things," the Roman soldier responded.

"They want . . ." His voice broke. He winced and shivered.

They were at the wall. Antony tapped it with his fist as the
men deployed for assault. The rain shattered on the bricks.
Their shadows danced and leaped as the electric strokes
crisscrossed into the boiling clouds.

"All right, men," Antony yelled down the line, but only his
raised arm actually made the point.

The Etruscan seer touched the wall. Shuddered and clutched
himself, shaking violently. His teeth clattered.

". . . they want . . ." He tried to say things. ". . . the child
. . . child . . . child to rule . . . rule . . ."

Antony squinted at him. The man seemed suddenly thin,
frail. Spasming.

"Have you fever?" Antony asked.

"Ahhhh," he hissed in terror, dropping to his knees, facing
the brick as if to pray. "Ahhhh . . . they see me. . . ." He fell
on his face in the mud, thrashing. ". . . hell . . . they want to
come out!" he shrieked. ". . . yes . . . yes . . . yes . . . gate
open . . . here . . ." He thrashed, kicked the earth to dark
foam, face down now as if trying to claw and chew his way
underground. ". . . they . . . have me . . ." Muttered and blew
mud bubbles.

"I'll be falling next," Antony snarled. *It's the fashion.*

"He'll drown like that," the nearest soldier yelled.

"Turn him over," commanded Antony. "Prop him on the
wall."

Two men obeyed. The younger, beardless, looked up:

"He's dead, sir," he shouted.

Antony wiped his face and sighed with frustration.

"That caps a well of wisdom and information," he said to
himself. He shook his head. But he wouldn't have denied (if
asked) that a shiver touched him, too. The leaping shadows
suddenly seemed ominous, suggesting forms and meanings he
tried to block out.

"This is not a good place," the young soldier said, standing
up by the contorted body. No one heard him.

Antony gestured again.

"Up and over, lads," he cried. *Or else I'll run home. . . .*

Up and over, then. Advance through the trees in the wild, overlapping shudders of light. Except (he gradually realized) more than the fists of wind seemed to slow them as the trees creaked and twisted in the sheeting rain. Everything hit straight into them. The storm suddenly seemed to have its furious source in the dark villa itself.

It got harder and harder to walk, the closer they came. Antony's heart pounded, breath went shallow. He could see by their faces in the flashes that the men felt it, too. He wanted to throw down his weapon and run. He felt like a scared boy. The young soldier to his left walked with clenched fists.

Break in, then work down level by level, was the gist of his instructions to the troops.

He shielded his face from the sting, squinted at the dark, low, wind-torn buildings about fifty yards ahead. There was a window open. Maybe a shutter had blown loose. He thought he saw a red eye of fire for a moment. *Some lamp . . . a torch . . .*

He looked to the side. Even that was an effort. His heart pounded. He saw less men than he should have. The leaping shadows seemed to show shapes other than trees, bushes, pillars, and sculptures.

Imagination, he thought. Perhaps the priest had just been more sensitive to some fearful forces, nightmare shapes the greenish-blue violence exposed: clawed movements, humped-up swirls; bat wings; fanged mouths.

He yelled from nervousness and anger and surprise. His troops were backing up, some fleeing headlong. The young soldier nearest him had shut his eyes and was screaming on his knees in the flooded garden. The statues seemed to caper in the mad light.

He yelled, heart sped, and nearly fainted with panic, panic pouring into him with each buffeting gust, while the shadows lunged, jumped, flew, ripped.

He saw something pale and strange. He squinted, wiped his eyes, feet trying to run, only his will holding him firm behind his drawn sword. Yes, there it was: a nude, smallish figure standing on the low wall that bounded the inner gardens. Looked like the rest of the statuary except it moved.

Iro, he thought. Had to be. Standing, one hand to hip in an oddly petulant pose, looking on while the shadows gathered and bounded.

"Go back, slave," Antony thought he heard across the surf of wind and rain that smashed over him. "We will call you here soon enough." Something like laughter. "Go back."

And wind and fear together smote the Roman leader and he staggered. The young soldier was screaming. Antony took his arm, helped him up.

"Come," he rasped, "come on. . . ."

They staggered back across the flooded, muddy grounds, tripping, splashing, dripping muck, gasping for air while terror squeezed their chests. As he stumbled away from the intensifying nightmare, Antony felt the sickening cold triumph of Iro at his back all the way to the wall, like a saw-toothed, poisoned dagger.

CHAPTER XXV

"It's a great risk," said Subius. They were side by side in a wagon drawn by two good mules. They wore stained tunics, light armor, and dusty traveling cloaks. "You should have waited for Caesar."

They'd just come to the street that wound along a rounded hillcrest, passing the modest homes and walled gardens in his family's neighborhood. The trees were skeletal, the few hanging leaves dry and gray. That was odd. Though there was a chill coming down from the mountains there was rarely anything like autumn or winter in Rome. There were palm trees standing in the city.

But the whitish-gray clouds, to Subius, felt like snow. The unseen sun was setting. A few lights already showed in some windows. Pedestrians all seemed in a hurry. A drunken plebeian rested with his back to a coppery cypress tree trunk. He sang under his breath, not looking up as the cart creaked past. A cat fled across a wall, stirring up a flurry of dark birds. Someone was calling a child in to supper a street away.

Leitus felt a strange nostalgia. This was home. These were old memories from sweet times.

"There's old Bono's place," he said, gesturing with his head. "I used to steal his chestnuts when a boy." He smiled.

"There'll be frost by morning," muttered the gladiator, "or I'm a Nubian with a foot-long penis." Subius chuckled. "Maybe snow. And you're a fool to think that centurion's outfit will defend you here."

"Snow? In Rome? There hasn't been snow here in . . . a long time ago."

"I smell it."

"I have to see my father and mother."

"Um," grunted the other. "You'll need a medium for that trick."

Leitus wasn't listening. "They raised me. I love them. I gave them little cause for joy."

"You had so much on your hands?"

"Much?"

"Joy. That you could spare it for others."

"Who was my mother, Subius?"

The massive man chucked the reins and winced.

"She died at your birth."

"But?"

"She was high-placed. A pale patrician who'd followed your father and had no real strength for it."

Leitus nodded. "That would make a tale in itself, I imagine."

"Hah. You'll not hear it from me, for I know it not."

Leitus pointed. "There's the house," he said.

Subius was remembering the day Spartacus had stood on a hilltop with a blood-colored sunset at his back and Rome across the river, thousands of slaves who'd just fought their way out of the city, waving and yelling "Hail, Spartacus! On to victory! Victory!"

"I remember," said Subius.

"By the gods, it seems an age." Leitus remembered eating December pudding with berry sauce. He tried to remember the time he'd seen snow: he'd been small. He'd caught the flakes and was amazed by how they'd vanished at his touch. Nothing had stayed. "I had to come here," he murmured. "I had to."

"You should have waited."

"Caesar will come soon. He'll see I have a fair trial before the Senate." He felt almost secure: a centurion, Caesar's chief bodyguard. The hell with Iro.

They drove under the rear, arched gate past the old cracking statue of a woman bearing water and the goddess Diana with one hand missing.

"No lights," he said. "Still, it's early." Except the gray was deepening fast, edgelessly, as if the city were submerging into tidal shadows. "I wonder if they've eaten yet."

"A sensible thought, at last."

The memory of Claudia, her blood and death, had receded to twilight remoteness. A stain of red behind all the shocks and sights since. He was still troubled by the blank period in Britain, the strange time in the village with the old wizard. He sometimes awoke in shudders from incomprehensible dreams, hints from that period. He shrugged it away for the moment and wondered if his old friend Marcellus still studied medicine. . . . Well, it hadn't been many months. It just seemed long and lost. He'd changed so much. It amazed him. His old life here seemed impossible now. He was better off in the army, he'd decided.

And then, what about that slave girl, that Bita? He sometimes thought about her. Wasn't sure what he felt. Wondered if he'd ever see her again. Wondered why he wondered. . . .

He went through almost all the rooms before accepting that the house was empty—no, deserted. Dusty. No slaves. Nothing in the kitchen where (as Subius pointed out) there hadn't been a fire in a week or more.

They'd lit torches and were heading back to the stable when Subius stopped and drew his blade. The night was getting quite cold. Gusts of wind soughed in the eaves, rattled bushes and trees. The flames made overlapping, shifting circles of glow around them.

"What is it?" Leitus wondered, whispering.

Subius spoke into the night beyond the flamelight. The wind stuttered the fire, bent and fluttered their shadows around them.

"Come forth," he commanded, "and show yourselves." Leitus was nervous. He sensed many men in the shrubbery, trees around them, and felt his body prepare to lash out.

"It seems you were right, Subius. I should have waited." But he wasn't afraid. Fear of ordinary death seemed to have been squeezed out of him.

Two or three men moved into the uncertain rim of torchlight. One was tall, bent to the side, somehow familiar.

Subius squinted, cocked his grizzled, scarred head. "You?" he grunted in disbelief.

"That's right, master chopper," the canted man said, stepping nearer so that reddish, gusting glow showed a long face, a patch over one eye, a set of thick scars that ran from hollow cheek to neck. He wore dark leather and cradled an ax over one of his high, narrow shoulders.

"By Jupiter's butt-hair," said Subius, "you're not altogether dead." Nodded with pleasure. "By Venus' split bottom!"

Leitus knew him now: Crato. He'd seen him fall at the
bridge, long ago; yes, months that were years or ages. "What
harm do you mean here?" he found himself asking. "Where is
my family?"

"This is he," said Crato to the men in the shadows. Two
short, stunted-looking fellows in front came full into the
wavering light.

"You are Leitus?" one said. He had no nose. It had been
chopped away. The other (who was nearly his twin in many
respects) had no ears.

"Yes. What—"

"Your father," said the second, No-ears.

"What," Leitus tried again, "happened to my—"

"You should never have come back," said Subius.

"Why, they're dead, boy," Crato told him. "Your fat uncle
took their property. They were under scrip." Raised an
eyebrow.

"What?" asked Leitus.

"Proscription, he means," said Subius.

"Ah," said Crato slyly, touching his uneven nose. "But
that's not all. There's more."

"My uncle," said Leitus. His heart sank.

"Rome is at war," said No-nose. "The tyrants have washed
the paint from their faces. They show their true looks and
teeth."

"War," hissed No-ears. "War!" He blinked as if stunned.
He often, Subius noted, looked stunned.

There's no escaping what the gods have set turning, Subius
thought. *Here is where I least hoped to bring him. . . .*

"Son of Spartacus," said No-nose, "your people are
ready."

"My what?" They all moved closer. He didn't understand.
He was thinking about how his uncle had murdered his
parents and stolen his property. Still a shock. Always a shock.
Who are these rogues?

"Your people," said Crato. "A city and country full." He
grinned, chewing something and swallowing.

"Riots have broken out," said No-ears. "Your people are

ready to rise again. We have swords and hate." He shook his head, suggesting a dog tearing meat from a carcass. "Swords and hate!" There was a whispered cheer among the others in the yard (maybe a dozen) and a soft clash of weapons. "The time is now, son of Spartacus. This is your hour!"

Leitus glanced at Subius, whose round head reflected the flames. His deep-set eyes were shadowed. He pushed the new ugly news down into his consciousness. He didn't want to deal with it yet. Couldn't. Subius was saying something to him:

". . . and I meant to spare you this." Touched his arm. The gladiator was thinking that these men here were capable of killing Leitus's family themselves just to bind him in hate to their cause. Not that they necessarily had, but what an idea! He sighed, looking at their faces. Yes, they had cause, but there was always good cause for bad deeds and there was no end to cause, since my vengeance purchased your vengeance . . . and on and on. . . .

"They killed my mother and father?" Leitus wondered vaguely, pushing it away, looking at nothing now, stare lost in the night beyond the torch flutters.

"Clodius and his rabble are fighting in the streets against Milo's men to see who is carried by the mob," declared No-nose. His eyes were small, hard. "But the slaves and the despised we're gathering everywhere." His voice broke and went shrill, short arms cut the air. "We only wait for you, Leitus, son of Spartacus, and we rise and topple the damned oppressors! The cursed Romans. The stranglers of the world!"

Other voices joined in. Violent whispers all around like (Leitus thought) suffering shades. And now (true to Subius's prediction) the first slight fluffs of snow swirled down through the turning wind.

Subius still stood with drawn sword as if half-minded to strike. *If he says no to them,* he thought, *I'll die beside him, because they'll never let him go. We must have been followed all the way, all the time.*

There was no life to return to; there was only an empty house, a cold season, and self-consuming fury. And he was a trespasser in his own life, on his own property. A trespasser. Leitus sighed.

"There were soldiers here to take you," said Crato, tilting to the side, grinning wolfishly, bunching the thick scars that ravaged his cheek and neck. Up close his face was truly terrible, Leitus thought. His jawline had been indented and shifted painfully sideways when he spoke.

"Ah," breathed Subius. That made sense.

"They want you badly, lad," Crato went on, jaw shifting. "Your uncle Flacchus."

"Yes, my uncle," Leitus whispered. The snow caught in hair and beards now. He hardly noted the wonder of it. He stared out at the circled, shadowy men who seemed poised for his words. The flakes touched specks of tiny cold to bare flesh.

"And Iro, and Pompey," put in No-ears. "And all the Roman devils."

No life to go back to . . . just cold rage. A trespasser. So there was no choice at all, and even if these men meant to use him they were (if not a keen sword) at least a club in his hands to crack his uncle's skull with. He stared as if he actually saw his stepfather and stepmother in the wisps of snow-ghosts.

"And what do you want with me?" he asked the burning, hurt, and haunted faces.

"Your commands," said No-nose. "We are all your army. You are your father's son."

"How will you lose this time?" Subius wanted to know.

"We won't," said No-ears. "We won't."

"Since you say it twice," agreed Subius, "it must be true." He spat into the chill wind. *The boy must see,* he thought, *that he's a banner they mean to wave and that there's no choice here.* "Command them to go home and give it up," he suggested.

"They are divided," shrilly put in No-nose.

"And ripe to fall," added Crato, jaw working.

Leitus was amazed at himself. He was cold. He watched them from a heatless calculating distance, saw their intentions. It didn't matter. He felt very powerful, suddenly. Felt almost contempt for their shallow scheming. Thought Caesar would understand and approve. If you knew how to touch him, any man would follow. The coldness in him was like a lens of perfect clarity: he would have his revenge . . . and more. Much more.

"They'll unite against you," Subius said. "That's clear." Also clear was that their plans were hazy. Was it just find the magical boy with the magical name and somehow the state would buckle? He spat again. *They're all half-mad with it.* "Think of Caesar or Pompey's legions. Think of that."

Leitus knew it was probably hopeless in the pause that followed Subius's advice. The pause was filled with wind and the scattered flakes of chill. Hopeless, perhaps, against the power he knew so well now, yet (perhaps his father's spirit, he later was to think, whispered to him at this crossing of fate) the enemy was ugly, senseless, cruelly unjust and not really the Romans (he believed) but some shadow that possessed them. Some poison, some hollow-hearted, rapacious evil that someone had to strike at, even if hopelessly, because it would have Iro's face and his uncle's body and a void for a heart. He saw this coldly, too. Without fear. He'd be destroyed. But he'd strike at that face and that gross body.

"Better to die like wolves," he found himself saying, "than sheep!"

Which startled Subius. Because he remembered that, a quote the boy could never have known. Standing on the hill with the red sun setting, thousands milling at his feet, Spartacus had whispered, not quite looking at Subius: *Better perish as hunting wolves than sleeping sheep*. Shouts and swords flashing on the hillside, sun like blood . . .

And now this moment. The wheel hung an instant, then swung on freely again. Because that was all he had to say. Now there was no way except forward and doom.

Subius shrugged as the others hissed savage cheers and crowded close. Now Leitus, he realized, was becoming a legend. Stepping into it. What a changed young patrician! A long way from the drunken, scared, confused, soft, and gripey medical student of maybe a year ago. Subius sighed. And now he was going to be dragged along to his doom by Leitus. *Irony mounts irony,* he thought, *and gives birth to Subius. Well, by rights I suppose I should have died with his father, so I owe this coming death. I should have stayed at home and run a tavern or been an armorer or* . . . He shrugged.

"Lead me," he heard Leitus say into the chill night with a voice that now filled with force and sureness, "and we'll begin." He saw the creature again in his mind, the darkness with Iro's paffy face and his uncle's sagging, puffed out body. "Lead me to my army!"

CHAPTER XXVI

So that's why the streets were empty, Subius was thinking as they marched rapidly across the suburbs. With about thirty men now. It was after midnight. The snow was still falling; in the fields and on scattered rooftops it was, incredibly, already inches deep. From the ridge the city was visible, tiny, wavering lights spread out over the hills and depressions, clustered in the low-lying sections, all blurred by the misty snowfall.

Walking beside him (Crato in front, No-nose and No-ears just behind), Leitus had remained silent since leaving his family's property a few hours ago. They'd half circled the city since then and were approaching the main body of escaped gladiators, slaves, and foreign prisoners.

Down in the central sections, torchlit crowds moved like streams of fire, collided, yelled, and battled. Muffled but audible on the chill, uncertain wind-rushes. Suddenly, as they watched, one house, then another . . . then a whole street seemed to explode into flame, and, after a pause, distant screams were tongued by the wind. More flames, bursting here and there, billowed up, leaping from alley to alley across the dense inner city where the packed buildings were mainly wooden.

"Well, it's begun," said Crato. His long face leaned into the torchlight, dramatizing the terrible scars that had twisted half his features into a permanent grimace of rage.

"Aye," said Subius. "More of what we've known too much of."

"It has to be," said his old companion.

That's true, meditated Leitus. Since accepting command he'd said almost nothing. *There's nothing else.* . . . Just long days and nights of emptiness, pain, and struggle. Until even to breathe was a battle, too. Everyone was dead or dying. He let himself go over it now: Claudia, Iro's sister, the girl he'd adored, cut into bloody steaks . . . his own life shattered . . . driven into exile . . . through his own stupidity and fate's harsh edge he'd lost that one sweet moment with his one and only virgin, that tender slave Bita . . . to British Gaul to wade in blood . . . memory suspended, used by some vicious cult— or priest, anyway . . . another girl in the night who seemed a dream now . . . a killer for Caesar . . . his parents betrayed and murdered. *More of what we've known too much of, indeed, by Juno.* . . . He remembered a quote from somewhere, some poet: "Seize today because I believe nothing about tomorrow."

So they might as well smash the rotten world to pieces as they perished themselves. Stand up to it. Break the powerful on their own wheels. Sometimes, by chance almost, he reflected, the sword can be just. At least he might be fate's grim hand if not fortune's darling.

He felt colder than the wind that puffed snow and billowed and steamed in the roaring fires below. *My father was history, but I never knew him, nor will I. But I won't disappoint any of them. I'll inhale this unaccustomed chill and hold it in my heart and weep no more boy's tears from this night on. They made me a weapon and I will grieve no more than a weapon grieves for the cuts I gouge from this black, stupid world of cruel fools.*

For some reason, unconnected to his train of thought, an image of Bita lightly teased his memory: her long oval face, slate-blue eyes looking quietly and calmly at him as she offered him hot soup she'd cooked while he was out learning the gladiatorial trade and starting to regret the days he'd wasted studying healing arts and maybe even the nights, too: deep in wine and lovemaking, licking Claudia like a honeyed sweetmeat, swimming into her as if to sink out of sight and thought in breasts, mouth, creases of spice and tang. Bita's eyes blurred all other recollections: hopeful eyes watching him, wanting him to like the soup (it was that simple) and so pleased when he did that he could now have wept for it.

Except there was only ice. She was probably dead, too. They'd pay for that and then he'd pay for their paying, and the snows of time would cover everyone. Everyone. Let the world be burned and bled clean, though, and then maybe the Bitas would have a chance. Like a garden of golden flowers planted on the ashes of weeds.

Someone had been talking to him. They filed through an almost circular arch in a dark stone wall as they moved back from the slope. The snow was piling in drifts against the stones.

"What's that?" he said, not looking back at the voice. It was No-nose.

"We're almost there," he told Leitus.

Subius took the flask from Crato again. Burned wine. They'd been passing it between them for some time. Something like the brandy of later centuries. He loved the hot sting of it, felt he needed to keep up with his drinking. He considered leaving them all once they reached the encampment (amazed, too, that these men had managed to come so close to the city itself) then went over his oath for the thousandth time and sighed. He'd had to guard Leitus until . . . until when? A good question. There was no date on that contract. He drank deep and relished the sting that gradually converted to a rush of peace and sweetness in his brain.

"So you lived," he finally said to Crato.

"I've got Romans still to kill before I give the last grunt."

"Why bother? They'll keep breeding more."

Crato grimaced and spat dryly into the white chill mist of flakes.

"It's futile work I don't mind," said the thin gladiator.

"There was a time," Subius recalled, "we spoke about better things."

"Ar, what time was that? Midnight?"

"We'll rule this land as is fit," put in No-ears. "When we've killed our full share."

Subius sucked down another burning slug. He heard the stirring sound of masses of people just before he glimpsed the tents on the field.

"Best to rule," he said, "when everybody's dead."

"What do you say, Commander Leitus?" No-nose wanted to hear.

Leitus didn't look up from his brooding. There was nothing

now. "Words are shit," he said. "I'm out of words."

"Ahh," breathed No-ears. "Your father's soul lives in you."

Subius didn't even sigh this time. *Comedy,* he thought. *Remind me to laugh.* . . .

"Tell me the battle plans," he decided to ask. He was just drunk enough now.

"Ar," grunted Crato, "General Subius Magnus himself."

No-nose picked it up:

"We stand behind Leitus. We march on the city."

"Aye," hissed No-ears, and others in the file nodded and sounded approval.

"Ah, yes," said Subius, deftly avoiding Crato's hand as it groped for the flask, "and then, when Pompey or Caesar turns up, you drive them off with speeches."

The bonfires ahead tossed long, wild shadows across the fields, the shapes of the gathered slaves and gladiators and barbarians, trees and tents on the smooth, pure snow surface. The reddish gleams showed on the low, fast clouds.

Leitus remembered the place. It was a park. He used to go there as a boy to ride horseback and play kickball. He shut down the memories, gritting his teeth.

"No speeches," he said, "just iron!"

"Did you hear that?" was whispered in a general wave of approval. Subius missed some, heard fragments: ". . . father . . . yes . . . the right one . . ."

And they would have slain him an hour ago, he thought, *had he spoken a word wrong.*

There were hundreds close and thousands beyond where the fires were dimmed by sheets of snow. People were huddled by the blazes and wrapped in cloaks. The word had gone around that Leitus was coming. There was tension and expectation in the air. Subius sensed a challenge.

"That one," he murmured to Leitus, shutting one eye to better focus as his drunkenness began disorganizing his senses. He gestured with his head. Leitus stood still, close to a fire. The snow was melted in a trampled circle around the crackling wood. He stared into the updraughting flames, the hot, crumbling embers, trying to bring something back. . . . There was a dark rock there that reminded him of something . . . a feeling from Britain . . . a blank spot that troubled him. "That one," Subius was saying, "the elephant's brother. He's not

going to step when you bang the drum, son of Spartacus.''
The gladiator's irony was lost on him. Crato snatched away
the wine flask this time and then cursed when he put it to his
lips.

"You selfish wart," he snarled. "You've not changed a
whit."

"And you've still got none."

"Eh?"

"Wit." Subius chuckled over his pun, then sobered slightly,
watching the huge man who stood with his back to the fire,
arms folded. *Were that one beef,* thought Subius, *we could
feed for a month off him.*

"You damned wart," Crato repeated.

Subius was enjoying the glow in his belly and the blur in his
brain. It was good not to think. "There's no place to retire
to," he suddenly said. "Everywhere stinks."

Crato laughed. He liked that. "Arena men never retire," he
said. "Except the one way."

Subius put one eye on Crato and thought he'd changed.
Gone snakelike and chilly. *We're all being ruined, piece by
piece. The world grows worse and the youth have no hope left.*

The huge man was suddenly speaking, harsh, calm, and certain:

"In the city we will be a mob. We're not trained to march.
We wait here for them."

That caused a stir, reflected Subius. Not that it was a bad
notion. This was as good a hill to die on as any other.

Leitus didn't look up from the flames. The men (a few
women on the outskirts) watched him and the giant. This was
a test. He didn't look up.

"Macen," said No-nose to the giant, "this is Leitus. Son of
Spartacus."

The giant stepped closer. He had a fringed, wiry beard.

"Send for his father, then," he said. A gust of snow hissed
into the flames. His back was to the heat and glow, his face
blanked in shadow. He held a long, iron-spiked club. Subius
took him for a gladiator at once by his shuffling step.

A circle formed around Leitus and Macen.

"Is there nothing more to drink?" Subius inquired in
general.

"Young Leitus may have come to the end of his string,"
said Crato.

"No," said Subius. His lips felt big and dull. He kept blinking rapidly. *After this they'll not only paint his father's face on him, they'll scrub his behind with their noses.* Because the big man, the killer-leader, the one who'd partly bent the bars to free the first slaves from the arena, hacked man and beast to get them this far, worth three normal soldiers at the least, would fall like a child to this (Subius thought) freak of the gods. He still had trouble believing what he'd seen Leitus do.

"We go to the city at once," Leitus said, not looking at any of them. "We will hold the capitol."

The giant loomed over him. "Where's the proof he's anybody's son?" Macen demanded, arms still folded, club over his shoulder.

No-nose and No-ears were close at hand. They both had shrewd, calculating eyes, Subius thought. He trusted neither one. Their mutilated faces were hollowed by the firelight.

"He's known to us," No-ears said.

"That's proof of little enough."

"He's known to Subius Magnus," said No-nose.

"You're in it now," muttered Crato. "Good luck to you."

"That's less proof," insisted Macen. "I lead here. I say we wait. I don't follow boys. No pretty youth claiming great birth slices shit here!" He looked down at Leitus. "I'll have you bare-butt in my tent, I think. You look fit for that. Son of whoever." He hefted the long club. The spikes glittered.

Silence. The snow billowed and hissed. The crowd waited and watched.

Leitus felt so distant. He kept picturing the city in flames, the huge columned buildings smashed to pieces, citizens frying, screaming. . . . There was still a blackness, a hole in him, his mind, like the almost round rock in the embers he stared at . . . a memory he'd avoided concentrating on. He'd tried to hold it back but the shock of his homecoming had revealed the void: a hole nothing could fill, no warmth could touch, a lens that showed him the ugly, dull meaninglessness of all existence. A lens that made all men mere meat for the blade, because they were stupid, weak, petty, cruel, and blind. He gazed through this lens now and saw the world destroyed, shattered to atoms, wiped dark and clean and smooth of all senseless flesh.

"Prepare to march," he said. "We will destroy the Romans. There's no more time for words." He glanced up at the giant now who was a club-length away. "Obey me or die."

Subius didn't like any of this, didn't like the alien chill in the young man. He rubbed his numbed face. The blood felt thick and warm in his flesh. They'd done something terrible, he believed, something terrible.

Macen said nothing. He just swung a blow that should have left Leitus mushed meat on the snow-smoothed ground. Leitus stepped in under the sweeping downstroke that flung shadows over the crowd and white air. Leitus struck in some way with his bare hand that even expert Crato missed. The impact echoed in his stomach. Seemed to shock his perceptions for an instant.

The giant spasmed and dropped the club, twitched wildly, gave a high, faint shriek, and spun (as if hit by a hundred-pound hammer) into the fire, where he thrashed and roasted in a dark stink of suddenly oily smoke. He kicked and struggled as if some unseen weight actually held his tremendous body pressed into the roaring logs. But these were only impressions in a mad moment of snow, shadow, and a suddenly cheering, wild mob that was an army, too.

"Victory will be ours!" yelled No-ears, dancing in glee to the howling. "Hail, Leitus! Hail, Leitus! Leitus the Great!"

The cry was echoed, spread across a quarter of a mile of encampment in moments, voices out in the swirling blizzard. "The world is rising!" No-ears shrieked on. "Rome will fall! Hail, Leitus! Hail!"

CHAPTER XXVII

Eyeless, earless, soundless, plugged with caked mud that had hardened like cement, bony arms still locked overhead, supporting the black sphere, the concentration of hate that had been Ulad shuffled and swayed across forest and field, unaware of dawn or evening, lost to wet or dry. In the choked red fury of its skull there was only a sense of Namolin (though there was no name attached), who was being followed as surely as a crawling, sightless worm crawls to its foul food.

Ulad didn't know that he was passing through a village south of where he'd lived when living. His stench preceded him. It was early evening and the red setting sun bent his contorted shadow over the pale grainfields where the autumn stubble lay in rough carpeting.

Children fled. Adults hid themselves. Warriors crouched behind lowered spears or raised swords. No one seemed to want to get too close. Namolin, by now, was a good hour ahead and gaining by slow limps. But Ulad was steady and sure as if the mass of turning world itself inched him on. Sealed in, he went, not even knowing that he went.

As the sun melted behind the hills, Ulad was tilting downslope toward the Thames. The water lay in a smooth, silvery curve. He never felt or sensed anything around him. He was drawn by the stone and found his way as if his spidery bones saw.

A young warrior had followed him, overriding his fear with anger and disgust. He darted from the cover of a laying-by shed full of grain (other armed men hung farther back in

superstitious awe) to fling a long spear completely through the
brittle, softened, spindle body. Dried mud puffed and the
spear stayed stuck halfway through. Ulad never lost a shuffling step. He went on steadily. The warriors went the other
way.

Locked invisibly by the stone to Namolin, the body went
straight for the river edge. The western sky had gone blood-
red, the water ephemeral bluish-silver. What had been Ulad
still held the sphere overhead as if about to fling it down.

He turned as if questing for a scent, though he had no
breath. He moved along the stony bank, crunching through
the stiff reeds.

Came to a battered sailboat with half a mast, drawn up on
the beach. He stepped into it and simply stood still. Waited.
The dark globe flared for an instant and the craft seemed to ig-
nite, glow like a coal, and then move, scraping slowly into the
evanescent water and sliding steadily out, following slightly
faster than the current so that the watchers on the shore saw
the bony figure with the thin spear shaft poked through it float
toward the reach, a mysterious shadow of terror.

Namolin kept peering back in deadly fear. He didn't understand the forces he'd unleashed or the reason the power sphere
had turned against him. He'd no idea the powers he'd played
with had vectors of their own, mock intelligence, will, and
purpose. The globe had absorbed the ambitions, weaknesses,
strengths, madness, pain, and anger of eons of wielders
back to the first nonhuman. The globe's ancient pseudomind
was using Ulad's shell.

Namolin was formulating vague plans for getting possession
of one of the remaining two globes. He'd have to reach the
gathering set for the eclipse night when Aataatana had promised to burst up into the world.

His feet were swollen, his breath hurt his lungs as he
climbed the steep slope along a path among massive pine trees,
the dark boles blended together by heavy ground fog. He
strained along, leaning on his broken staff, feeling (some of
his wizard's senses were still keen) pursuit too close to pause.
He kept twisting to look back as the twilight closed around
him. The ground was damp and cold. At any moment he expected to see the tall, spidery, undead thing loom out of the
mist.

•   •   •

He was right and wrong: the hunter was there, just out of sight, intent, determined, and steady with hate. But it was Tirb the Strong, the scar from the blow Namolin had given him a vivid rent on his side. It gave the impression he might have been nearly burned through.

Tirb was armed and careful, listening, pausing, easily following the tracks and stick marks that the Druid made no effort to conceal, since he believed his only tracker was supernatural.

Tirb was thinking about losing two daughters because of this false priest. The first, Bita, stolen; the second lying in some strange trance, with child. He'd wept when he left. His wife had said nothing, standing by her daughter who'd lain there, wrapped in furs, while the child grew. They could feed her soup and soft foods, but she never really woke. The mother's eyes said it all, watching her.

A spell, he snarled to himself, *that I'll end with the watery blood of that treacherous beast. Soon.*

He reached the top of the hill. The trail showed the old man knew someone was at his heels. He smiled with no more humor than a shark. He touched the hilt of his dagger. *Soon.*

He tracked the wizard quickly, despite the massed fog that wet his skin and beard. The traces veered suddenly into the trees. *He's gone to ground,* he thought. *He's tired out. Soon he'll have his rest in the hell-world.*

A little farther and the trees opened out. It was nearly night, but from the vague outlines he sensed the trees curved around this space: a rounded bulge on the high hilltop.

Muffled, distant, Tirb was certain he heard the surf hitting the cliffs. He wasn't quite sure where he was now. They'd apparently circled back to the coast when he thought they'd been heading due west, inland. No matter.

He passed between two huge standing stones, square pillars holding up nothing. He felt cold. A wizard's spot, he thought. *A good place for one to die,* he concluded.

The tracks led to the center of the mound he now realized was not natural. He unslung his spear and crouched forward to what seemed a well.

He's gone down there. He leaned over. Yes, there were stone steps, spiraling. Tirb reslung his spear across his back, kept the dagger in his left hand, hooked his legs over the rim, and carefully padded down into darkness. He would never turn back. Fear wouldn't penetrate his cold, hunting frenzy.

So he went down, blade first, into whatever depths lay ahead.

After too many turns to keep track of (if he'd tried), he paused. Listened. Sure enough, pittering footsteps down below.

I have you, false priest, he thought and went on, going a little faster than he intended, finding it easier to speed on the tiny, slick steps and let the momentum keep him close to the wall. After a while the steps seemed to circle of themselves under his feet while he floated, suspended, just keeping his place . . . down . . . down . . . giddy, his mind wandering into strange sidetracks, memories of Bita, how he'd chased her captors right to the edge of the water where the pirate ships had lost themselves in the incoming mist. . . . Tirb always believed Namolin had known more than he'd said about the incident. And he'd made a whore and dead meat out of his second daughter. . . . He remembered, vaguely, his meeting with the woman, witch or spirit (he never decided) in the woods just behind the beach after the pirates had vanished with Bita. She'd told him he would seek her. Well, he hadn't, so that was wrong. Perhaps he should have. She'd said something about a dowry, too. . . .

He spun on down the pitch-black, insanely spiraling stairs. How could he have been so blind to that priest's intent? He now asked himself. *It must have been a spell to dull my senses. But now I'll soon repay everything.*

Fleeing too fast, light-headed, going down as if into a whirlpool, he never realized he'd reached bottom until he'd spun and staggered across a smooth flooring, noticing a faint reddish light spinning by, slowing as he slowed and finally fell . . . slowed but didn't quite stop. When it did it was already too late: he glimpsed his quarry looking back at him, lit by a witchlight glimmering at the top of his broken staff, so that his long, razor-sharp face was hollowed. He seemed, as Tirb cursed and wobbled to his feet, dagger still gripped in his left hand, to drift magically away, shrinking into the blackness of the tunnel.

Tirb staggered after him, and then there was nothing under him but air and he understood that the wizard must be in a boat. He hit a warmish, brackish surface and went under the river. Came up sputtering. The current was swift, the gritty taste bitter. He was swept along in the wake of the boat. He paddled and kicked, watching the tiny spot of illumination shrink to a wink of light that finally became indistinguishable

from the spots and flashes of his straining sight. It was dark.
He swam expertly on, grimly determined not to give up, vowing that wherever the wizard was going he'd get there, too . . .
on and on . . . hearing only the rush of the bitter water until
time lost itself and his mind wandered as if he dozed. Dreams
flashed at him as he struggled on. At one point he felt he was
sinking, dropping into a golden glimmering, seeing a bright
city and beautiful female figures swimming or floating in
golden space. Then he was back in utter blackness.

In distant Avalon the three leaders no longer floated above
the round pool that was the gateway between worlds. Neither
were they blended together into a single consciousness of
brilliant light and power.

They lay on the silvery-green softness surrounding the pool
which had grayed noticeably, the colors paler, the sky thinned
to a kind of rusty-gold. The perfect trees and ornamental
structures were sketchier now, detail lost, blurred. Even the
pool showed dull streakings.

They were weary. The shimmers that surrounded them
reflected the draining of their world. They all understood,
even the lesser members of the army of light. Something had
reached into all the worlds from the black heart of the earth
and hurt all creation. The laws of nature were changing, the
balance of the multiuniverses had been skewed. The perfect
spheres spinning in eternal symmetry were scraping together in
places. Olloa was meditating, watching the shifting patterns in
himself that reflected the total external effects.

"*Ah,*" he expressed, "*Ata touched what was forbidden. He
has freed what will eat us all.*"

He perceived the stains that were scars, permanent rips in
the subtle, shining field of his being. He knew those marks
were scored on all the worlds. They could never be healed.

Adellee agreed. She shuddered at the spidery traces of black
annihilation in herself and on the landscape softly surrounding them.

"*The surface earth,*" she added, sickened, "*will gradually
darken. The humans will dull their inner senses even more.
The grinding harshness of their environment of pain, greed,
and endless war will wear them away. . . .*" She saw that love
itself would go black, in the end, and the last link, hope,
flicker between the shining worlds and the humans would be
blotted away. A dead and empty philosophy and blind religion

would wall them off from the subtle glory until (they all saw) a terrible magic and science from the depths would dominate them completely and leave the earth a smoking, dark coal.

"It is finished," expressed Olloa.

"He will be ruined, too," put in Lillila, "by what he released in his stupid pride."

"So will we all," added Olloa needlessly. Though they existed in a timeless land they seemed weighed down, faded.

"We have to fight once more," she expressed.

"Can we?" he wondered. His color pulsed slow, weary.

"We must. We must fuse again. The moment is coming. The eclipse your brother waits for. They will all meet at that creature's home in the human city. At the gate to Hell."

"But we just failed at that," Adellee expressed.

"We try again," Lillila insisted.

"If we do," Olloa put in, "all our substance will be spent and our home"—his color wept—"the wonders and nooks and joys will fade and crumble like a human's dreaming when he awakes to that deeper sleep they call the day."

"Yes," she told him. "But we must."

"Cannot we have peace?" wondered Adellee. "We have done all we could. Cannot we enjoy what little brightness is left?" Her light wept, too. What pain to see this strange and sudden autumn in a land of unending and infinite summer.

Lillila didn't reply. Didn't have to because they all felt the inexplicable touch of purest compassion. The light within color. The love that echoed everywhere. That grew like spring shoots in rich soil, or soil blasted and barren after all the fires of hate had burned into ash. The glory that awakened in a child's eye or a flower's tilt, the same everywhere for everything alive. There was no choice for them. This was a voice they didn't know was a voice. A thought too fine to feel. Yet it was there. The pure ones, the ones unseen, were speaking to them.

"Arise, soul of my soul," Lillila told them, gathering her strength, starting to gently suck the color from the landscape to rebuild the grayed-out parts of herself. The nearest sketch of sward, touched by the beams of her soul, began to empty, the trees and flowers going to pale, crystalline translucence, looking brittle as ice.

The others sighed in almost somber tones. But they made no protest now. They would absorb the remains of this landscape to fight the battle with. They sighed. . . .

CHAPTER XXVIII

The flames from the burning city showed in the huge Senate windows and flung magnified shadows on the marble walls and domed ceiling. Not quite a quorum was present, not that it mattered. Dour Casca was there and Brutus, bony Cassius, Livian Argenteus Saccus, and others. Some stood in the windows and doorways, watching the carnage below. Some kept their seats and stared at nothing, afraid or angry or hopeful according to their natures, giving the impression that the state was functioning smoothly.

Someone was shouting over the mob yells and clashes outside:

". . . and now they've invaded the city itself! We must fly and—"

"Coward!" yelled Casca from a window where he'd been watching the flames and the amazing fact that it had started snowing again. How much portent did they need? Two days of heavy fall in a place that rarely saw a single flake. "Let the mob eat itself."

There were some shouts of "Yes!" Saccus, weaving slightly, toga askew, leaned in the main entrance.

"Antony," he called, "went to meet Caesar's legions."

"What?" demanded Cassius. "Now Caesar dares bring an army into Rome?"

"Disbanded returnees," someone corrected.

"Ha, ha," scoffed Cassius, "that's a child's tale." He waved long, bony arms above his head. The flamelight painted

his enlarged outline on the far wall, where he seemed about to
hurl something down on the troubled lawmakers.

Now another shadow, from the doorway, bigger, rounded
. . . a fat senator came puffing into the chamber. His shadow
blotted over Cassius. His voice was hoarse, reedy, overexcited:

"Gentlemen," he cried, and Saccus, to his infinite disgust,
recognized Leitus's uncle Flacchus rushing past him. He had
an urge to trip the sweaty man and send him sprawling down
the short flight of steps to the forum floor. "Gentlemen of
Rome!" His bug eyes bugged. "The Republic is saved!
Pompey is here! Pompey!"

"Him, too," snarled Cassius. "And do we next make Iro
consul for life?"

Saccus leaned on the edge of the doorway. He didn't want
to hear arguments. All these windsacks knew to do was bellow
and be sly and endlessly talk. He'd ever prefer to endlessly
drink, given a choice. He thought about the wine jug his body
servant was bringing him. Where was the young bastard?

Then he peered out and saw more than he bargained for.
"Pompey better move double-step," he muttered to no one
because no one was close enough. Because coming up from the
burning city, charging from low, rolling billows of smoke and
snow-ghosts (with dawn still an hour off at least) was a solid
mass of armed, armored, and semiarmored men. Obviously
the wrong side. Whichever, he passingly considered, that
was. . . .

He stared as they came past the statues and smashed aside
the line of praetorians holding the steps. These were nobody's
regular troops: soot-blackened, bloody men with a mob of
crazed slaves at their backs.

"These," he muttered, "don't much look like talkers . . . or
listeners, either." He almost ran, but that wasn't his nature.
Anyway, seeing fat Flacchus brought low could be worth a
little discomfort.

Too bad about the wine, he thought, as they flooded up the
steps, snow-gusts driving around them as if they'd material-
ized from some wild, freezing hell.

Subius wasn't surprised that the mob joined them after the
first impact carried the gladiator-led army deep into the central city in a single slash. They'd hit the civil guards, who were
trying to contain the risings in the plebeian sections where the

fires were driving them uphill, frantic, terrified, furious.

With Leitus at their head, mounted on a big black-and-white cart horse, they smashed all resistance and followed the main streets up the hill to the capitol itself.

The city was a nightmare of burning buildings, gushes of superheated air that turned the amazing snow to rain and steam. Streets flashed past, bodies jammed, adding an acrid roast flesh stink to the chaos; knots of fighting where armed gangs clashed with slaves . . . blood and screams . . . on and on . . . breathless, choking on smoke, climbing the capitol hill. Leitus kept ahead on the massive, heavy-stepping horse. He seemed to look at nothing, lost in some inner brooding, only glancing up twice when soldiers broke through and tried to cut him down. Then he moved with that deadly, fluid speed his people were already building into instant legend. He stabbed each attacker once, in the face, and they fell, bubbling blood into the fresh snowbanks.

We have the city, Leitus was thinking as he reached the crest of the capitol area, moving among the huge state buildings, the flames below now, the dark smoke crossed by spuming white shapes of snow-gust. *Let them come and take it back from me.*

His coldness was his power. He saw that. Nothing would turn him aside. Nothing. There was a cold, empty place in him and he carefully focused through it. He'd level this world, plough under all its cruel stupidity. Level it. He'd have a seat set up for himself in the Senate. He'd rule from there. Who could stand against him? Who could slay him? He grimly smiled. *Leitus the First,* he thought. So be it. Because he didn't really care if he lived or died anymore. That was the point. The void waited behind every human folly and dream. Rich went poor, poor rich, kings fell, rose, decayed, men cut each other to bloody meat with void slogans on their lips. And all were ground under in the end. What illusions! Madness.

He rode, brooding, right to the door and into the Senate chamber. His men surged around him. The senators fell back to the far end of the place. Some kept their seats as Leitus urged the stolid, barrel-bodied animal to the forum center where it stopped and stood still as if carved.

Subius stopped in the gallery. The slaves, freebooters, gladiators, renegades, barbarians overran the seats, clashing weapons and cheering: grimy, bloody, hungry.

Crato stood beside Subius in the mad, stinking press. His scarred face was twisted with elation.

"Saturn's butt-hairs," he muttered, close to Subius's ear, "will we actually do it?"

"No," said the gladiator, rubbing his tired eyes under their deep browshelf. "Not this rabble. It will slip through their fingers. It always does." *Yet here I am. And he's already worse than his father. Madder.*

The cheering went on. They really believed, he realized, that they had won something. The senators, for the most part, bunched together. The flamelight drew Leitus and the horse's outline on the wall and dome.

When Leitus looked around the chamber they all seemed pale and remote. Small with fear.

Subius was watching his eyes, and didn't like what he saw. He had an idea he instantly rejected as imagination: a sense that something had been forced into Leitus, something strange and deadly.

Small and pale and feeble, Leitus was thinking. He managed to not quite sneer.

A fisherman told the story to his wife, folding his nets on the dock by torchlight, his catch in wicker baskets ready to unload. The wife was dark, squarish, young, and strong. He was balding, bent-nosed, restless.

The bay was calm, sky clear. The city (Naples) was a warren of narrow, twisting streets where candle and torchlight flickered.

The fisherman was sucking a piece of salted cod while he spoke, big hands working the webbed knots and meshed strings. The floats clunked dully on the stone pier as he carefully measured and folded.

"It was just at sunset, I tell you," he was saying. "A ghost craft."

"Ghost?" She squatted beside him, looking out over the moon-laced water.

"No sail. No oars. Coming down across what wind there was. Passed a cable-length from where I'd made my last cast this day." He sucked the stinging salt fish, relishing the burn of his gums.

"You did well today."

He grunted. "And stranger still . . ."

"Stranger?"

"A skinny thing, a ghost, standing in the prow. Not moving. Hands up in the air." He demonstrated. "Just standing while that boat went right across the wind and passed me." He nodded. Pointed. "Straight to shore."

She looked around nervously. "This shore? I don't like such tales."

"It's no tale, woman. But he put in, I think, above the harbor. I lost track in the mist." He shrugged his hands. "I had my own business to trouble about."

"A ghost," she repeated, squinting out across the silver-dappled bay.

On and on, floating through unrelieved blackness, drawn by the current of that acrid, underground river, Tirb the Strong wondered if this would end short of death—or had he already died? Was this Hades' stream of forgetfulness? How many days had passed . . . or were they hours? Minutes? No way to tell.

From time to time things that might have been fish touched his feet and legs. He'd kick and splash and the touching would stop. For a while. That and sinking were the only real breaks in the monotony. On and on. . . . And then he knew he was accelerating by the sound: the sloshing water sound gathered gradually into a hissing. He understood. Cursed to himself and struck out against the current. He'd tried before but there'd been no shoreline—only slick, wet, cold walls of worn stone.

He heard the falls ahead, the unmistakable booming magnified by the cavern. It struck him that the wizard had obviously turned aside or landed somewhere. He'd lost him. He ground his teeth and nearly burst his heart and lungs trying to save himself, but his hands skidded over smooth rock-face again. No way out. And moments later he went over and down into unseen depths. He may have screamed. The fall was sickening. For a few moments it seemed to be bottomless . . . and then came the foaming blow of bottoming under a crushing weight of water. He knew he was dead this time and (according to his religion) he already saw light in the darkness which (in his stunned consciousness) he took for the doorway to the next existence: a golden, pulsing, superb illumination spilling up from below, spilling around him as he was tossed and sucked deeper.

His final thoughts were furyless regrets that Namolin had escaped his wrath. He saw images of Bita, a memory of holding her in the surf on a smooth summer beach, delighting in her squeals as the waves broke into them, scintillant in sunlight. Then he was gone.

Leitus was exhausted. He'd given orders all night from the Senate floor in the mad red light of the burning city. He'd dictated terms to assembled senators and tribunes. Sent his men to hold key positions along the Capitoline hill. Sent other groups to pacify the other districts. Sent men to capture and loot the patrician villas along the Tiber. He hoped to take all the shipping on the river by blockade. He was (Subius had noted) an endless fount of strategic and tactical ideas, almost none of which the men he commanded were capable of executing. When the gladiator brought that point up he'd been ignored by Leitus, shrugged at by Crato, and glowered at by No-nose and No-ears and other instant true believers.

Now he watched his former charge striding along the wide wall that ran beside the main building. He kicked the snow idly, his newfound captains following his pacing in the snow-covered garden below him. Their heads were about level with his feet.

Subius had just cracked a fresh wine jug so the dawn was blurry gray with a few streaks of gold. The sun broke through the clouds now and then to glitter on the snow that had stopped about an hour ago and was already melting. The fires were smoldering in the fresh light. A black, thick cloud lay over the lower city and blotted out the river.

He let Leitus's words become blurs, too. The senseless, incisive orders, the cruel commands to slaughter all patricians and bring the children to the countryside. Leitus planned to take personal charge of their upbringing. The only way was through the children. He had to make a new world as rapidly as possible. Despite the fact that it was manifestly impossible.

Leitus stood, hands on hips, overlooking all the other hills. He'd just sent messengers to gather slaves in the countryside to march to Rome. His voice was raw, raspy now. He proclaimed the city a fortress that Italy would bleed to death besieging.

No-nose and No-ears and the others grimly applauded. One

man walked on his hands with delight before toppling into a drift.

"There's a little overoptimizing," a high-pitched voice said at Subius's shoulder. The gladiator was leaning on the building, squinting into his jug with one eye shut tight. "May I have a taste of that, good man?"

Subius raised his squint to the thin, prematurely balding young senator. He looked friendly enough. The gladiator grunted. "His father's son," he said, holding the jug out. The other took it.

"I am Livian Argenteus Saccus." The man drank deep. Burped. "And I thank you."

"That's fine," grunted Subius. "We're all doomed."

"I agree," said Saccus, squatting, leaning on the same wall, "but anything is better than being bored. I'm terrified of that. That's why I drink." He looked bleary. "I remember the last time it snowed in Rome." He passed the jug back to Subius. "It's already melting."

Subius felt the blurring, tender touch of the wine hit his eyes and brain. He smiled. His lips felt thick. Leitus on the wall across the garden reminded him of a statue. It was all so hopeless. The men below him making plans that were dreamings. . . .

"We're going to be destroyed," he said.

Saccus nodded vaguely. "That's probably true," he agreed.

"Something happened to him."

"Ah," said the senator, prying the wine loose again from the gladiator's great hand.

"In Britain . . ." A flicker of sun and then a humping of the smoke blotted it out. The rising black clouds were sinking the scene back into artificial twilight, rolling toward the hill, mounting.

Leitus watched it come with a strange joy: the smoke was covering everything and he imagined it dissolving whatever it touched so that the land (he pictured) after it passed would be sooty and rubbed clean of all traces of human effort and existence. The idea filled him with a thrilling swell of power.

Wipe the earth clean, he said to himself. He considered enlisting Caesar. Let him govern the outlying provinces. *Then I can organize the legions under myself and sail to Egypt and Persia. Like the smoke, I can spread out and cover all countries, grind the world smooth and start building new with only*

*the best human material. Build a true empire on noble lines.
. . . Yes . . . grind away all other ancient evil cultures, all the
hopeless ages of stupidity and vice and weakness. A new world
must be born and I will be the father of it!*

He glanced up at the massing smoke. His symbol. Out of
the ashes a new substance rising from the flames, higher and
higher, covering everything. He smiled, enjoying the conceit.
Himself as smoke. He ignored the obvious flaw. The fire had
burned him, made ashes of his life, of everything he'd hoped
for, cared for; but he'd risen, like smoke, from his destruc-
tion. . . .

And then he saw him, on the far side of the wall at the base
of the capitol steps where a blank-facaded state building stood
with terraced gardens fronted on the open space that the snow
had smoothed edgelessly together. He knew him instantly,
even at that distance. He didn't need details of the paffy face
and empty eyes, slouching mien.

"Iro Jacsa," he hissed.

Alone, too. Standing among the statues and pillars in a
white-smoothed garden.

"What do we do with the fat one?" No-nose was just asking
him, straining to look up at where Leitus paced the high wall.

"What is it?" Leitus snapped, distracted. He stared at the
robed figure down the slope.

"Your uncle, the senator."

"Pull off his legs like a bug," Leitus told him. He started to
pace along the wall top, which took him a few yards closer,
while the others followed on their side, unable to see what he
was looking at.

"Yes, Commander Leitus."

"No," he responded. "Imperator." The inspiration hit
him. "Call me that now." Yes, it had to be Iro. He was sure
now. What good fortune! All things were bending his way
because his purpose was finally clear. "But don't kill him
yet," he commanded, jumping down on the other side of the
ten-foot wall. He headed down the steps, pleased. *He's in my
power. Poor Iro. He should have fled.*

He was halfway down, watching the bland, round face, the
loose-lipped smile that showed one buck tooth, the mole under
the left eye, the feminine slouch. He just stood there, obviously recognizing his hated enemy. Not moving.

Leitus wasn't even going to draw his sword. Just hands on

the soft throat would do. Running now, skidding on the part-melted surface, the smoke overhead, a fine grayish ash falling, whirling in the twists and turns of the breeze.

He leaped over several bodies of rebels and guardsmen sprawled on blood-spattered, trampled snow. Nearly fell, almost on top of Iro now, seeing only the hated face, the glinting tooth, pit eyes that showed nothing.

"Iro!" he yelled. "Murderer!"

Iro waited. Twenty-five feet of flat terrace lay between them. The snow was stained with frozen blood.

As he crossed the last gap he realized Iro was actually laughing, and then the thin layer of ice under the snow shattered and a shock knocked his breath out. He broke the surface, bloody snow in his face and chill water in his eyes. Stiff, strange hands clutched at him. He screamed in pure terror because he was wrestling with frozen bodies that clogged the pool.

In panic he climbed over them, cracking the ice, spraying crimson snow until he dragged himself with shudders and shivering over the rim. By the time he thought of Iro or even to look up there was a thunder of feet, clash of arms, creak of leather, flashing bronze and steel. Hundreds of troops (he didn't yet know were Pompey's legions) charged past him, driving into the masses of his fighters and slaves gathered on the steps.

He realized the enemy had been in the city all the time. He'd fallen for a feint, spread his army out to hold the perimeter of Rome. And was taken from within.

He snarled, shivering and outraged. But how could Iro have known to bait him like that? Could that be mere luck? Bad luck. He twisted around, looking for the little man as troops thundered past. He drew his sword.

"Come on and die, bastards!" he shouted. *How blind . . . how could I have been so blind?* "Come on!"

He gathered his terrible killing force and flung himself at the nearest group, slamming aside their big bronze shields, his sword bursting through armor effortlessly as the day became night under the cloud-mass, and falling, choking ash rolled over them so that they fought like phantoms in blinded, shadowy flurries. His eyes watered and burned. His lungs hurt and he coughed desperately to breathe. He struck at shadows and they at him. He hit a wall. But which, where? He was totally disoriented. The roar of combat was muffled all around. He was alone now. He groped along the wall, sick from cold and smoke, bleeding from several nicks . . . then a swirl in the blinding soot clouds. He squinted, waved his hand to try and clear a space to see. A vague outline. No armor or weapons. He hesitated. A small man. Iro. Except it was too late: the little man was already too close. Leitus tried to slash and punch at the same time, but the soft-looking necromancer, seemingly undisturbed by the choking gases, had already placed his hand firmly on the other's chest and a hammer blow boomed in his heart and blanked his mind. He was vaguely aware of falling into utter void. Down to nothingness. His last thought, as in a dream: *How could I have not seen it? All for nothing. . . .*

When Subius opened his eyes the day was cold and clear. He was still sitting against the capitol building under a high window where he'd passed out from the wine he'd shared with that (he thought, dimly brought it back) odd patrician.

He rubbed his face, shook his head, and stared. It was late in the day. Fire smoldered on in the city but the wind was now pulling the smoke away from the Capitoline hill.

He realized fortunes had changed when he noticed the heaps of dead on the capitol steps and lines of Roman soldiers at the entrance and down in the streets. He stood up. Wobbled. Touched his big skull tenderly. His delicate mouth felt gummed together. No-nose himself lay a few feet ahead, locked with a dead legionary, both stiffening, bluish-toned.

Dead as stone, he thought. *Here's a mystery. Why am I alive?*

He looked around. No one was near him. He coughed. Cleared his throat and spat phlegm. Glanced up as Senator Saccus came out of the Senate behind him, walked over and half smiled.

"You passed into unconsciousness," he said.

Subius nodded. "I suspected as much."

"You are a good fellow." Saccus blinked pale, ingenuous eyes. "You can go home if you like. No one will trouble you. I'll give you a pass."

"Home?" *What an idea. Where would that be? My home is among the dead and dying; I can live anywhere in equal comfort.*

"What were you doing before all this?" wondered Saccus.

A pair of senators emerged and walked past, staring down at the slow masses of smoke that hung over the ruined inner city. Subius didn't recognize Cassius and the famous Brutus. They were followed by Pompey and Flacchus: Leitus's false (in more ways than one) uncle.

"Singing and dancing," said the gladiator. He heard Pompey talking as the group went past:

". . . was taken. The crosses are being set up."

Subius recognized Flacchus and stared after him, only half hearing the young senator responding behind him.

"Have they taken the leader?" Flacchus asked.

"Yes. His mistake was not killing you when he had a chance. He must have overfine sentiments. I'd have squashed you like a bug, were I in his place."

The voices were harder to follow as they went down the wide steps. Saccus was at Subius's elbow.

"He was insane," Flacchus was saying, a little shrill.

"Was he?" Pompey rejoined. "Speaking of madness, where is Claudius Iro? Taking a bath?"

The following statements were swallowed by the general sounds of wind and crowd murmur below.

"Well, what do you say?" Saccus repeated.

"Say? You want me to say more?" Subius almost smiled, staring at the fellow. *Home,* he was thinking. *Had I the power to pray or space in my heart for it, I'd pray for a home to return to.*

"Will you join Antony's side?" Saccus asked, whispering now. "He can use such as yourself."

"Why is it that the victors never invite me along?" Subius rubbed his hurting eyes. Then it hit him through the blur of sleep and drink. "By Mars," he said, "they meant Leitus."

"Whom?"

"What became of Leitus?"

"Your leader, the son of Spartacus?" Saccus looked interested. "Was he mad?"

Subius grunted. *If he's dead already, why I'm free.*

"Not mad. Ruined, Senator. Ruined."

"He's to be raised above the city," said the younger man, curious and strangely neutral. "I doubt he'll enjoy the view."

"The what?"

"The view from so high. His slaves fled or were shattered to pieces." He shrugged. "The thing is to forget all that and hold off Pompey's bid for dictatorship until Caesar can—"

"Raised? *Raised?*" Subius understood that now, too. His inner fog had lifted. He licked his lips. Awareness hurt. *Of course, of course,* he thought, already running across the terraced side of the Senate, down the side steps. It hurt. All of it, and now this. *Not even a clean death at the end of it for him.* The terrible irony he thought might burst his heart—because he loved the young, silly, hopeless man. In spite of everything.

Now there was nothing left to do except die for him, at last. That had just been postponed, he thought, running through the slush of the street now. Just postponed.

And so he always believed it was his own mind, as he trotted massively down lanes, across squares, up alleys, circling to where he knew he'd find him, always believing he'd had the idea himself in the jumble of his thoughts and that nothing had whispered to him.

He'd just come from behind a high wall and the sun had flashed in his face, stinging his vision with a spatter of gold as the desperate plan came to him full-blown, instantly. The plan that contained both hope and doom.

CHAPTER XXIX

The pain was a dim background in lightless awareness. Sounds and movement were distant, infinite, and part of the pain. Everything was part of the pain. A roaring sound. A bending, hurting. And the weight. The weight bent him, pressed him down. He was drowning under tons of darkness.

He struggled suddenly, kicked against the crushing density, and swam for the surface, for a breath. A single sweet breath. Swimming toward the roaring brightness so far above . . . swimming up into the bright hurting so that his heavy eyes opened and the next agony was the stabbing sun above the blurry hills . . . and then the meaningless sounds of the blurry people on what he barely remembered was a road (he'd even known the name once) in what he still knew was Rome. Yes, Rome and agony.

Memory hurt like his crusted, numb hands where they were pinned to the wooden arms that wrenched his limbs into an X. His swollen feet had not been nailed to the wood, just his hands. He remembered screaming now. The terrible outrage and shock of the nails at each impact of the hammer. Screamed . . . shut his eyes, trying to sink back down again, to escape this intolerable present and the faces that craned up to watch him as the X cross (not yet named St. Andrews) was tilted upright and the weight of his bloody body tore raw, dry screams from him as the flesh and bone sagged around the terrible nails. There were faces he didn't know watching with expressions that meant nothing to him (disgust, satisfaction, amusement, dread) and one face he did: Iro. Iro, looking smug in the early-morning light, eating a piece of soft, dried fruit (for some reason he remembered that clearly), a plum probably, staining the buck tooth purple.

"Leitus," a voice was saying now. "Leitus, can you hear?"

He could, but chose not to. He let himself sink again, down into the waiting, heavy lightlessness. Down under the pain and meanings of words or names until it was all a distant, mixed, senseless roaring far away again.

He let the weight push him down this time without resistance. Went deeper. How far, how long had no meaning. It could have been forever. And then there was faint, fitful, reddish gleaming. A jagged landscape, razor peaks, molten rivers and lakes, a sky like blood. He knew the place. Batlike, flapping things soared in the crushing atmosphere. He touched bottom, able to see but not move. He couldn't tell if he actually had a body. Near and far were strangely mixed, as in a dream. Suddenly he was close (though he hadn't moved) to a dark, seamless wall where the atmosphere was swirling in slow motion. Pale human forms, caught in this whirlwind, flickered and tumbled helplessly. Next he perceived a woman on her back across a carved cube of basaltic stone. She was chained. She seemed to have more substance to her than the others. Illumination glowed steadily within her, faintly, palely gold like a northern autumn sunrise. He knew her. Black chains held her to the block. Her knees were up and parted. Her belly was full and round. Three of the winged, beetle-skinned lords stood around her. One towered over the others. The helpless, flimsy human phantoms floated past in the puddinglike atmosphere.

Though Leitus had no physical substance there himself he felt the hot rush that would have burst into weeping in the world above. He heard their soundless speech while far, far away and above his body was dying on the cross.

He wanted to weep for the sweet, sweet shimmer of her outline. Wanted to reach, touch her. Her light was peaceful, gentle, easing the suffocating agony of this stifling place.

Voices, had there been words, would have been saying:

"Its substance is a stink, Lord," said General Zeleb to the king, meaning the human female shape at their feet. Her golden luminescence was like a foul smell to him, though he had no nose.

"Speak better of my bride," Aataatana insisted sardonically. The glare in his eyes rhythmically pulsed with amusement. *"Or I'll send you to herd Zugs in the great crevice."*

"I abase myself, Lord," replied the other carefully.

"What will you do with her?" inquired Luvnac, the crippled scientist. He was slighter than most of them and showed signs of age. When he moved he twisted to the side in an exaggerated limp. *"What is her purpose in the Plan?"*

"Her child. My son. My regent in the upper world." He raised one taloned hand with casual contempt. *"This human will be born here, in the heart of my kingdom, and at the moment of his birth I will mount his mother and pour my flame and force into the child."*

Somehow Leitus understood the gist of all this. Knew that faintly golden mother would be destroyed, drained to nothing, left less than the least of the phantasmal, pathetic, trapped beings tumbling helplessly on the dense black winds of ash and smoke.

"Ah," commented Luvnac, *"so he will rule the surface where we cannot stand."*

"He will hasten the day when we can." Aataatana made two immense fists and held them trembling before his long, semihuman face. *"From where we can reach for that cursed, burning ball of false fire and put it out!"*

His pseudovoice shook the massed rocks and almost solid air. His red eyes poured out burning beams into the boiling sky.

Luvnac lurched a step or two. Zeleb nodded furiously.

"Our enemies," Luvnac pointed out, *"are not weak as we hoped. Time has shown us that. You say yourself, Aataatana, never underestimate the foe. You say it yourself."*

"What is your point, old one?" Zeleb wanted to know.

Luvnac wasn't sure. He shook his long head and did their equivalent of sighing. He shrugged a rather stunted wing. His thoughts were clearly inward.

"I sense something. . . . A danger in this."

"There is danger in all things," declared Aataatana, *"but we will have our day! We will thicken the gulf and cross it! We will squeeze the stars. My will is—"*

But Leitus was gone on a shift of the dream. He was trying to cry out, to weep. Pity and love sang in him. How could they crush something so precious? O to weep, to weep! Something

sweet as all springtimes and the slow, golden-hued summer
days, the full perfume of steeping life. . . .

And then he awoke into flooding, golden light, a supernal
rush of singing brilliance. His eyes were open. The pain was
nothing, remote, meaningless because there was only the sun
streaming into him as it burned pure in a cloudless, stainless
sky above the ravaged hills of Rome.

His cracked, blood-caked lips moved. Swollen tongue
strained. His breath gasped it like a prayer into the glory that
filled and fired all things into life:

". . . B . . . B . . . Bita . . ."

He was crying now. Tears welled and broke free. He hadn't
wept in so long. He'd dried up inside. And now tears followed
one another down his swollen, sunburned, blood-clotted
cheeks and chin. How sad to finally know that he loved her,
that he could have had such . . . But now it was lost forever.

The thirst and cramping pain was dull and distant. He fell
asleep, at times, without dreaming. Partly woke. Thought
about her. Blinked at the warm circle of sun. Waited for death
in a soft half doze. Without fear. Voices came and went.
Blurred figures watched him from the road and went away.
And when his brain went to think and hurt himself with thinking, he'd see only the echoed sun-disk in his head, burned into
his eyes, a muted gold memory that soothed and blessed and
lifted him above the intolerable body, the twisted, broken
agony of heavy flesh. . . .

So night and new sounds made no difference, either. They
could have been anything, to him. Everything moved suddenly. There was crashing, shouts . . . then a cracking noise
and he was jarred. Voices. He was irritated because his soft,
edgeless concentration on the pale gold memory, the lingering
sun-circle, was broken.

There was pain again. His hand wounds ripped open again.
His body thrashed and blew out a hoarse, meaningless sound.
Eyes unglued themselves. Opened. Saw two blurred, silent,
silvery circles in the sky. He didn't know it was the moon.
Then strange, detailless faces bent over him.

"Easy there," one said. A round one. He remembered.
Remembered and made another inarticulate noise in his chest.

"The nails are out," said another. "What a mess."

They sat him up on the center X of the cross. Three men:
Subius and two others he didn't know at all. There was just

enough moonlight to show their faces, as his painful focus returned.

"Good job they only bound your feet," Subius said. "You'll be walking in an hour. I know a few oils to rub in."

He tried to say "Subius." Almost managed. He saw the dead guards in the road. Four, it looked like.

The second man, thinnish, balding, youthful, held his legs as the gladiator took him under the armpits. The third man wore armor. He was smooth-faced, stocky, held a stained sword, unsheathed. The second wore senatorial robes, spotted with blood, colorless in the moonlight.

As they lifted him he glimpsed the roadway and saw other crosses lining both sides where men hung dying and dead in the wash of silver light.

Leitus felt pity and upset. He tried to point. Croaked this time because Subius touched a wet cloth to his lips and wrung some water and wine out. He felt a shock of something like ecstasy. He sucked like a newborn child.

"H . . . help them . . ." he finally managed. "Them . . ."

"Too late for that," said the third man, the soldier, as they carried him gently to a waiting, closed cart. They laid him inside and it was dark again.

No, he kept thinking, *have to help . . . help . . . too much pain . . . too much . . .*

Outside, the third man, Marc Antony, spoke to Subius:

"Lose no time."

"Yes. Everybody likes to tell me that."

"Saccus?" Antony said.

The young senator came closer. "Yes, Antony?"

"You can do no more. You can go. You owe no more. You didn't even owe this much."

"I know," was the reply. "It wasn't a debt. There's such a thing as acting honorably."

"And as often met with," said Subius, "as egg-laying dogs." He studied Antony's face as the cart started down the steep cobbled street, clattering, creaking, the single mule's hooves sparking.

Subius had run all the way from the Capitoline hill to the Appian Way. He'd trotted up the long slope, panting along the broad, block-paved roadway, not looking up at the rows of crosses that tilted from a terrible dream revisited. He'd known Leitus would be the last one, as his father had been. Iro would have seen to that. For irony's sake.

He'd never looked up. Hadn't dared. Hadn't even been
drunk. He'd jostled past the gawking citizens. Down below
parts of the old city still lay under a smoke haze. He'd smelled
the acrid ash. The day was cloudy, raw, but most of the aber-
rant snowfall had melted away.

It had been dusk by the time he'd reached the last cross and
seen the guards: three had been sitting, eating supper while
one stood, leaning on his spear looking out over the city. The
last sunbeams sank into blood-colored gleaming and spreading shadows.

He'd already drawn his sword, not really thinking about
what would happen even if he actually managed to kill all the
guards. He'd supposed if Leitus were still suffering he'd end
that at least. He'd shut his eyes, dizzy for an instant with the
memory of Leitus's father. He'd run Spartacus through while
he'd hung bleeding in delirium. While the woman had wept
and soldiers jeered, Gracchus had hissed at him: "Do it now,
gladiator!" He'd been very quick then. Young. He'd burst
through the line of troops as Spartacus had tried dully to move
his head, to speak again, his mouth a dark silence as Subius
leaped into the next row of legionaries and smashed two or
three flat, fleeing on into the crowd and diving over a wall,
getting away. Just like that. Only later had he noted the blood
spattered on his arm, shoulder, chest, face.

Ah, Spartacus, he'd thought, with a deep sigh. And then
(the past replaying) he'd been among them, glancing once at
Leitus (perhaps dead), head hanging, sagged on the X, the
ruby sunset glow making an ember of his outline.

He'd drawn and stabbed in one motion, grunting. The man
had turned, jerked down in agony, his spear clattering on the
stones.

As he'd turned the others had already been on their feet.
Fast. Too fast. He wasn't going to win this time. These were
real praetorians.

"Leitus," he'd said, "I tried." And then the shadows had
moved in the twilight and giant, dark shapes flung over the
wall in deadly silence. For an instant he had believed they were
devils from Hades, then had known they were Nubians. Seven
feet tall. Naked. Swift. A *shoosh* of flung spears, cries, curses,
groans. Then two robed Romans had chopped at the
wounded. Orders had been hissed and the black men had gone

like shades into the falling night.

"For you, Antony," Saccus now said, saluting. The cart was moving, the mule delicately step-stepping.

"Why, Antony?" Subius asked. Because he hadn't had time to ask until now. And he had to know. Why Marc Antony would risk his life, family, estates, everything for a condemned traitor and murderer.

"For pity, gladiator."

"Pity?" Subius was hoarse. Whispered the word. "Honor and pity."

They followed the cart. A Nubian drove the mule. Around a bend, click-clack, rattle-rap-creak. This had been a slave quarter and the houses were dark. Any that still lived were not showing themselves. The city was still in shock and there were sporadic, isolated outbreaks of violence in various sections.

"It may be a hopeless world, but I'm not a hopeless man," Antony said, remembering Spartacus in his child's clear, shocked sight.

Then Leitus's bloody, swollen hands gripped the two sides of the cart back and he sat up, gasping.

It was one of the hardest things he'd ever done, forcing himself up, forcing his stiffening paws to work. His breath burned. He shifted himself toward the two men, thinking: *Subius, Subius . . . help me.*

"Subius," he croaked, "help me. . . ."

"Easy, Leitus." Was that the first time he'd used his name? "What is it?"

Antony held his wrist to help support him upright.

"Bita," said Leitus. Swollen tongue moistened his cracked lips. ". . . I . . . where . . . where's Bita?"

"*Now* you ask?" Subius whispered. He wanted to press Antony further. Still, don't look for silt in a free cup of wine.

Antony leaned close to the young man's face. Held the wrist firmly. Watched his eyes. "I tried to help her," he said intensely. "I failed. I know where she is but we couldn't break through to her." He thought about it: the terrible shadows, the pulsing fear as he and his men had fled from Iro's walled gardens. He'd rationalized as best he could but had no desire to go back there again, into that wind (he thought) of madness.

"What did you want with her?" Subius put in, as the cart tilted around another steep turn. Saccus kept pace a few yards back. They passed a soldier who was eating on a bench by oil-lamp light. He stood up and saluted Antony's uniform automatically.

"Never mind," Antony said to Subius. "That's all dead past. The fact is, she's supposed to be with child." He still leaned in under the hide top, close to Leitus. It smelled like grain and wet wood in there.

"Oh," whispered Leitus.

"You're supposed to be the father. That's what she says." Antony shrugged. "I'm impressed, in any case." He smiled, remembering what she'd done to him in the garden. After this, no more dealing with seers and wizards and their friends or relatives. Because he sensed he was being drawn in.

"Jove's hind end," said the gladiator. "What a world!"

"Take me to her," Leitus said and surprised himself by not fainting, because he was sure he was about to. "I . . . was a fool."

"Part of a large family," Subius said.

"Yes," agreed Antony. "We've all the same father, I think." He studied the young man's face. "Lie back and rest, now."

"Take me . . ."

"Yes," he promised. "For pity and history. Or whatever it was." *Mystery.*

Antony stepped around to the driver and gave instructions after Leitus settled back down on the sacking.

"My father was a slave," Leitus said to Subius.

"Like myself. Sometimes."

"Yet I was less free than he."

Subius agreed.

"Save your strength. Heal." He sat up beside him on the floorboards and put a big, iron-hard hand gently on his forehead.

Leitus shut his eyes. Still saw the faint circle the sun had burned into his vision. Remembered Bita's face, the last time he'd seen her. Remembered. "I have to find her," he whispered again, as the hooves and wheels hammered slowly down the cobbled hill.

A man and wife, in full togas, stood by torchlight holding their front gate half-open. They'd been going to visit their neighbors in the villa just across the wide street. Due to the uprising they were suffering somewhat from a servant problem.

They'd been waiting for the hired freeman bodyguard to bring the cart for the quarter-mile ride up the entrance drive. Now they were staring at each other, almost afraid to comment. He looked (she knew the look) as if he were about to simply blink and forget anything had ever happened. "One is stronger in life," he liked to say, "when one takes a narrow view of it. A blade is sharp because it is thin and straight." He had both fingers on his bumped nose, which usually meant he was getting a headache. But she had to say something. So:

"Did we actually . . ." She stopped and waited.

He sniffed and looked away, vaguely, as if for the cart. He was erect, thin, gone gray. She was soft-faced, puff-breasted. The taper they held hollowed their faces.

"Hmn," he responded.

A bony stick figure had passed on the road, feet sluffing on the smooth stones. He'd limped and wobbled through the damp night, lath-thin, arms holding something above his head. He'd never put them down.

"How odd," she said, looking at where the night had swallowed the figure.

"Just some mad slave," her husband assured her.

"Or unholy spirit."

"Nonsense," he said. "Just some low-life from the pigsty." She knew he meant Iro's place, their neighbor in the other direction. That was their name for it. No one liked to pass by there, even in full daylight. "Some low-life. . . ."

Ulad was a hundred yards up the road from the couple now. The hate reached out and felt the hated one was closer. The hate stirred thickly within itself, hungry and thirsty for the hated. The hate that was Ulad had come so far yet felt no weariness. Only appetite.

Not far away, and hundreds of feet underground, Tirb the Strong (once again proving the aptness of his name) was climbing in total darkness up a twisting stair like the one he'd descended in Britain. Up tiny, slimy steps.

He'd come to the end of the tunnel where the river had drained through an ancient, mossy metal grating. He worked his way along the grating to the unseen, rocky shore, found, touched, and scrambled over the abandoned boat beached

there that had to be the wizard Namolin's. Some magic must
have passed him through the falls, he decided.

Tirb had groped to an archway and found the stairs. He
never thought this was all too easy because it had already been
too strange. He'd held the weapon. That was the point. The
sword. He'd held it in his left hand because he couldn't open
his grip. The joints and muscles had locked around the scabbard. When he'd been sucked over the waterfall and whirled
to the bottom (or near it), sure he was doomed, he'd glimpsed
strange glimmers of golden light and then his hand had closed
on something in a burst of brilliance, as if the sun had ex-
ploded underwater in those black depths and then he had risen
with an impression that the metal rod (he hadn't known was a
sword yet) had somehow buoyed him. . . .

He climbed and climbed, aching, groggy, panting, keeping
one thought: the picture of Namolin at his sword's point.
Namolin's head bouncing on the ground. This kept him moving, shivering, drained to a flicker by hundreds of miles of
drifting, half-drowned, in that fetid river though the incredible trip had taken less than two days.

He had no idea where he was. He'd vaguely concluded he
was in some wizard's world or the land of the dead. He didn't
care. He climbed and survived like a man fleeing through a
nightmare.

At some point, high on the endless, circling steps, he simply
crouched over and slept, the sheathed blade still clutched in his
hand as if the metal itself had frozen the fingers. Once he'd
tried to draw the sword but it seemed rusted tight.

Namolin felt safe but frustrated by the time he reached the
top of the stairwell. His lungs hurt, eyes kept blurring, general
strength drained away. He'd come close to fainting on the
same stairs Tirb was laboring up behind him. He kept forgetting things, too. Had to stop and make himself recall once or
twice just what he was doing there. . . .

He came out in the bottom of a series of massive chambers
carved from the living rock of the hill in some immemorial
age. None of the present wizards had any notion of what manner of race had lived here except to judge from the scale of the
steps and pillars and doorways. They were very large.

More stairs were followed by slanting passages. He lit his
way with his broken, nimbus-headed staff. He'd been here

once before, a decade ago. He'd never gone as high as the levels Iro haunted. They'd watched him from a distance, the three wizards. Ata had told them not to directly contact Iro. Iro, he'd said, was a tool being sharpened for a task. Now the time of the eclipse had come at last and the tool was ready. Namolin only vaguely recalled the details of all this now. His memory was bothering him increasingly.

But he felt safe because his pursuer (he assumed it was Ulad) had to be at the bottom of the river. His frustration was that the power stone was hopelessly lost.

He sensed that the other two Druids, his fellows of the inner circle, had already arrived and were waiting above by the sacred well that led down to the central dark world. The eclipse tomorrow night, when the full moon would be caught in the shaft, was the moment when the power of the hated sun-people, the Avalonians, would be at its weakest in centuries. Ata had told them he would be able to rise and thicken himself on the surface of the earth. Even crafty old Namolin had believed him. Took it literally. His not having the stone might be a problem, he thought, might make a fatal difference. He wasn't sure. But it was too late for that. If nothing else, he had to gamble, trick one of the other two and get possession of another sphere. After all, he reasoned, the stones had been stolen in the first place. Even the dark lord himself who said he created them might be lying to secure his claim.

He wanted to rest. The partly healed stab wound (that Tirb had given him in the village street) was a cold, deep ache. But he wouldn't stop for fear he'd never rise again. Without the power stone his life meant nothing. Nothing left then but an old, failing man staring through dimming sight as the world hummed on without him. Left and lost without hope or in-fluence. Alone. Dying by degrees . . . sinking, shivering into emptiness and the nightmare of his fading memories.

The wizard shook his head, drooling a little. Never. He'd have a sphere again, speak to the great ones, probe the future, restore his vigor, command the stupid mass of humanity . . . yes. Muttering, he came out through a low doorway into a far corner of the chamber where they were to meet around the lip of the pit that reached to (they believed) the bottom of the world.

He leaned there, gasping, intent, looking around the dim space. Gray light filtered down the overhead shaft that led up to an enclosed garden in the center of Iro's sprawling villa.

Namolin knew there was something he had to recall. Thoughts kept slipping through the loosened fingers of his mind. He knew each hour without the power sphere was costing him years of knowledge as his memories melted away forever. It was slow death. The power had held him together and now he was unraveling.

He had to concentrate, and his need was doing that for him. His body and soul screamed for the stone, each nerve and cell raw. There was nothing real but that as he limped silently into the hall, leaning one unsteady hand on the cool, smooth wall, following the perimeter. Nothing but his need was real.

He limped and muttered. His right hand clutched the broken staff convulsively, the other left the wall at times to feel under his mire-caked cloak for the absent globe. He believed he felt it, now and then, that he touched the cool, vibrant surface. He felt the energy pouring up into his arm. He'd straighten up then, scowling with triumph and confidence. He'd soon have thousands of slaves to do his bidding. His future was filled with new purpose. The dark ones would rise. His body would be remade.

Then his eyes would blank again and he'd shuffle on, bent and hurting, forgetting even that he was forgetting.

Back in their doomed, fading landscape, the three Avalonians who made the fusion, the composite mind, were seated on a violet grasslike sward under delicate trees whose tints had run thin like diluted paint. The once steady, pulsing, golden glow that filled the vast dome of sky had dimmed. Thin streaks of actual shadow showed here and there, spidery scars left by the black beams of annihilation loosed by Aataatana.

They didn't discuss it. There was no healing the wounds. Though ten thousand years might pass on earth before it actually crumbled into colorless fluff and shards, Avalon was doomed. The thought was the hue of weeping.

Lillila was contemplative. Since her encounter with the shape of glory in the spilling rainbow water, the being that had written on her mind with fingers of light, she'd lost her fear of loss, of ending. Because she'd seen a hint, a flash of ineffable, unending glory and ecstasy that needed no form, no substance, subtler than the subtlest nuance of Avalonian light.

"But have we strength enough?" Adellee was asking. She

looked at the pool, now the color of a rainy sky on earth.

"We must have," Lillila expressed. *"One more time."*

"Can we succeed? We are hurt."

"Yet so are they," put in Olloa. *"But not so badly."*

"Ata, the cursed, has the girl and the child," Lillila reminded them.

"And do we now deliver the boy as well?" Adellee wondered. *"Then he'll have all he's played for."*

"My deception worked, to some extent," Lillila responded. Her colors were like old, worn, coppery gold. All their faces showed a kind of aging. Care had marked what time could not. *"The bait was taken. The foul wizard's fouler spawn has undone him."* She meant Aataatana and Iro.

"But Ata cares little for that," put in Olloa. *"That's a pinprick in his dense hide."*

"Yes," she agreed. *"Yet he will take the next bait, too. They all lie to each other. Do not forget, my brother Olloa, this bait has a poisoned fang that will pierce even his thickness."* She shuddered with disgust.

She'd given the mortal, Tirb, the sword. The fang, she called it. They understood. *"Oh, Aataatana, you stupid, senseless, false, insane, pathetic fool!"* She sighed. *"Thick, dark, dull Ata. He hears and sees nothing. Nothing."* She was thinking about tenderness and joy. The joy that had touched her and left her longing. Aataatana had sealed himself off from any hint of that, she thought. She sighed again.

"What sense to rail?" Olloa wondered. *"He was not always as he now is. But he cannot be reached. What he loosed and manufactured now rules him, can move without him. He's a slave to his machinery. He's doomed, too."*

"So," sadly expressed Adellee, *"we have to be extinguished in that dark, dull, terrible place to help guide a hopeless hero on a hopeless quest?"*

"Not hopeless!" Lillila was almost fierce now. *"One spark of light in that hole of night will never die out! It will haunt them until the time—"* She floated to her feet, graceful, delicate, colors catching sweet fire, flashing in the pool. *"Until the vault is opened and we reawake the inner sun in all its lost glory! And pass beyond crude forms like"*—she indicated herself, her awesome beauty—*"these."* The inner sun, the counterpart of the one that hung in space, would be relit (the legends stated) in the hollow heart of the earth after all

Aataatana's works had passed away forever. Then would the
earth be pure and full of glory and men on the surface would
never die.

"*But annihilation cannot be reversed,*" cried Adellee. "*The
worlds will slow and thicken or fade and die! Heaven is
dying!*" She was upright now, too. Her colors were sobs.

"*No!*" Lillila's eyes sang with golden ecstasy. She was being
touched by a light too intense to be visible to any of them: the
light behind all myths and dreams, the light that created light
itself. "*No, I tell you, all this will pass and be as nothing, yet
the light will never be extinguished! Nor shall we, who are all
mirrors of glory, ever be shattered!*" Had she breath she
would have been breathless. "*Join me!*" she cried in a gust of
shimmering flame.

They all rose into the lucent atmosphere. Poured themselves
together, fused into a union that would have made human
orgasm a dullness. Plunged into the brightening pool, drawn
by her sudden and mysterious strength, which was a shock and
delight to the other two.

CHAPTER XXX

The next night the nearly full moon had just risen as Senator Flacchus arrived at Iro's doorstep. The gate and walk was manned by private troops and some praetorian guards on loan from Pompey. There were none at all in the gardens or inside. Iro had warned Flacchus not to venture off the path. He hadn't said why.

The senator was thinking about his wife just then. Thinking of ways to send her south to her family. She'd been listing his errors and shortcomings lately. She'd somehow found new ones. Amazing. He shook his head, pondering these and other weighty matters, such as how to break with Iro and depose Pompey in favor of someone more tractable.

The air was cool. His palms were wet when he rubbed them together nervously. He peered through the open door into the thickening dimness and blinked several times. Then he glanced into the gardens. They seemed still enough, but he felt a chill finger his spine. The soldiers were quiet. Some were eating. A few were gambling by oil lamps near the statues. Normal.

But why no lights inside? He didn't like that. He paused at the doorway and wiped his hands on his robe. The last spots and streaks of sunset stained the dark walls. He thought about good reasons for going home right then. After all, the battle was won. He'd nearly died as it was, at the hands of his miserable and insane nephew. Ah, yes, who called himself the "son of Spartacus"! Son of Poppycock. The world was constant war and his brother, Gracchus, and his wife had lost the

battle. That was all. Gracchus would have done the same to
him, he reasoned, if he'd had the chance. As long as one
enemy lived you were not safe. Iro was right about that, and
little else, he reflected, feeling beads of cool sweat crawl down
his thick neck. They'd always mocked him, Flacchus. Called
him a fat coward and fool. *Well, dear brother,* he thought,
who was the fool after all? He remembered how as boys they'd
tied him to the tail of a placid cow. After a few struggles the
beast had ignored him, but for over an hour he'd been trapped
(shouting his voice raw, but the adults had gone for the day)
with the evil stinks of that vantage point and vicious hoards of
green flies. Stinging flies. A nightmare he'd never forgotten.
Who's the fool?

He wiped his hands on his robe again. He hated sweating.
Everyone had always said how he sweated. Now young Leitus
could discuss his inheritance with the crows, from his lofty
perch above the city. Flacchus smiled and sweated some more.

I won't need any of them soon, he thought. Particularly
that weasel-faced, sinister, and insane Iro.

He made up his mind to leave at once. Give the senatorial
scroll to a guard, yes, good idea. As he was turning to go Iro
spoke from the shadows just inside.

"Flacchus, enter."

He turned and saw the small, pale figure. His eyes, when his
head shifted, seemed to flash a last ember of sunset.

"I can't stay," Flacchus said uneasily. He fumbled out the
rolled-up scroll and held it for Iro, who paid no attention. His
mind was full of red glare and excitement. It was almost time.
Almost. The promises were about to be fulfilled. It was time
to begin the open rule of the great hand. The redness in his
brain was eloquent on this point. Iro was the hand of the great
lord Aataatana and would rule, side by side, with his sister and
queen-to-be, Claudia. This was the promise. All others would
be lackeys and slaves. Tonight, when the moon was round and
sat in the hole above the pit, exactly at the moment of total
eclipse (a configuration possible only once an age) Aataatana
would manifest himself. While the three wizards (slated to be
Iro's vassals, he'd been told) directed beams of control to hold
the minds of the kings and princes of the surface world and
spread fainter fogs to influence the mindless masses. Iro could
have danced with delight. The hand soothed and stroked his
hot brain. He smiled. The redness pulsed within.

Now that the fool, the scum, the swine-spawn was dead on the cross there could be no question of Iro's right. Because he'd known about the stupid plan to use that Leitus creature as regent, although the boy had never known it. Iro had learned about the plan years ago during an argument with one of the wizards. The fellow had taunted him with it. Well, he'd dealt with that problem pretty well.

And now this fat senator, this boob who imagined wealth could purchase the spears of darkness . . . Time for him to learn to walk on his knees.

"Can't stay? Important business, flaccid one?"

"I . . . yes, I . . ."

"Can you bark?"

"Can I . . ."

"Like a dog?"

"I don't quite . . ." The stare held him: twin coals in the thickening dusk. Hurt to look at. Flacchus's thoughts slowed. Trying to follow things was a terrible strain. He couldn't remember what he wanted to say. His ideas stirred sluggishly. Iro was suddenly closer; his pale, soft hand touched the senator's bulging forehead.

"To your knees, dog," he said, sniggering wetly. "Down, boy!"

The senator dropped, trying to scream a protest. As Iro strolled away he found himself crawling behind on hands and knees, scraping and clunking awkwardly across the floor. Iro paused once to gesture. "Come," he whispered to the gathering night outside. "Come closer." And instantly, outside, several soldiers deserted their posts, backing off, then fled down the road because (they later swore) terrible ghosts had moved, flowed in from the grounds, gathered close to the villa and poured inside like smoke.

Flacchus was now banging down steep stone steps, past feeble oil lamps that barely melted back the shadows. His knees and hands were bleeding, and though he felt the pain he couldn't control his spasmodic movements, as if he were jerked along by unseen strings. Now and then something seemed to grip his chest, squeezing, and he'd emit little, squeaky yips like a hurt puppy.

He tried to break away, but he kept forgetting why or how. . . . His ideas would thicken and there'd be nothing to do but crawl and yipe, scurrying to follow the quick, soft, bare feet

just ahead as his naked master fled down to the chamber of
destiny to meet the moon's ultimate culmination. The crawling senator's fat body wobbled, bloody palms splatting on the
stone. He panted, tongue lolling, saliva drooling.

That same night, not quite twenty-four hours after being
taken down from the cross, Leitus was walking satisfactorily.
Stiff, sore, but moving without dizziness beside Subius. Antony had wished them well and left the city to meet Caesar.
Saccus had returned to his life. What he called his "circus."

Antony had loaned them two of his prized Nubian warriors,
so there were four of them coming across the grounds of the
deserted villa opposite Iro's huge palace.

They'd soaked Leitus's hands all night, first in ice, then in a
vinegar balm Subius had learned about in his arena days.
Leitus had a feeling that if he once closed his hand around a
sword he wouldn't be able to open it again. He thought how
this was a second life (or was it third or fourth?) for him. So
he owed it. He was amazed at how much he loved Bita. After
such a strange and terrible gap of time. Less than a year and
yet it seemed past reckoning. But it was easy now because all
he had to think about was her.

They heard the soldiers running before they saw them, sandals slapping the pavement, then a faint glint of bronze plate.
Others called after them in the dusk from the villa gate.

The four of them paused, crouched in a screen of hedges.

"I count at least a dozen," said Subius. "There may be
more inside and hidden in the trees."

Leitus shrugged. "One way looks like another," he said.

Subius glanced at him and suddenly realized he hadn't had a
drink since the day before. Didn't want one but should have,
because if he'd ever needed to be dulled it was tonight. "We
who are about to die," he voiced, almost inaudibly.

And then the rest of the soldiers were running, too, or, at
least, backing off under the trees and shrubs. Subius caught
the stench of raw decay, thick enough to gag on, spilling
across the road on the breeze. Leitus made a choking sound.
The two black warriors from Africa shifted and muttered,
almost invisible in the dark.

Then they all saw the spidery stick figure swaying along the
road. The long, bone-thin, reeking shape was just entering
the gate, outlined against the pale gleaming of the lightless,

marble building. Its twig arms were still locked over its head, clenching something that only Leitus came close to actually perceiving because he'd been open and intimate with the stone.

He stood up. Terror squeezed his heart. The spider fingers (he thought he saw) enclosed a round, utterly dark spot of something. The dark thing somehow was alive, he sensed. It reached out with dark rays into the night. One seemed to touch his forehead and tug at his mind. It ached like an old wound . . . which angered him so that the fear focused into disgust. Again, blurred memories of shameful desires, ugly needs came back . . . blurred. . . . He nudged the gladiator.

"Come on," he said, snarled, "I'd like to smash that thing."

Subius, still on one knee, was baffled. "What is it?"

And then the Nubians seemed to know, suddenly backpedaling, then running, crying out:

"Ju'ja! Ju'ja!"

And then they were gone as if swallowed up. Ulad was shambling up the walk past the statues of the gods with Iro's face on each.

The last troops gave ground as the stone (now close to the great pit that led down to the world of its making) came nearer. The stone held imprints of all who had possessed or been possessed by it. All the distorted wisdom, madness, terror. A shell of warped intelligence, because it had no insights absorbed into its lightlessness but only strains, tortured hints and hopes, desperate destinies. The impressions in it, for all their sheer intensity, had developed only a contradictory cunning with no purpose but the last violent mental outpouring it had sucked into itself, so now, and until the next, it was Ulad's hate and despair in dying which gave it a mad semblance of personality. And purpose. It radiated those terrors while it thirsted for more energy, more violent drives. As it pulled at their minds they broke and ran. Subius, on the other hand, automatically said "No!" with unconscious outrage at the thing's lightest touch and blocked it out. Leitus charged, Subius at his heels. Neither even glanced up as they gave the stinking outline a wide berth, taking advantage of the scattering guards. They ran outside the line of sculptures toward the dark, open door about fifty yards farther on. Subius noticed the spear poked through the thing's brittle, stinking body.

Somehow it didn't surprise him.

Three soldiers had held their ground on the steps of the villa. None dared go inside. There were horrors inside. The men were near panic now as the stick shape moved up the walk, trapping them. So they welcomed (in a way) the normal problem of combat, flinging themselves on the newcomers, cutting and stabbing in a kind of desperate relief.

Leitus never even had to draw his blade and test the stiffened hand; Subius hit them spinning and sticking. Two fell at once and the third was driven back almost through the doorway, biting his lips, rolling his eyes. Subius charged in one compact thrust and the soldier staggered into the dark house. They heard him running, blundering, crashing into walls . . . screaming . . . then silence.

Subius glanced back at the weird, lurching shape only a few yards away now. Then he turned to go inside behind Leitus, who was standing framed in the doorway. He'd just stopped. One of the fallen soldiers on the stairs gasped, tried to crawl away. The other lay still in a spreading wet shadow. The moon was clear of clouds now and glowed ghostly on the marble. The dry, scraping footsteps *schluss*ed closer.

Leitus sucked in his breath, holding his swollen hands before his face as if to fend off the sudden, icy wind that blasted through the doorway into their faces. Subius felt only the strange air which flapped the leather pieces of their armor and fluttered Leitus's hair. Breathing it somehow sickened and weakened him. Leitus (because he'd been changed) half saw gusts of things *swoosh*ing past and into them. He moved back. Things like coils and black rags, shapeless, sucking at his vitality.

He was sure they were beaten. There was no way to pass inside. They both were forced back from the door.

Bita, he kept thinking, *Bita, I've failed you again and you'll never even know it.*

And then the teetering, spidery thing of mud, slime, and bone, rotting, lurched past them, up the steps they'd just been driven down, and into the villa. The foul wind instantly ceased. Subius thought it had met its match. The flapping rag shapes that Leitus semisaw seemed to withdraw. He sensed how his senses had been changed by the blot of darkness and the golden insight of the sun on the cross. He perceived that the dark beams from the sphere were chewing up the horrors inside.

"What, in the name of Pluto, is this?" Subius asked in awe.

"Madness and death," said Leitus as they both inched forward again. "But I think the gods are clearing the way." He went in, following Ulad, resisting the black beams of the sphere that he didn't actually see so much as feel. Subius gritted his teeth and followed. Kept saying "no" over and over. Both of them tensed with strain, walking behind the wobbling, scraping, stinking shape that (they didn't know) was drawn in insane hate to find the crippled, failing wizard. "Even burning dung," whispered Leitus, "casts light."

They wandered on through unlit corridors touched here and there by flecks of bilious moonlight. The eclipse had begun. . . . They followed the creature down stairs and ramps, moving by touch except when passing a stray oil lamp or ten-day taper in a sconce.

They passed bodies, dead slaves. Men and women lying twisted on the hard floors and stairs. They didn't pause, concentrating on defending their minds and souls and keeping the pace of dead Ulad.

As they went, Subius finally gave in and freed a flask from his belt and made up for lost time in a series of long, desperate swallows.

And, finally, the twisting staircase came out in the vast bowl-shaped chamber of the pit. With the stench of Ulad in their nostrils, sweating, they reached bottom just as the moon was shining down the shaft, fainter and fainter as the eclipse neared totality in a tinted, sickly, reddish glow.

Ulad teetered ahead. Leitus and the gladiator slowed, peering into the semigloom. Straight ahead, in the center, under the round opening where the moon showed, was the pit opening. The shaft into the dark kingdom. They counted at least three figures there . . . no . . . four, and what looked like a high-backed seat to one side. A throne? Odd.

Three of the outlines were the Druidic wizards spaced equidistant around the lip of the hole. Iro stood apart, near the chair. Leitus, straining his sight into the steadily dimming eclipse light, thought now that someone was seated. Couldn't be sure. And something else was there, on the floor, some large animal.

"Well, here we are," murmured Subius. His head still retained the circling of the stairs amplified by drink. "But I swear, I think we'd do well to give it up." His world was nicely blurred now. He was thankful for that, at least. When he walked his feet had a floaty feeling. He liked that.

"No," said Leitus. "This is the way to Bita." Briefly, he shut his eyes so the memory from what he saw on the cross sharpened: the massed weight of darkness stifling him as he watched the lovely, glowing female on the black stone surrounded by glossy, winged beings. He believed it was Bita he'd seen. That she was somewhere under here, trapped, and that those creatures were some kind of phantoms like the rag-flopping shadows they'd met at the entrance upstairs.

He winced, testing his right hand by crooking the fingers slightly. Not good.

"As you say," Subius grunted. "I am bound to you, it seems, to the end. The end of what, I'm not sure. . . ." He started walking again. "But I think it's close at hand." He drew his sword just to feel comfortable. The burned wine soothed and mellowed even the prospect of doom. "Let's go on to meet more freaks of nature and smelly creatures and awful men. . . . No doubt there's a limitless supply in this place." Subius laughed without smiling. Rubbed his bald skull-top. Squinted.

And then a cry, a curse. Someone plunged into the reddened, sickly moonlight. Someone running from back in the blackness behind the tall chair. Subius caught a flash of steel. Yelled curses. Venom. Felt the fury in his own stomach, echoed.

It was Tirb the Strong. Bita's father. He'd crept close, inching across the chamber on his belly, his dagger in his belt, the mysterious sword locked in his left hand, undrawn. Frozen (he believed) in the scabbard.

He'd just recognized Namolin. Saw the beaked profile when his hood had parted. The wizards had just begun chanting, a low, hoarse, wordless noise that seemed at times (to Subius, for one) the growling of some great (but possibly ridiculous) beast that was trying to force speech from its blocked throat.

This was the moment Namolin had waited for, holding himself under control as best he could. The time of ceremony. He'd forgotten so much already. At times he mumbled and wept to half realize it. . . . Other times he just wept with no sense of why. A moment later he might feel supremely confident contemplating how he'd wrest the sphere from soft, greedy, fearful priest Haartweal, the weakest of his peers. A perfect plan, he'd think, without the least idea of how he'd implement it. Then he might forget he'd ever lost the thing and reach under his robe to touch the vital, vitalizing smoothness and feel his mind grow cold, clear, and superhumanly quick. Ah. . . . Then blank spaces sometimes, which could have been dreamless sleep, and he'd awaken to find himself collapsed on cold, damp stone.

But now was the moment, during the opening chant, to raise dread Aataatana from the murk below. He twitched, thinking about how he'd slip around while they were totally absorbed in the spell.

He nodded to himself, holding his thoughts fixed on what he had to do next. The nearness of the power stones drew at him, burned and chilled his brain and nerves. He was drooling slightly with need and sickness. His nose ran unnoticed. He remembered nothing now but his sucking, hot, clawing desire. Once he had it, he assured himself, he'd rule them all. He chortled and nodded. He'd have slaves to wipe him when he passed waste. Yes. He'd have kings and queens do that office. Yes. . . .

He'd just turned to move around the rim to reach despised Haartweal when Tirb spotted him, spotted his beak nose against the ominous, dimming moonglow. Just before the ceremony the three had bowed to one another.

"It is time," Haartweal had said, mind to mind.

"We will become one with the lord of reality," declared the second. They each stood with left hands under their robes holding their power stones as if these were their hearts. In which case Namolin was truly heart-less, as he closed his grip on nothing. Said nothing. Just stared, trying to stem the steady melting away of his memories.

"Behold," said Haartweal, pointing to Iro, who stood, nude, smiling in the dull light with Flacchus crouched at his feet, a naked woman on the throne behind him who (Tirb, creeping past, would notice a few minutes later) was as still as a stone carving. *"Behold Iro, the hand of the lord, who will help us pull him up."*

The "hand" himself was paying no attention to them. He couldn't hear their thoughts, in any case not clearly. Just a murmuring feeling. He was thinking how these greedy little priestlings would soon learn to grovel like this broken, fat dog, Flacchus. How sweet that would be. He unconsciously cupped his soft palms over his feminine pectorals. *And Claudia will rule beside me,* he thought, asking the red fire in

his head and absorbing its soothing response. His sister would
rise. Hadn't he done his lord's bidding? Hadn't he slain what
he desired most? Hadn't he slain Claudia? He had. He had.
And with Leitus gone, who could compete for the stewardship
of the earth?

Oh, how sweetly sly he was. His blunt-tipped fingers gently
tweaked his nipples. He sighed with pleasure, watching the
priests prepare the call to the depths as the moon darkened.

This way she would be only his. Immortal. Bound to him.
He'd proven his faith and kept her from that Leitus creature,
that nameless filth. He understood how all the products of the
ages of breeding had been drawn together. It was bred into
them. Their mutual blood was like the hand of fate. He had
some of that blood in himself. And Claudia. But they were being passed over for these upstarts. He gritted his teeth. Well,
he'd dealt with both. The girl and Leitus. He stroked his soft
chest.

Iro remembered submitting to his sister. Remembered her
long-limbed, sugary flesh that suggested a slightly overripe
grape: sweet but with the first faint hint of sour. He gazed
complacently at Namolin and his pards. These smelly barbarian wizards had a few tricks to learn! They'd leaned too
long on those power stones. Iro had the red jewel in his brain.
The red jewel of Aataatana, which would lick up the black
beams and lap up the shriveled souls of those doddering
savages.

He turned to drink in Claudia's perfectly preserved body,
naked on the throne. Was it only to his eyes that she was
not dried out and decayed? Or had the ceremony of blood
worked?

As he turned he missed Tirb's snarling, berserk charge.

Namolin was just sidling toward Haartweal, hand under his
robe as if holding the power stone.

Now, he kept thinking, *now is the time. . . . Now. . . .*

Then he heard a bellow and turned, not actually recognizing
his own name, which he'd forgotten in any event.

"An enemy," thought the other two wizards as one. *"Form
together and destroy!"*

Namolin glared at mad-eyed, foaming Tirb, struggling now
to draw the long blade locked in his left hand. Failing. He
slowed slightly because he wanted to get it free and chop, stab,
slice, rip the hated Druid.

Namolin felt the sphere in his empty grip again. He snarled in wrath and tried to form the magic joining with the other two. But it lumped; the circle went squarish as they hurled a killing beam at the wild Briton, who spun and skidded (half-insane from his experiences), straining at the sword hilt and foaming.

The death beam, a mental mace, sprang from the partially crippled union (they now knew one of them was stoneless), and the impact knocked the crazed warrior onto his back like a blow from a catapult. But it didn't quite kill him. It choked, blinded, and burned out his nervous system, however. He was doomed, destroyed.

"The joining failed!" cried Haartweal.

The moon had dimmed and died to the tone of dried blood. Centered in the shaft, it was now an eaten sliver.

Leitus and Subius had moved closer, unnoticed. They watched the spindly, stiff shape reel straight toward the priests. Leitus squinted and thought he recognized the pale outline (faintly red-tinted in the eclipse glow) that he didn't yet know was Iro.

"Did you make sense of anything here?" Subius wondered.

"He just flopped down," Leitus responded, whispering. "Must have hit his head." Though he'd felt something strange. A sudden pressure. His heart had missed a beat, as if he'd been struck in the chest.

Subius blinked. He wasn't that drunk, he was thinking. But things mattered less and less. Here, in this dismal underground inhabited by Jove-knew-what. . . . Better this way, he decided. *I'll fight when I have to and see only what comes close enough to cut.* Shadows and devils, too. He'd cut them if they had skins. And, on the subject, what was that skinny, stinking bone-sack up ahead? He sniffed and winced.

"What a stench," he muttered.

"Mn?" whispered Leitus, amazed no one had paid attention to them yet.

"That creaking skeleton must have been rubbed with bad fish."

Namolin had just noticed. His wandering, thinning consciousness felt a shock like recognition without having a what, where, or name attached. He felt, then saw, in the moon-tinted umbrage, the sphere. *His* sphere!

Mine, his brain said again and again as he dragged his worn-

out body forward, arms clawed, reaching as a shriek of need
bubbled up and burst in his throat into wordless howling.
Mine, as he fled at Ulad as if rushing to a lover.

"Ah," said Subius, "old friends meet, eh?"

Down in utter denseness, Aataatana hung on vast slow
wings over the greenish, globular construction that contained
the impossible plug of solid emptiness. He hadn't realized (as
the Avalonians had) that each touch of his will was loosening
the restraints and that the annihilation force had begun leak-
ing. Each concentric sphere of existence was starting to touch
and clash with the others. The highest and most delicate first.

Aataatana swam in his sluggish air, pouring himself into
nothingness. Flickers of jet black reflected into him and he
drank the energy to form his projection on the surface world:
the head and limbs that would appear above, the hand that
gripped Iro's brain and was normally maintained by a corner
of the dark master's consciousness.

But now he was concentrating totally. The moment of
eclipse was helping him thicken his projected images to
semisolidity. If he managed it perfectly he'd virtually exist as
flesh on earth long enough to spring his next surprise. Iro was
bait this time. That smug weakling imagined he would rule!
How purile. A poor instrument, reflected Aataatana, too
cheaply possessed.

Here, pouring his palpable will into the terrible hole, he had
ten thousand eyes. He saw above and below, peered into
remoteness. This was his joy.

Even now he watched Bita chained below to the black block
waiting to give birth. He gazed over his whole, fitfully molten
kingdom and glanced up into the bright worlds he despised.

Now, he expressed to himself, *is the moment!*

Aataatana hurled his projected head up the shaft, his long,
almost lipless face thickening as it zipped in a blink up to the
chamber under Iro's house; where all the players, witting and
unwitting, unwound through their interlocked destinies. Like
meshed gears.

Aataatana felt the hand he'd held casually in Iro's puppet
head grow firmer, surer. He could now simply wrench him
around at will. No longer need he whisper and persuade. How
pleasant. In time he'd develop countless such hands holding
unbreakable grips on all rebels, all confused cowards afraid to
join a battle for the universe. Now could he start to shape a

true race of warriors and heros . . . yes, or, failing, smash the worthless lot to bloody mush.

The rotted, slime-slick stick figure that had been Ulad spat forth its blind, amplified hate. The spider arms snapped down in a terrific spasm, arcing the small, dense ball into Namolin's convulsed, greed-wracked, senile face.

Subius knew the burst melon sound. There was nothing else quite like a splitting skull. He blurrily noted that the stick man with the spear angled through his body dropped flat in the wake of the killing blow and fell in pieces on the pavement.

At the same moment, moving toward Iro, hoping his hurt hands would be able to close around that paffy neck, Leitus tripped and sprawled over something elastic, limp, that an instant later he realized was the fallen warrior.

Leitus groped around on hands and knees. Glanced up the shaft at the swollen, blood-tinted, shadow-eaten moon. Then bent his face close as the man gasped gutterals, words. Something else was just happening that Leitus missed: a cry from the priests, a sickening impact, Iro suddenly moving away. . . .

Hands clawed a foot or two from the blissful energy of the stone, the power and red-fire wonder that promised joy, a crackling, thrilling fire. Namolin had sighed like a lover the instant before the terrific blow had smashed the black globe into his head. It expanded instantly and then there was nothing but empty night. Then not even night.

Subius heard the globe bounce hard enough to chip stone, then roll across the floor. He didn't see what Aataatana saw through his almost solid image-face as his shoulders popped (like some mad jack-in-the-box) out of the bottomless well. Ata's empty image-eyes watched the sphere roll straight to the spiral steps set flush with the floor (where both Tirb and Namolin had climbed from the underground river), and his thickened hand jerked Iro to chase the precious thing that he finally had a chance (a bonus for his planning) to recover and bring to the underworld. The wizards would never willingly surrender them and even Ata couldn't force the issue. Iro's body was too soft, too slow. Aataatana snapped his hand free and reached for the sphere directly. Iro, free from Ata for the first time in decades, sprawled on his belly in front of the throne that held the body of his sister Claudia sitting in macabre state.

The tenebrous hand and arm whipped across the chamber

and snatched at the dark ball as it rolled over the lip and went
crashing down the tight-curving steps.

The hand clutched, closed. No effect. Cupped and gripped
softly but even thickened as it was (with the eclipse in force),
there was no holding the slippery, massively dense stone.

Meanwhile, Iro went into shock: the torch was gone, the red
fire extinguished that had comforted and soothed his mind.
He shivered and croaked out senseless sounds for a few moments of shuddering panic. He was cold, exposed. Isolated.

Blindly, he gripped his sister's bare, lifeless feet. Pressed his
face to them. Moaned and shut his eyes because life hurt now.
Hurt. All he'd ever seen and done squeezed and suffocated
him. He was sobbing, trembling with grief, pity, and a deep,
unbearable sorrow.

"Help me, Claudia," he said, sobbing. ". . . please . . .
please . . . please come back . . . help me . . . aiiii . . ."
Holding the dead feet that their shadowy powers had restored
to meaningless fullness. "He promised. . . . He did . . .
aiiiiiiii . . ."

He had no redness now. He was alone. Shriveled. Prey to
his terrible memories.

"Help me!" he screamed through shudders of weeping.

Why is that one howling over there? Subius shut one eye to
try and fix his focus. What now? What next?

He noted something that reminded him of faint smoke
pouring out of the round hole in the floor. What next?

Subius didn't see the long, hollow-eyed face there. Leitus
wasn't looking, because Tirb (whose face was faintly familiar
from that still blacked-out period) had just gasped and muttered something again in that incomprehensible tongue, then a
name:

"Bita . . . ahhh . . . Bita . . ."

He knelt over the fallen Briton. "What's this?" he demanded of the dying man. "What did you say?" He touched
the bearded, seamed, tough face with one stiff, swollen hand.

". . . Bita . . ." and more unintelligibilities. Then two
Briton words he seemed to know: ". . . her father."

"You?" Leitus said. Then found himself saying it:

"You are Bita's *father*?"

"Ah," breathed Tirb. *"Her father."* Tirb tried to draw the
blade where it lay across his body, his left hand still frozen to
the scabbard.

By now the two remaining priests had recovered and were gathering their strength. They greeted the head in the well with joy. The glossy, gleaming blackness, the emberglow of the hollow stare. They were sure he was about to emerge, that he was present in person.

The dark scarlet eclipselight showed them cross-clasping right hands as they gave welcome:

"Great one, how can we serve thee?"

"Strike the intruders!" came the echoing command.

Aataatana, far below, concentrating into the plug of emptiness, pouring his whole energy into it, was making a last try at getting his image on earth solid enough to hold the sphere that was accelerating down the steps, crashing around the tight circle, pounding down and down.

Then he gave up. It was hopeless. He took a fresh, fierce, contemptuous grip on Iro, who still lay sobbing at his dead sister's feet, yanked him upright like a toy. Iro struggled faintly.

Flacchus, still on hands and knees, had begun crawling in quiet panic the instant Iro had collapsed, releasing him. He left a scrawling trail from his bloody palms and knees, spatters and scribbles as he headed straight for the stairwell as if he were actually following the sphere down. . . .

The wizards inhaled, prepared to launch a killing bolt at Subius just as Tirb's hand fell lifeless from the hilt and Leitus noticed, in the haunted light, nude Iro hopping, jerking madly toward him in the impatient, frustrated, furious grip of his semisolid master. The little man seemed to be in torment, as if dancing on coals, when in fact he was drinking in the pure, rich redness that was the burning ring (brighter, hotter now) on the black finger crooked in his skull.

Aataatana had recognized Leitus through the captive eyes of Iro. His plan had worked again. The boy was in his hands. He'd deceived both enemies and allies alike. Leitus had been drawn to the one place where the dark master could physically touch him despite whatever guardians sprang to his defense. Here and now he had them all: the girl, the baby about to be born in his prison below, and Leitus, the last hope of Avalon.

He jerked and flung his soft-bodied thrall straight at Leitus, who stood up, whipping out the sword from the sheath held by dead Tirb. The blade was much longer and thinner than the gladius he was used to, but he liked the balance instantly. And the golden flash of the metal seemed bright even in the dull, phantasmal eclipselight.

His hand flared in agony then locked so tight on the hilt it shocked him. The pain was white fire, but he was already crouching to meet Iro's strange, hopping charge.

As he raised the blade high it seemed to flash as if struck by a sunbeam. He half noticed runes cut into the steel.

No time for questions: fast, spastic, like a berserk marionette, Iro was flung on him. He remembered what had happened last time that little hand had touched him in the smoke and snowstorm by the Senate. So Leitus was ready, all pain forgotten. Ready and raging.

Iro was in ecstasy. He knew Leitus through the red glare in his skull. He snarled, adding his own furious efforts to Aataatana's purpose, gnashing his teeth, clawing his fingers, wanting only to taste hot blood, to rip hated flesh to tatters. The sword meant nothing in the face of the red power that rode him forward.

Simultaneously, the wizard priests struck at Subius. But the sword burst into shattering brightness for an instant that seemed to suspend all breath and movement, a sunburst that blazed through flesh and showed the ghostly bones beneath all of them. The shadow face recoiled. Iro seemed to hang in midspring. And then there was only the afterglow and sickly, tinted, tainted moongleaming again.

Except the two priests were gone. Subius, blurred and blinded now, imagined he'd seen their empty robes flopping down.

Ah, well, he thought, *that's sufficient. That's plenty. No more, I beg you, gods . . . no more tonight.*

Subius slammed his blade back in the sheath and shook his big, bald, thoughtful head. His sight was full of dancing golden specks. No more insanity, he decided. All debts were paid. No more skeletal creatures hobbling in stink; no more reeking winds of shadow; vanishing tricks; bursts of sunlight underground and at night. . . . No, no, too much for him. All debts were discharged.

No more.

The old gladiator started walking away, wobbling from the velvety blows of the strong wine he'd last guzzled. . . .

The golden fusion had struck. They'd tuned themselves to the long sword. That had been Lillila's last touch. The blade could draw them past Aataatana's webs of awareness.

Now the fusion withdrew to the metal again in less than an eye-blink, as Iro leaped unnaturally high (showing what seemed a sudden beat of dim wings and searing red eyes). To Leitus the sword seemed to swing itself in a terrific downcut that almost effortlessly sliced through the flesh and bone in a percussive impact.

Iro dropped, spurting and splatting on the stones. Broken meat. His mouth vomited a black death sound.

Leitus stood there swaying. The first sliver of unblocked moonlight was showing in the shaft as the eclipse separated. He was partly aware of the giant face in the well at the edge of his sight, because something was still in front of him, a flicker of hard ruby color, something (his stunned mind tried to focus) like a huge, taloned hand, which flashed toward him.

He cut and missed and felt a numbing grip enclose him with the strength of a natural calamity. The finger that reached for his mind slipped its grip. A golden shimmer defended him. But it had his body, bone and nerve, and he staggered, stumbled, jerked, and was dragged across the smooth paving toward where (he vaguely perceived) the shadowy arm reached from the pit. The face was fading as the eclipse passed, but he was caught. He kicked, twisted, weaved, staggered, fell flat and hard, cracking his forehead in a blinding shock.

Subius saw him flinging past, too dim for details. He realized it was Leitus and veered in his general direction, instinctively. Then he weaved abruptly to the side, moving as if an improbable wind blew his massive body here and there.

"Leitus," he muttered, "hail and farewell. . . ." The wine and an empty gut finally caught completely up with him, hit him on the skull with a big, soft club. ". . . I cannot," he said to the blurry, cool, velvety darkness as he wandered across the huge chamber. ". . . I cannot look at any more of this. No more. . . ." He shook his head. Didn't realize he was crying. Just blinked out tears. Choked with emotions he couldn't have defined: vague things, thoughts of Leitus . . . Spartacus . . . his own sister when he was a boy sharing a cup of cool, wood-rich water in the dry mountain sunlight, relaxed, content, thinking about leaving the village, hiking beyond the farthest hills he'd seen from the highest point he knew . . . yes. Eventually he had and had never been able to return. So long ago, that was. He sighed. Flashed the face of the woman (whose name he never knew) who'd slept with him before the games and taught him to regret and grieve for a dream through all the violent, burning, brass days of his life. "Enough!" he cried to all blurs and dreams as—

—Leitus went into the pit holding the glowing sword, dropping too fast for reality, as if he'd been sucked out of himself, zipping down endlessly as in a nightmare, the grip tightening, the hand thickening as he neared the inner kingdom . . . down . . . down . . . into forever and a night past understanding—

—Subius remembered, twisted around, cocked himself, then let his body fall forward in the general direction of where he'd last seen Leitus, catching himself as he fell with his feet in a stiff-legged, spasmodic run.

He had to tell Leitus the things he was feeling. That was important. The understandings that suddenly made the meaning of everything clear. The love and tears that had flashed like that blinding light a few moments ago. They all had to weep for each other, for all pain and lost love.

"Leitus," he called, groping at the blurs. He stepped past the rim of the well. But there was no shaft, just solid stonework.

He shrugged. One more absurdity. He almost managed to stop falling forward and then slipped on something he didn't know was part of Iro. He skidded to his big knees in front of the throne, looking up at two pale, thin, featureless women. Shapes, outlines. He shut an eye and there was just one. He tilted his head, amazed for the last time that night.

His lips felt thick and dull. "My lady," he said to the unmoving figure on the throne, "did you enjoy the show?" He tried to smile. Waved a hand. "I want . . . money back . . ."

Elsewhere in the black, thick grip, sinking slowly now through a sky shot with smoke and crimson gleamings above a tortured landscape, Leitus could see the world he'd glimpsed in dreams and agonized flashes of vision.

He felt Bita down there. The darkness pressed on his mind, but the faintly golden light of the sword held it back like a shield. Moving body or mind was a strain. Required concentration to force it through the pressure. But he could think. And his memory held, so far.

He saw the arm of the hand that clutched him stretching off into the cloudy, burning distances as it pulled him deeper.

"Free yourself, Leitus," a voice seemed to tell him. Sparkled in his mind.

"Who are you?" he thought in return.

"We will help you. We are the fusion. We will cease to be here. Yet nothing will be lost, in the end."

"I must be mad or passed out. Or dying somewhere."

"It is all one thing. All your worlds are dreamings. Yet what you do here now is forever. Find your true wife and son-to-be. Free them and yourself. You are strong now and we will help you be stronger."

"What is happening?" Thinking was still in slow motion, as was his fall. Nothing could hold back all the pressure of the red-streaked blackness.

"We are now the light of your son's sword that you hold in trust for him. It is the promised dowry for your true wife. Fight, child, fight! If you are held here and they take your soul-body, whole worlds will darken and fail. We love you, child.

"Strike!"

And he swung the two-handed sword through the crushing atmosphere. The blade seemed an immense weight that once started would smash through any substance.

The golden cut severed the black, clawed hand from the incredibly long arm. Leitus felt a shudder in the whole underworld, a crack of stone, a shock that shook the rivers of fire, a cry of pain hard as stone ground together. The golden light flared up and he dropped like a falling star, streaking the everlasting night with a perfect arc of brightness.

And then he was, instantly, on the bleak volcanic surface where faint wisps of green luminescence flickered spectrally. Nearby, a molten spring bubbled slowly, boiling rock. The heat beat against him.

Holding the glowing blade like a torch he went straight toward immense steps that climbed a carven wall. He was at the base of the hundred-mile fortress that had been hacked and melted out of the black mountains by virtually limitless forces.

He leaned against the soupy air. Heard faint, lost, hopeless wails all around. Glimpsed flickering, phantasmal victims. Noticed beetle-shiny, winged warriors beating rapidly toward him. He felt their wrath and outrage.

He also felt Bita. He could have, he suspected, found her if he were blind. She was near.

Then a winged, harsh, clattering creature, face full of fangs, gusted down over him and the blade again seemed almost to swing itself, crashing into the hard neck with a tremendous sound as a black, knotted fist cracked a glancing blow off the side of his head.

He reeled. The landscape wavered, tore in places, and he was rebounding from a dim, hard surface, the thinnest, faintest illumination showing the winged shape frozen in the dimness. A suddenly narrow place. A different place.

His head rang with pain-light. A narrow place. *Magic or a dream?* he asked himself. Groping with the (here) faintly gleaming blade, reaching ahead with it like a blind man's staff, probing the shapes and shadows, he hit a wall. He thought he knew where he was . . . then not sure again because the solid things kept melting and leaving him walking under the blood sky of the underworld.

An undulate, ghostly form drooped menacingly above him. His blade ripped it to silvery tatters: a huge cobweb. He plunged on through a doorway, went up a short flight of stairs, and then another winged shape stood before him. He made it out in the gleam of faint moonlight straining in from somewhere up high. He saw it was a dark statue. A rippling tremble and the winged thing leaped, wailing red fury and hate down the steps of the smoke-torn fortress.

He cut and chopped off a wing. Then he tried to run the last few yards to the top, half swimming in the thickness . . . except he was in another narrow, twisting passageway. A bat had just thumped past his face. He'd struck blindly at it.

"Bita!" he shouted, voice muffled, echoing ahead and behind. "Bita!" Because he felt her, loved her, through even the blinding pain in his battered head.

He struggled on, blade scraping sparks from the walls, passing more of the carven things, monuments to the ancient race in those eons-old tunnels and chambers that had been a fortress when the earth was new.

"Bita . . ."

Creaking wings fluttered all around his head. He swung wildly, spattered small bodies. Then one flew into his face and he was out on the square top of the citadel again where three winged, merciless lords stood around the block of stone where pale Bita lay chained, legs up and parted, round belly showing she was near her time. She seemed asleep.

Head beating and blurred, flashing in and out of what seemed a two-sided nightmare, Leitus staggered forward. He spun, chopped, stabbed, the sword burning gold, as talons ripped him, stone-hard fists banging him sideways. He blocked, twisted free, hacked insanely at the flame-eyed, solid creatures. But the blade cut them and they wailed to feel it. And fell back, dripping molten blood from their rent shells.

Above him giant wings beat cyclones in the clouds as Aataatana dropped like a hunting hawk, screaming doom, vomiting fury, crashing through the shocked sky to smash him to cindered dust.

Leitus staggered to Bita and fell against the altarlike block. Though he didn't breathe in this world he felt breathless. Her flesh had no heat or cold to his touch. The shadow fell closer, covered most of the sky.

Then the dim chamber was back: a faint glow and cobwebs. The *squee* and rustle of troubled bats. He was panting here, dizzy. Felt her chains. Got up, wobbling. A shattered statue of a black demon stood near him, one long arm broken on the floor. Two more tilted together, one missing a foot, the other a wing. Had he actually chopped stone with this strange blade? His hand seemed glued to the hilt. He was afraid to try and open the fingers, in any case. Was he mad? Were the visions coming back at any moment? He was terrified of being trapped in that dark, oppressive world, in a dream he would never be able to awaken from.

While I'm still here, wherever here is, he thought, *I better use my time well.* Here had to be under Iro's huge villa. These passages obviously were cut into the steep hillside.

He hacked her chains. Left her wearing bracelets and anklets. Bent over her. She was motionless. Was she actually breathing? He put a gentle, fearful hand on her bare, grape-round belly. Made a slight, unconscious, sighing sound—

—and was back in the dark pressure of the underworld. The golden light from the sword shimmered around him and her as the winged lord's tremendous pinions crashed onto the slick, black stone, slashing one great hand to rip Leitus to tatters. The dark lord had given up his plan to use Leitus. The blade changed everything. It was too deadly. It hurt and maddened

him while carving up his folk; the golden radiance spread
terror and unrest everywhere. Even the pathetic phantoms
stirred with hope and wonder, catching sun-bright glimpses
whenever Leitus swung the sword. Aataatana bent low over
the pair, glaring flame.

Leitus's hand was still touching Bita's pregnant stomach.
She stirred now, opened her eyes. The golden sword shimmer
reflected there.

"Flee," the fusion, the shimmer told them. *"You are only a
single step from freedom."*

Leitus raised up Bita. Her arms hung at her sides. She
seemed to float lightly in the strange atmosphere. Her eyes
were open but she didn't seem really awake or aware.

He felt shrunken, pitiful, as that huge hand slammed down
on them. Other beings swarmed toward them from all parts of
the underworld. The three lords he'd injured moved closer,
spewing flame and hate.

He clutched Bita with his left arm and struck straight up
into the black, hot, hard palm, expecting the metal to shatter.
He was small, pitiful, lost. . . .

But the steel held. A golden flash and he felt the vibrating
length drive deep. He was tugged into the air several feet as
Aataatana recoiled. He glimpsed the gaping, flaming, fanged
mouth and glaring stare that ripped into his mind, searing it.
He knew those red beams would dissolve his consciousness,
leave his skull a cindered shell. Had there been sound there he
would have screamed.

"Now!" a musical shimmer of golden unvoice called,
sparkled. The fusion streamed from the still upraised blade
and (as he reflexively stabbed again) burst in one blinding
flash, a sun-blast that filled the whole vast underworld. For an
instant, as they spent all their substance, the sun came out in
that sealed, damned place. For an instant there was no spot or
space of darkness. The fusion (as mortals call it) died. All the
trapped and hopeless beings, phantoms, blazed bright for that
moment; knew themselves and were briefly free. And the light
would linger in them and leave a mark for ages in the endless
night.

Leitus felt the shock and pain echo among the great race;
felt them waver and spin and fall blinded. He knew he was
moving, holding her, moving fast, seeing only afterglow himself, a brightness, a vague image of Aataatana reeling back,

hands pressed to his eyes, wings flailing.

They floated faster and faster through the thickness, still gripping the sword that seemed to be drawing them along at his arm's length. The massed rocks seemed to melt away . . .

. . . back in the dark again before time was melted by the blast of glory (the times and places had run together) and he was holding her, unstirring, as he thrust blindly at solid blankness, throwing himself forward with all his force, desperate to escape.

The blow numbed his arm to the shoulder. Something gave way, and he had an impression of a door opening (superimposed on an image of a shadowy, winged creature towering above them, striking down) and then a blinding shock of brilliance. Holding her tightly, he stepped out into the gold blaze. He fell for a long, sickening instant, clutching her and the sword. Then, somehow, he slowed, was eased softly, tenderly, down by a scented touch, slowing . . . slowing to a sweet stop, swaying gently, nothing underneath or anywhere in reach but an elastic, perfumed cushion.

He saw a little now as his sight recovered from the shock of daylight . . . flashes, flickers of sunbeams through golden blurs like fluffy clouds (was this some perfect world high above the earth?), and when he moved they both sank and swayed and were lifted again as if on gentle sea swells. He saw a spot of blue sky, too . . . and flowers, massed flowers, thick enough to hold their weight aloft on the crushed sweetness.

How high? He couldn't see down, the huge bower was too thick. And they'd sunk so deep he only had glimpses of the sky. If he strained his neck back, bits of the steep slope of cliff they'd fallen out of was visible. It had to have been a door or window, he realized. Incredible.

He had to wake her, if he could. She was in his arms and he discovered she was holding him now. They lay there as on a magical cushion in the soothing, warm, stray sunbeams. The dark images of the dark places were purged by day, fading blurs in this fantastic afternoon.

He wanted just to lie there and rest. Sleep. He laid the sword across their bodies. She winced slightly when the flat steel touched her swollen belly. He noticed the words, runes, carved on the blade. Didn't try to read them. Was thinking how there was going to be time to get to know her well. What a wonderful idea.

"Dear Bita," he said gently, drinking in the sight of her hair, oval face, bare, small breasts in the reflected, honey-soft flower-light. "Bita, Bita...."

Her eyes were open. She found his face inches away.

"Hello," he said. "I found you."

She blinked. Nodded. "It seems," she whispered. "I remember..."

He moved and kissed her cheek. They rocked gently like children in a cradle. He liked the clean, warm, dry taste of her skin.

"Don't remember," he told her.

"Leitus," she said, amazed and yet not amazed. "Leitus."

"Yes. Don't remember."

"If you say not to, I won't," she responded.

It was nice to imagine they were miles above the world. He refused to really remember, either. Everything had to start from now. This was their first day.

He understood part of what had happened. She'd been chained deep under the villa which was on top of the hill at their backs. He knew about where they were because this side, the cliff, opened out into a valley. Amazing. And yet, now, it really didn't seem so strange or to matter much.

"We'll leave here soon," he told her, touching the elastic, soft belly again, fascinated, just above where the naked sword crossed over them. "We'll go away." He kissed her again. "With our child."

"Soon," she whispered near his ear.

"If you like." He yawned. "Soon," he repeated.

"Yes, Leitus." She seemed very composed. She wasn't remembering; she was content with the secret she held within herself. Bita nuzzled his shoulder.

He felt like a man risen from a long fever. His pierced hands still throbbed and he didn't dare let go of the sword yet for fear his hand would lock open, but he felt warm and stronger. He started planning a little: find the ground, walk to the nearest farm, get food and clothes for her and then ... then ... then make their way to safety, far from Rome. He felt confident he could protect her. In a little while after a little rest.

And then this child. Tentatively, he touched her again. The roundness was firm and warm. He thought something moved inside. She was smiling.

"Not yet," she said, voice knowing and tender. "He has a little time yet."

And then she remembered (though she wanted to please him) that they'd only have him—what was it—fifteen years? Could that really be true? Were the golden people really gone? She sighed. Time would tell. What mattered now was the baby and Leitus. Because it was as if she'd surrounded the precious gold with her body, too, with all her love and life. They'd already told her what to name him, and said he wouldn't die as other men died. Time would have to tell that tale, too, she reasoned.

"Arturus," she whispered into the flesh of her husband and the rich, dizzying sweetness of the cloudy flowers.

"Hmn?" he murmured, glancing at the blade that lay across them. A sunbeam caught it and the mirror-flash hit his eye. He turned the metal to study the runic inscription. It meant nothing to him, just barbarian marks. Perhaps Subius could read it. He wondered if he'd find the gladiator again. He depended on the man, and liked him, too. They'd certainly been through enough together. Leitus hoped the gladiator was all right, but he was still too comfortable lying there, as if enchanted, to focus well on other matters.

"Are you ready to go on?" he asked her.

"A little longer, my love. It's so sweet to lie here."

"Yes," he agreed, taking a long, slow, perfumed breath. "I was such a fool."

She smiled, eyes closed, nuzzling. "Oh, yes," she said, kissing his bare shoulder. "You were."

He wanted to talk, tell her things, all about his life and hopes. . . . But there was time for that. Time. . . .

Subius stirred. Groaned. Licked fuzzy, sticky lips. He was still flat on his face under the open shaft to the surface. Daylight poured down over him, cut the dank, stone chill.

After listening to his heartbeat and breath rasp for a while, he tried thinking. It was hard to tell his thoughts from a dull, steady headache.

He considered getting up. This was the power of reasoning. If he got up, he might find something to drink; if he lay here he'd have to hope someone would happen by with a jug and loaf. He burped thoughtfully.

He discovered a craving for eggs. He decided he could easily accommodate a basket of goose eggs. He loved goose eggs. Baked with mushrooms and peppery herbs and small onions.

Thinking hard about these issues, he rolled onto his back. Sighed, winced, blinked up at the perfect circle of blue. Under him the floor was still solid brick. He decided it had to have been a drunken dream last night. There was never any hole in the floor here. In which case, where was the boy? He groaned. He'd get to that a little later.

His eyes didn't hurt so much now and he gazed up at the view: the soft fluff of sun-bright clouds winking past the opening.

"Eggs," he muttered. Wine was less important. Eggs were the thing. And good hot bread and honey.

So he had to sit up. That wasn't easy. His head throbbed and back cricked. He glanced at what he knew were bodies outside the circle of daylight that enclosed him. He rubbed his face and spat dryly.

"Curse the gods," he muttered. He didn't care about bodies anymore. "Let all bodies lie as fallen." Someone had scribbled that with torch smoke on the wall of the first arena he'd fought in. Good advice. "Curse the devils, too."

Still alive, that's a feat in itself where I travel. Made him part of an ever-shrinking group. *A plate of eggs and then look for Leitus, that's the first order of business.*

He finally stood up. Didn't wobble much. Thought he'd look up Crato as well. He liked Crato. He smiled, thinking about him.

"And then," he said quite loudly into the emptiness around him, "we'll all retire to a farm and stir shit with a spoon together and ponder the backsides of countless pigs." He laughed and started walking out of the circle of illumination. "But first," he said profoundly, "eggs."

Far below at the bottom of the spiral stairs, in total darkness, crouched on his side, fat knees drawn up, fat body shivering slightly on the damp rocks, fat arms clutched close to his saggy chest, wrapped in his tattered, wet, greasy toga, Flacchus lay feverish, neither asleep nor awake. His mind was strange with shock and sickness. He imagined the roarings of the underground river were voices telling him things, making profound promises. The air was dank with brackish water.

He shivered as the fever shaped and cooked his mind. Spoke

with voices, understood deep matters. He grasped all these things as the blackness squeezed his soul.

His fat hands gripped the perfectly round, cool stone, holding it tight to his breasts as if it were a suckling child and he a mother. He caressed it, stroked its smoothness with gentle, fat fingers.

He listened. Murmured. Shook. Burned.

In Britain, in the chief's long hut (though Tirb had been replaced) in the semidarkness of shuttered windows, bloodless, stiff and silent, Bita's pregnant sister lay on the lumpy pallet. She was not dead. Her belly filled month by month. The women no longer even keened. Just waited. Waited and lit herb candles every morning.

He'd given Bita ragged garments torn from his clothes and made a loincloth from the rest. Good thing it was warm, he thought. Well, the snow had been a portentous freak. Roman winters were like a northern spring.

He held the strange, inscribed sword over his shoulder as they padded together down a long, grassy slope through stands of cypress, eucalyptus, and olive trees. The city was above and behind. He knew there were a few farms not far ahead.

He had a plan now to head south after the child was born. He'd discovered the sword hilt was crusted with gems. His ruined hand had been locked around a fortune. The bloody jewels would purchase their freedom ten times over, he realized. And chop a way to it, if it came back to that.

He felt tough, relaxed, content, and dedicated. He'd come of age, he decided. He knew now what to value, what to fight for.

He held her delicate but strong hand as they descended the angle of hill into the slant of broken sunbeams. Wild grass *swoosh*ed under their bare feet. The sun glowed on the coppery trees and glinted in her fine hair. The air was fresh with a tang from the earth. The warm breeze seemed to lift him as he went. They'd come to a clear stream that creased down the hillside and looped in front of them. The branches crossed over and interlocked their feathery tips, so that spots and speckles of sunlight lit the water here and there.

They stopped and bent to drink. She stared into the rich,

green depths. Their reflections seemed formed from the waterflow, a gathering of ripples and soft tints.

She cupped a double palmful from where his heart would
have been, and drank.

I don't care for any more visions, she thought. *I don't want
anything but this child and this man.*

Fronds and colors stirred and wavered in the current.
Specks of gold flickered as the leaves riffled overhead.

She looked up when he sighed with pain. He'd just released
the sword. She saw the hilt was printed with his blood. She
took both hurt hands in both of hers; looked at him in speaking silence. He smiled. She couldn't believe he was really here
with her. Really. At last. Out of a dream.

The wounds were almost closed but still dark, puffy. She
kissed each palm and felt tears blot her sight. Nothing needed
to be said.

They knelt there together like that, getting ready to go on
into what waited that she refused to even try and see. No more
leaving footsteps on a path before they actually walked it. . . .

She felt it, a slight elastic bump that wasn't quite pain. It
showed in her eyes and he was instantly attentive.

"What is it?" he asked. The sword lay beside him. He'd
been about to take it up again.

She smiled. Shook her head.

"Your son," she said. "He's restless."

Leitus freed his hands and gently touched where he was. He
bit his lower lip lightly, startled, when he felt the movement,
then grinned with delight. She was pleased.

"Ah," he sighed. He couldn't express what he felt. Didn't
try. He put his face there next and kissed, then turned his ear
as if to listen to her living flesh and the new life that had
gathered there, condensed from a dew of promise into eternal
miracle.

The water sparkled with flickers of broken gold. She held
his curly head close to herself. Listened to the water rush as he
listened to the beat and mystery of her and what lived in her.

"I love you," he whispered.

Notes for <u>Runes</u>

Even in a fantasy novel, why have Arthur of the Britons born
so many centuries too early and to such unlikely parents? A
myth, you might ask, is a myth, but why stretch it so out of
shape? The sequels, I hope, will explain. Arthur is a mystery
and at the heart of one. There's history there as well as myth
because the man did exist, after all. His birth is the first
mystery: his father, Pendragon, supposedly made love to his
mother (someone else's wife) while under a spell of Merlin's,
so that he seemed to be the husband. The wife, the story goes,
was fooled. That's a little thin. Pendragon seemed to want to
lay claim to this special child. Literary device? Myth? Of
course. But behind it a mystery, nevertheless. There are hints
that Arthur may have turned up in his world as inexplicably as
Kaspar Hauser.

The strongest Arthurian tales are involved with literal and
semiliteral history as much as with metaphor. They are anything but "pure adventure" stories. They are images of initiation; spiritual alchemy; journeys into the secrets of the soul
and the actual world. It's no accident that many of the finest
works of any literature depend on the quest structure so central to Arthurian tales. The quest, generally, in all cultures,
seems to lead through mystery, darkness, and terror into en-
lightenment and self-discovery. Homer, in a way, begat
Dante. The Grail hunters begat Melville, Conrad, Kafka, and
the like. For many years now I've been chasing the Grail
myself, with mixed results.

The projected *Runes* series will fill some of the gaps on the map of an imaginary landscape. The landscape compresses time and space between the birth of Christ and the rebirth (so to speak) of Arthur and Merlin. The roads all lead to the Grail and, ultimately, to the twentieth-century Armageddon when the myths collide in the final battle for our civilization's soul.

To answer some questions about my work that have been asked many times in the years since Parsival was first published:

1) *Are the books meant to be genre fantasy? Does it really matter? If so, what is a "genre," anyway?*

Yes and no, I'd have to say, to the first query. To the second: It really doesn't matter, because if there is life and truth in the books then that's good enough. But, since it interests some people, a genre is something you can feel but barely define. Whatever you can say about a tree, for example, or a person, is not the tree or the person; but just what you say. There is some fantasy that stays in generic bounds like water in a narrow channel; other works overlap the banks and spread across the literary fields into the "mainstream." As above, great fantasy writers include Homer, Dante, Milton, Melville, Conrad, Kafka, Shakespeare, and Dickens . . . and the list can be extended effortlessly.

2) *Were the books really meant to be Arthurian tales?*

Yes and no, again. Years ago I asked Fellini some questions about his fantasy, *Satyricon*, and he replied, at one point, that while the means were complex, dense, subtle, the effect was ". . . very easy, very honest. It's just a picture about love, about life, about fear, desperation, friendship, the necessity to be in love with life. . . ." Unlike the anemic retellings that devolve from Malory, most original Arthurian stories are quite brutal expressions of a brutal existence with love and the Grail quest as a redemptive hope.

Some of us confuse fantasy with escape from reality. Some readers mistook a medieval and contemporary blunt sexuality and violence (side by side with dreaming romance) as a disparagement of some strange Camelot illusions we're supposed to maintain in the genre. Escape? But to where? Into your own mind and images, in the end. And you'll have to deal with the facts and fears, agonies, frustrations, and hopes. There's no real escape. Even if you move to Hollywood. Daydreaming about fairies or ruthless, tireless, indestructible barbarians is harmless fun, but sooner or later you're wide awake again. The sweet dope wears off and there's that factual, point-blank glare of life in your face. All the real excitement and wonder of it. Life is the secret, the Grail, I think, if you go back to it without illusion or fear. So I opt for that redemptive hope, the quest that leads toward inner freedom and an intensity that brings more joy and real passion than you'll ever find in any literature of daydreams.

—Richard Monaco
New York City
June 1983

About the Author

Richard Monaco has been a writer of poetry, short stories, novels, plays, screenplays, and musical compositions. He hosted a radio program on poetry for four years and was the fiction and poetry editor of *The University Review*. He is currently the editor of the fantasy magazine *Imago* with his wife, Adele Leone. In addition to *Runes*, Monaco had written *Parsival, The Grail War*, and *The Final Quest. Blood and Dreams,* the fourth book in the Parsival series, is in progress as well as the sequel to *Runes*.